# DIVINITY
# AND THE PYTHON

2013 December
Merry Christmas,
Kara!

# DIVINITY AND THE PYTHON

Bonnie Randall

PANVERSE

# DIVINITY AND THE PYTHON



Cover by Janice Hardy

This book is a work of fiction. Names, characters, places, and events in this book either are products of the author's imagination or are used fictitiously. Any resemblance to actual events, places, or persons living or dead, is purely coincidental.



Published by Panverse Publishing
2207 Holbrook Dr., Concord, CA 94519
www.panversepublishing.com

First edition: September 2013

Printed in the U.S.A.

ISBN 978-1-940581-99-6

*Every woman should experience a friendship that was hard won, fought battles, and became bulletproof. Ah, McToner. You and I have seen so much trauma together. Thank you for feeling confidence in me when I had none for myself. For shoving me (kicking and screaming) to my first writer's conference. For reminding me that I still had compassion during times when I was sure I'd run out. And, mostly, thank you for teaching me the inimitable power of one word: BELIEVE.*

*I love you, Heather, my soul sister and dearest friend. Divinity & The Python was, from its inception, your book.*

*(she shoots/she scores)*
*love, b*

# ACKNOWLEDGEMENTS

I am so grateful that Divinity & The Python has the opportunity to soar!

First, to Panverse Publishing and all the players thereof, thank you, thank you, thank you, for taking on my novel and helping it become the best it could be. I owe special gratitude to my editor and friend, Dario Ciriello. Your judicious eye has enlivened so many passages in this book and every addition, elimination, or plucked word was spot-on. It is a privilege and a pleasure to work with you.

To Ann Meier—unlike Cele, your love of the Tarot really was eclipsed by your love for Cameron Weste (and I still think that's so cool!) Ann, you are more my Cele than you know and I love you. Thank you for reading, re-reading, critiquing, and championing this project from first-vomit-draft until polished.

To Heather McFadzen, Leighanne McDonald, Linda Miersch, Patti Shea, Erica Snook-Pennings, Erin Haig-Sather, and Christine LeBlanc, beta-readers extraordinaire. Your input, feedback, and enthusiasm became part of the energy that lives in these pages. I am so thankful.

Lastly, mostly, and always, thank you to my James and our girls for indulging all the times when I am a quirky writer instead of a sensible social worker, and for your willingness to share me with an imagination that holds court far too much of the time. Loving you and being loved back is the best gift I could ever have.

For all of you, any of you—there are not enough colored stones or jars. I am so grateful.

br— May, 2013

# CHAPTER ONE

The Python hung in the air, a hologram of green light with an illusion of movement enhanced by wind from a generator. Shaynie Gavin glared into its cavernous eyes. "Well, Python?" Her Tarot cards *whish-whished* in her hands. "You gonna help me or hurt me tonight?"

"Let *me* answer that." Gray Ward, Python music man, moved through the light of the hologram snake to plop his elbows on her bar.

She stopped shuffling cards to flick the brim of his fedora then mimicked him with his deejay's voice. "'Ah, Shaynie,'" she quoted "'It's not a matter of *if* The Python will hurt you. It's a matter of *when*'."

"Yet you're still here. Grab that carpentry degree—"

"It's called a Journeyman's Master Builder Ticket—"

"—and get the hell out. You have your own business—"

"No, I don't, Gray. Not yet."

"Close enough."

She wished. "Right now I'm barely covering expenses and the bank's still on my back. I might have enough to get the next phase of my operating loan, but here's a crazy quirk: I also like to eat. So much that I've become convinced it's a basic necessity."

He tapped her garnish tray of cherries. "So stuff these in a Ziploc and go."

Why oh why did she always argue? She already knew this whole script.

"And take me with you."

Whoa. That wasn't in the lines. She stared at him, stage-struck by an actor who'd suddenly ad-libbed.

"The Python will swallow you or strangle you," he said quietly. "Nothing in between."

She set her Tarot cards aside. "Gray, has something happened? What's—"

"Same old, same old." He looked away. "Nothing new."

Bull. The way he wouldn't make eye contact was new. And the complete lack of humor, that was new too.

He jutted his chin at her deck. "Ask your question."

She didn't reach for her cards, instead peered at him, forced eye contact.

"Shaynie, c'mon." A bit of sparkle that *was* Gray, her oldest friend Gray, shone in the gaze he lifted. He pushed her deck with a finger. "Ask."

Keeping eye contact she shuffled, sent her question back into the cards. Would The Python help or hurt? Meaning would it be a slow night, hopping night, or mere mediocre? The cards *whish-whished* until she felt it, the familiar hum that said the answer was present. She dealt three, face down. Gray hovered as she turned the first. "The Queen of Pentacles. Pentacles mean money. So the Python Pack will be generous tonight."

"Oh?" Gray turned her next card. "And will they also spill all their booze?" The card revealed eight Cups, all askew.

"Emotional risk." Shaynie frowned, confused by its meaning but proud to recite it like a pro. She was getting better and better. "Emotional risk, or the need to set limits."

"'Limits'? No kidding. Tonight will be how many shifts Jude's had you work without a night off?"

"Does your cousin know how much you complain about him?"

"Is the ocean wet?"

*Sarcasm, thy name is Gray Ward.* Yet the look he shot over to Jude—part annoyance, part affection—was one Shaynie knew. She often wore it herself when she peered at her brother, Andrew. Keeping quiet she flipped her last card. They each caught a breath.

*"Summum malum."* The Devil glared up from the counter, one hand raised in a jaunty little wave. "The sum of all evil."

"Strangled or swallowed whole." Gray tapped the card. "Shaynie when you decided to work for Jude I told you to stay a few months, not a few years."

And she'd agreed, but…she glanced at the overblown brandy snifter she used as a tip jar. Shift after shift it was filled.

Gray looked at it too. "The Pentacles, as you call them, come with a price. This place is a bad habit, and take it from someone who knows bad habits; they change who you are."

"The Python is *not* my addiction and it *hasn't* changed me."

His incredulity hung between them, but she didn't lower her chin. 'Cause she was right. The Python hadn't changed her. It had only marked her. One dark footprint on her soul. A lesson learned one black Hellnight. *And for it I am grateful.* A small dish of gratitude stones was under her counter. She reached blindly and took one, dropped it into a jar.

The audible click made Gray's nostrils flare. "This place is nothing to be grateful for," he said and turned, steps echoing in the pre-opening silence as he stalked to his music booth on the other side of the dance floor.

Shaynie watched him. What had happened to launch his ever-present Python superstitions into overdrive? Or—and she sighed here—maybe they weren't in overdrive at all. Gray blamed every missed opportunity and unanswered résumé on the club, believing the place somehow sabotaged him, kept him trapped by paying him well. "But you forget that The Python's not a person," she murmured to his figure, moving briskly now, and tight-mouthed, through his pre-opening prep.

The Python. Not human. Although…her gaze tracked the dance floor, sought its dark corners. What would Gray say if she told him that sometimes, in pre-open moments like this, she could swear the walls slithered? And that other times she heard them hiss her name? A prickle straightened her spine and she shooed it, gathered her Tarot and squared the cards into a neat little stack. Outside the Python Pack would be waiting, queued up in front of a cut glass entrance that looked like a fanged snake mouth. The Pack, willing to be "swallowed whole", would soon be gulped into the club with two goals in mind. Get drunk. Get laid.

*'Cause' The Python changes who you are.* "And maybe you've tried." Her eyes scored the walls. "But you did *not* succeed." She slipped her Tarot deck into its bag, tucked it into its spot between her stones and a photo. The picture pulled a smile forth and she lifted it. A weathered brick building. Stained glass cathedral windows. *"Your own business."* Yes. Yet right now its very existence was what kept her tethered to her role in The Python: Shaynie Gavin, the bartender who poured vino like a vamp. A different entity entirely than Shaynie Gavin the carpenter who took old things, dead things, and crafted them into pieces beautifully brand new. "Soon," she whispered to the ethereal old building. "I'll have our money soon."

"Ahem!" A throat clearing over her shoulder made her jump. "That place still doesn't scare you?"

Jude Kevlin, Gray's cousin and Python front man, had a cherub's face with dancing dimples. He poked a finger at the photo. "Divinity scary," he said. "Python merry."

Spoken like a true salesman. She slid the photo back into place, nose twitching as a scent, lavender, drifted up from it. Divinity. She enjoyed an inner smile. It, unlike The Python, *was* alive. But no one seemed to believe it but her.

Then again, maybe no one knew it but her.

Jude grinned. "Don't you look mysterious. Now, are you done with that voodoo you do? There's a line up outside. We need to throw wide the doors!"

Doors. To her they symbolized transport from one world to another. What, she wondered, did they mean to The Python?

*Summum Malum.*

A tremor jittered on her shoulders. *God, Shaynie.* She shook it off. *Get a grip. Ditch Gray's melodrama.*

"Shaynes?" said Jude.

"One sec." Melodrama or not, she struck a match, its smell acrid as she lowered the wee flame to a candle. Black, always black. "For protection."

"From what?"

*Your scary bar.* "You never know."

Jude rolled his eyes then looked across the dance floor. "Maestro?"

Gray nodded and The Python erupted, a techno beat like a tribal pulse. Shaynie's body rocked along with it before she stilled herself with an ironic smile. *Ah, The Devil's voice. Sweet to the ear.*

The rush of strobe lights that formed the hologram drew together and the green python raced across the dance floor, its tongue licking the bar with wind that blew her hair into a riot of glossy chocolate. Jude laughed. "Sexy," he said.

She scowled, finger combing her tresses back into order. "I hate that damn thing."

"Aw." He affected a pout. "But look how it loves you." And, like a techno-light pet, the snake licked her once more then splintered, became countless strobes illuminating more snakes everywhere. The pewter rail around the bar was a python. The iron table legs were pythons. Even the swizzle sticks, silver metallic, were pythons.

"And we're open!" Jude called.

The Python Pack flooded the place with titties, tushies, and—Damn!—only a little testosterone? What the heck had The Pentacle Queen been talking about? Gals didn't tip. *Well, Python?* Shaynie mixed the first drink of the night. *Help me or hurt me?*

Her first customer took the hi-ball—and her change.

Guess that's my answer.

Jude, from his station, caught her eye. "I feel outnumbered."

"I wish you weren't."

"Don't worry. It's a game night." His dimples danced in time to Gray's music. "It'll change."

Would it? Typically when the city's pro hockey team played at home their tills sang, but tonight...she glanced around, feeling as glum as the gaggle of girls who stood wallflower-esque beside the dance floor. All dressed up in the wrong place to go. She almost felt sorry until—

"Omigod! Jude!" One, a sky-scraper blonde, deliberately stretched high enough to lift her skirt, flash an electric hued thong. "Did you see that?"

He grinned. "God bless The Python."

God? Whatever or whoever *He* was, He had *nothing* to do with The Python. "God bless her with a little self respect," Shaynie muttered, but as Panties the Blonde snake-danced toward her station she pasted on a glittering, please-tip-me smile.

Panties beamed back. "Martini, please."

Her voice, high and breathy, made Shaynie cringe. Affected baby-doll. Far from feminist. "What kind of martini?"

"Oooh…" Panties' features crunched. "The one with the berry. *You* know—that turkey berry."

Oh, Lord. Not a feminist or a Mensa member. *Yet who the heck am I to talk?* Shaynie glanced down at her own barely-there costume. It hardly screamed, "women's rights," and nothing about wearing it in a meat market club was smart. "I think you mean cranberry."

"Right!" Panties' bleached teeth were as white as her hair. "You make them even better than Jude."

Shaynie blinked. "I've served you before?"

"Well, 'course, silly!" Panties fired change into the tip goblet. "We chat most weekends."

They did? And she'd never paid a whit of attention. So much for The Python not changing who she was. Shame lit her cheeks and she plopped an extra-fat cranberry into the martini, presented it with a flourish. "Here you are. One turkey martini."

Panties giggled and something; maybe the baby-doll voice, perhaps the little girl way she lifted her finger when she took a sip, made Shaynie flash a hand out, clasp hers. "Hey," she said.

Panties blinked saucer eyes.

"Play safe tonight."

"Aw! Thanks, sweetie!" In the work of a second Panties' belly was flat on the bar and Shaynie leapt back but too late. Panties seized her by the shoulders with surprising strength, and the kiss she planted on Shaynie's mouth was lip-gloss gooey. A sparse crowd of men cheered at what had to be another crotch-shot, one crying "Thank you, honey! Now can you do that again? With some tongue?"

Not bloody likely! Mopping her mouth, Shaynie scurried back, out of reach. "Pentacle Queen, did you see that?" she muttered. "I deserve to make money tonight."

Flopping back to her feet Panties drained her turkey martini. "See you," she tittered.

"Uh-huh. I see you alright." Shaynie watched as Panties' swinging fanny melted back into colored lights and bared flesh. "For God's sake look after yourself." She glanced down at her protection candle. Its flame flickered in mutinous time to the music. So, in fact, did her foot. *Dammit!* She planted her stilettos firmly on the floor. How was it that The Python always got the last laugh?

'Cause it changes who you are.

Hours slid by on girlie drinks and a tip goblet so empty she could see through it. *Pentacle Queen, where are you?*

The hologram licked her, blew her hair.

She bared her teeth at it.

"Hey, Shaynes, why so glum?" Jude poured a bottle from over his head.

She watched the liquor hit the glass and splash high enough to paint the sides but not leap the rim. Expert, she thought, but called back "Show off."

He grinned and slid the glass, also without spilling, to a buxom down the bar. "Told you this place would rock."

Rock? There was no one at her station. She slumped, elbows on the bar, then jolted upright when Gray, over the speakers, boomed "Ladies and Gentleman! Eyes to the door!"

Every head turned and six notes split the air, the intro of the vintage classic, *Bad To The Bone.* Aha! Python theme music for the city's pro hockey team.

"Whoa, *baby*!" Jude hooted. "Edmonton's pride and joy has *arrived*!"

Oh, thank you Pentacle Queen! And hello, professional athletes! Shaynie reached under her counter, patted her Tarot bag.

"Nelson here?" Jude asked, looking.

*God.* Shaynie's smile shriveled. *That's all this night needs.* Noel Nelson, Jude's oldest buddy, was Edmonton's biggest ego. The rumor mill implied that gobs of family money had secured his spot in the Big League far more than had any athletic talent, and Shaynie, a lifelong hockey fan, believed it. Noel had been the epitome of entitlement since they were all just teens and that he and Jude remained friends was astonishing. Moneyed pedigrees were all they shared; Jude, a workhorse who never breathed a word of his wealth, was polar opposite to Nelson who paraded his coinage like a badge of honor. She couldn't stand him, and Gray, with good reason, flat-out hated him.

"Huh." Jude scanned the players. "No Noel. Just King Pussyhound."

Cameron Weste, this season's newest star centre, led the stroll of players into The Python.

"Now *that's* arrogance," Jude stated, and Shaynie laughed. How was Weste any different than Noel? In fact, cocksure and strutting, all these pro athletes were exactly the same. Well…almost the same. She took in Weste. The other players did not have big, blue bedroom eyes that were always come-hither. Or pout-mouths that wickedly flashed whiplash smiles. And that body. Her tongue came out. Ripped, defined, and oh-so big.

She quickly stopped licking her lips. *Seriously, Shaynie? He's not on the menu and, more importantly, neither are you.* Still she watched Weste's eyes cut through the crowd, seeing everyone without really seeing anyone at all. Skating over her like she was furniture. *Ah, for I am but a servant to The Ice Deity.* On impulse she bowed. His brow was furrowed when she rose. *Oops!* She chomped back a giggle. *Guess he did see me after all.* Not that it mattered. Their eye contact was rapidly eclipsed by the boobs and bums bouncing toward him, Panties leading the parade. "Wes-teee!" she cried.

"Oh, dear." said Shaynie. "*This* can't miss."

The corner of Weste's pout-mouth cocked—*yep, there's the whiplash smile*—and Sky-High Panties draped her arms around his neck. *She likes turkey martinis, Weste. Please let her steer you over here.* 'Cause the radio said he made seven million a year, yet not once in the months he'd been coming to The Python had he graced her station with his presence. Seemed to categorically avoid her, actually; the nearest he'd been was to once hover at the elbow of Noel Nelson as the latter draped himself on her bar: "So Shaynie, you've teased me for what—thirteen years? Why not just give it up?" Nelson's gaze had zeroed in on her crotch. "Let me make your dreams come true."

"Nightmares are dreams too." She'd looked at *his* crotch. "Thanks, but I'll pass, Ladykiller."

Nelson had snarled, but Weste, oblivious to the double meaning, had laughed and laughed, the thunder-rumble so infectious she'd laughed too.

But apparently not hard enough. He hadn't ordered a drink, hadn't said a single word, and with no drink and no dialogue there was absolutely no tip. *So how about tonight, Pentacle Queen? Can I see Weste's wallet?* She tapped her Tarot deck and Panties, as if on cue, swiveled to lead him toward her bar. *Yes!*

Jude, juggling shots at his station, called "Hey, honey, need a drink?"

Shaynie glared—*Panties is mine!*—and The Pentacle Queen held court, for while the blonde blew Jude a kiss she continued her beeline for Shaynie, Weste on her arm. *Oh, yes! Oh excellent! Queen, I will never doubt you again!* "You're back!" She beamed at Panties. "Turkey Martini?"

"No." Panties flopped on the bar. "I want a Dong."

*Oh. My. God.* "Well." Shaynie tucked her tongue in her cheek. "So much for gobble gobble." She flicked Weste a look.

Amusement glittered in his eyes.

"And you'll have...?"

"Depends. If you're gonna bow to me again, champagne."

And that's what I get for being a wise ass to a wise ass. "Sorry, but my quota is one bow a night."

"Really?" The whiplash smile flashed. "That's not what I heard."

Ah. Shades of Noel Nelson. Her grin shattered.

"C'mon," he said. "Make me feel special."

"I think you feel special enough." And why it bugged her that he'd just proven to be as big an ass as Nelson was anyone's guess. *Must be The Python, changing things again.* From seeing a baby doll in Panties to a potential bedmate in a pro hockey player. Right. Like she'd pick up anyone *here.* After all, how many footprints on her soul did she need? A chill lanced her shoulders.

Weste said "Well, since no champagne how about gin and tonic? With lemon."

"Twisted g'n't." She flipped a hi-ball, filled the glass, then impaled a lemon wedge with a silver plastic python. "And now," She nodded at Panties. "Your Dong." She selected a shot glass, rolled it end over end down her knuckles.

"Cool trick," Weste rumbled.

She did not reply and instead whirled two bottles, one in each hand, then layered a bit of Bailey's beneath a longer shot of Minze. *Beat that, Jude.* She plucked Weste's twenty from Panties' fingers. "How much change, Sweetie?"

"Oh, keep it," Panties tittered.

Shaynie rained the change into her tip goblet with a smirk. "Costly Dong."

"You have no idea." Weste looped an arm around Panties, steered her into the crowd. *Tried* to steer her into the crowd. Panties' flamingo legs teetered, and then when she reeled he had to stop, right her.

"Oh, damn." The smirk danced off Shaynie's face. "Wasn't that me who said 'play safe'? Some watchdog *I* am. Hey, Jude?"

"Yes, m'love?" He twirled a bottle of Curacao like a baton.

"That blonde with Weste. Cut off."

His brow hopped and the Curacao flashed, bright blue.

She approached him, found his ear. "She just knocked back a shooter I had no business making. She's staggering."

He frowned. "Did you know before you served?" When Panties had flopped, boneless on her bar? "No," she said but not quick enough.

"Shaynes! That's a rookie gaffe! What the hell were you thinking?"

About The Queen. "I—"

"Media converges when the hockey boys come and you know it. Keep pouring booze for stumbling drunks and the paper will write. The liquor inspector will check. And suddenly, my liquor license—" he snapped his fingers "—Poof!"

She hung her head. "It, uh, it was Weste's enticing wallet."

"No, Shaynes. It was your enticing old funeral parlor."

Spat with so much venom her head snapped back.

He mistook shock for anger. "I am *not* the one who's wrong here."

True. A muscle twitched in her jaw.

"Don't do it again."

She pivoted, marched back to her station.

Her photo was beaded by spilled booze. She swiped it with a bar rag. *Soon,* she said, silent, and for a heartbeat dove through its stained glass, felt peace and smelled lavender.

"Hey!"

Serenity splintered, she jerked up.

Weste's storm eyes danced. "You know what I want."

"Ah, yes. Daiquiri, right? Strawberry?"

"Hilarious."

"I try." She shot gin into a hi-ball, filled it with tonic. "With lemon or without?"

"Put your finger in it. That'll make it tart."

"Put a sock in it. That'll shut it up."

He grinned and handed her a twenty.

She made change. He waved it to her tip goblet.

She bowed, low and long, then showered his money atop all the rest. "You shouldn't drink so fast."

"I didn't drink fast. I just like to buy things in twos."

Interesting. Although— "You did buy two. A g'n t and a shooter."

"Two of the same thing. Trust me, I'm not interested in Dongs."

She bit back a grin. "Well, for the record, your tanked typical won't be interested in dongs either unless you take her this." She filled a beer mug with water. "Sober her up."

He spun the mug upon bar top condensation "You really playing cupid? Or just covering your ass?"

"*My* derriere? Those aren't *my* undies peeking out for the whole Python Pack to see."

"Maybe they should be." He hoisted the mug, drained the water. "Then you wouldn't leave here like Nelson says you always do. Alone."

He swaggered away before she could slice him with a comeback—or shoot him in the face with her soda dispenser. He'd gossiped about her with Nelson? "Alone is a *choice,*" she called after his broad shoulders.

He didn't turn.

Grumbling, she fake-smiled her way through the rest of the night; a flurry of sold booze, spilled booze and sticky booze rings on the bar. But by the time Jude flicked the houselights— "Going once! Going twice!"—she saw The Queen had been right; her tip goblet was stuffed. And *she* was wiped. Over the speakers The Python finale song pierced the air and she was grateful that the Pack knew just what to do. To the tune of *People Are Strange,* various boobs and bums found the door, some with hockey players in tow, some with just girlfriends as guides. *Don't sweat it, sisters.* She saluted them with her customary beer mug of water. *Alone is not necessarily lonely.* Contrary to what Cameron Weste had implied.

She looked around for him. Nowhere in sight. Possibly already naked with Panties.

She captured a yawn as Gray, looking as wasted as she felt, linked arms with two stragglers who weren't quite willing to find the door. He led them in a chorus-line kick to the snake mouth. "G'night dolls!" he bade.

They draped over him, matching boas of teased hair and bare arms.

Shaynie shook her head. "Good luck getting rid of them now, Grayson."

Jude, beside her, did not reply, had not said a word since she 'fessed up to Panties' Dong. Pouting. His least lovable feature. Although... The Python was his baby just as much as Divinity was hers. "Hey, my friend." She ventured over, slid an arm 'round his waist. "How about you cash out and let me clean house tonight?" There. A peace offering. She waited to see how it would be taken.

His stiff features melted. "The Python Pack's trashed this place, Shaynes. I'll count the cash, but no way do you mop up alone."

*Truce.* She released a held breath then reached under the bar, seized the t-shirt she kept for all the work the Python Pack didn't see. A men's double XL, it draped well past her knees, hid her Python provocateur. "Can't wait for tunics." She kicked off her stilettos. "And moccasins." Grabbing a cleaning bucket, she got started.

She was halfway down the bar when a shadow fell across granite. She looked up.

Cameron Weste looked back.

"Bar's closed, Weste."

"Yeah, but I want to know something."

"Library's downtown."

He planted his palms on the bar. "You mocked me."

"Uh-huh. And you mocked me. What's your point?"

"My point is I was teasing but you weren't. And I want to know why."

She rocked back, bar rag dripping on her t-shirt. Was he serious?

He crossed his arms over his chest.

Oh, yeah. He was serious. "Weste, I didn't mock *you.* I mocked the things you *do.*"

He jacked one brow over a storm-sky eye.

She fired her rag in the bucket. "When you—and your cohorts—strut through that door it's like you follow a script. Same buddies, same drink, and, before long same-different girl: long legs, tight tushie and hair; blonde with a side of no brains. You're Python-predictable. It's funny."

"So I'm boring. Shallow."

"I said predictable, not shallow. And you are. I always know what's going to happen next."

He stood there, a human thunderstorm that loomed over her for what felt like a full minute.

She wondered if she was supposed to feel intimidated.

"You," he said finally, "Have *no idea* what I'm going to do next."

## CHAPTER TWO

SUNSHINE SPILLED a brand new day into Divinity, stained glass light warm on Shaynie's face. "The Devil was in The Python last night," she said.

*"Diable?"* Cele Boisvert, her teacher, her friend, pursed ageless lips. "And who were his companions?"

*A sky-high pair of Panties and a few Knights of the Round Ice Rink.* Shaynie shoved Weste's storm eyes and slick smile away. "Eight Cups and the Pentacle Queen."

"An Eight?"

An eight was more alarming than The Devil? Yet it seemed that something outside agreed. The flood of window sun vanished beneath a scudding January cloud, left Shaynie standing in a pool of shadows.

"Eight is a karmic number," said Cele. "Its very appearance a mirror image, top and bottom. Past reflected in the present." She paused. "Meaning The Devil, who you've seen in The Poison before, visited you. And Pentacles—money—, too."

"You're saying that I saw The Devil *literally* last night?"

"*Oui.* Possibly."

A rash of goosebumps raced over her skin. What would the cards say today? "Let's get into my reading-lesson."

Cele's caftan was a swirling cloud as she led them to a table tucked against a street-facing window seat. "Call your question into the deck," she murmured and Shaynie shuffled the cards, let them *whish* between her hands until they hummed. The Devil. Where was he? Who was he? She dealt a spread, breath suspended as she turned the first card.

The Ten of Swords, each blade rammed into a prone figure's spine. "Stabbed in the back," murmured Shaynie. "Betrayal."

Cele, nodding, circled the number on the card with her fingernail. "A lesson on the number Ten, *Cheri.* Where the Eight is a mirror, past reflected in present, the Ten is a reflection of opposites. Look." She tapped the number one. "Something." Her finger moved to the zero. "Next to nothing. A ten represents the duality which exists in us all."

"Dark and light," said Shaynie. "Innocence and depravity." *A carpenter and a vamp.*

Cele said "Beauty and brutality? Something that hides its brutality behind, or within, its beauty?"

"Or can be brutal despite its beauty?"

Cele looked up, stunned or shaken, it was hard to tell. "*Oui,*" she said softly. "That too."

Shaynie smiled, pleased and strangely comforted by her intuition. She turned the middle card, wincing. "Damn swords!" Life's challenges. And this one, the Seven, was one of the worst.

"Someone is feeding you lies."

Which the Tarot reminded her of in almost every spread, but— "These are new." she tapped the last two. "The Ace of Cups. A beginning. Divinity."

"Tut, *Cheri!* Cups mean *amour,* not business."

"Divinity is my love *and* business." Sunbeams rushed through stained glass. "See?" she said, then laughed when scent joined the sunshine. Lavender, everywhere. "And smell that?"

"*Non.*" Cele impatiently tapped the next card. "Focus, *Cheri!* The Two of Cups is next, see? *Amour.* Love. A partner."

"A partner?" Shaynie recoiled. "No. No partners. Divinity is *mine.*" A fact she'd known the moment the realtor had unlocked the old morgue—reluctantly, and with a hasty speech about the place being slated for a wrecking ball. "No!" she'd cried, shocking him as they stood near where she and Cele sat now, in the upper floor funeral parlor, colored light fuzzy through the then-grimy windows. "This building is sacred." A place where both the living and dead had once received equal reverence. A place which would understand her love of taking things dead and abandoned—neglected items, old wood—and crafting them into beauty. Life from death. Resurrection. *Divinity.* The name had whispered itself to her as she stood, enveloped in dusty window light. Divinity, the lounge of her dreams, a place that would showcase her furniture and offer Tarot readings, reiki healings, and, most importantly, respite from a world that eschewed spirituality and scoffed at New Age.

Cele cleared her throat. "Shaynie," she said. "Not everything is Divinity."

Nonsense. Everything was *absolutely* Divinity.

"Darling, a Tarot reading is a living thing—it cannot be limited to one wish in your heart."

"But Divinity's all I want."

"Yet love is what you need. Look." Cele pointed to the Two. "A woman and a man—not a building."

Shaynie stayed stubbornly silent. Cele sighed. "You choose not to believe me. So flip the last card, heed its direction."

*Summum malum.*

The breath she drew somehow sounded like frost.

"Lust," Cele intoned. "The Devil is utter devotion but *not* like love. More like obsession."

Obsession? Divinity? Surely not. Although…who had served drunk Panties in pursuit of Weste's fat wallet? She hung her head.

Cele, at her side, read the reading. "Full circle. Your usual cards except this time with love and joy in between. You'll be so blindly happy that you'll be vulnerable. Protect yourself, *Cheri*."

"I do protect myself. Cele, you know that—"

"—that you're alone now, always? *Oui.* It breaks my heart. And it is clearly not working."

"Then what will?"

"Eyes open. Heart open."

"Heart open? When something's out to betray me?" She read the cards, from the swords to *summum malum.* Deception. Obsession. Fooled by the Devil? The thought felt like a shiver.

Cele watched her. "Your heart can be closed to evil too. Keep it open. Keep it wise." She gathered the cards, wrapped them in their silk scabbard. "And one more thing, *Cheri.* A necklace or a choker. Something to encircle your neck, guard it." She reached out, and when she lifted Shaynie's hair the sensation was a jolt. It felt like the hologram python, blowing her tresses off her nape. Would a necklace keep *that* thing away?

"Well," she said lightly, and cast the thought away, chastising herself for sounding so much like Gray. *Speaking of obsessive….* "Between protection and poison, how am I supposed to paint this place today?"

"Why, with your usual tenacity of course."

Tenacity. Some would say foolishness. Like the loans officer who was coming. He had accepted the thirteen years of saved Orphan's Benefits she'd used to secure the morgue but had laughed when she'd requested a traditional loan for the rest. "Funding? For the hospitality industry? Ms. Gavin, you are an optimist!" The best he could offer was a draw mortgage which demanded proof of progress at scheduled intervals.

"Today the bank needs to see eighty percent painted, the wiring complete, and a few samples of furniture in the showroom." Her gaze moved to an armoire and *étagère* she'd set out, both fashioned from salvaged barn wood. The two tables standing between them were crafted out of vintage doors.

Cele said "The wiring, *Cheri?* It is done?"

"Absolutely. It pays to keep one's old buddies from tech school."

"You mean Stephen?"

"Uh, no." Ex boyfriends did not do favors. And besides, "Steve's a welder, not an electrician."

"Ah, of course. Now what of the paint?"

Her least favorite job. "I thought I'd finish our divining rooms." She grabbed a paint bucket she'd set by the door.

"Ah, amethyst." Cele beamed. "A red mother, a blue father. A color suspended between hot and cold."

"A Ten," Shaynie said.

Cele blinked then laughed. "*Oui,* my star pupil. A Ten. Purple," she said, "Is the Diviner's shade. Now, tell me—which room do *I* paint?"

Shaynie gaped. Cele sniffed. "One of those Divining Rooms is mine."

"Cele, you know you don't have to."

"I know that I want to."

"You pity me."

"*Non.* I *love* you. *Je t'aime.* I want to see you succeed. Now. Paint!" She clapped bejeweled hands. "And the radio. This silence must be killing you."

Shaynie's lips quirked. "I've been at The Python too long."

"*Oui.* You certainly have."

The radio was a companion as they dove into color. "Looks like our team's in for a tough game this evening," said the announcer. "Their opponents have never looked better."

Another home game? Shaynie rolled an amethyst stroke up one wall. The Python would be hopping tonight. A smile tickled her mouth. *Wonder how Mr. You-Have-No-Idea-What-I'll-Do-Next made out with Panties?*

The announcer broke in. "Cameron Weste's lucky to be back in the lineup. He was slated to be a healthy scratch due to lackluster performance."

"Ha!" Her roller made a purple splotch on the wall.

"Something funny, *Cheri*?"

"That hockey player they're talking about—Cameron Weste. I met him last night."

"Really? Snaking his delicious self through The Poison? Shaynie-*Cheri,* you did not tell me this."

"Py-thon," Shaynie enunciated. "And did you just call Weste 'delicious'?"

"You have a better word?"

*Uh-huh. Smart ass. Predictable. A Nelson clone.* "Why didn't you ever mention that you follow hockey?"

"I am French-Canadian." Cele sniffed. "You should know I follow hockey."

It came out "'ockey" Shaynie hid a giggle. "Weste's not my style."

"A body that would make angels weep is not your style?"

Shaynie jerked her roller up. Too hard. Purple beads spattered on her arm. She swiped the dots with a rag. "I didn't say he wasn't good looking. What I meant was he knows it."

"He deserves to know it. He is beautiful."

"Cele! He's a man-slut."

"Ah. Sexually astute too?"

"'Beautiful'? 'Sexually *astute*'? What's with these euphemisms? What Weste probably is, is a two pump chump."

Cele laughed, wind chimes in the breeze. "Why not find out?"

"Please. I don't do man-sluts."

"You don't do anyone, *Cheri.* You're alone all the time."

*Alone.* An echo of the cards—and of Weste's jab. Her smile died.

"The way you giggle," Cele added. "You enjoyed him."

"I laughed at him." Mocked him, to be precise.

"Ah. He made you smile."

"And for a smile I should have sex with him? Really, Cele. Making me smile and making me scream are two different things."

Silence exploded. Then "'Scream,' Shaynie?"

"Slip of the tongue." She didn't look at her, rolled paint up the wall.

Cele set her own paintbrush down. "There are no accidents, Darling. Especially not ones that are screams."

Shaking suddenly, Shaynie slipped her roller back into its tray.

Cele drifted over, sequins and silks impossibly absent of any amethyst mistakes. "Forgive me, *Cheri.* It was thoughtless to tease about your god Cameron Weste."

Now he was a God? And, more specifically, *her* god? *Not in this lifetime.* Still, it dissolved the darkness. "It's okay," she said. "I'm okay. But really, Cele, I'm not interested—even if Weste sports the naughty of a god."

"Ooh, but he must. So much that angels weep. Now, this, Darling, this I would like to see."

Shaynie laughed. "Then maybe you should come to The Python. He's bound to be there tonight after the game."

Cele's eyes popped. "You forget Barnabas?"

Barnabas. A black-clad, mile high presence who did not walk so much as lurk. He was the sweetest gentleman Shaynie knew, yet the first time she'd met him she'd been tempted to search for batwings. "Cele," she said, "I could never forget Barnabas."

"Who, by the way, also makes angels weep."

A bat with a big penis? A gale of giggles stormed and she swallowed once, twice, and was losing the battle when "Lattes!" was called out from the entrance.

"Ah!" Laughter disguised itself as delight. "Sustenance. We're back here, Jude!"

"*Cheri,*" Cele looked at a jewel-encrusted watch. "I must go."

"No latte?"

"Caffeine?" She looked horrified.

"You'll drink wine, but you won't have a coffee?"

"*Spiritus contra spiritum.*"

"Yes, yes. Alcohol is both the highest religious experience and the most depraving poison, but what, *mon ami*, does *spiritus contra spiritum* have to do with caffeine?"

"Alcohol serves a purpose, albeit a delicately balanced one. Caffeine, however, is an unnecessary agent. The lazy man's path to alertness."

"Yowch." Shaynie wrinkled her nose. "I'll be sure to feel guilty with every sip."

Cele tsked.

Shaynie grinned. "*Merci* for all of your help." She kissed her cheek. "And your beautiful heart. Hey, Jude." He'd entered the parlor. She relieved him of a cardboard tray rich with lattes and scones. "You're a welcome surprise."

"I know how you bow to the coffee gods." He smiled at Cele. "Madame Boisvert, I didn't know you were here. Please," He gestured to the tray. "Have mine."

"*Non. Merci.* I really must run. Barnabas waits."

The bat with the big penis. Shaynie clamped her teeth against giggles and Jude nodded, not so much as a twinkle in his eye. *He's learning.* She selected a scone.

Cele, wrapped in a cloak, drifted to her. "A necklace, *Cheri.* Do not forget."

"I won't. Here." Shaynie split the scone, quickly buttered it. "Try. It's still warm."

Cele bit into the baking. "Mmm." Her eyelids fluttered much like they had when they'd spoken of Weste. And, as though she read Shaynie's mind, she said, "This would make angels weep."

Shaynie grinned. "It seems a lot of things do."

"*Oui,"* Cele's smile became as sober as *spiritus contra spiritum.* "Many things do. *Au revoir, Cheri. Monsieur* Kevlin."

She glided to the door and only when it swooped shut did Jude say "She's spooky, Shaynes."

"No, she's wonderful."

He shuddered, grabbed a scone. "Getting lots done?"

"Getting there. And you? Been to The Python yet?"

"Been there, headed back. Owning a business means it's your bride." He sighed, looked around. "You sure you're ready for that?"

God, she knew *this* script too. "Why do you always assume I'm not?"

"I don't. I just know the sort of sacrifice business means—and I don't wish it on anyone."

He knew sacrifices? He'd been born to a property mogul. He'd never had to sacrifice a damn thing.

"It gets lonely sometimes."

A stab of shame lanced her belly. No sacrifices? Yeah, right. Ever since they were kids there had been nothing in his life—no hobbies, no leisure, not even a girlfriend. Just work. The result was a man who now had a knack for knowing exactly what type of venue would make money—and what type wouldn't. She held a breath as he looked around, released it when he said "I'd had doubts about black for the showroom, but it really works."

She grinned. "Just like snakes work for The Python."

He toasted her with his coffee. "Hey, speaking of my snake, we received a memento there this morning. Or rather, you did."

She hiked both brows.

"From Pussyhound Weste."

Weste again? He was haunting her. "This would be his 'something next,' I'd presume. Tell me, what did he send? A signed hockey stick to hang over my bar? To mark his territory with one of those phallic symbols he swings night after night?"

Jude choked on his coffee. "Uh...no. It's not exactly a stick."

"Oh? So exactly what is it?"

He said something that got muffled by another choking fit, but what she thought she heard..."Pardon?"

"A vibrator."

She spat latte all over the floor. *"You lie!"*

He reached into a bag she'd barely noticed, pulled out an object.

Her eyes widened. *"Oh my God."*

"He sent a letter too."

"Well wasn't that big of him."

Jude hacked on her choice of words. She winced too. "What's the letter say?"

"I don't know. I didn't open it. Here." He handed her an envelope.

To My Brunette Bartender, it said.

She tore it open, read aloud.

"Judging from your countenance I've little doubt you know what this is."

"My 'countenance'? What, did a dictionary fall open in the locker room and Weste just happen to see it? 'Countenance'." She rolled her eyes, kept reading.

"Save a hapless hockey player. Hand THIS out to girls who strictly want Dongs."

Because *he* was neither predictable nor shallow. She laughed, shook her head. "Did he leave a number?" She flipped the note over.

"Not if it's not on there."

"Hmph." She folded the note. "Guess I'll have to wait till tonight to razz Mr. Complicated."

Jude snorted. "If he comes back. If he didn't like the, uh, *wares*, he may slip his dong somewhere else."

"Oh, ye of little faith—or knowledge of your own species. Of course he'll be back."

Jude jacked a brow. She tsked. "Weste's got something to prove and so now—" She leapt into a fighting stance, wielded the sex toy like a sword. "*Engarde,* puck bunnies! The Ice Deity doth cometh…but too soon, sadly, for while he may masquerade as a thoughtful lover he is but a two pump chump."

Jude stared. "How much time have you spent in a small room with paint?"

"Not enough." She tossed the toy aside. "And as ungrateful as it seems I have to kick you out. I need to get at least two more walls done before the bank's here at three."

"The bank's coming? Why?"

*Because I am but a mere mortal who needed a loan while all you needed was a Dad who had an extra club kicking around.* She bit the ugly thought back. Where the heck was all this snot-green jealousy coming from today?

The Devil.

She drew her bottom lip into her mouth. "Draw mortgage," she said. "They need to see progress."

"And do you *have* enough progress?"

Oh, those skeptical eyes. She scowled. "No, Jude, I don't. That's why I need to paint."

"Shit." Color raced to his cheeks. "I didn't mean to sound condescending."

*Right.* She took a sip of coffee. "'s'okay."

No, it wasn't. And he knew it. "Know what's not okay?" His tone clearly shot for a smile. "The Python. 'Cause it's sure going to miss you when you give it a run for its money over here."

Because the crowd she was aiming for would rival The Python? She laughed. For a business maven he could, from time to time, be shockingly naïve.

He grinned too. "Here you'll be, surrounded by spirits and longing for the days when vibrators appeared out of thin air."

And slick whiplash smiles. What would Cele say if she knew her god frequented sex shops? Probably cheer. "Can you believe Weste told me I had no idea what he'd do next?"

Jude clucked his tongue. "He mustn't know that you behave yourself now."

"I beg your pardon?"

"Crap." His cheeks turned brick red. "Why is everything I'm saying today ten shades of asshat? What I meant was you don't party anymore."

She never really had. Just once. It had been enough.

And her expression must have said it because Jude tried a new tack. "You don't even dance with Gray anymore."

True. Prior to Hellnight she and Gray's hot salsa dance had been a predictable part of their work night. They'd always chortled merrily at the money they made in the hat they passed.

"—and you don't drink with us after we close," Jude went on.

"Drink with *you,*" she corrected. Gray didn't drink. And as for her, one nightcap as she cleaned up could hardly qualify as drinking, although… she *had* once enjoyed that sole drink after shift, far more than the bland mug of water she chugged now. She'd also enjoyed being the joy-filled gal who'd once embraced everything, even The Python, with deep spiritual gratitude. Now…*Eyes open. Heart open.* Now gratitude took a different form. Discernment. Sobriety. And she'd never told Gray or Jude why.

"The old you would've had great fun cutting Weste down," Jude stated.

She pursed her lips. The old her would actually have just had fun with Weste. And not necessarily sexually. Although…the cards did say she needed *amour,* and Cele had been right. Cameron Weste had made her smile. She retrieved the sex toy. It was goofball orange. "You know, Jude?" She twirled it. "Maybe you're right. Maybe it *is* time for a little fun."

## CHAPTER THREE

THE SINKING SUN stole her swagger. She should have known Jude's doubtful eye would forecast the loan officer's funding denial: "Ms. Gavin, I really thought I'd see more." Driving home, the cloud of that conversation hung over her. How was she supposed to manage "more", she had asked, without released funding? The banker's answer was a pained face. "Could I see all the finish carpentry completed and all the furniture in the showroom by next week?"

That was a lot more than the vague "eighty percent completed" he'd initially requested, and as he'd bustled out into the cold she'd wondered if even a hundred percent done would keep him in the old morgue long enough to assess her craftsmanship and skill.

Sighing, she pulled off Whyte and parked in the lot of her brownstone apartment. Snow lumped the front steps, made them muddy and uneven. "God, this place is a dump." She'd snap an ankle navigating those stairs in stilettos. "Note to self," she muttered. "Wear snow boots to The Python and *carry* stilettos." *And tonight will be how many shifts Jude's had you work without a night off?* Not enough, she reflected grimly. Because finish carpentry meant baseboards, crown molding...and what she hadn't been able to salvage from Divinity's initial reno she'd need to buy—with money she didn't yet have. "Pentacle Queen, I really need you tonight."

Showering felt more like drowning than baptism, and once she finished she stared at the candle she'd lit. Blue for intuition. *Yeah, right.* It illuminated nothing more than dingy walls and places where condensate had peeled all the paint. Sighing, she toweled her arms, frowning at the amethyst spatters that stayed behind. Body glitter. That's what she'd need. 'Cause Pentacle Queen or not, long sleeves were never tip friendly at The Python.

*And you're gorgeous when you dress like a whore.*

With a gasp she dropped hard to the edge of the tub. Those words, hissing through her memory like dead leaves rustling on a breeze, were Hellnight. A *memory.* Heart hammering, she held her breath, willing silence and stillness to perhaps conjure more.

They did not.

The gaping hole in her memory yawned, wider it seemed with the attempt to remember. But those words—"You're gorgeous when you dress like a whore." They'd come from *somewhere.*

She reached back, a year ago, grasped what she knew. A liquor-soaked party. Hot bodies, hot lights. Then a voice, *her* voice, drunk on booze and bravado, "Will you do me rough?" All she'd wanted was to have some fun. *Fun? Be honest.* Okay. All she'd wanted was something that would seem racy but feel right, something that would justify the way she'd refused that practical ring and sensible life her then-boyfriend Steve had proposed just that afternoon.

All she'd ended up with was something more—something new— to feel guilty about.

Waking up the next morning she'd heard the strains of *Let it Be,* repeating itself from her stereo. She'd been all alone. But when she'd crawled from her bed, looked at herself...

Shaking, she opened her towel, certain the bruises would be resurrected there, every color the same shade as a scream.

But her skin, creamy in the candlelight, was every bit as blank as the empty memory erasing the face of her Hellnight lover. She exhaled audibly, rose. Two jars perched on her vanity and, ignoring the one winking with rainbow-colored stones, she reached instead to the left for the one full of ink-black obsidians. "Burdens." She fished a rock from a bag of stones which, like the jars, she kept stashed everywhere. "Take this burden I call Hellnight." She held the rock up in the candlelight. "Lift its footprint from my soul."

The obsidian, glossy like a mirror, reflected her wide eyes, shamed and sad. She looked into them and spoke. "Burdens only magnify gratitude," she announced, but the edict, usually strong, resounded as lifelessly as the click the black stone made when it hit all the others. *So change the tone. End with gratitude.* Exhaling she selected a colored rock, closed her eyes to conjure an image.

Good God. Weste's florescent sex toy? And what she said stunned her even more. "I'm grateful for someone who made me laugh at being lonely." The colored stone made a lively little click as it landed in the jar. She stared at it. *"Lonely?"*

Her cell, not the stones, answered, vibrating from where she'd set it on the toilet tank.

"Shaynes!" Jude, sounding harried, pulled her from the pit she'd been blown into. "I hate to ask, but we're two hours from open and I've already got a line stretched 'round the block. Could you skip your ritual latte tonight? Come in early?"

Her latte at Has Beans. Her sedate drive—no music, just sports radio—to The Python. These predictabilities, these normalcies, ushered her completely back to the present. "I...yeah, I guess. What's with all the people?"

"Hockey's with all the people. The game's a barn-burner and your sweetheart is stealing the show."

"Weste?"

"God, no. Not Pussyhound. He's underperforming. Again. I'm talking about Noel."

Her sweetheart? An unexpected shudder made her tighten her towel. "Why do you insist on teasing me when you know I detest that grease stain?"

"Because the way you and Gray make him out to be the devil is funny."

The Devil. *Summum malum.* Hair stood on the back of her neck. "Gray has good reasons for hating Noel," she said stiffly. "And not one of them is funny."

Jude sighed. "You're right, Shaynes. The fact that Gray can't get over Noel stealing his girlfriend a hundred years ago when we were all sixteen isn't funny. It's pathetic."

A stolen girlfriend? That was so far from all of it—

He spoke over her speechlessness. "The real devil was Jen." The way he said it, so wearily, struck her. Maybe all old friends had scripts they knew. "She screwed around while wearing Gray's ring. She, my dear, was a whore."

*Whore.* It howled in her head like an ice breeze.

"Noel's not a villain." Jude clucked his tongue. "Case in point: he's not the one sending you smarmy sex toys."

*Seriously?* Of all straws to grasp. "You're tossing Weste into this? He's got nothing to do wi—"

"My point? Yes, he does. Pussyhound would bang *you* just for sport. Noel, however, has more scruples. He teases, but he knows your forbidden fruit act isn't an act."

But so did Weste. It was the message between the lines of the goofball vibrator, now a gelatinous sentry on her key table; a statement that said her "countenance" didn't run from bed to bed. Or to any bed at all. *All alone.* She tightened her towel again. "Weste's no devil, either."

"Right, Shaynes. Just keep telling yourself that."

"To hell with The Devil," she muttered at her station an hour later. The hologram python trolled the floor, roaring with wind and green light. Shielding her cards from it she dealt a rapid-fire spread. "Quickly," she whispered. "Show me past-present-future." Her eyes skipped the cards like a stone over water.

The Two of Wands and a couple of Knights, Cups and Swords. Good news, bad news, in that order. But the Two.... The hair on her arms stood, electric. Why shudder over such an innocent card?

"Shaynes?" Jude called. "You set for swizzles and straws?"

Gold like the python swizzles, her straws looked, right now, like tiny wands. Wands. Wands meant work. *And shivers.* She swung her eyes back to the card.

"Shaynes!"

"Uh—yeah. Yes. Lots of wands."

"*Huh*?"

She ignored him, rummaged for her cell.

"What about condiments? Got what you need?"

Hitting speed dial for Cele she raised the lid of her garnish tray. Citrus scent rose, sickly sweet. *Poison.* She wrinkled her nose.

"Shaynie! Condiments?"

"They're fine, Jude," she spoke over the ring tone in her ear. "Good to go."

"Okay then." He beamed. "Get ready for the countdown 'cause we're open in—"

"*Salut, Cheri*!" said Cele, on her cell.

She cupped a hand over her other ear. "Cele, I just did a spread and—"

"Ten!" bellowed Jude.

"—the Two of Wands. I laid it for the past and I know it's innocent, but it feels—"

"Nine!"

"—sinister," she said, then cringed. Aloud, her concerns sounded melodramatic. *Foolish.*

But Cele didn't scoff. "Ambiguity is *le deux de* wand. A surprise. A nasty surprise."

"Eight!" boomed Jude and Shaynie shivered. Eight. Past and present, both at once.

"*Cheri*?" said Cele. "What surrounds *le deux de* wand?"

"Knights—Cups and Swords. Good news, bad news."

"*Non.* These would be a lover and an aggressor. Light and dark. Which is," she said, "one more ten."

"And five!" Jude called. Shaynie swallowed.

"And look, *Cheri*, on *le deux*. What is present in symbol?"

Shaynie looked at the card. A wand stood in the nobleman's left hand while a globe was in his right, effectively creating "….a Ten," she breathed.

"Three!" yelled Jude.

Shaynie covered her ear tighter while Cele spoke "A present lover. A past aggressor. And *le deux* may be a warning that you must choose between them."

"A warning? But that's obvious, isn't it? Why would I choose the aggressor?"

"Because the Devil *looks* like an angel." Cele paused. "And he acts like one too."

"Two!" Jude echoed, as though he agreed.

"Remember, Darling—eyes open. *Heart* open."

"And we're *open!*"

The Pack flooded in, skin and adrenaline, and when the hologram roared it sent the two Knights on the bar flying. "I have to go," said Shaynie and the last thing she heard Cele say was "Protection, *Cheri!* Your neck!"

Her free hand flew to her bare throat as the other whisked the Two of Wands from the bar. Then the night was underway. The Python Pack, parched, kept her hopping, and when the last period of the hockey game, visible from the TV over her station, ended with a hometown win, there was a frenzy of hiballs, high fives, and Pentacles raining into her tip goblet. *Thank you Pentacle Queen.*

The revelry drew on for hours, it seemed, until Gray's music halted. Then the customary beat of anticipation hung in the air before the team's song—and the team—filled The Python. Cheers drowned the music as player after player filed through the door. Shaynie watched. Some players she recognized, a few she didn't, and she waited, waited…. but the snake mouth slid shut and her belly dipped, disappointment so sharp it surprised her. No Weste. She'd even dug his goofy sex toy from her bag, had planned to wag it like a finger. Now she jabbed it back into her purse. So much for trumping him tonight.

A new cheer arose. Her eyes raced to the door.

Noel Nelson high fived his way in, all teeth and testosterone. Shaynie's toes curled. *Narcissist Noel.* She rolled her eyes at the big wave he exchanged with Jude then glanced over the dance floor to Gray. He shared her loathing in the form of a sneer then smiled, commiserative. *Good luck,* he mouthed. They shared a silent laugh before the entrance swooped open once more.

Cameron Weste did not so much strut as slink, head ducked as though he hoped not to be seen. *Hmm.* Shaynie watched him. *Something's off.*

He raised his eyes as though he had heard her.

*Whoa. Ice Deity, what's with your countenance?* No strut, no eye sparkle, and definitely no smile. Still, she flung her arms wide, bowed so low her plunged neckline met her thighs.

It worked. When she straightened his frown had flown and when he laughed she did too. Grinning, she retrieved the vibrator and was about to wave it when a face stuck itself between them.

"Bowing to me?" Noel Nelson grinned. "Why? Did you see me… score?"

Good grief. Did guys never get tired of the ol' double entendre? "You scored, I poured. You did your job and I did mine. None of it's worth a bow, Noel. Not even a curtsey."

His flash of teeth lost their shine. "Christ, Shaynie. Don't you ever get tired of acting like such a little bi—"

"Nice bow." Weste, pushing through the crowd, stood beside Noel. "You're catching on."

She grinned. "What'll it be?"

"An answer," Noel, between them again, leaned over the counter much like Panties the night before. "After all these years, tell me—" His hand flashed, cupped her chin. "—what color *are* your eyes, Gorgeous? Gold? Or green?"

"Neither," said Weste, batting Nelson's hand down. "They're an eclipse. Gold *behind* green. Sun on a meadow."

The statement, its poetry, erased the way her skin curdled where Noel touched her. Still she shielded her chin as she gazed back at Weste.

No eye glitter, no whiplash smile, instead…*The Moon.* The words shivered into her ear as though her Tarot had breathed them. The Moon hid its depth by reflecting the sun. So what did Weste keep locked behind a swagger, a smile, and a stupid orange sex toy? A reading would tell her.

Her hands crept to her cards. An old Cele-warning swatted them back. "Never query the Tarot because you want your querent's answers." Chastened, she clasped her own hands while her gaze—*an "eclipse"? Really?*—skittered away from him.

The longing to turn his cards, however, remained.

"Put that smile away, Gorgeous," Nelson advised, dry. "Don't waste it on this guy. He's given more rides than Greyhound." He thunked Weste on the shoulder. "You should try channeling that energy onto the ice. If I could I'd lend you one of *my* goals."

*God, what an ass.* Shaynie took a read of Weste's face.

Amused, yet a chill lurked there, she could feel it, The Moon, drifting behind his storm eyes. *So what would your cards say Weste? What's beneath your façade?* She probed him, and only when Nelson laughed did she realize he was scrutinizing her, too. She crossed her arms over her navel-cut costume—*who shows the façade?*—and cleared her throat. "You guys drinking or yapping?"

Noel looked at Weste. "Buy me a beer?"

"Pfft. You shoot your wallet into the net tonight too? Get your own."

Noel eyed her. "Draw a draught. Give it good head."

If loathing were lethal he'd drop dead on the spot. She looked away from him. "Weste?"

"Ginger ale. Two of them."

She blinked. He stared. "That a problem?" He folded a crisp twenty into a peak.

"Only the money." She waved the twenty away. "Virgins are free."

"Huh. Where was *that* advice in high school?"

She flashed a droll little smile and he laughed, mercurial once more. *The Moon.* She glanced at her Tarot. *It'd be the first card he'd draw.*

"Hey!" Nelson was back between them. "My beer." He snapped his fingers in her face.

She smacked his hand. "Back off, Ladykiller."

Yes, if loathing were lethal *she'd* be dead. "Don't you call me that," he hissed. "You know how I felt about Jen."

"Yeah? Gray felt that way too," she said, and—as though he'd heard them—the latter spoke into his microphone, over the music.

"Temptress of The Taps," he said. "Are all your customers being good to you?" A thread of warning laced the words together, and from the corner of her eye Shaynie saw Jude cast a startled look over. Before her, Weste's brow climbed. She sought Gray. *I'm okay,* she mouthed. He wouldn't hear her, but over the years they'd become experts at lip-reading.

Nelson sneered. "Of course you're still on side with that druggie loser."

She bared her teeth, but any retort was lost to a swarm of short-skirts wedging between he and Weste. "Noel!" One fingered his collar. "Great game. Autograph?"

"No—a dance!" said another and grabbed him.

They melted into the crowd. Shaynie exhaled.

"You know," Weste nursed one of his sodas. "He really does like you."

"Noel likes himself."

He smiled The Smile. "Sounds like someone's been dumped."

"By *Nelson?"* If her eyes popped any further they'd shoot out of her face. "He said that?"

"Nah, just a guess, Gorgeous. Take it easy. I'm only trying to peace-make."

By hooking her up with Nelson? And here she'd thought *he'd* been interested. *Two of Cups. Uh-huh. Right.* "Thanks, Cupid, but I know Noel—not by choice—and trust me, I couldn't be less interested."

"Aw, c'mon." The Smile danced. "Nelson's better than no one."

"Oh, but I *have* someone, remember?" She twirled the orange toy in the air and it made a perfect double gainer into his soda. The cherry garnish surfed overboard and, plucking it up from where it made a fizzy plop on the bar, she popped it into his gaping mouth. "Thank you," she said, "For the thoughtful gift."

"You're welcome." He grinned and, chewing cherry, snatched up the vibrator, fired it arrow style over the crowd.

It landed on the dance floor and "Hey!" someone yelled. "What the hell is *that*?"

Weste collapsed on the bar, eyes streaming. Shaynie shook her head. "What an overgrown teenager you are."

"And what perfect entertainment *you* are." The Smile beamed. "Especially on a crap night like tonight in cold Deadmonton."

The slur to her city sailed by on a word. 'Entertainment'? *Whore.* Her grin faltered. *Hellnight.* Why was it back? She visualized a black stone. *Take this burden!*

Before her, Weste snapped a scarlet fifty. "For you," he said. "For enticing, then entertaining way too much ego."

Enticing. Entertaining. *Whoring.* The Knight of Swords rode and "Cock tease," she sputtered.

Weste's eyes widened.

"I-I mean, *cocktails.*" She pushed his fifty back. "I'm paid to make *cocktails* not—"

"Ladies, gentlemen, Python Prowlers of all ages." Gray, speaking on his microphone again, but this time his voice was paired with a collective crowd-gasp as he soared over the dance floor, holding fast to a zip-line aimed at the bar.

*Oh, no.* Shaynie's gut sank. *Not this.*

"It has been a very long time since my lady and I entertained you."

"*His* lady?" Weste's eyebrows went up.

Gray plopped his feet on her counter and offered one hand, covering his headset with the other. "Looks like right now may be a good time to—"

"Dance! Dance!" The Python Pack chanted. They remembered.

"Gray..." She didn't do this anymore. Not since Hellni—

"Say you still love me!" Gray, back into his mic, dramatized, clutched his heart.

The Python Pack screamed.

Nelson, back at her bar, snorted, "Seriously, Gorgeous?" He eyed Gray with derision. Weste, also watching, eyed *her* with derision.

And the decision was made.

Gray's zip line yanked them both up, away. Then her feet got cold. "Grayson—"

"No thanks necessary. It's not the first time I've rescued you from horny hockey players."

"Huh—"

"Hush!" He let go of the zip line, and as their feet hit the dance floor their old song hit the air. "Perfect timing." He beamed. "I've still got the knack."

She hesitated. He saw it. "Shaynie!" he admonished. "No backing out! Think money."

Money. The banker. *Divinity.* The hologram blew through the club and with it her feet moved, their old routine that was really an inside joke, their mockery of The Python and everything it stood for.

When the song ended she heard The Pack cheer as Gray grabbed her around the waist and sailed again over the crowd. She took in the sea of upturned faces—and one whiplash smile of reality. *Entertainment.* And she'd just proved him right.

Gray didn't appear to notice the hot embarrassment on her face as he deposited her at her station, just gave her a kiss that drew cheers anew. "Python Prowlers!" he called. "Give it up for the loveliest lady to ever have concocted a cocktail!"

The Pack went wild.

"Thank you for giving us love!" he cried. "Now show us that love!" With a flick of his wrist he passed his hat, headset never so much as twitching. Again he covered his mic. "We'll split the spoils in the back?"

"Y-yeah. Okay."

"Hey." He frowned. "You okay?"

"Yeah," she said again, but didn't look at him. "Fine."

He hesitated. She gave him a wee shove. "Dead air," she said. "We need music."

He grabbed the zipline and was off, just a deejay once more.

"Well that was interesting." Weste, no smile, no eye-sparkle, assessed her. "You're all starched-shirt about being called entertainment yet you'll lapdance for money?"

"I—" She shrank within the lack of clothing she wore. "That wasn't lap—"

"You're quite the contradiction."

A contradiction. A Ten.

Affecting curiosity, he tapped his chin. "So if entertainment is a no, but lapdancing is a yes, then where does stripping fall? And how much would it cost me?"

Her head snapped back and "Whoa!" Nelson, to her shock, glared at him. "Over the line, Weste. Let it be."

*Let it Be.* Never—ever—had she actually felt the blood drain from her face. "W-why'd you say that?" Her heart was pounding.

Nelson scowled. "Because he didn't need to be such a prick—"

"Hey!" Jude, swooping over, got between them. "What's up?" His voice held the practiced tone of one used to balancing diplomacy with authority. "Fellas?" He looked from one to the other. "Is there trouble?" A bouncer, clearly cued, hovered to his one side.

"Nope," Weste volleyed a steady gaze between security and Jude. "No trouble at all." He drained both sodas then swaggered away and Nelson, after a beat of apologetic discomfort, sauntered after him.

Jude snapped his fingers at a barmaid, a redhead Shaynie didn't recognize. "You,' he said. "Spell Shaynie off. And you," He turned back to her. "Come with me." He steered her to the staff room, closed the door.

"What the hell did they say to you?"

*Let it Be.* "N-nothing," she croaked. "It was nothing."

"Bullshit. Do you need me to ban them?"

"Ban Noel?" She tried to laugh.

"For you, Shaynes? Yeah, I'd ban Noel."

"I—no. Forget it." *Let it Be.* That and stripping. Whoring. Hellnight. *Please!* She envisioned an inky stone. *Take this burden!*

Jude watched her face. "Gather your tips," he said quietly. "Go home."

"But—" Her tip goblet wasn't nearly as full as she needed.

"Shaynie, I'll pay you till closing. Just...go. You look like crap."

Crap? But weren't lap-dancers supposed to be gorgeous? She reached for the ice vat, grabbed a cube to slide against her hot cheeks.

"Go home," Jude reissued. "This place is nowhere to make yourself sick over."

Sick. *Poison.* She slipped the melting ice cube in her mouth as though it were an antidote.

Jude leaned in, kissed the top of her head in a way that reminded her of her brother. "Drive safe," he said.

She should argue. Stand her ground. 'Cause dammit, there was money to be made, face to be saved, and yet...she was grateful that no one seemed to see her skulk back out, grab her tips and her purse, then was relieved to sit alone in the empty staff room with only Jude's collection of faux snakes for company as she rolled all her change, securing the bills with elastics.

The amount she slid into the canvas deposit bag was nowhere near what she'd needed. *Damn!* She would *not* cry. *I thought the Knight of Cups meant good news too.*

*"Le deux de wand is a nasty surprise,"* had said Cele. "No kidding." She buttoned her coat to the throat, scoured the floor for her boots.

No boots. Right. Because in her rush to get to The Python early she'd forgotten to wear them instead of stilettos. "So now I get to leave dressed like the lap dancer I am." She shoved the back door open.

A blast of Edmonton cold stole her breath and made her uncovered toes cringe. "Knight of Swords, you caught and killed my Knight of Cups." She wended her way down the stairs, steps slow and careful on the ice.

"Hey, Gorgeous!"

She jerked around, heels teetering.

Nelson and a few other hockey players congregated beneath a green spotlight. "Want to come with us? Go party?"

Was he kidding? And who the hell had authorized them to park in the staff lot? Jude, of course. She wanted to bark at them to leave, but

Weste, present and watching her, struck her silent. His arm was around a more platinum—and more sober—version of Panties. *'Grats on finding yourself a lap dancer, Dildo.* She lifted her collar, looked away.

"Gorgeous!" Nelson called. "C'mon! Don't be mad."

Again she looked over, but it was not his gaze she sought. "I don't perform off the clock," she said, then turned back to her truck, opaque with frost and waiting, alone and frozen. Its appearance somehow made her want to cry.

"Hey!"

The shout came from behind her and she did not look back. Knew precisely who it was.

"*Hey!*" he called again, and she dove into her truck. The ignition was stiff, reluctant to turn over, and the engine whined as she jammed it into gear.

"Wait!"

The shout reverberated over the whir of defrost blasting cold air against thick ice on the windshield. She twisted her wipers to high and, peeking through the wee hole they made in the frost, stepped on it, tires spitting snow as she raced away.

In her rearview she could see Weste, arms thrown up in a *What the hell?* gesture.

"Screw off, Ice Deity. The only whore I see is *you*."

She cranked out onto Gateway, and as the defrost thawed her windows it wasn't just the beads of moisture that blurred her vision. She reached up, swiped her cheeks. Damn it! Damn *him*. It was all *his* fault she didn't make enough money, and thanks to that prissy banker and his renewed ransom list of demands, she couldn't go home, either.

Bypassing Whyte and her scabby little brownstone she stayed on Gateway, made the hairpin onto Sask Drive to downtown.

Divinity. Tonight it felt less like a haven and more like just one more job, yet as she parked in the shadow of the old morgue she automatically felt her spirit rise, could almost *see* it float atop the evening's ice crystals. "Thank you," she whispered, and visualized a jewel-colored rock. As she stepped from her truck her eyes caressed the old building. Then squinted. Then adjusted.

"What..." Sharp angles were scrawled—no, *carved*—upon the regal front door.

She raced over, feet numbed by cold as she vaulted the front steps.

The sharp angle scratches took form.

STAY AWAY DEVIL'S WHORE

The icy damp of night carried her scream.

## CHAPTER FOUR

*CALL CELE! CALL ANDREW!* Her breath blasted frost as she scrambled for her cell, blindly stabbing speed dial for her brother.

When he answered—"Detective Gavin"—her words were one long run-on sentence.

"*Whoa,*" he said. "Slow. Breathe. What happened?"

She tried keeping it calm, but her voice rose anew in the recount. He cued her again.

"Stop. Breathe."

She stopped. Breathed.

"Do you have what I gave you?"

"Y-yes." She reached in her pocket, grabbed her taser.

"I want you to take it out and start back for your truck. And I want you to keep talking to me while you do it. Do you hear me Shaynie Grace?"

"Y-yes, Andrew. I hear you." Taser out, she walked.

"Head up," he barked. "Eyes open."

Echoes of Cele. She obeyed without question.

"Are you at your truck?"

"Y-yeah." She popped the door.

"Good. Now lock yourself in. I'm on my way."

Minutes, *centuries*, crept by, and around her the night sky was alive with wisps of exhaust that hovered over high rises, colliding with the dark like malevolent spirits. Occasionally a sweep of headlights from the odd late night driver would make her flinch, and when Andrew pulled into her lot his unfamiliar unmarked launched a scream into her throat. Then he exited, caught her gaze with eyes as familiar as her own. She exhaled, nodding when he signaled for her to stay put.

He vaulted the steps to the door and, unable to look as he read the scrawl, Shaynie instead shoved her stilettos up high on the floorboard, resting them beneath the blasting heater. It didn't help. Shivering, she stared at the dashboard until from the corner of her eye her brother loped back down the stairs then disappeared around the back of the building.

When he came back she unlocked the passenger door. He flopped inside.

"Everything's clean except the door. Vandals," he spat.

"V-vandals?"

He looked at her, sharp. "Any reason to think otherwise?"

*Yeah, Gorgeous whore, is there?* "I…" A million times she'd started to tell him. A million more shame shut her up. Now here it was again, a scarlet wash on her cheeks. Grateful for the dark confines of her truck, she shook her head. "No."

"You're lying."

"I don't lie to you, Andrew." Which was why it hurt to do it now.

He blew a harsh breath. "Have there been rednecks wigging out about a witchy place? Hassling you? Threatening you?"

"No," she reissued, relieved that this *was* true. "Nothing like that."

He assessed her, far less brother than cop. "Give me your key. I need to look inside."

Dammit! He'd see that the alarm he'd paid for wasn't set. "Can I come?" she hedged.

"You think I *want* to skulk through a morgue in the middle of the night all alone?"

She scowled.

"That was a joke, Shaynie Grace."

"Yeah, well, I don't feel much like laughing."

He dragged a hand down his face. "Listen, vandals are assholes but also cowards."

Cowards? Like a guy who'd seduce a drunk woman for brutal sex then disappear? She chewed her bottom lip.

"C'mon." He shot a rare smile. "Be my partner and we'll make sure some dick didn't get inside."

She accompanied him to the door, grateful when he splayed a hand over the carved scrawl. "Thanks." She worked the key in the lock.

"You're gonna get crap like this, Shaynie Grace."

Crap, yes. But like *this*? She peeked at the letters spilling out from under his hand, the 'r' and 'e' of "whore". *Hellnight. Could it be?* She opened the front door.

The alarm panel in the entrance should have emitted a warning shriek, and its silence was not lost on Andrew. He glared at it, then at her. "Goddamn it, Shaynie!"

*Oh, damn.* Whenever he choked out only her first name she knew she was in trouble.

"I pay a monthly fee for security you don't bother to use?"

"I never asked for this alarm." He'd imposed it on her and she'd cried when it had been installed, an ugly panel clinging to the wall like some sort of digitalized insect. "Oh, Divinity," she had said, once the security tech had left. "Nothing can move freely now."

The old morgue had responded, its embrace stained glass and lavender. The same scent which now floated between she and her brother.

"Smell that?" she ventured, voice small.

He rolled a deadpan gaze over her face.

She smiled in spite of it. "This place is its own security."

"So then why didn't some spook scare the shit out of the asshole who wrecked your front door?"

She gave him a death stare.

He gave it back. "Stop pissing me off and get rid of those idiot shoes." He jabbed a finger at her stilettos. "Those stupid things make *my* feet cold."

Wordless, she shucked the heels and slipped into her moccasins. They melted, comfort around her feet, one more extension of Divinity. "Where do you want to look first?" She already felt stronger.

Andrew hiked a thumb in the direction of the staircase. "Let's get *that* over with."

Downstairs, her current workroom. The once-upon-a-time embalming room. She swallowed a sudden grin. "Need me to lead?"

He glared and, chomping back a smile, she obediently trailed as he marched, all bravado, toward the staircase, flicking lights on in the divining rooms as he passed. "Whoa." He winced at the first one. "There's a whole lotta purple in there."

*"Ms. Gavin, I thought I'd see more."* Resurrected worry nagged her gut. "Not enough."

"Well I can't help you there. Suck at painting."

"'s'okay," she replied, but anxiety spiked along with the worry in her belly. A wrecked door. Furniture to retrieve. Painting which *she* sucked at, too and...*How? How will I ever get this done?*

*Let it Be* re-awakened, a head-serenade and, *shut up!* she told it, creaking down the stairs with her brother. *Shut up, shut up, shut—*

"*Christ!*" Andrew yelled and a crash like cymbals rang out.

"What?" She rushed to keep up. "What did you find?"

"These." He clapped a hand against something that clanged. "I thought you were getting rid of these damn things."

*Oh.* The body drawers. "I am. I just haven't thought of anything reverent to render them into."

"Render them *into*? Jesus, Shaynie Grace, is nothing sacred to you?"

"Everything is sacred to me, Andrew. That's why I can't just take them to a landfill."

He looked skyward, seemingly for strength. "Okay." He peeked into the old lavatory. "This place is clean. Can I follow you home now?"

So spooked. It would have been amusing but..."I'm actually going to stay."

He made a show of gaping at his watch.

"I have work."

Silence roared. She sighed. "The bank, Andrew. They want more than I've given, and now I have a door to fix too."

He folded his arms. "Bullshit."

Her brow jumped.

"There's something else—or something more—eating you. Not just the bank or the jackass who trashed your door."

Yeah. It's a jackass who implied I was whoring. A bastard before that who called me a whore.

*Gorgeous whore,* memory corrected. *Devil's whore,* it added. She shivered.

"Shaynie Grace..."

Several wordless seconds ticked by. He sighed. "I saw upstairs in the purple room that you still have a cot for when you sleep in this place."

"Yeah, but why—"

"So go ahead and work. I'm gonna find that cot and crash."

"You're not on duty?"

"Nope. Just cleaning up paperwork when you called."

And now rather than go home and have a decent rest he'd sleep in a place he admitted scared the bejesus out of him. "Andrew, you don't have to—"

"Just wake me up before you leave 'cause I sure as hell don't want to sleep in this place all alo—" Her cell rang, cut him off. He frowned. "You always get calls this late?"

"Hardly." She fished for her phone. "Hello?"

"Shaynes!" Jude exhaled audibly. "You weren't answering your land-line. You okay?"

*No. A vandal somehow saw my cards. And my mind.* "Yeah," she lied. "Fine. Tonight…it was just an off night. I needed Divinity." God. Lie after lie. What was wrong with her?

A beat of silence, then, "A morgue. After midnight. Only Shaynie. You sure you're okay? I'm on my way home soon. I'd be company."

"I have company. Andrew's here."

"Oh?"

As in, "why's the cop there?" But damned if she was going to 'fess up to her biggest Divinity naysayer that she'd just endured her first vandal. "Sure." She kept it light. "We're spending a little brother-sister time."

"In a morgue," Jude repeated, and laughed a bit. "Well, whatever flies your family's kite, Shaynes and, uh—hey, can you call Gray? He thinks something's up because you didn't stick around to split your money, and I tried deflecting, but he's making up what he doesn't know and now he wants to kick Noel's ass. As usual."

"Tell him—" *to kick Weste's too* "—tell him not to fret. And that I'll call him tomorrow, okay?" He agreed, and, "'Night," she said, then slipped the cell into her pocket.

Her brother was examining her. "I'm surprised he didn't want you to go over there, clean that shit-pit."

"I'm the one who always offers extra shifts, he rarely asks."

"I hate that skin buffet."

One more script she knew. She wrapped her arms around herself, thankful her coat covered her. "You—uh—gonna crash on my cot or stay awake for a card reading?"

"Consider me crashed." He climbed the stairs two at a time and as he retreated into her divining room she traced an ankh in the air, over his shoulders.

"I'm grateful for you, Andrew."

"Uh-huh. Bill's in the mail."

❧

Her brother slept while she stewed through the rest of the night, the rhythm of her tools carrying her through a room's worth of re-attached baseboards and half a pile of crown molding before dawn finally awakened the sky, a palette of rose and tangerine. She lost herself in the shifting colors a moment then padded into her divining room, gently shook Andrew's shoulder. "Morning, Guardian. Sure you don't want me to turn a few cards for you before you go?"

He smoothed his wild hair. "How come in Shaynie-speak 'no' always means 'maybe'?"

She grinned.

He followed her out into the parlor, slid on his boots, then unlatched the front door. "Hey!" He beamed at the offended panel, now smooth. "You're a fast operator."

"Nothing a planer and some good old sandpaper couldn't obliterate."

"'Obliterate'." He dropped his voice low. "To erase for all eternity."

It sounded like a final benediction. A chill waltzed on her neck.

He didn't notice. "How's *that* for Shaynie-speak?" He shot her an Andrew-grin, there and then gone, then slipped out into the cold.

The rising sun lit drifting ice crystals, transfigured them into tiny glass fairies. She leaned against the door jamb and watched them.

Her brother assessed her glassy-eyed slump. "What time do you work tonight?"

"Night off." Her smile was as lazy as the ice fairies. "Hard to believe, eh?"

"Go home." He unlocked his unmarked. "Get some sleep. But before you do, set the damn alarm."

An answering crack resonated above and a glistening shape hurtled from eaves to ground. An icicle, stabbed into the snow, looking like a sword. *Swords. Life's warnings.*

"I—uh—I'll call you," said Andrew. His voice held the same uncertain waver as her breath.

Nodding, she waved absently as he pulled away then looked down at the ice sword. "Was that a yes or no to the alarm?"

Silence drifted along with the ice crystals.

"What are you trying to tell me?"

An answering prickle sizzled on her skin, a feeling inexplicable yet unmistakable. *Someone's watching.* She darted a look north up Jasper Ave, then south toward the river. No cars, no pedestrians, yet the prickle—

*watching me!*— was so strong her skin screamed. She slammed the door and bolted it, jabbed the code into the alarm. *Watching me.* She peeked through glowing stained glass. Who? The same Andrew-labeled redneck who'd carved into her door?

Outside traffic awakened on Jasper Ave, the rhythm of whishing tires making sounds like words. *Let—it—Be.* Let it Be? That was *Hellnight.* Breath hissed through her teeth and she flinched away from the window.

Deep in the old embalming room the ancient furnace growled.

THE REST OF THE DAY, warmth, lavender, and talk radio, turned Hellnight into a distant bad dream and, relieved by the things she could both see and hear in the tangible present, Shaynie turned her companion, the radio, up. "A night off for our team this evening and what does the future hold?" asked a peppy jock. "Two contenders are vying for superstar status: Nelson, hungry to be hometown hero, and Weste, who seems to want to perform but for whatever reasons just can't for this team."

"Because he's a contradiction like The Moon," said Shaynie. "And an ass."

"Inconsistency will hang him," agreed the jock's sidekick. "For the salary he commands Weste must step up and deliver."

An echo of what the bank wanted from *her.* Feeling vaguely chastened, Shaynie rolled amethyst onto one final wall. "Trade day is looming," continued the lead sportscaster. "And if Weste doesn't pick it up, Edmonton won't want to keep him—and no one else will want him either."

A pang of pity surprised her. She flicked it off along with the radio. "Sympathy? Right. For seven million a year I'd not only score goals, I'd turn axels out on the ice too."

Ah. Like a stripper?

She dropped her roller in the paint tray, startled by the thought that felt more external than internal. She looked around. "Are you planting reprimands in my head?"

A beat of silence elapsed. She retrieved her roller. "Not undeserved. After all, what do *I* know about how to play hockey? I can't even skate." She cleaned the roller and stretched, feeling loose for the first time in days. "I love being with you, Divinity." She kissed her fingertips then pressed them against an inconspicuous spot near a door jamb, purposely leaving an impression of fingerprints in the wet paint. "Cele was wrong. You *are* the only partner I need."

Scent accompanied her down the stairs and rushed through the water when she showered in what had been the scrub area in the old embalming room. Then, when she curled on her cot for a nap, lavender remained there too—and stained glass color. A chorus of comfort that lulled her to sleep.

The sky was velvet black when her cell woke her and, scrambling for it, she groaned at Jude's name on the screen. Because she'd lied to Andrew when she'd said he rarely asked for extra shifts. "Hey there," she purposely made herself sound breathless, busy. "Calling to see if I've fallen in my money pit and can't get out?"

Silence, yet in it she could hear befuddlement. "Jude?"

"A money pit?" rumbled back. "Where *are* you?"

Whoa. That thunder timbre was *not* Jude. "Divinity," she answered, automatic. "Who's—"

"How am I supposed to mock you if you're not here?"

Cameron Weste? "Why do you have Jude's phone?"

"'Cause he wouldn't give me your number to call you from *my* phone. What's Divinity?"

"My club. What do you want?"

"Your *club*? What sort of club? You never said you had a club."

Because she owed him the details of her life? "It's under construction. And *not* a meat market."

He snorted. "Every club is a meat market."

"Not mine."

"So what is it then?"

"It's—" What the hell? She was going to answer him? Talk to him at all? "What do you want?"

He didn't answer and for a moment she wondered if her cell had dropped the call. Then— "What I want is to tell you I was a jerk to piss you off."

An apology? She wandered out into the parlor, plopped hard onto the window seat.

Weste cleared his throat. "Now tell me: how's this Divinity not a meat market?"

"You don't want to know."

"Did I not just ask?"

She tapped a foot. *Tell him. Let him laugh. Get it over with.* "Divinity will be a metaphysical lounge and retail shop," she announced. "A place for Tarot readings, Reiki healings, and spirits—the liquid kind, not the phantom kind." There. She squeezed her eyes shut. *Now here comes the smart ass.*

"I want to see it."

Her lids flew open. "Wha—no. *No.* It—it's not ready for guests."

"Doesn't matter. I want to come over."

"Listen Weste, Divinity is *not* something to harass me about."

"I'm hardly harassing you. Where is it? I'm coming over."

"Yes, you *are* harassing me. You want to come over here, crack a few jokes about flakes and spooks, make me feel like an idiot then go back to The Python and laugh about it with Nelson and whatever same-different girl you scoop up. No."

He was quiet a moment then "Believe it or not, I'm hardly a prick."

"And I'm hardly a rube."

He sighed, a noisy crackle in her ear. "You may as well tell me how to get there 'cause I'll find out anyway. All I gotta do is ask."

"Jude's not going to tell you."

"Rasputin's not the only one here."

*Rasputin?* She gave the phone a look. "Weste, rock The Python. It's far more your style."

He emitted another staticky sigh. "Do you not know *anything* about athletes?"

What did that have to do with it?

"We're a superstitious lot."

"So?"

"So you have a Tarot lounge. *I* want a reading."

*See his cards.* An electric crackle danced through her fingers. Still— "I don't do readings," she lied.

"Well you must have someone who does."

"She's home. Probably sleeping."

"Call her."

"I am not going to call her. It's late."

"Not *that* late. Tell her I'll pay double."

"What? Can you even guess her base price?"

"I don't care. In fact I'll triple it. Quadruple it if she seems too lazy to get out of bed. Tell her that when you call her."

Her cell clicked to dead air. "Weste," she said. "You are *far* too used to getting what you want." Although…a smile, faint as firelight, flickered on her mouth. What he wanted was Cele. "Hear that, angels?" Grinning, she hit speed dial on her phone. "Get ready to weep." The phone rang once, twice—

"'allo?"

Triple, he had said. *Triple, my ass.* "Cele," she said. "How would you like to quadruple your rate tonight?"

"But I read you for free!" Cele, fuggy as if she was wrestling sleep cotton out of her mouth, sounded alarmed. "Darling, what's wro—"

"Nothing's wrong and it's not for me." She paused, wished she could conjure a drum roll. "Cameron Weste."

A tonne of silence fell. *"Himself?"* Cele croaked.

Shaynie bit her tongue.

"His beautiful self…where will he be?"

So much for sleep cotton. She sounded wide awake now. "Divinity."

"He is with you?"

"On his way. Can you co—"

"Barnabas!" Cele lilted. "A God has summoned me!"

*I guess that's a yes.* Shaynie bit her tongue then, in the background heard Barnabas say, "A god? Then let us burn mace, my adored."

Giggles came out, she couldn't hold them. "I—uh—guess I'll see you shortly?"

No reply. Cele had hung up. Shaynie laughed and Divinity joined her, a chug of heat ducts. "A God." She grabbed a broom, began sweeping the showroom. Ten to one he wouldn't even show—there were Python panties to distract him on his way to the door—but on the off chance he did, he'd be her first paying customer. "So we need to make you presentable," she told Divinity, and ran a dust rag over her furniture, stuttering over one armoire's crooked hinge. "How did *this* escape me?" She plucked a screwdriver from her tool belt.

"Told you I'd find you," rumbled from over her shoulder.

Shrieking, she whirled.

Weste cocked his head. "Why so jumpy? You think I wouldn't show?"

She pointed, shakily, at the door. "That was locked."

"Nope." He flicked it a glance.

She frowned. The alarm had been set too—hadn't it? Her gaze tracked from corner to corner.

Weste examined her, not the room, and as his eyes swept her she knew what he saw. A scrubbed face and blue jeans. Ponytail and sweatshirt. She looked like The Anti-Python.

He, of course, looked every bit like the God Cele believed him to be.

She tucked a lock of hair, an escapee from her ponytail, behind one ear. "Welcome to Divinity."

"Thanks for the invite." The Smile played with his mouth.

"Got your checkbook?"

"Cash."

She jacked a brow. He jacked one back. "You thought I was joking?"

She wasn't entirely sure what to think. Especially about that open door. "Cele's not here yet."

He flicked a shoulder. "Then how about a tour?" He surveyed the room from his spot at the door. "I'm dying to see what could seduce you away from The Python."

*Dying.* Was *that* mockery? She examined his eyes.

Fathomless. Frowning, she beckoned him down the short steps into the lounge, swept an arm out. "Main seating area and showroom."

He assessed it, also frowning. "People will have their cards read amongst one another?"

"No, this is where they'll mingle. Shop. Have a drink—or ten." She grinned.

He didn't. "Won't booze mess with the mojo?"

Good grief. He was worse than the bank. "House rule: You drink *after* your reading."

This he chewed on, then— "That works."

"So glad you approve."

He gave her a look then crouched, eye level with one of her creations. "Quite the table." He ran a hand over the pebbled stained glass she'd inlaid on top. "Custom made?"

"Yes. And thank you."

His eyebrows flew up and she bowed, low and long. His lips hitched and he ambled over to a cut glass wind chime she'd affixed in one lonely corner. He flicked it, eliciting a pitch-perfect peal. "Ambience," he uttered.

Ambience. Countenance. So much for predictable.

Unaware of—or maybe ignoring— her scrutiny, he eyed a group of sconces she'd centered on the wall that would face the eventual bar. She had needed a ladder to install them. He, however, faced them dead on. "Electric, yet they *look* like candles." He slid her The Smile. "Nice touch, clever Shaynie."

She had not heard him use her name before. Was half surprised he knew it. Rattled, she pointed. "The bar will be over there," she told him, mostly because she just wanted something to say. "It'll be marble and teak, but I—uh—I've had to hold off." She pulled a face. "Things don't always go as planned."

"Huh. Have I ever been to *that* movie." Not seeing, or again maybe ignoring, the question on her face, he assessed a bare wall. "You need something here. A wall hanging. Copper or metal—"

"Yes!"

He flinched.

"Sorry." Her cheeks heated. "It's just…the body drawers. That's *perfect* for them. I'll haul them to my old tech school, have someone in the welding department fabricate them into—" A visual occurred. "—the four suits! Wands, Swords, Pentacles and Cups. Fantastic!"

He stared. "Did you just say *body* drawers?"

Oh, no. Not another Andrew. "Weste, you, uh, you can see what this building was, can't you?"

His expression moved, from blank to befuddled then to beaming and he laughed, a little incredulous and a whole lot…sexy? "Ah…" He nodded. "I do now."

And he was neither spooked like Andrew nor repulsed like Jude. She beamed too. "Want to see the body drawers?"

"No." Laughing, he held up his hands. "I'll take your word for them. You don't seem like the type that would lie."

*I don't do readings.* Guilt painted her cheeks. "So," she smiled, too bright. "Why query the Tarot?"

The sparkle stole out of his eyes. "Ever listen to the radio?"

*"…no one will want him."* That earlier shard of pity found her belly again and she looked at him, *really* looked at him, a chiseled hockey god whose storm eyes saw things metaphysical that she had *not* expected. *The Moon.* "You really do want this reading."

"Why would you think I was lying?"

She didn't really know. And whatever she might have said was lost as the door reopened and Cele drifted inside.

He blinked. "Your reader?"

"Cele," she confirmed.

"Is she…is she *floating*?"

"Possibly."

He gaped, stunned. She swatted him.

"Of course she's not floating! God." She rolled her eyes. "It's just her caftan. It creates an illusion."

He grinned. "You gonna wear one of those too when you open this place?"

Yep, The Moon. From sincerity to smart ass in a nanosecond. She skewered him with a glare.

"Or maybe you'll just run with this look—pixie meets blue collar. You need a ball cap, by the way."

"And you need a slap." She turned to Cele. "Allow me to introduce—"

"—*Monsieur* Weste." Cele curtseyed.

"Cameron." He took her outstretched hand, raised it to his mouth.

Shaynie stared. "How come you weren't charming when you met me?"

"'Cause you never told me you'd show me my future."

"So instead you sent me a vile present?"

"That vile present wasn't for *you.*" He grinned. "I'm sure you look after yourself."

Good God, but she wanted to slug him.

Cele cleared her throat. "It grows late," she announced.

An unbidden shiver skated up Shaynie's arms.

"Shall we get started?"

"Go ahead," said Shaynie. She should have known Cele's moony eyes would evaporate the moment she headed to the Divining Room. Her devotion to Tarot eclipsed even her love for Barnabas, and Cameron Weste certainly wasn't about to hijack *that* ship. Giving them a little bow, she turned back to the crooked hinge on her armoire. "I have a job to finish. Take your time."

"No," said Weste.

She swiveled and, framed by soft light spilling from Cele's divining room, he beckoned her with a hand. "Come."

Another shiver, eerie or enchantment, she wasn't sure, lit the hair on her neck. Still— "Readings are private."

"I don't mind, and besides…" He looked beyond her, out the window, smart ass gone and sincerity back. And something else too.

Unease.

Her nape tingled.

"Shaynie," he said. "Humor me."

She followed his gaze to where street lights shone innocently through the stained glass.

This morning's eyes peered back. *I see you, Devil's Whore.*

Swallowing a gasp she strode to the door, flicked the deadbolt into place. "Customer's always right," she quipped, but was grateful to follow him, mentally casting colored stones as the morning's eyes burned a hole in her back.

## CHAPTER FIVE

WESTE SANK opposite Cele. Shaynie sat by the door.

"The chair, *Cheri,"* said Cele. "Bring it closer."

Weste slid over to make room and Shaynie hesitated—readings were private!—before lifting her chair, placing it next to him.

He knocked a playful knee against hers and shot The Smile.

She jerked her leg away. "Behave!"

Cele lit a candle. "Now, Cameron," She handed him cards. "Shuffle your question into the deck."

He obeyed, fingers not dwarfed by the cards like Shaynie's always were, and she watched him, struck by a scarlet slash on his right knuckle, livid in the candlelight. "How did—"

"Hush, *Cheri,*" said Cele.

Chastened, she hushed while Weste soberly selected his cards, smile and eye sparkle gone. "Done," he said at last, and righted the stack he'd created.

Shaynie itched to flip his first card—*The Moon, got to be—and* to stroke that harsh knuckle gash. She knitted her hands tight together.

And, as if he knew, he shot The Smile.

Cele cleared her throat. "We begin." She turned his first card.

The Tower, shattered by lightning and with windows belching flames, was a study of shock-shades against a black background. "Prison break," Cele said. "Change you do not expect, yet it liberates, for that which you crave, you will no longer need, and that which you need, you will crave." She revealed the next card, laughed. "Ah, yes. the Nine of Cups, see?"

But he clearly did *not* see for he looked at Shaynie, quizzical.

"That's the wish card," she told him. "It trumps every card in the deck."

His mouth split into a grin. "So my wish will come true?"

The sparkle in his eyes made her want to lie, say 'absolutely,' but—"The Tower means change. So that means your wish might change too."

"Excellent, Shaynie!" Cele clapped. Weste snorted.

"Change my wish? Doubt it."

Cele regarded him. "Let us see." She turned the next card.

A familiar figure, stabbed and prone beneath ten swords. Shaynie's breath caught and she cringed when the next two cards—the Nine of Swords and Three of Swords appeared right beside it.

"That's a whole lotta knives," Weste murmured.

Shaynie flicked Cele a glance. "I shouldn't have come."

"Tut! Cameron picked and shuffled them. His energy, Darling. Not yours."

His energy? Shaynie stared at the Ten, swords in the back.

Weste looked at her, not the cards. "What do they mean?"

*Nelson.* The name splashed up in her head, intuitive certainty.

"Shaynie?" Cele prompted.

Nelson's face in her mind was smug. Entitled. Nonetheless, as she sought Cele's eyes she saw the warning. *Never frighten your querent.* She cleared her throat, recited the cards' textbook meaning in order. "Betrayal, fear, and—" Her finger hovered over the Three. "Heartbreak."

"Huh," said Weste. "What fun."

Her shoulders prickled, but whether it was from his spread or the coldness in his tone, she wasn't sure.

"Turn the next one," he said, and stuck his chin out, a challenge.

Death, its skeletal face eyeless yet somehow aware.

Weste snorted. "No surprise considering all those knives."

"*Non.*" Cele assessed the cards, thoughtful. "Death is the most misinterpreted card of the Tarot. See?" She pointed to the flag Death was toting. "Victory. The change, complete."

He eyed Death dubiously. Cele watched him.

"Not literal," she said. "But this change that threads your cards… Shaynie is right; it is something—conscious or, more likely *un*conscious—that you have wished for. And," one finger underlined the Swords. "Not easily achieved."

*Because Nelson's up to something.* Shaynie eyed Weste. With no whiplash smile and no eye-dance, he looked bleak. "There's one left," she reminded and, using a Cele-trick, flipped it with a fingernail.

"Oho!" Cele laughed lustily. "Recognize it, *Cheri*?"

"Of course," Shaynie pulled a face. "It's the card I never get."

Cele grinned. "*Oui,*" she said. "Go on."

"The Sun," said Shaynie. "Another trump card, and I believe here to remind you that before all those Swords—"

"—was my wish card," he said.

She smiled, impressed.

He took up The Sun. "I like this."

She laughed. "You *should* like it. The Sun means everything's worked out in the best possible way."

"Really? So could it be a *place*?"

The way he asked, she couldn't tell if he was hoping it was or hoping it wasn't. She looked to Cele for direction.

Her teacher said nothing.

"Well...I guess it *could* be a place, but like Cele said, the Tarot is rarely literal."

"What you need you will crave," Cele added. "And The Sun says you shall have it."

Again neither smiling nor frowning, he kept the card, looked at it.

Cele gently plucked it from his fingers. "Is there anything else you'd like to ask?"

"Is there anything else I need to know?"

"*Oui,*" she said. "That chain around your neck. You believe it is a talisman. It is not. Take it off, *s'il vous plait.*"

His brow arched.

"It's from an old lover. And the protection that's in it is as dead as what you feel for her now."

He cast startled eyes Shaynie's way.

"Okay, so maybe she floats a *little* bit."

Cele's hand flashed out, jerked her ponytail.

"Ouch! What the heck was that for?"

"Everyone floats," Cele said sharply. "They need only accept it."

Scowling, Shaynie tried fixing her mussed ponytail, succeeding only in messing it up more. She yanked the elastic out, shook her hair free.

"Much better," said Cele, still sharp. "You're loveliest with your hair down."

"Sexy thang." Cameron tweaked her nose.

"Shut up." Self-conscious, she readjusted her shapeless sweatshirt. "So? Has Divinity been everything you expected?"

"Yeah." Sobering, he looked at Cele. "Your fee. Let's rack it up with some zeros."

*"Non!* And don't rush off quite yet. I'm going to prepare you something." She opened a drawer, rummaged through it. "And Shaynie?"

"Uh-huh?"

"Do not think I've not noticed the absence of protection I told you to wear."

Her hands flew to her bare neck. "Uh—"

"A necklace, Darling. It's imperative."

Cameron's gaze volleyed between them. "Why?"

"Because my—uh—my cards weren't quite as benevolent as yours."

"Benevolent? Death looked me in the eye."

"And The Devil looked at *me.* So did all your swords. But—" She offered a shrug. "—The wish card and Sun did not."

"So wear the protection," said Cele.

"I will. I promise."

"Promise! You promised before."

Shaynie looked at the floor.

Cele leaned over, pecked her smartly on the cheek. "Obey," she said, then turned to Cameron. "For you. This." She held a tiny, braided labyrinth of red silk, purple hemp, and shiny threads Shaynie could not identify.

"Under your clothing. Next to your skin."

"What will it do?"

"What you need you will crave. This will bring what you want close to you."

He took the little charm, tucked it in his hand. "Your fee and some zeros."

Cele laughed. "Sometimes, Cameron Weste, I read for free."

Shaynie shook her head. Such a flirt.

"The cards said things you needed to hear," Cele told him. "Now." She clapped her hands. "Barnabas will believe I've transfigured if I don't get home."

Shaynie rose, drew her close. "Love you, friend. Thank you for venturing out in the cold dark."

"Protection." Cele drew a line over Shaynie's jugular. "My Darling, *please* don't forget."

Cameron rose, took Cele's arm. "May I walk you to your car?"

"*Merci*," she replied, visibly, and very dramatically, swooning.

Oh, my. Shaking her head, Shaynie smiled. "*Au revoir.*"

Cele blew her a kiss and was gone.

She was straightening the chairs and extinguishing the candle when Cameron returned.

"I did pay her," he said.

"That's between you and her." She set the candle on a shelf, caught a yawn in her palm.

"Tired?"

"Yeah. I was up late last night, dealing with my own deck of Swords." Including the one that had sliced a word in her door. And the one that had been that set of eyes, glaring at her through the stained glass.

"Swords," he said. "Is that what you call the idiot who sparred too hard in The Python last night, hurt your feelings?"

More apology. It caught her off guard.

He ducked his head, caught her eyes. "I told you: I'm not a prick. Thanks, incidentally, for letting me pirate your club."

"Because you gave me such choice?"

He laughed. "Can I walk you out to your truck?"

"Me? Oh, I can't—" Go? Why not? She'd worked all last night and most of today. "Home before midnight. What a concept."

"You're usually not?"

"I'm usually at The Python."

"Ah, right. The Python."

The scorn that crossed his face was a surprise, yet not a surprise. She laughed a bit. "I cannot believe you didn't turn The Moon."

His eyebrows climbed, a question.

"The Moon is the inner world that goes on behind slick smiles. It reminds us that sometimes when we step into a mud puddle we find out it's an ocean."

"Thanks—I think. And if that's The Moon then I'm surprised *you* don't get it."

It was her turn to wear a question in her eyes.

He jacked a thumb toward her showroom. "You're an artist who serves beer."

An *artist*. A delighted little quiver danced inside.

"A contradiction," he said. "Except tonight I mean it completely as a compliment."

A contradiction. Her smile faltered. Like a redneck vs. a resurrection of Hellnight. The rogue thought caught her cold. Weste didn't notice her shudder.

"Contradictions." He looked beyond her, into the morgue. "Just like Divinity and The Python."

More opposites. *Another ten.*

"—*and* like The Sun and Edmonton." He dragged a hand through his hair.

"The wish card trumps the whole deck," she reminded.

He rewarded her with a smile as brilliant as The Sun, and another rogue thought intruded. *How would someone my size ever kiss him?* "I-I what did you say?"

The sweet smile was gone. "I was going to ask you for coffee."

*Was* going to? Now he didn't look too sure. Her phone shrilled—"Hold that thought," she said, and pulled it from her pocket.

"Hey," said Andrew. "You still at your spook factory?"

"It's called Divinity, and yes—the alarm is set."

"That's not why I'm calling. Last night I forgot to tell you—one of the uniforms' wives opened a boutique and I scored you an order. Six door tables."

"Six?"

"A grand apiece."

"A gran—Andrew! I only charge five hundred!"

"So tell me: how much do you love your big brother? They're due in two weeks."

"Two—I can't meet that sort of deadline! And it's winter. I can't even scavenge doors in all this snow."

"You don't have to. I showed him your brochure a while ago and it turns out wifey had access to an old farmhouse. She scavenged her own doors."

"She has her own material and you *still* charged her double? What are you, a cop or a criminal?"

"A good detective is a bit of both. As for the price, she does want stained glass inserts."

Which were tricky to accomplish. And needed in two weeks?

Andrew said "Gets the bank off your ass."

"And a customer on it."

"So take time off from the shit pit."

"I want to kill you."

"Pfft. Pack a lunch. And stick around, eh? Buddy was banking on my shitty memory and brought the doors tonight. We'll be over in twenty."

"But I was going to go home!" Or on a date? Maybe? She peeked at Weste.

He didn't look terribly happy.

"You still can go home," said Andrew. "Only later." He hung up. She looked at Cameron.

"My brother tries to bail me out, but just digs my grave deeper. And he's ripped some poor woman off—charged *way* more than my pieces are worth."

His lips twitched, neither smile nor grimace. "Sounds like an agent."

Her brow wrinkled.

"An agent," he repeated. "Someone who touts you as being far more capable than you really are then sells you to the highest bidder no matter what *you* want."

Oh. A hockey term. She slumped back against Divinity. "I wish my life was as easy as playing a game."

"'Easy'?" he echoed. "Is that what my life is?"

"I—"

"Funny. Lately I've found it kind of hard."

Oh, boy. We're back on the moody Moon. "Weste—Cameron—I'm sor—"

"So these hot ticket tables you make. Why doors?"

Neutral ground? Somehow she didn't think so. "Because doors are portals," she answered, carefully. "Access between one place—one *dimension*—and another. For example: ever walk into a room and forgot why you've entered it? Folklore says it's because you just moved through a door—and that by doing so you've entered a brand new dimension."

"Like the Death card. Leave one state of being for another."

"Ah. He learns."

"He isn't a stunned puck."

She gaped. "I never said that you wer—"

"You know for someone who doesn't do readings you sure seem to know a lot about Tarot and stuff."

What was with the offensive? “I—”

“And, speaking of The Devil, here.” He pulled his chain from his pocket, a glitter of gold in the winking snow. “Cele’s sincere and honest. You should listen to her.” He dropped the chain into her palm then turned, crunched through the snow to where he’d parked.

She gawked after him, feeling the way he’d looked last night when she’d peeled away from him in The Python parking lot. “Cam—”

“G’night, Shaynie.”

Goodnight? Sounded more like “goodbye”. He drove away, left her gaping. “What the heck did I say? Mercurial.” She twined his chain through her fingers. “He *is* The Moon.”

And you’re The Devil.

Startled, she whirled.

Crouched in the dark, Divinity was a seductress in a snow globe. A jury of one.

The Devil? Her? Although…selfishness: *I wish my life was as easy as playing a game.* Deception: *I don’t do readings.* And, maybe most importantly, there’d been Nelson, slithering amongst the swords in his reading and she’d said nothing. She’d *Let it Be.*

Divinity’s stained glass eyes did not look away. “I’m sorry,” she told them. “Tomorrow I’ll track him down, tell him everything.”

## CHAPTER SIX

THE NIGHT HAD SENT dreamscapes of screams through her sleep with Cele’s voice underscoring every shadowy image. *“The liar’s card, Cheri. Someone’s telling lies.”* “Yeah. Apparently me.”

In the dusky morning she faced Divinity again, standing right where she and Cameron had been. Silently she traced one booted toe over two sets of footprints still visible in the snow—hers, small, and his, twice as big. Side by side until his could be seen leaving hers to stand alone. It stung, and she turned from them, trudged up the morgue’s steps. The door opened before she could unlock it.

“Bonjour *Cheri!”* Cele beamed.

Startled, Shaynie shucked her boots. “You’re here early. I didn’t see your car.”

“In the back and yes, Darling, very early. ’Imself the Hockey God called, needed to meet."

Good grief. This morning she really *was* floating. And damned if it wasn't kind of irritating. "So what did he want? Another reading? Wasn't the wish card en—"

"*Non.* Not a reading. He came to bring this."

This. An envelope with "Seely" on the front, misspelled but penned with much grandeur. A helpless smile found Shaynie's mouth. "Look inside," Cele said.

"Oh. Oh *my.*" Hockey tickets. And not just *any* tickets. "Ice level." She whistled. "I'd have to forfeit a payment on Divinity for these."

"*Oui.* And all because I would not take extra payment for his reading."

Oh, yeah, she was floating all right. And it was *not* irritating. It was sweet. "So? Have you called Barnabas? Told him you have tickets for the hottest show in town?" An image, pale, veiny Barnabas craning his long neck to see the ice action, was so absurd that it tickled her tongue with giggles.

Cele's slim shoulders fell. "*Oui.* And Barnabas reminded me about Reiki tonight."

"Aw, but Cele, you *love* the 'ockey game."

"Ridiculous accent, and anyway, my beloved is right; we cannot neglect our Reiki students, so—" She shrugged, palms up, the gesture pure French-Canadian. "Perhaps *you* would like to see 'imself play?"

And tell him everything she'd promised Divinity she'd 'fess up to? Lift the word "liar"?

She couldn't.

"I work tonight, and even if I wasn't you are not going to believe the order Andrew set me up for." She told Cele of the door tables.

Cele beamed. "Ah, he *is* the Knight of Pentacles, your brother, in so many ways."

"He'll be thrilled to hear it."

"Why not offer *him* the God's gift?"

Shaynie slid the glossy tickets between thumb and finger.

"Go on!" Cele clapped bejeweled hands. "Call the Knight of Pentacles."

Andrew was a no— "Can't. Supervising a stakeout." And when Cele said, "How about your friend Grayson?" Shaynie pulled a face. Anything connected to Noel Nelson won no points with Gray.

"Gray hates hockey." And Jude wasn't a real fan either, but— "Jude would know someone who could afford to pay you what these tickets are worth."

"Scalp Cameron's tickets?"

Shaynie cringed. "I know it's scabby, but better than letting them go to waste, right?"

Cele slumped onto the window seat.

"That a yes?" asked Shaynie, small.

"*Oui.* Call The Poison."

Jude's greeting was cloudy and she tsked—did no one besides she, Cele, and apparently Cameron Weste crawl out of bed early? "Got comped by our first divination client," she told him. "Hockey tickets."

"Oh?" was issued 'round a yawn. "Weste?"

"Uh-huh. Ice level. Know anyone who would want them?"

"Sure. Me."

"You? You don't even *like* hockey."

"For seats like that? Access to club level? I *love* hockey."

Ah. He wanted bragging rights. Typical man. "Hate to burst your bubble, but you're working tonight."

"*Was* working. I'm the owner. Want to come?"

"Funny guy. I'm *not* the owner."

"Consider it another comp. You've busted your butt lately. Take a few hours off, come along. After all, it's you Weste gave the tickets to."

Not exactly. "Who's going to tend bar if we're both gone?"

"The barmaid I'm training to replace you."

"You're going to let a rookie tend bar on a game night?"

"She'll thank me later. You did."

Yeah, but not until well after the fact. That first night...talk about Hell. She'd spilled a swimming pool of beer and by last call smelled like she'd swam in it too. She'd been ready to quit, but Jude, laughing, had merely pointed to her then-small tip jar, dumped into a larger container at least three times that shift. Looking back she smiled. "I hope your new girl makes a whack of money."

"And I hope you buy me one of those stupid-priced popcorns when we sit at ice level."

She laughed.

"Or maybe Pussyhound will spring for that too?"

Her smile died. She had lied to Cameron, invalidated the concerns he'd brought to the Tarot, and kept what she knew of Nelson to herself. Now she was not only about to use tickets not meant for her but also with someone who called him filthy names. Karma may make her *choke* on popcorn. "You said we have club level access. That means we can see the players, right?"

"Well...kind of. They walk through the club to their locker room—but it's not like they *talk* to the fans."

No matter. Fans could talk to them. "Pick me up at six."

She slid her phone in her bag. "Guess I'm going to the game after all."

Cele was sitting at the window seat turning cards. Shaynie joined her, dismayed that now, like yesterday, she automatically scanned the window for eyes. *Redneck vandal. Andrew said so. The rest was just old shame and crap.* She tore her eyes from the window. Nothing was out there. Nothing had ever been out there. "You turned The Magician."

"The Magician reversed," corrected Cele, and her fingers, full of rings, flashed as she crisply drew back. "What does he mean?"

An impromptu exam delivered starchly. Yikes. She really *had* wanted to use her own tickets. "Well," Shaynie examined the card, culling through the endless lessons filed in her memory. "Reversed, the Magician is a charlatan. A liar." *Lies.* There was that word again.

"Um-hm. The Magician is all about illusions, *Cheri.* Showing one face while wearing another."

Like an artist who served beer? Shaynie sat back. "Oh, crap. Is this... is this me?"

Cele blinked, surprise in her onyx eyes. "Darling, The Magician reversed is not like The Moon."

The Moon. The card both she and Cameron, just last night, had defined each other by. *Does she float?* Sometimes it seemed so. She plucked the upended Magician from the table and the eyes, outside, suddenly felt as if they were awakened and alive. "A redneck vandal who's really someone more sinister."

Cele did not contradict the speculation. Nor did she minimize or dismiss it as Andrew might have done. Instead—"So tell me how one protects herself from someone sinister."

"With intuition. You mentioned The Moon. Let *it* discern toxin from elixir."

"Use The Moon so that her heart will recognize poison even before her head makes the connection?"

"Yes."

A heartbeat of silence elapsed and Divinity's furnace awakened, not a growl but a soft gasp of breath. Then Cele spoke. "Sweet *Cheri,* I think that is most excellent advice."

~

By the time her watch alarm called an end to the day any guilt over going to the game versus working was gone. Two of Andrew's doors were complete and had earned their bloated price; inlaid with stained glass and standing upon antique clawed feet, they were a chic contradiction of elegant and battered. "Beautiful," she breathed, then called her brother, told him so.

"Glad to hear it. Although I still think you're pathological for believing that anything other than a *person* has a *personality*."

"Really? Yet it's you who always looks like you're going to wet yourself in my morgue."

Silence sizzled and she laughed but before she rushed home to change for the game she set the alarm, a salute to him, then tossed a colored stone in a jar, too. "*Je t'aime,* my big brother."

Less than an hour later, as she hustled alongside Jude off cold January concrete into the arena, Andrew was still on her mind. "My brother would have loved these tickets," she mused. "Him and I have never sat anywhere but the nosebleed section."

"Tell him to wear something cut to the navel and a pair of super-tight slacks. Then maybe Pussyhound will comp him too." Jude grinned.

She didn't. "Our section is this way." She led through the bump of bodies alive with game night electricity and air redolent with the aroma of popcorn and burgers. Her belly rumbled, a reminder that in her marathon of building all she'd eaten all day were a few soup crackers and a handful of granola. Pausing before a concession, her mouth watered over the cloud of buttery popcorn behind glass and she became momentarily hypnotized by a spinning showcase of pizza. A fan clad in cutoffs and face paint mowed into her.

"Careful!" Jude admonished, scowling.

Cut-offs flashed a big, gap-toothed grin— "Sorry Sweetie!"—then snagged her arm, raised it in solidarity. "Home team for the win!" he cried, then disappeared into the crowd.

She laughed. Jude rolled his eyes. "Fanatical nutbar." He grasped her wrist. "C'mon. We need to hurry."

She looked longingly back at the food then lurched forward as he pulled her past fifty-fifty barkers, program sellers, and an endless sea of fan jerseys like hers. On the air an undercurrent hummed, game night glitter, and it was a feeling that said anything could happen. Jogging to keep up with Jude she wondered—if electricity was what it felt like to be a fan, then what was it like to be a *player?*

One more thing to ask Cameron.

They met their section and as she trailed Jude to their seats her jaw dropped. The ice surface was *huge.* So were the players. Big men turned giant by the added height of their skates, they sailed past the glass like titans. "So *this* is ice level." A different planet than the nosebleed section.

"Told you it was cool." Jude flopped to the seat beside her, scanned the ice. "Hey—there's your man."

She peered through the Plexiglas and Noel Nelson glided by, teeth flashed to the crowd. Jude roared. She smacked him. "Why do I hang out with you?"

"Pity? Meeting your quota of good deeds? Or, dare I hope—," he clutched his chest, "—love?"

She rolled her eyes. "I will never—*ever*—understand what you see in Noel."

"A fool," he answered, shocking her. She'd meant it to be rhetorical. "I see a blowhard and a butthead, just like you do. But, unlike you, I also see that underneath all that pretence is a little boy who just wants people to like him."

The compassion there made her assessment seem cruel. Yet from the corner of her eye she could see Nelson, still grandstanding. "So you think that stealing the limelight on every occasion is just 'cause poor Noel has crappy self esteem?"

"Yes," Jude said simply. "And I never said he made *good* decisions, Shaynie. God knows I've had to weigh in more than once, make decisions for him."

A conclusion then struck her. "You like that he needs you."

Jude smiled. Shrugged. "Everybody needs somebody. And unlike you, I never had a sibling."

"You've had Gray."

He gaped. "Talk about someone who has crappy self esteem and makes shitty choices."

Defensiveness made her bristle. Jude leapt up. "I also like when *you* need me," he said. "For things like popcorn." He sprinted away before any retort about Gray could form.

THE GAME ROCKED. Seventy-one shots on net by the end of the second and countless checks, each making the boards shudder and the crowd roar. Ice level took her breath away and, in the flurry of skates, sticks, and a bullet-fast puck, Cameron flew past their seats twice, once ringing an opponent into the glass hard enough to make popcorn rain onto her lap.

"Wow." She caught her breath. "I thought that whole wall of Plexiglas would shatter."

"Frustration." Jude watched Weste. "He's underperforming and he knows it. Team needs to trade him."

Shaynie jacked a brow. For someone who wasn't a bona-fide hockey fan, Jude could sure trash-talk like an expert. Or maybe he was just parroting lines brought to him by good buddy Nelson. 'Cause God knew that once Weste found his groove Noel would quickly be outshone. She kept her mouth shut, though, and watched the game. But when the horn blew to end the second period she had to concur with Jude; Cameron wore slumped defeat in his shoulders that was palpable as he skated to the bench. *"What you need you will crave,"* Cele had told him, and Shaynie knew what to do. Time to clean up his Karma—and her own. "Come on," she told Jude.

Club Level was chaos. Fans clamored for a closer look at the players; fellows in fan jerseys trying to high-five them while women reminiscent of Panties stretched manicured fingers out, hoping to capture jerseys separated by only a blue velvet rope—and several burly security guards. Unbelievable. Staring in wonder, Shaynie watched for Cameron, flinching when a hand flashed from the row of players and snagged her shirt.

"Hey Gorgeous!" Noel Nelson see-sawed on skate blades. "That jersey looks *way* good on you."

She jerked away, arms shooting across her breasts. Beside her Jude choked.

"I hope you wet yourself," she hissed.

"It'd be worth it." He guffawed.

She stomped a heel backward, hoping for his toes, then launched back on tiptoe to peer at the players. There! "Weste!" She bobbed her head to catch his eye, but two sky-high hotties knocked her askew. Scowling, she elbowed in front of them. "Cameron!"

His storm eyes did not waver and it was tough to tell if he was ignoring her or simply locked in his head. She weaved left and right—*C'mon! Look at me!*—and was grateful when Jude plopped a hand on her shoulder to keep her from being knocked flat. "Weste!" she called. "Your charm!" She ignored the sneers and hostile tsks from the hotties she'd elbowed. "Wear your charm!"

He did not so much as flick a glance backward. She sank back to her heels. Had he heard her? Or ignored her?

Jude pulled her back out of the crowd. "Nachos before the third?"

"I need to talk to him."

He gaped. "They're a little busy, Shaynes."

"I know, but..." She drew a breath and decided to breach. "When Weste turned the Tarot I was far from a benevolent reader."

"Ah." he nodded, sage. "So comp him at The Python. Drinks on the house." He threaded them back up the stairs. "C'mon. By the time we get through the concession they'll be back on the ice."

She trailed him, frowning. Free drinks at The Python? Let the bartender mask she wore speak for the artist she was? "You get nachos," she told him, pensive. "I'll wait." She squeezed past an usher. An *usher.* "Excuse me." She placed a hand on the sleeve of his uniform. "Could you help me?"

"Of course." The usher crouched beside her while Jude, clearly thinking he was out of the range of her vision, rolled his eyes, bemusement all over his face.

She ignored him. "I need to get a message to a player."

The usher blinked. "A *player* player?" He hiked a questioning thumb out to where, on the ice, the swish-thwack of skate blades and sticks signaled pre-period warm up.

"Yes. To Cameron Weste. He gave me these tickets and I…lost his number." She crossed her fingers, distilled the lie. "I'd like to say thank you."

The usher did not say "bullshit". He didn't need to.

"Truly!" She rummaged in her purse, found a pen and scrap of paper. *I owe you a latte and a lesson on The Sun,* she scribbled, then quickly added her cell number, shoved the note into the usher's hand. "Thank you," she said, eyes pleading.

"Uh—yeah. Sure" He tucked the note into his pocket.

She slumped. No way did he plan on giving her message to Weste.

"Uh, Shaynes?" Jude was tapping his foot. She looked up.

"They're starting." He sank back to his seat. "No time for nach—oh. Oh, *damn.*"

"What?"

"My cell." He flipped it open, pulled a face at the screen.

"I didn't even hear it."

"Text," he said distractedly, and heaved a sigh. "The Python. 'Scuse me again, Shaynes. I need to go out on the concourse, call Gray. He's saying 'urgent'."

Her brow rose. "Hope it's nothing seri—" she began, but he was already gone, and by the time she sensed his presence again the third period was almost over and her gaze was fixed on the ice. Cameron was back out on shift, chasing the puck. "C'mon," she breathed. "Nab that thing."

Yes! He blew past her, puck on his stick. She slid to the edge of her seat.

"Shaynes?" Jude tapped the top of her thigh.

She held up a finger, staved him off. Weste was on a breakaway! "Go!" she cried.

"Shaynie!" Jude grasped her knee. "We—uh—we need to leave."

Leave? She turned to face him and fifteen thousand bodies flew into the air. The floor rumbled beneath her feet. Weste had scored. Scored and she'd *missed* it. *"Damn!"*

Jude grabbed her hand. "C'mon."

She pulled away. "But the game's almost over."

"I know, but the Fire Marshal is at The Python. Rookie staff let it get *way* over numbers. *Please,* Shaynes. I've got to go, straighten this out."

She cast a look over her shoulder, onto the ice. Just the top of Weste's helmet was visible, the rest of him hidden by an embrace from his teammates. *Way to go!* she called silently then rose.

Jude was gone.

*Oh, damn!* She bolted up the stairs and onto the concourse. He was already meters away, on his cell, and making long strides to the north exit. Sprinting to catch up, she was sent reeling by a concession straggler who lumbered into her path. "'Bout time Weste did something," he, a man with a mammoth belly, grumbled to a skinny sidekick. "That's a fat paycheck we're cutting him."

*We*? Shaynie shot him a look. "Gee," she muttered. "You don't *look* like you're on the team's payroll."

"What's that Sugar?" Belly pinned her with piggy eyes.

She pinned him back. "I said I'm sure the team knows what it's doing with payroll."

"Shaynes!" Jude, breathless, had doubled back. "Excuse us." He caught her wrists, pulled her past Belly. "What the hell are you doing?" he side-mouthed. "I gotta fly and you're starting a brawl?"

"That idiot's never even *met* Cameron."

"Oh my God, Shaynes." He laughed. "Well, I guess if anyone could use your voodoo, it *is* Weste. Underperforming and overpaid. Far from a fan favorite. But—" he popped the exit open, hit them with a shock of cold air, "—let's just make sure *Gray* doesn't hear that you're making mojo for hockey players. Sacrilege." He shook his hands, theatrical, then latched onto her. "Crap, it's cold. Let's run."

They bolted, every inhalation cold fire in her lungs. Why oh why did arenas world over insist on parking people so crazy-far from their structures? "So," she panted, reaching his car, "how are we going to thin out The Python?"

"'We'?" Fumbling with his keyless lock, he lifted bewildered eyes. "Shaynes, I'm dropping you off at home."

"*What?* But it's my work night."

"And I'm over numbers."

"Jude, I'm staff!"

"No, tonight you're just one more body that I really don't—" Unlocking the car, he whipped his cell from his belt. "Damn it! Gray *again*." He smacked it to his ear. "I'm coming!" he barked, then stabbed it off, swiped a hand through his hair. "I'm going to end up with a fine over this, I just know it."

And she'd end up broke. "Jude, I really can't afford—"

"Oh, for Christ's sake, Shaynie, I'll pay you, okay? My God. I've never seen someone so obsessed with turning a buck."

As far as slaps went, it was as cold as the air outside and she couldn't think of one thing to say. He, occupied by his cell the entire length of 75$^{th}$, didn't speak either, and she was glad. Gladder still when the familiar quirk and charm of Whyte became visible. *Home. Fine. Take me there.* But when he pulled to the curb instead of rounding the corner, she stared at him.

He looked meek. "Shaynie I am so, so, sorry, but that Marshal is wigging…"

"So you're just going to drop me off *here?*" Her apartment was five blocks away.

He cringed. "I'll make it up to you. I promise. I—"

"Whatever." Talk about someone obsessed with turning a buck. "Hope you don't lose any money to the Fire Marshal." She got out, slammed the door.

Whyte Avenue was a plunge into ice water. This was what she got for trying to clean up her Karma? "Please." She threw her head back, faced an ink sky luminescent with exhaust. "I am trying so hard."

Red taillights and illumination from late night shops glowed against pearly air, and the effect of colors, subtle and beautiful, was like stained glass. *Stained glass.* Her feet halted, a crunch in the snow. What was she thinking, mourning a night away from The Python? She should be grateful. Andrew's door order and its bloated price made her Python tip jar look silly. Mentally she cast a colored stone, and above her the sky lights danced as she broke into a jog, covering the five blocks to her door easily. The security door was unlocked—big surprise—but she was grateful for that too. The foyer was so toasty that the moment the air hit her stiff, scarlet fingers pain shot through the joints, respite and agony, and when her cell phone erupted in her pocket, the sensation curiously matched her shivers. She drew it out.

UNKNOWN NAME, UNKNOWN NUMBER.

A tremor skated through her belly on a thought—*Don't answer*— and she frowned. Don't answer? *Don't be stupid,* was more like it. It may well be Jude, calling her to come to work anyway. "Hello?"

"Latte isn't even a word. It's just a couple hoity-toity syllables that make people feel sophisticated when all they're really doing is ordering coffee with cream."

She sagged against the security door. "So I take it you don't want a lesson on The Sun?"

"I didn't know The Python served lah-tay-dahs."

"It doesn't. Has Beans."

"Pardon?"

She laughed, couldn't help it. "It's a place, not an insult. A coffee house on Whyte. Need an address?"

"Nope."

"Are you determined to be difficult?"

"Yep."

"Well then go ahead and sulk. I, on the other hand, will be sipping a lah-tay-dah in Has Beans and looking out at all this glorious snow. I guess I'll either see you or I won't."

## CHAPTER SEVEN

*Guess that's a "won't"*. Thirty minutes had bled into an hour. An hour seeped into two. The coffee crowd had dwindled, and though the barista behind the counter looked busy, stacking cardboard cups and shining machines, her covert peeks let Shaynie know that she wanted to close up and go home. Sighing she peered one last time out the window.

A *noir* night, still opaque with frost but with its enchanting stained glass colors long gone. Now it was just a big burden stone. She mentally cast it into a jar and rose.

The barista cleared her throat. "Guess your date was too scared to see his future."

Too scared? Nope. Too *done*. Tossing another imagined stone, Shaynie handed over her untouched pie. "Please wrap this?"

The pie was in Styrofoam and the lights were killed before Shaynie could shrug her coat on. She hurried to the door, cheeks on fire. That toe-tapping impatience, she'd felt it herself at The Python, waiting for the last stragglers to *please* go *home*. "Have a good night." Stuffing the Styrofoam into her tote, she fled.

The temperature had plummeted and cold shredded her lungs. Still she looked, once more, down the street.

Something looked back.

She gasped, the sound erupting as a puff of ice crystals. The street was deserted, yet...she fell perfectly still, silence swallowing her feet's crunch of snow. "Hello?" she called.

The question floated, an ice ghost of frost, and nothing replied, yet she could feel them—Eyes, alive in the cold.

"Weste?" She shifted, one booted foot to the other. "Not funny."

But that was just it. It *wasn't* funny. Which meant it wasn't Weste. A dark feeling, not unlike the Eyes themselves, slithered inside, and her hand crept to her pocket, finger curling around the taser trigger. *Head up. Eyes open.* Andrew's mantra, and she heeded it as she crunched, one step then another, breaths hanging in the air like visible heartbeats.

The distance between her and her apartment building shrank, but the Eyes…

*Behind you!* She whirled—*no one? How can there be no one?*—then bolted, dove into her truck and fired the engine in one seamless motion. *Safe! Safe I'm safe I'm...*

Her cell rang.

Swallowing a shriek, she jerked into gear. The engine screamed, unwilling against the cold, and as her cell rang again she shoved the gearshift back into park—*don't die don't die!* She tapped the gas, gunned the engine.

Her cell phone kept ringing.

*Damn it!* Foot hopping on the gas she wrestled it from her bag. "Hello?"

"Duzithert?"

A hiss, indistinguishable. Nonsensical. Her truck purred. "Pardo—"

"I said—," the annunciation crackled with clarity, "—Does. It. *HURT?*"

Her ear burst, and with a little cry she yanked the cell away, jerked her truck into drive. Cranking out onto Whyte, she re-engaged the phone, eyes half on and half off the road as she scrolled through features—*last call, last call*—then jabbed it.

CALLER BLOCKED

That and a red light stopped her short. *C'mon!* She glared at the street light. *Change!* Out her windshield, out of reach, the downtown core glittered over the river, alive with lit high rises and the movement of taillights.

And no Eyes.

On green she squeal-wheeled the hairpin onto Walterdale Bridge, hit '0' on her cell.

"Operator, may I help you?"

"Yes." She sailed over the North Saskatchewan, into the life of lights. "My last call. It was blocked and I need to access the number."

"Ma'am, privacy laws prevent us from tracing blocked num—"

"*Privacy?* What about *my* privacy?"

"Was this a *threatening* call?"

"Uh—"

"—because threatening calls *can* be traced. But only by the police."

*The police!* She hung up, hit speed dial.

"Gavin," said her brother.

"Andrew, I just got a freaky call on my cell and—"

"Your cell? Aren't you at the shit pit?"

"No. Long story. Anyway, I—"

"A freaky call? What kind?

What *kind?* The kind with *Eyes*. "I...just freaky. He—she—asked me if it *hurt.*"

"If what hurt?"

*Being stood up*. It was knee-jerk, and as she parked at Divinity she rocked back in her seat. *Does it hurt?* It had been about a no show for a date. About walking home all alone. The intuitive place inside—*The Moon's* place inside—knew it, and yet why would anyone take pleasure, or even care, that she'd just been humiliated in Has Beans?

"Shaynie Grace?"

"I—I don't know." She had no idea whether it was truth or lie.

Her brother sighed, and the same tears she'd felt sitting in the silence of Jude's car, then alone in Has Beans, threatened to fall. Being a nuisance. Being unwanted. *Does it hurt?* She caught a sniffle. "Listen, for all I know it was a wrong number. I'm probably just being a *pita*—"

"Yeah, but you're still my favorite little pain in the ass," Andrew said, and the grin in his voice was real. "I'll check, okay? But it won't be immediate."

Gratitude showered an array of clear colored stones on her heart. "Andrew, I…I'll build you something beautiful."

"Huh. Just remember me the next time you get free hockey tickets." He hung up.

The next time? There wouldn't be a next time. "Our lah-tay-dah was a lah-tay-don't." The joke, uttered aloud, sounded lame. Pathetic even. *Does it hurt?* She slipped from her truck, trudged up the stone stairs to unlock the morgue.

Warm air rushed to kiss both her cheeks. "Thanks," she murmured, and punched in the alarm code. "I tried with Weste tonight, to make amends."

The alarm, chirping deactivation, sounded a lot like dismay.

"Not to worry. He…he just didn't want to see me. But that's okay." She affixed a bright smile, flicked the light on. "'Cause now it's just you and me."

Familiar scents, sawdust, paint, and lavender, didn't answer. Instead something else was there, vibrating. A held-breath something. A hung heartbeat something.

Worry. The sensation was worry. Her throat went to dust. Divinity knew—*how* did it know?—about the Whyte Avenue Eyes. "It—it's okay," she announced. "Andrew's on it."

Overhead, the light flickered, then *plink!* The morgue plunged into darkness.

Skin quivering, she reached out, jiggled the switch.

The light flared back on only to *pop!* burn out altogether.

"O-kay…" Cloaked in shadows, she looked around. "You don't *want* lights on?"

Deep within the quiet she felt it. Reproach. As though the place wagged a finger.

"I hear you," she whispered. "You're worried. Don't want me seen. What else?" She was shaking but forced herself to breathe, to close her eyes. To become one with the place. *Show me. You know I believe in you. Let me see what I'm supposed to see.*

Her eyes opened.

Cele's candle, still at its morning spot by the window, was directly in the path of her gaze. Black. The color of protection. She approached it, struck a match.

The wick grabbed the flame hungrily, and soft light licked the table, illuminated the card left behind. The Magician, upside down. She examined it while outside late night vehicles whished, tires hissing sounds that could not be coincidence: *Charlatan. Illusions.* Shuddering, she reached out, flicked the radio on.

Noel Nelson joined her in the old parlor. "If Weste can just accept that being in Edmonton doesn't hurt, he'll continue to play as good as he did in the third."

*"Edmonton doesn't hurt."* Does *it hurt?* Another coincidence that was no coincidence? Every sense sharpened and *charlatan* continued to whish from outside. "Who's a charlatan?" she called out. "Nelson? Or Weste?"

Below her the candle flame seemed to brighten, its small purple heart glowing. Then a breeze out of nowhere snuffed it out.

She relit it. "Again with no lights? What are you saying?"

Sensation, a presence, crackled around her then abruptly withdrew. Just as if the old morgue pulled back into itself, distant and closed.

And angry.

She gingerly sank to the window seat, tongue between teeth. "The charlatan isn't Weste," she announced, as certain as she was when the cards would fall still in her hands, answers ready. "It isn't him, and you're irritated that I thought it was. You *like* him."

The candlelight babbled, bopping up and down like a nod.

Her smile was grim. "Cut me a wee bit of slack. As far as fits, it wasn't a bad one; Weste *is* a player in both actions and deeds."

The candle flame stretched, piously straight, and with it memory resounded—her question: "Do you need an address?" and his answer: "Nope."

She scowled. "Alright, so he's *not* a liar."

The flame, back on the move, bopped brightness.

"But did I really deserve to be stood up?"

The flame quivered then drooped, defeated. She laughed a bit, grim. "Don't feel bad. I liked him too. Although—," she slumped back against the wall "—why being ditched by someone who gave me a sex toy makes me sad is also beyond me." Her eyes sought the scrolled ceiling. "Seems these days everything is beyond me. Except you." Her smile was wistful. *Grateful.* "Divinity, I love you."

Warmth whispered back.

"Centre me." She opened her palms. "I'm screwing up, getting dumped, seeing Eyes, for goodness's sake...*please,* Divinity, centre me. Give me what I need."

Peace. Protection. They were upon her within seconds. "Thank you." She closed her eyes.

Lavender rushed through the air.

"Thank you, thank you, thank...you..." She drifted, weightless, timeless...and when a blue flash lit the backs of her eyes, she flew from her spot, heart hammering.

Illumination she recognized poured through the stained glass. *The motion light! The Eyes!* Scampering from the window she dove for her coat, plunged her hand into the pocket. "Okay," she panted, and, taser in hand, crept to the door. "Game over, redneck. You are *done* scaring me." She lunged for the latch, wrenched it open.

"Hey!" The figure looming there ducked. "Don't shoot!"

## CHAPTER EIGHT

"WESTE!" SHE CHOKED on a scream. "What the hell are you doing, skulking around here at night?"

"*Morning.*" He batted a hand at her taser and, missing miserably, had to catch the doorjamb to get his balance.

It groaned against his weight and "Hey!" she righted him, bore his weight. "Are you—oh, damn. You *are.*" Drunk. *Seriously?* She glanced around. *This is my karma?*

Deep in the basement the old furnace chugged to life. It sounded a lot like a chuckle. She shot a glare in its vicinity. *Right. Funny one.* "Weste—"

"I'm not drunk," he rasped, anticipating her and surprisingly lucid. "I—I'm *dizzy."* He leaned against her. His weight made her feel as though she, like the doorjamb, would groan and splinter.

"I...I gotta sit down."

"Wrong," she grunted, straightening him. "You gotta go home."

"Hush." He touched a weak hand to her mouth. "Shaynie, I got something to say."

Why oh why did drunks always think they were full of revelations? "You want to talk? Call me." She tried wheeling him for the door.

It was like pushing bricks. She struggled, and at first he sighed, then he tapped his foot, then at last he simply lifted her, set her aside. "If I did call..." He looked down at her, again jarringly lucid. "Would you still answer?"

*Does it hurt?* The night beyond his shoulder loomed, an abandoned inkwell. With Eyes.

"Get in here." She hauled him over the threshold, scowling when his track suit, frozen nylon, crackled in protest. "A spring jacket and running shoes. It's *winter,* Ice Deity. Where's your coat?"

"Wish I knew." He tried to step, but had to stop, plop a hand on her shoulder.

Her knees buckled, but she managed to tow him to the window seat. "Looks like new staff don't know enough not to let their customers get drunk," she muttered.

He hissed, the breath setting her candle flame dancing. She glanced at it. Glanced again, a double take. No longer tall and straight, the candle was a spent waterfall of wax. Which meant— "It *is* morning."

"Told you." He flopped to the seat.

*Give me what I need.* She peered around. "And you thought I needed sleep?"

"I don't know *what* you need other than to believe I'm not drunk," Cameron replied. "God, Shaynie, look at me. Do you know how much booze I've gotta pound to even get a buzz?"

Fair enough. He wasn't drunk. It was morning. By now he was hung over.

"I'm just...dizzy," he said again, and the back of his head hit the wall with a clunk.

She could not help a tiny smile. "What," she said, "happened?"

"The Python. The Python happened."

Something—a green sort of something—slithered through her gut. "Ah. The Python. Of course. How could a lesson on The Sun ever win over The Python?"

He opened one eye. "I didn't choose it over you. I went there to see you."

"Uh-huh. Last time I checked Has Beans was a coffee house on Whyte."

"Yeah, and last time I checked Shaynie Gavin wasn't terribly truthful."

"You thought I'd set you up?"

"Crossed my mind." His lids drifted back shut.

She glared. "Give me—just *one*—reason to not boot your butt outta here."

"I outweigh you." He yawned, stretched his legs out. "My God, I feel like sh—"

"Yeah, well, you look like it too."

He opened one eye again. "You need to get a leash for your tongue."

"And lend it to you. If I'm such a bi—"

"Don't say it, Shaynie. I did *not* call you that."

"—a *bitch*," she said, anyway, "then why are you here?"

Silence shimmered in the candlelight. "Why," he said, "did *you* want a lah-tay-dah?"

Good question. Her gaze fell, landed on his lap where his hands, folded and massive, still had that one knuckle seething with a gash. She stared at it, caught once again by the need to touch it. *Heal* it.

"Shaynie? Why?"

Why did she want to touch him? She had no idea. All she did know was "'Cause I did lie." Nelson's face flashed in her head. "Lied then I invalidated your call to the Tarot, and that...that may be the role I play in The Python, but it's not who I am."

"So the bartender—little Python Princess—she's completely illusion?"

Was that disappointment or relief? "Yes," she said, and stuck out her chin. "So much that I used Cele's hockey tickets just so you could see that."

A heartbeat elapsed and within it she felt it, footing between them that was all brand new. "How about the Python Prowler?" she ventured. "Is *he* an illusion too?"

"The Python Prowler?"

"You know, the strutter. The guy with the hot smile and sharp tongue—which needs a leash."

"Pfft." His lids fell back shut. "He sounds like a moron."

"Nah. He's actually a pretty good guy."

He opened that same eye. "Newsflash. He doesn't exist."

And back was the mercurial Moon. She stared at the floor, at the footing that was new.

"I found you tonight for the same reason you wanted coffee," he said, quiet. "'Cause 'sorry' isn't something you say on the phone."

An unexpected storm, opposite to the tears after trudging home from Jude's car, hit her eyes. She tried looking away, out the window.

Impossible.

His gaze caught hers, kept it, and she tripped on their new footing, hands working, fingers knitting this way and that. "You...you're really pale." It was more than just something to say. The candlelight licking his cheeks illuminated pallor so translucent it glowed. "Here." She dug in a cooler she kept under the table, cracked a bottle of water.

He knocked it back in one go.

"Slow," she scolded, then opened the tote she'd had at Has Beans. The barista had been thoughtful enough to include a plastic fork with the ganache. "This too."

"Food?" He recoiled.

"Food," she said firmly. "Your body needs to digest something other than booze."

"I told you I didn't—"

"Hush." She popped a forkful of pie in his mouth.

He tried to scowl, tried to speak, but "Oh," was all he managed then "*Oh.*" His mouth worked, swallowed. "What *is* that?"

"Ganache."

"Ganache," he echoed, tasting the word. Then he beckoned for more.

She could have handed him the fork. Probably *should* have handed him the fork. But feeding him...it was just automatic. And he liked it. It was in the way his mouth closed around the ganache, the way his head fell back. The *sounds* he made. It was like spying on something secret, something sacred; and when he licked his lips her tongue came out too, like an echo.

"Straight out of a fantasy." He opened his eyes, plucked the fork from her fingers. "*You* try."

There was no time to say no. The fork slipped between her lips and her mouth flooded with silken chocolate. Her eyes flooded with his satisfied smile.

He forked up more pie for himself. "This is what I missed in Has Beans?"

*And this is what* I *missed in Has Beans?* God. Her heart was pounding.

"There's only a bit left." He offered it.

"Go...go ahead." She looked at the ganache, not him.

"Uh-uh. It's yours." He stabbed it. "My punishment for standing you up."

"No." She shook her head, eyes averted. "My gift to my guest."

"Uninvited, unannounced guest."

She met his gaze. "That's okay."

His smile, not The Smile but a real, gentle, smile, made her heart flip. "We good now?" he asked.

"Yeah." There was chocolate on his lip. She reached out, reflex.

His tongue darted, also reflex.

Skin hunger.

The contact was like an internal gasp and she could taste it; sweet chocolate, salty skin. Her mouth went arid and she looked up, *stretched* up.

He jerked back. "Nuh-uh. *No.* Bad plan, Shaynie."

She flinched, face on fire. He captured her chin before she could turn away. "Don't. It's just...Shaynie, I like you *way* too much for that."

For what? A kiss in the candlelight? Weren't you *supposed* to like people you kissed in the candlelight? Cheeks hot, she tried squirming away.

He stilled her, a hand on each shoulder. "I meant what I said last night," He looked her in the eye. "I'm not a prick."

In other words, one night stands were what he had with women he didn't give a damn about, not ones he "liked". But this...this was just a kiss in the candlelight.

Yeah, right. Subtle scent, *his* scent, rode the air. Fresh rain and sweet chocolate. They were bury-your-face-in-his-neck smells. Lick his neck smells. She wiggled backward, floundering on footing that was again all brand new. "So." Sliding distance between them she primly clasped her hands. "You're clearly *not* drunk. So why dizzy? Concussion?"

"Hardly. I *delivered* checks tonight, not the reverse. You saw the game."

"Not all of it."

His brow rose.

"Story for another day." She shrugged. "We were talking about you."

"Yeah, well," The pillar of his throat worked, Adam's apple bobbing, and at last he merely opened empty palms *à la* Cele. "We got to The Python and there were a couple of red-headed robots behind your bar. I was going to leave, but then your dancing deejay—who's a sarcastic bastard, by the way—yelled for them to pour me a shot. To celebrate my 'miracle goal.'"

*Oh, Grayson.* Talk about someone whose tongue needed a leash. She rubbed her temples. "Where was Jude?"

"Rasputin wasn't there. Or..." He searched the unseen distance. "Is there a back room in The Python?"

"The staff room. Our exit." Then it dawned. Of course Jude would have been there, placating the Fire Marshal. But— "What were *you* doing in there?"

"I don't know. I don't even know if I was. I just remember wanting to leave, but then Nelson—"

"Nelson," she spat. "Every gutter always drains back to the same cesspool."

He blinked. She folded her arms. "Cameron, you need to understand something about Noel Nelson."

"Shaynie, save your breath. I understand *everything* about Nelson—from his TV shows to his toilet habits. We're roommates on the road."

He had to sleep in the same room as that grease stain? Good Lord. Now how to tell him. *What* to tell him. What she had—instinct and conjecture—was the stuff Jude said turned her and Gray into paranoid harpies. Then there was Cele. She'd scold her six ways from Sunday for worrying or, worse, *scaring,* a client.

Still, his cards, all those swords, had been abundantly clear.

"There are people," she began carefully. "Who will do anything—and I mean *anything*—to win."

"Yeah." He nodded. "Every professional athlete I know. Including me."

She scowled. "*You* are not like Nelson. Cameron, think...hmm. Think of Noel as the Knight of Swords."

"Nelson, a *knight*? Court Jester, maybe. But a *kni—*"

"Weste!" She glared. "I'm trying to help you." She was surprised at how wounded she sounded.

He was too. It was in the way the sparkle left his eyes. "And I'm listening. Truly. After all, Nelson *is* kicking my ass for points out on the ice."

"Yeah, but he knows that won't last. He's not stupid; he knows that of the two of you you're the one with more talent. And trust me, it's making him crazy. He..." Her thoughts strayed to Gray, less wealthy than Nelson, less star-power than Nelson, yet he'd always been the nicer guy. Noel had *hated* it. "He'll make it his mission to humble you. It's what he does. Believe me, I...I've seen him do it before."

"Shaynie, you don't have to tell me. I know your history."

Her history? An image popped like an old time flash cube. Blood on the bathroom floor. A blank slate of memory. Hellnight. A night which she, like Weste, could not remember. Her heart pounded a blood rush through her ears and before them the candle flame jiggered then fizzled out altogether. She stared at it. Exhaled. Hellnight? No. Of *course* not. She *was* being a 'paranoid harpy'. Heck, bordering on obsessive. What he'd obviously meant was— "Noel clearly told you about when we were all teenagers."

He hesitated—or maybe he didn't—it was hard to think straight with her heart still in her ears, but then, "I know what he told me," he said. "But what's your version?"

"Probably one that's a whole lot more objective than anything Noel *or* Gray would say."

A quirk, confusion, rippled on his brow. She smiled with no mirth. "Here's the truth: Once upon a time Gray had a girlfriend. Noel got her pregnant. Then neither one of them wanted her and she drove herself off a cliff back in the mountains. Ever since then they've changed their tunes, both claiming she was the love of their lives and blaming each other. Jude has always been the voice of reason. He thought Jen was poison for them both and has spent a lifetime trying to peace-make between them. So there. Now you know."

Cameron, chewing his tongue visibly, was wordless for several seconds. "That's a story without you in it," he said finally.

"Thank God for that," she replied.

He frowned and she could see an internal debate, alive on his face, then, finally— "I guess I shouldn't be surprised that Nelson would inject himself in the middle of a soap opera," he said. "After all, I've known him every bit as long as you and your friend Gray. Maybe longer."

Her brow hopped. He shrugged. "The hockey world isn't big, Shaynie. No professional sports world is. Noel and I have been in and out of each other's circles since Juniors and he's always been an attention whore. But—" he dragged a hand down his face, "he's basically harmless."

*Harmless?* "Tonight he was on the radio, sounding off about you. He—"

"Whoa. Now you're basing a judgment on trash talk?"

Among a million other things. "What I heard—"

"—was a taunt. Build someone up by tearing him down. Sports Psych 101."

"Spirituality 101: that which is hidden actually exists all around you. The most important life lessons hide in plain sight."

A beat elapsed, then "Just open your eyes," he said softly. "Then you'll see."

A chill—and a tingle—waged war on her shoulders.

He didn't notice. "Trust me, I know Nelson can be a prick. In fact – " He stopped himself. "I know him. But thank you," He reached out, trailed a finger down her cheek. "For the loyalty."

Shoulda seen the rumble I almost started at the arena with Belly. "Choose better friends."

"Nah." He smiled and more chills and tingles abounded. "I already pick good friends."

Friends. And friends did *not* kiss in the candlelight, no matter how many times their eyes met and clung. She dragged her gaze away. He did too.

"Got any more water?" he asked, and she wondered if he, like she, needed distraction. She rummaged in the cooler and he cracked the bottle she handed him, drank slower than before, but then flopped bonelessly backward. "Flu?" he asked the ceiling. "Does flu come with these disappearing then reappearing headaches? Black you out?"

"Weste, *alcohol* blacks you out despite how little you think you drank. *Spiritus contra spiritum*. Next time stick to lah-tay-dahs." *Like I've learned to do.*

"Coffee?" He pulled a face. "I can't choke that crap down even with cream and sugar."

She laughed, a feeling like the sun dancing out from under clouds. "Ah, the 'ockey God is a coffee hater. Like Cele needed one *more* reason to love you."

He shot a weak whiplash smile. "Always listen to a woman who floats."

"Oh, but I do." She dug it out from beneath the fan jersey she still wore, his discarded gold chain.

He hooked it onto a finger, smile gone. “The Devil. Who is he?”

“I don’t know.”

*Yes you do.* It was more than a thought. The words were a zephyr, breathed by the walls. She looked around, heart hammering.

The chain on his finger caught stained glass light, flashed colored starpoints in his hand. He looked at them. “Is The Devil why you don’t have a guy?”

*Let it Be.* She swallowed the lyric, as loud as a scream. “H-how do you know I don’t?”

“’Cause if you did you’d be home sleeping with him tonight, not in a morgue all alone.”

*Does it hurt?* Yes. It did. Yet— “I’m not alone, Cameron.” Again their eyes caught and clung. “I’m with you.”

Kiss in the candlelight. She reached for him. He reached back. Her cell shrilled.

He jerked away as though awakened, and her cell rang again. “You—uh—gonna answer that?”

She reached for it, read the screen. Andrew. Her heart bolted. The phone call. The *Eyes.* “Hello?”

“You at Divinity?”

Divinity. Not Spook Factory, not Skeleton Parade. The distinction sat her up straight. “Yes. I’m—”

“Lock the door, do not leave and for God’s sake don’t let anyone—*anyone*—in there.”

She snared Cameron’s eyes. “W-why?”

“Because your so-called crank call, the location was kicked back.”

She held her breath

“Shaynie Grace, it came from your apartment.”

## CHAPTER NINE

Crisp cop questions curdled the scream in her gut.

“What were you doing when you got the call?”

“Walking home. I was at Has Beans.”

“Having coffee with who?”

“No one. My...my date didn’t show.”

Beside her, Weste softly tsked. Andrew said "Did you see anyone—*anything* suspicious?"

Not seen. *Sensed.* Eyes. From her window! They had been *in her window!* The scream clawed her throat.

"Shaynie Grace?"

"I—I was sure someone was watching me as I walked home."

*"What?"* came from beside her while, "Why the *hell* didn't you tell me that?" blasted her ear.

She winced, held the phone away.

"Who *is* that?" Weste growled.

"Who's with you?" Andrew barked.

"No one." The lie was not premeditated. It just fell out.

"Shaynie Gr—"

"*No one*," she repeated, and looked at Cameron, placed a finger to her lips.

He glared at the phone.

She turned her back to him. "I want to see my apartment."

"No," said Andrew. "*I'll* see your apartment, with backup, and you'll stay put till I say otherwise. Now sit tight, let nobody in, and keep your door locked."

He hung up. Weste cleared his throat. "That The Agent?"

"Detective," she managed through frozen lips. "Andrew's a cop."

"A cop?" His track suit rustled as he leaned forward, found her face. "What the hell's going on? People are watching you?"

Not 'people'. 'Person'. There'd been only one set of eyes. That much she was sure of. She slashed a hand through her hair. "Tonight, when I left Has Beans." Her voice was brittle, like broken match sticks. She swallowed its dry taste. "And then they, *he...*" *Broke into my apartment! He was in my apartment!* A scream crackled in her throat. "...he crank called me."

He was wordless and for a beat she wondered if he knew that wasn't all. Then, "Scary." He nodded. "I've been there."

She gaped.

"Crazy fan," he added, smile tight.

"Crazy—"

"—fan. Like the freakshows who hang outside the locker room after every game, hop planes and follow the team, sometimes even across the country."

She stared at him. He sighed. "They're stalkers. People who show up where we eat, hang around the hotels where we sleep, manage to get private things like our addresses—*and* phone numbers. Doesn't happen so much down in the 'States where no one gives a damn about hockey, but up here, where you're a rock star…" He let it trail off as if the answer were obvious.

But for her it *wasn't* obvious. "Cameron, I'm no rock star."

"Guess again, Python Princess."

He read the horror on her face with a wince. "Shaynie, you didn't need to tell *me* that the wise-mouth hottie who dances with deejay is all an act. I'd figured that out even before I was such a jerk to you the other night. But some people...some people don't get it."

"So you…you think I set myself up for this?" But…had she? How many times had Gray told her to get out of the Python? How often did Andrew tell her she'd end up in trouble there?

Cameron made an impatient noise. "No," he said. "You didn't ask for this any more than I ask for every private aspect of my life—right down to my damn bank account—to be bleated out by some color commentator on TV."

She shook her head. "You're comparing two different worlds."

"Not really. Consider your Python self, but more to the point consider the crazy fan. He thinks that based on only what he sees, he knows you. Has a right to you." He curled his lip. "Case in point: how many times have I got to a hotel room and found a naked puck bunny in my bed?"

In his *bed*? Had Eyes been in *her* bed?

*Yes.* The answer came straight from the place where intuition lived, right between her gut and her heart.

"Shaynie?" He ducked to catch her eyes. "You just gasped. Did you think of someone?"

Not someone. Some*thing*. Hellnight. And this time it was not paranoia. She drew the pieces together, the Eyes, the vandalism…Andrew had said redneck, and over her own intuition she'd *believed* redneck. Now…. She breathed deep, forced herself to reason. *How* could it be Hellnight? Whoever she'd been with didn't know where she lived now 'cause after that night she'd moved, fled that fantastic loft she'd lived in, just blocks from where they sat right now. It had been a way to wash away her bad choices, her shame, and she'd explained to no one—except Cele—why she'd left. And as for the shabby little brownstone she resided in now, it had hosted only two visitors since she'd moved in: Cele and Andrew. Because irrational or not, *paranoid* or not, it had felt safest to keep it a secret, even from her best friends.

So *how* could someone know?

*Someone does.*

Another zephyr and, as if to prove itself, the candle she'd re-lit flickered out. Cameron—and she—stared at it. "Shaynie?" he tried, tentative. "What's going through your head?"

"Andrew. He...he said the call came from my apartment."

He swore and sat back.

She nodded, eyes locked on the dead candle. "Know what's ironic?"

He shook his head, and even from the corner of her eye she could see his expression, *careful, careful,* all over his face.

"It's ironic that someone was eager enough to break into a place that I'm not even willing to invite people to. Because I—" *I'm scared.* She shoved this away. "Because it's a dump." Both truth and lie. "There's structural problems everywhere. Cosmetic issues out the wazoo. It's the last place in the world that I, a ticketed carpenter, should be living, and I...I'm ashamed of it. Or at least I *was* ashamed. But...know what else is ironic?"

Again he shook his head.

"That now it's like some kind of palace that some scumbag's defiled and I...I'd like to kick his ass for it."

His mouth twitched, a movement that badly wanted to be a grin, and she was touched when he tried coughing to hide it. "So now what?" she asked, more to herself than him. "Palace or pit, I don't want to go back there."

Sunshine color awakened the windows. An answer. She spoke to it. "Move in here? Wouldn't *that* make Andrew's hair curl?"

Cameron made a noise of assent, and she remembered that he thought she was talking to him. She looked at him. "My brother and I have this thing, dinner once a week. Living here I'd need to knock a hole in the wall, make a take-out window so he could get his to go."

"Complete with his coffee in a take-away urn?"

Laughter took her by surprise, wicked but oh-so welcome.

He grinned too, but in a wink The Moon was back and his expression was grave. "I know what you can do."

## CHAPTER TEN

"I'M GOING ON a road trip. My condo will be empty."

Her wide eyes spoke for her. He splayed his hands. "The Agent would think it's a great idea."

"Andrew would kick my tush if he even knew you were here. Then he'd want to kick yours."

"Pfft. Tell him he'd better bring a friend."

"He has a gun."

"And I have a *stick,*" he stage-whispered.

Laughter, again out of place and certainly fleeting, but it felt good. Felt *grounding*. "Cameron, thank you, but—"

"Your crazy fan was *in your apartment*, Shaynie."

Like she'd forgotten. A shiver tracked her neck. "I-I'm a carpenter. I can change all the locks."

"My place has security."

And her little brownstone had that busted security door. But *Divinity…* her eyes skated to the alarm panel. His did too. "People," he said. "Not electronics."

The alarm's red light blinked, a neon heartbeat that thrummed. '*Does—it—hurt?*' Goosebumps iced her arms. "Yes," she whispered. "It does."

Cameron questioned her with his eyes. She faced him. "I was just reflecting: 'Does it hurt?' That's what my caller asked me."

"Does what hurt?"

Andrew had asked too. Would no doubt ask her again once he was done at her apartment. And the answer, when she considered it, stayed the same. "Being stood up," she said quietly.

He winced, guilt all over his face. "Shaynie, I'm so—"

"It's not your fault." She took herself back to cold Whyte Ave, but instead of being the person who left Has Beans, alone and rejected, she became the omniscient presence in her window. Watching. Waiting.

*Waiting.*

A dark thought dropped her gut. She'd been in her apartment for mere seconds before sprinting over to Has Beans, excited to meet Cameron. Had Eyes already been there? Heard her make plans to go out? Is that how he knew she'd been stood up? Panic seized her breath. If that had been the scenario then what if she'd stayed? What if no date had been planned and she'd locked herself—*them*—in the apartment together? Her teeth began chattering.

"Here." Cameron shrugged his track jacket off, dropped it over her shoulders.

The scents rain and chocolate warmed her far more than the thin, useless fabric.

"How long do you think you've had this crazy fan?" he asked.

*Since Hellnight,* answered intuition. She shuddered under his jacket. That could be right, but panic, on the other hand, could be wrong. "I... don't know."

She could practically hear him debating, and when he spoke it was with that same careful-careful he'd worn on his face. "Shaynie, I may just be armchair analyzing with a psych degree I didn't finish, but crazy fans are just that: Crazy. So if you're thinking of being some self-reliant little detective? That's not bravery. That's stupidity."

She flinched.

He didn't apologize. "It's The Agent's job to figure this out," he said. "*Your* job is to keep yourself safe. Which means stay at my place till your brother finds this guy, brings him to you so you *can* kick his ass."

He was aiming for a smile, but she was fresh out. "Say I do hide in your condo. Wouldn't that just reward this guy? Prove he can scare me?"

"What difference does it make if you're scared so long as you're safe?"

A good point, worthy of Andrew. In fact, if her brother were there he'd likely applaud—and she'd be powerless to argue. She swallowed, unable to speak.

Cameron shifted so he faced the window. "See the high rise three down?"

She barely had to look. She knew each of those high rises, had long appreciated the stately grace with which they hovered over the river valley.

"Find the window second from the top, on the corner," he said.

A small glowing square was gilded by eastern rising sun.

"My bedroom."

A cartwheel vaulted her stomach. He mistook the shudder for surprise. "I know. It threw me too when Dancing Deejay coughed up this address and I saw that it was practically next door."

She stiffened, belly shimmer gone. "Gray gave my address to you?" *To a hockey player?*

"Don't hang him for it. I had to grovel and even then all he'd do was landmark this place, threatening my throat unless I promised to lick your boots."

Throat threatening? Now *that* sounded like Gray talking to a player. But to send one to her door?

"Sarcastic bastard or not, he is a good friend," said Cameron.

She was speechless.

"So am I," he ventured and smiled, neither sexed up nor sheepish but a combination of both. "C'mon, Shaynie. Who hasn't crashed at a buddy's? You'd even be able to keep an eye on Divinity all night."

Because she'd sleep in his bed? Phantom scents, rain and chocolate, were so strong she could taste them. She slipped his coat off. "Cameron that—that's really generous, but really, I barely know you—"

"Disagree. And besides, *I* won't be there."

Scent. *Skin hunger.* Oh, yes. He'd be there. She looked at the floor. "Weste—"

"A minute ago I was Cameron. A minute before that you said, 'what if I did stay at your condo'." He reached out, swept up her cards with one large paw. "What would these say? They *are* Tarot, right?"

"Yeah. Yes. But..." But what? Why not turn the Tarot and seek direction—especially now?

He squared the deck's corners, frowning over its fairies and nymphs. "They don't look like Cele's."

"The deck chooses the dealer." It sounded hollow, like reciting by rote.

He nodded, sifted through the cards. "These suit you," he said, then placed them in her hand. "Shuffle. And if they say you shouldn't stay, I'll shut up."

The cards felt too big, too bulky, and her fingers were trembling and stiff. Still, she forced them, and soon the sound—*whish, whish*—caught and calmed her until a hum as familiar as a heartbeat reverberated in her hands.

She stopped, turned the top card. The Lovers.

"Hmph," he said. "My offer didn't mean you could bring a friend."

She slashed him a look. He wore a grin. "C'mon, Shaynie. That was *funny*."

No, it was as unfunny as she'd be if she tossed a knee over his lap, found his mouth like a literal lover.

A *literal* lover? Good God. What *was* she thinking?

*Bad choices.* The little Lovers gazed up at her, tiny eyes judging. *That's why we're here.*

*No kidding.* She drew a breath. "This card—like all of them—isn't literal. And it's telling me that the Tarot won't make the choice for me.

I have to do that on my own and use either my head—" She pointed to the male on the card. "—or my heart." Her finger slid to the female.

"Or maybe it means listen to a man *and* a woman." He gave the card a speculative little tap. "Cele and I both think you need protection."

She hooked a thumb beneath her collar, pulled out his chain.

"Not *that.*" He scowled. "That's *useless.*"

"That's not what you said last night."

"Last night I didn't know you had a stalker." He sneered at the chain. "Toss it. It's probably doing you more harm than good."

Her eyes widened. He flicked a shoulder. "What did you say to me earlier? 'Story for another day'?" He rose. "I'll tell you another time. But right now I need to go. I'll have to make arrangements for you with my building security before I pack and leave."

Just like that? She hadn't green-lit anything. She scrambled after him. "Wait!"

He paused in the pool of morning light now pouring through the stained glass.

"Weste—*Cameron*—please don't think I'm unappreciative. And I'm not trying to be argumentative. It's just…"

"Would it help if I had an ulterior motive?"

He did? She sagged. Yet...an ulterior motive. It actually *would* help.

"I want another reading."

"Another—you were dealt the best cards in the deck!"

"A vague Sun, then betrayal and heartbreak. Yeah. Fantastic."

"But the wish card—"

"Shaynie, I've had enough heartbreak."

Pain. Little more than a ghost in his eyes, still she saw it. *Felt* it, a sharp stitch in her side.

"I'd like you to watch my next game. *And* turn a card."

"With what question?" she asked, yet something—some visceral sort of something—told her she didn't want to hear. Didn't want to know.

He hesitated a beat. "How about I tell you when I see the answer?"

*Superstitious athlete.* Yet not knowing was somehow a relief. She nodded.

He misread her face. "Selfish lunatic, eh? Asking you to take your cards and watch a hockey game after everything tonight."

Who was the selfish lunatic? *She* didn't want the answer he was looking for. Faking a smile she hoped didn't look as twitchy as it felt she said "It'll be a good distraction," A lie but when he beamed, his smile, sexy and sweet, was two opposites. A 'Ten'. *My Python Prowler,* she thought. *My pal.* Blinking, she was astonished that her lashes were suddenly cold and wet. She swallowed the mystery of tears. "H-how will I get hold of you to tell you about your reading?"

"Easy. I'll leave my number in my condo."

Which slickly eliminated all choice. "My God, you're stubborn."

"Some people might call me helpful."

She chewed her lip. Going to his condo didn't mean she had to sleep there. "One card for a whole condo. Sweet deal. Anything else you need?"

He softly smiled. "Yeah. Same thing you need. One good friend." He found her eyes. "Want to apply?"

The mystery tears flooded back. "Yes." Her head bobbed. "Sure."

"Thanks," he said, and this time when their eyes clung he leaned down.

She stretched up, lips parted, but his mouth didn't go there, instead landed prayer-soft on her cheek. *One good friend.* She touched the spot, held the kiss there. "You—you really don't need a new reading, Cameron. The wish card will give you whatever you want."

A wistful smile pulled the light from his eyes. "If that's true then I wish *you* had it."

A lump leapt to her throat. "Thanks, but...I'd rather have your Sun."

He looked confused.

"Then I'd know I'd made all the right choices."

Stubbornness reclaimed his jaw. "I already made the choice for you. Security will make sure you're let into my place."

His place. The perfect solution. The worst possible plan. "Cameron—"

"He scores!" cried a canned voice, and he pulled a face, brought a cell phone out of pocket. "Hockey humor." He shut the alarm off. "Means my flight leaves in just a few hours. If I'm going to arrange my condo for you I really gotta go."

'Go'. Leave her alone. Ice scored her neck. "Cam—"

"Shaynie, *please* don't argue with me about this."

"I...wasn't. I was just....Thank you." Oh, damn. Her chin was wobbling. "For finding me. For staying with me." She needed to turn. Hide her eyes.

No chance. He caught her, and what she knew next was body heat. Heartbeat. Chocolate and rain. "Hey," he said. "It's okay." He wrapped her close, breath lifting her hair. "It'll work out."

A tear slipped out and she tried squeezing it back, but another joined it. Then another.

"Aw, Shaynie." He tilted her face back.

"He scores!"

"Oh, shut *up.*" He dropped his arms and she stepped back too, tempted to grab the doorjamb and steady herself like he had when he'd come in. What sort of emotional funhouse *was* this? A few minutes ago she'd have stiffened if even *Andrew* tried to give her a hug. And now to be craving it? Craving more? Craving *everything*?

Does it hurt?

Yes. Yes, dammit, it does. Happy now?

The Eyes, wherever they were, laughed. She felt them. Wrapping her arms around herself, she took one more step away. "When—when will you be back?"

"A week. Lots of time for The Agent to catch your crazy fan, shove a boot up his ass."

She grimaced. "Sounds like you've *met* Andrew."

He did not smile. "Be safe, Clever Shaynie."

He opened the door and— "Whoa," he said. Cele was on the threshold. Jude too, arms loaded with predictable coffee and scones. Their eyes, wide and wondering, traveled up Weste's large presence then down to Shaynie's smaller one. But before either could say anything, a vehicle roared into the lot.

Uh-oh. Her belly pitched. Andrew.

Her brother slammed his car door so hard it cracked like a gunshot. "Well." His eyes raked the small crowd on her stoop. "I guess in Shaynie-speak 'let no one in' means go ahead and throw a big goddamn party. Pita, are you brain dead?"

Beside her a hiss of breath whistled and she sensed, rather than saw, Cameron stiffen. She slipped him a look. "Go," she mouthed, as obliquely as possible.

He peered directly down into the lot, at her brother. "I don't think so," he rumbled.

Her gut hit her shoes. "Andrew." She tried catching his eyes. "What did you find?"

Her brother's close-mouthed appraisal of her onlookers did all the talking for him.

She swiped a hand through her hair. "You know everyone here." Well, almost everyone. "And you know I'm going to tell them everything anyway."

He was silent for another beat, then, "Robbery," he spat. "Looks like jewelry."

"*Mon dieu*!" Cele was bug-eyed, and *"Robbery?"* this echo was Jude's. "Shaynes, *what* is going *on*?"

She stared at her brother. "Andrew, I don't even own jewelry. Just costume garbage. Nothing worth stealing."

"Yeah, well, a crack head wouldn't know pearls from piss."

"A crack head? Why would a crack head call me?"

"Why would a crack head call *anyone* connected to The Python?"

"What the hell does that mean?" Again Jude, and this time he stepped forward. "There aren't any drugs in my club."

"Please. There're drugs in *every* club."

"Well there aren't any drugs on me." Dragging the issue back to the point, Shaynie glared at Andrew. "Or anybody I know." Anymore. Gray had been clean for a decade.

Andrew looked at her. "Really? And you know that how, Shaynie Grace? You well versed in how someone on meth acts? Or crack?" He slid a look to Cameron. "How about steroids?"

Her jaw dropped, but to her astonishment Cameron laughed. "Trash talk," he side-mouthed. "Let it go."

Andrew cocked his head. "What was that, Goliath? You look like you're just dying to say something."

"Yeah," said Cameron. "I am."

*Oh, God.* Shaynie squeezed the bridge of her nose.

"Shaynie didn't invite *anyone* over here to party—or do anything else, for that matter. It's business hours." He tapped his watch. "We all just showed up. For business."

A bald-faced lie, yet neither Cele nor Jude contradicted him. Flashing Andrew a big smile, he turned to her. "Thank you for setting up that Tarot appointment," he said, loud enough and formally enough so that everyone could hear.

"You're welcome." She matched his tone then dropped her voice several octaves. "*Go*," she whispered, but smiled, ever so slight. "The Sun is waiting for you."

Softness sailed through his storm eyes and then he was gone, down the stairs and across the lot, long strides eating up the snow in big crunching bites. Her eyes clung to his back—*See ya, "friend"*—and a phantom taste, not rain or chocolate, but her all-alone lah-tay-dah in Has Beans, found her tongue.

Behind her Cele's throat cleared. It brought her back to reality and she turned to her brother. "You said, crack head. Why?"

"Irrationality. Jewelry strewn out while a wad of cash laid untouched on your table. Not bright, by the way, leaving money out like that."

She ignored the slur on her intelligence for "wad of cash". *What* wad of cash? The only money she had was the change from the ten she'd broken on her lonely latte. "There was no cash on my table."

A thread of alarm wiped *pissed off* from Andrew's face and he bounded up the stairs, whipped out his phone, a twin to Cameron's. "Here," he said. "Look."

A picture popped onto the screen: a tidy roll of cash centered on her familiar barn-board table. She gasped, but the sound was lost when he said, "And this."

The cash scrolled off the screen and there was her bed skirt, snowy against drab carpet. She squinted, unable to make out the small object he pointed to.

"Here." He enlarged it. "This is what was dropped in the jewelry grab."

Her gut spasmed. "It's not mine," she mumbled, yet she too had a picture of the necklace Andrew was showing her. Had snapped the shot so she could research the saint etched on the pendant then present what she'd learned in a long handwritten note, a surprise because—

"He's a good friend," had said Cameron.

"A crackhead." Andrew had spat.

Yes, to both. And that pendant in the picture, it was *his* chain, *his* patron saint.

Saint Cecelia, Patroness of Music.

Patroness of Gray.

## CHAPTER ELEVEN

NOT A REDNECK. Not Hellnight. *Gray.* It had to be a joke.

She followed Andrew from Divinity to the south side, dialing and re-dialing Gray's number despite what had been her brother's curt direction otherwise. "Please pick up." *This has to be a joke.* "C'mon, Gray. Pick *up."* *'Cause this is a joke. A stupid joke. A mean joke. But still just a joke!*

The phone rang on and on and at last she had to slip it into her pocket. They'd reached her apartment, and when she saw the two uniformed officers waiting there, the word 'joke' burnt and flew, black ashes on the breeze.

Cops in your house were no joke.

They were oh-so-compassionate as they trailed her through the minuscule square footage to see if anything was taken or harmed.

Nothing was.

Then they asked her to recount everything that had happened from the aborted hockey game till now. She delivered it all in a voice crisp and cold, omitting only the part where Divinity had protected her by dousing its lights. And how, when she'd asked it to give her what she needed, it had brought her Cameron Weste: *"One good friend"*.

No need to have cops think you were crazy.

Her brother, however, was another matter. "You're sure there's nothing else?"

"I'm sure."

He looked at her, hard.

She looked straight back.

"Alright." He folded his arms. "Tell us about Gray."

"If it was Gray then it's a joke."

"No one here's laughing."

"Neither am I. Andrew—" She turned to face him, but the uniforms craned their necks too.

"We're all here because this is an investigation, Shaynie," he said.

'Shaynie', not 'Shaynie Grace'. *You know you're in trouble when...* She massaged the back of her neck. "Just now, back at Divinity, Jude was right when he said Gray would never hurt me."

Jude had actually said more than that. After she'd blurted her shock over St. Cecelia he'd been vehement. "My cousin would throw himself in front of a bus for you, Shaynes."

She knew it. But St. Cecelia was still Gray's. "Jude, did he leave The Python last night?"

There was a scramble behind his eyes as though he were searching for something, *anything,* plausible to say. She said it for him. "You don't know." For it had dawned. "'Cause you were in the back with the Fire Marshal."

But Gray *had* been in the club—he'd bought Cameron that smart-assed shooter. So could he have left? But how? His deejay equipment was digital, complicated, no layperson or barmaid could operate it—could they?

*Think, Shaynie.* She'd stared into Jude's silent eyes.

"Shaynie Grace," Andrew had cued her with a look that said *shut up,* then a directive to get into his unmarked, "Now", and head with him over to her apartment.

She'd started her own truck instead but not before encouraging a fretting Cele to go inside, to remain in Divinity. Jude had popped in the old morgue too, to retrieve her coat, a helpful gesture that only added to the chaos when the alarm went off, audio shrapnel resonating as though Divinity echoed her confusion, fear, and ever-growing anger.

"Shut that off!" Andrew had barked and with that the alarm was just an alarm, screeching only because it was wired to pick up anomalies like the door being ajar for too long. She'd taken her coat from Jude, shook it as though the fear and confusion would scurry out with the wrinkles. Andrew's tires spat snow in the parking lot as he'd led the way.

Now they stood toe-to-toe.

"Does Gray owe you money?"

"No." Wait. Their dance. "Yes."

He raised the evidence bag, sealed with the cash inside. "This much?"

Well, his hat *had* been full.

Andrew watched her. "It's starting to make sense," he said, and she marveled at how readily he plucked the comprehension off her face. He'd likely seen the look on dozens—maybe hundreds—of victims before.

"Shaynie Grace," he said, gentler. "You know I've got to go pick him up."

"No." She shook her head.

He made a rough sound.

"Andrew, please." She took his elbow, steered him away from his colleagues. "I don't know why Gray would do this. But I know him. You do too."

"Who I know is someone likable, yes, but still a guy who was sketchy and unstable the whole time you were in high school."

"Only after Nelson stole Jen and then she was killed in that car wreck—"

"—*and* after he stuck his face in a bowl full of blow."

"He's been clean a long time!"

"Was he clean when he got you the job at the shit-pit Python?"

"Yes. And he nags me to quit more than you do. You should hear him."

"You should hear yourself. What the hell possesses you to defend him? And what the hell would possess him to do this in the first place?"

She didn't know. Unless.... Maybe Jude's joke when they'd left the arena— "Don't let Gray know you're making mojo for hockey players."— wasn't a joke at all. Still, could Gray really be that petty? If so, why had he landmarked Divinity for Cameron? Unless that night he, like she, had not really thought he'd show up? Or...

"What?" said Andrew, reading her.

"He...he may be mad that I was hanging with a hockey player." Because if he *had* thought Cameron would show up and then heard, last night, through Jude—because God knew they gossiped together—that she was trying to make a date with Cameron after the game...

"Is he jealous?" Andrew asked, breaking the thought.

"No. *No.* We've never—*he's* never—no. Not jealous. More...protective." And pushy. So if he'd seen her walking home hangdog and humiliated from Has Beans, "I told you so" would be the first thing he'd say. Or some Gray variation of it. *Does it hurt,* indeed.

"Protective?" Andrew echoed. "Shaynie Grace, *I'm* protective. And it would never occur to me to break into your place and call you, scream something weird. Know why? 'Cause it would *scare* you. And I want to *protect* you."

"I didn't say I agreed with what he did. All I'm saying is that I know him." Although Gray didn't know that she now lived in the brownstone off Whyte. And for that matter, how the hell did he get in?

"Shaynie Grace," Andrew watched her. "*Is* Gray still using?"

"No." That much she was sure of. "He's been clean since he left Jasper." Which had been a year before she had; he had graduated high school and left their mountain town in his rear view mirror, anxious to start a new, sober life in Edmonton. He'd succeeded. Between broadcasting school and a position at his cousin Jude's Python, what little free time he'd had he'd spent attending twelve step groups, so many that whenever she'd come to the city their visits were short—"Can't hang out, Shaynie. I've got a meeting."

To this day he still attended groups, perhaps quieter now and with less enthusiasm, but he still referenced them from time to time. In fact just a couple years ago (almost to the day, she noted with mild surprise), they'd watched a big league hockey trade together on the Python's TV, a trade that had landed Noel Nelson back home in Edmonton. "Never thought I'd have to deal with that douchebag again," Gray had said then flashed an ironic grin. "Good thing I have group tonight."

She blew out a breath. "Gray's the first one on the phone to the police if he even *thinks* someone's brought drugs into The Python. He wears St. Cecelia like a talisman—the way some Alcoholics Anonymous people carry coins and whatnot. He—he'll be devastated when he sees that he's lost her."

Andrew shook his head. "There you go again, sympathizing with the perp."

She flopped backward, out of answers. Out of everything.

He surveyed her. "You look as wasted as that hockey player at your door."

She wondered when he'd bring Cameron up.

"He's a real train wreck too. Waste of talent. I picked him in my hockey pool and now he decides to play with no heart. For that alone I should have beat him with my billy club."

"You made detective over a year ago, Corporal Gavin. You no longer *carry* a bully club."

"*Billy* club. He keeps playing like a plug and he'll never get that trade he supposedly wants to California."

"C-California?" 'Could The Sun be a place?'

Andrew vaulted a brow. "Thought he would've told you that—being a client and all."

*Nope. He didn't tell me a thing.* But, then again, he hadn't *not* told her either. "W-we're straying from the point and into irrelevant."

"Fair enough. So: do you think he's the one who vandalized your door?"

*"Cameron?"* she squeaked. And why did Cameron's name linked to *Devil's Whore* make every intuitive flag start to wave?

"No. Your good friend Gray."

"No. No way. Absolutely not." At Andrew's long look of *"yeah right"* she went on. "Gray wants me out of The Python. Why sabotage Divinity?"

Her brother snorted and she knew the sound. Knew the expression. "I'm not being stupid," she said clearly.

"I never said you were."

"Yes, Andrew, you did. You *do.* And I'm frankly sick of my intelligence being questioned. It doesn't seem to matter that I've figured out how to make my menial job—which I know you hate—pay like a slot machine. Doesn't matter that I managed to secure a loan for a business the banker called risky—right before he went ahead and ordered a table from me, *and* a mirror. Doesn't matter that I've picked friends who care enough to show up in the morning, check and see how I'm doing. Nope. I'm still flaky Shaynie Grace, a poor judge of character, naïve, reckless, and *stupid*."

He fired a hand through his hair, another gesture she recognized, for it was a trait that they shared. "Stupid," he echoed on a quiet, mirthless laugh. "You think I call you *stupid.* Shaynie Grace, I'm prouder of you than anybody I know. You're an amazing craftsman, crazily creative, and you're decent and kind to everyone you know. You are everything about Dad that I miss. Everything I wish I could be." He looked her in the eye. "You say Gray is protective? I say he doesn't know the meaning of the word. There is so much of you that I wish was me but, Shaynie Grace, those same things drive me nuts. Like the way your heart blinds your head."

Her chin was wobbling and right now she wished she could be tough—like him.

And he knew it. It was in the way he flicked the end of her nose. "Little sister, I have to be the cynical bastard *for* you. And damn right I'd use my 'bully club'. Or my boot, if I had to, for you."

*"The Agent will stick a boot up his ass."* Cameron had no idea how well he already knew her big brother. She reached for Andrew's hands. "I am grateful for you every day."

He squeezed her hands back. "I'll let you know when I track Gray down. It's the most I can promise."

## CHAPTER TWELVE

SHE CLUTCHED HER CELL PHONE like prayer beads once Andrew and the uniforms left, keeping it with her as she paced, holding it when she finally collapsed into sleep, and setting it on the edge of the tub when she showered.

Andrew didn't call. Nor did Gray.

The radio accompanied her to The Python, sportscasters with predictions to rival the most seasoned psychics. "When looking ahead to play-off hockey our boys are shaky, but every team coming out of California looks like a contender."

"Why, how *special* for California." She slowed over the speed bumps in the customer lot.

"Our correspondent has traveled to La-La Land with the team. Let's hear him."

"Oh, yes. 'Cause we're dying to know what it's like in Utopifornia." She cranked it.

"Watched our boys practice today and was Cameron Weste hot! If he plays like he practiced for the game tomorrow he'll light the arena on fire! And that, ladies and gentlemen, is how you advance a career!"

"Advance a career"? Double-speak for "hire the movers"? She shut the radio off, parked. With the team gone no crowd waited outside The Python. She gazed at the empty curb. Did the Ice Gods know how subdued their city was without them? Did they care? A spider's web of frost iced her windshield as soon as she killed the ignition, and she shivered as she slipped from the truck. January in Edmonton. Maybe *lots* of people would prefer California. Crunching over ice she climbed the back stairs, pushed the service door open.

"Why the *hell* didn't you call before now?"

"Wha—" Oh. Jude wasn't talking to her. There was a phone at his ear.

"Well apparently it *wasn't* enough, was it?" he said. "And if this keeps up guess what? You're screwed!"

She blinked and it was like he sensed it, for he looked up. "I gotta go." He shoved the cell in his pocket. "Shaynes, what are you doing here? After this morning I'm the *last* person you need to convince that you need some time off."

"I need normal." She looked at his pocket. "Was that Gray?"

Hesitation, then— "I promised I wouldn't call him."

Said quick. Too quick. Her gut sank. "Jude—" The rest was drowned out by shout from the main club.

"Do *not* move!"

She bolted, Jude on her heels.

Gray, spread-eagled against a wall, yelped as a familiar figure kicked his feet apart.

"Andrew!" Damn him! He'd said he'd call!

He spared her a look— "Get back"—and Gray, peeking over his shoulder, said "Shaynie? What *is* this?"

Andrew slammed him back against the wall. "I've tracked you all day, that's what this is and you've slip-slid all over town. Now you owe me some goddamn answers."

"Wha—Shaynie?"

"She's not talking right now. *I* am." Andrew jerked him upright. "You've ran the city all day long. An apartment on the west side. Residential in the south. The hospital. What the fuck are you up to?"

"What—*nothing!*" Gray struggled, chin against the wall. "Since when is it illegal to go to the hospital? Shaynie," he tried another look over his shoulder, "what—"

"Leave her out of it!"

"I'm already in it." She clamped a hand on Andrew's arm, keenly aware of the crowd that had gathered; wait-staff, bouncers, and a distraught-looking Jude. "Andrew, what is *wrong* with you?"

"Wrong with *me?*" He shook her off, whipped out the bagged St. Cecelia. "Let's hear about *this.*" He dangled the bag in Gray's periphery.

Gray froze, and the look he wore. Shock. *Hurt*? "Grayson?" She got close to him. "What—"

"—the hell were you doing in her apartment last night?" Andrew forced his way back between them.

She bared her teeth "Andrew—"

He drew out his handcuffs and Gray's eyes ripped so wide it looked like his lids had been stapled to his forehead. She grabbed his wrists before Andrew could. "Grayson, *were you* at my place last night?"

"My necklace—" He shot a look to the evidence bag.

"Was on my bedroom floor. And cash was on my table."

"Shaynie Grace!"

She hissed a *shut up* at her brother. "—then you called me. Or *someone* called me. And scared me."

"Scared you?"

His eyes were blank. God. *Was he* on something?

"Wh-what did I say when I called?" he asked.

"What did you....don't you know?"

"I..." He dragged his gaze away, cheeks heat-colored. "I can't remember."

"Oh, Grayson. No." He h*ad* used. After so long—

"Shaynie." He couldn't seem to look at her. "I...I'd never scare you. Not on purpose."

But he might do it stoned.

"So let's get this straight." Andrew wedged between them once more. "You went to her place with money, but instead of just ringing her buzzer like a normal person you broke in and called her?"

*No.* The answer, unbidden, sprang into her head. But Gray said "Y-yeah. Yes."

"Why?" she asked and the question seemed to startle both he and Andrew. Gray's Adam's apple vaulted and she watched it, narrow-eyed. "It's a simple question, Grayson. *Why*?"

A flicker, rapid-fire and fleeting, moved through his eyes and she recognized it: the scurry of the brain racing ahead of the mouth, trying to think up a lie. Her stare sharpened. "And more than the why, *how?* As in how did you get in?"

"Your door." The sentence shot out the same way one would exhale in relief. "It... wasn't locked. It never is."

No. It never *used* to be. Yet last night, in her excitement to see Cameron—had she forgot? "So you just went on in?"

"I've done it before."

Bravado. All bravado—wasn't it? She chewed the inside of her cheek.

He looked steadily back at her. "Don't you remember, Shaynie? The last time I visited I let myself in and you were downstairs, doing laundry."

In her old place. "Yes," she said. "I remember."

He blew out an audible breath. She pinned him with her eyes. "When you called you blocked my number. Why?"

The change in gears set him back and there it was again, *scurry-scurry* in his eyes. But then— "That wouldn't have been me, Shaynie. That would have been *you.*"

Her turn to be taken aback.

"You have a private number," he said solidly. "When you call me—or anyone, I suppose—it comes up 'caller blocked'."

She sagged. He was right. Still—*scurry-scurry.* She knew what she saw.

And he knew that she knew. As she stared at him, he stared back, an unmistakable plea in his eyes.

Andrew cleared his throat. "Shaynie Grace, do you want to press charges?"

"I don't know." She held Gray's gaze, held his plea, in the air between them. *C'mon. Explain this. Say something—anything—different.*

He didn't.

"Shaynie Grace!"

"No," she said slowly, then chose the rest with double-edged care. "Other than being stupid—" and what sounded like stoned "— Gray really didn't do anything wrong. Did you?"

"I...I'd hang anybody who hurt you Shaynie," he answered.

The truth in a land field of lies. She did not break their eye contact and Andrew, hissing, clicked his cuffs back in place. "You should bend over and kiss her ass right now." He whipped Gray around to face him, poking a finger in his chest. "'Cause it is *only* because she's my sister that I'm not hauling you in."

"I wouldn't blame you," Gray, looking at her, not Andrew, held her gaze a second longer then tore his eyes away, sought Jude. "Can… I have the night off? All of this—"

"Isn't my problem," Jude said coldly. "We're ten minutes from opening. If you take off who covers for you?"

"I do," piped a voice. Shaynie turned.

One of the bartenders Cameron had described, a "red-headed robot", stood with her chin out. "I covered for him last night."

Shaynie's brow rose. An accomplice? Interesting.

"Let Gray go home," the redhead went on. "He's endured enough." She shot an acid glare at Shaynie that opened a floodgate. Around her the crowd of staff began murmuring, low-pitched and feral.

Gray fled amidst the hissing.

## CHAPTER THIRTEEN

SHE TRIED TO BOLT after him, but Andrew clamped a hand on her arm. She smacked him away. "You," she spat, "made me a promise—"

"—which you should have seen through just from watching cop shows on TV. C'mon, Shaynie Grace. Like I could let you be an active part of an investiga—"

"You lied to me!"

"And you haven't lied to me? Haven't manipulated this entire charade, spoon feeding your good friend every goddamn answer he needed?"

So he'd seen it too, the scurry-scurry.

"I don't know what the hell is going on here, but if this is the way you're going to play it, lying and covering for someone who's clearly guilty of *something*, you're on your own." He pivoted, and the glass doors of the snake's mouth whished open and shut. He was gone.

The strobe lights whirled, made the dance floor yawn and stretch at odd angles along with the choices that remained. Chase him or chase Gray?

Definitely Gray.

The sizzling scrutiny of waitstaff tracked her all the way to the back room where Jude, shrugging into his jacket, spared her a glance. "Manage in my absence," he said tersely. "I need to go after my cousin. God only knows what else he'll do when he's rattled like this."

The thread of blame in his tone was unmistakable, and it made her wonder— if someone other than herself had been victim of this…whatever it was, would she too be protective of Gray? Shield him because she believed he was fragile? *You already did,* spat her inner Andrew, and it was true: Just like the rest of The Python staff, she had ignored the fact that it was *she* who'd been terrorized, *her* apartment that Gray had broken into.

Correction: Had been *party* to breaking into. "*I'll* go after him," she said.

"Shaynes," Jude turned to her, exasperation obvious. "You know he's sensitive—"

"Yeah? Well, so am *I*."

Jude looked at the floor.

"And incidentally, if you think your rabid staff is going to let me manage this place now that their favorite child's been shaken down by my bad-ass cop brother, then you're more naïve in business then me." She reached for her coat.

Behind them the door out to the main club slammed open with a bang startling enough to make her not only drop her jacket but knock a few more off the coat tree too. A grating voice said "Running away, you little bitch?"

Shaynie turned. The robots, spiked hair siren bright, towered over her.

"Girls," Jude began.

"Don't." Shaynie held up a hand. "They've got something to say." But which one would cough it out? Right Robot was so furious she vibrated, but her clone merely jittered, dart-eyed. Shaynie shook her head. Just this morning Andrew had asked about drugs in The Python and now here were two new employees, one of them obviously—and colossally—stoned. "Well?"

Right Robot sneered. "Little Miss Perfect ditches work last night then glides in tonight with her ball-busting brother, sniveling because somebody scared her."

Shaynie jacked a brow. "Interesting interpretation." She glanced over at Jude. Would it kill him to clarify to these fools that she hadn't blown last night off but rather been dumped out on Whyte in the cold?

He did not say a word.

"I don't have time for this." She stooped for her coat.

A robot hand clamped onto her shoulder. "Don't you flounce away from me. Humiliate sweetness like Gray? I'm gonna kick your perfect little ass."

"Hey!" Jude at last dove between them, one hand on the Robot's forearm, the other wrapped around Shaynie.

Oh, so now *she* was the favored child. She wriggled away.

Jude was pointing a finger in Right Robot's face. "Rule one: I don't tolerate threats in my club. Rule Two? Asses don't get kicked. They get kissed. And not only customers. Senior employees too. Now get *your* ass out behind the bar before it gets fired."

Left Robot swiveled. Right Robot did not. Shaynie marched up to her. "Touch me again and I'll see you on your knees."

"Oh? Whatcha gonna do, Perfect? Call big brother?"

"Yes. And charge you with assault—and whatever else he can come up with once he searches your stuff. After all, it doesn't take much to trump a simple possession charge up to intention to traffic." She smiled, cold and big. "Want to risk it?"

Right tried holding her gaze, but only lasted a few seconds. Turning with a snort she slammed out the door.

Shaynie released a shaky breath.

Jude cleared his throat. "Uh—Shaynes?" He held up his cell. "Gray just texted. He's okay."

"He say where he was?" She bent again for her jacket, now buried beneath the avalanche of others that had spilled from the coat tree.

Jude crouched with her. "I'd guess at home, but Shaynes—" He scooped up a ski coat and another with a crest she recognized. "I don't think, given what you and Andrew just pulled, that you should be the one to see Gray."

What she and Andrew just *pulled*? "Jude, did you not hear what *Gray* 'pulled'?"

He winced. "Yeah, but—"

"Breaking into my place was a crime."

"No, it was a stunt." He dumped the coats in a heap on the staff sofa.

She gave them half a glance then decided not to bother. Where Cameron was—Utopifornia—he didn't need his coat anyway. "I can't believe you're minimizing this."

"I'm not. But...don't you think you're overreacting?"

Her eyes popped.

"God, Shaynes. It's just Gray."

"God, Jude, it was just *my apartment.*" She jerked her coat on, jammed her feet into boots.

"Aw, Shaynes, come on. I'm not picking sides! I'm just saying that if you go see him it's not going to go well. Cool off. Let *him* cool off."

While he thought up more lies? Uh-uh. She grabbed her purse.

Jude stepped in front of her. "At least let me know if he even lets you in."

"Well if he doesn't, maybe I'll *break* in. You know—just a stunt."

Jude looked miserable. "Shaynes if he doesn't cooperate—"

"What should I do? Come back to work? Get threatened some more?"

"No." He scowled. "What I was actually going to say is go to Divinity. Immerse yourself in something you love. In fact I—uh—I even have a project for you."

A project? How convenient. What was that he'd said about asses getting kissed?

He flicked lint off his arm. "Last night we had trouble with crowding, as you know. And it's happened before, as you also know. So I've been racking my brain trying to think of solutions, because lecturing the bouncers to be on top of their counters clearly isn't working. I need my own eyes all over this place."

*Eyes.* She shuddered. "Try video."

"I tend bar. I can't have screens lined up on the marble."

She looked at her watch.

"The hall to the snakepit is the biggest offender because right now it's blind. But if I lined it—with mirrors—then I'd be able to keep track of the crowd. Keep my butt out of a sling."

"Full length mirrors are ten bucks a piece at most box stores." She opened the back door.

He pulled it closed. "The Python is no different than Divinity. It needs aesthetics too."

"So…?"

"So when I say mirrors, I'm thinking more in *your* style. Out of doors. Creepy, antique doors." He paused. "Got any?"

She wanted to tell him to stick it, but her carpenter's brain was already clicking. Six mahogany doors with baroque cherubs carved deep in the wood at each corner. She'd scored them at an auction in an old hotel in Banff, a place alleged to be haunted. They fit the bill of creepy. *And* magnificent. "They'll cost you."

"Toss a figure."

"Fifteen hundred each."

"Ouch! Try eight."

"Twelve."

"Eight fifty."

"Ten fifty. Final. I'm not in the mood to dicker."

"With a dickhead."

"I didn't say that."

He grinned and, helplessly, her lips twitched too.

"Croissants and coffee in the morning?" A smile crinkled his eyes at the corners.

"I'll be at Divinity." Not a yes nor a no. She opened the back door then paused, turned back.

Jude frowned. "Forget something?"

"Yeah. My dignity. I'm not sneaking out the back like I've done something wrong."

He nodded. "Want me to walk out there with you?"

"Nope." She opened the door to the main club, stepped out beneath the hot strobes. One Robot was at her station, Right Robot or Left she wasn't sure, but she spat as Shaynie walked by. *Charming.* She moved through the crowd, perversely pleased to see more waitstaff on the floor than customers. *Thank you, Ice Gods, for being away.* Colleagues' allegiance obviously turned on a dime but so, apparently, did karma. She held her head up and ignored the dagger eyes and muttered insults.

It was The Python she could not ignore. For even though strobe lights slashed the air and the hologram python was roaring, it still felt as though darkness fell, and as she quickened her pace her hair billowed every time the hologram licked its rounds, its wind hotter—and stronger—than usual.

*Stay away from me.* She glanced at it over her shoulder.

The snake roared, a blast of hellfire strong enough to propel her into the sensors that opened the front doors. She rushed to the curb while a bouncer, stationed by the entrance, surveyed her. "Adios," he said dispassionately then the doors swallowed him back up just as readily as they'd spit her out. She stood, breathed January air that was harsh and real. And safe.

"'Cause *you're* not safe," she said to The Python.

The club pulsed with life, its glass snake mouth alive with the movement of strobes and its snake eyes peering down, creating a scarlet bloodbath on the street where she stood.

"You're evil," she whispered.

The hologram roared, a shock of light against the windows, and she bolted, head up and eyes open as she made for her truck in the back staff lot. Pulling out her cell, she hit Gray's number.

"Hey!" he answered.

"Gray! I—"

"—I'm away! But you know what to say!" A long beep shrilled and she left a message— "No: *You* know what to say,"—then climbed into her truck, fired the ignition.

The motor sputtered then died. Too cold. She cranked it again and jacked the heat, shivering as the vents blew icy air. "C'mon." She patted the dash then squinted from a sudden glare in her rearview. The Python's back door motion light. Curious, she looked in the mirror to see what, or who, had tripped it. "Really," she said, and pursed her lips. In the pool of illumination was Panties, a handbag in her arms that was larger than her dress, a glittery affair that resembled a large tube sock. "My God." Shaynie rubbed her cold hands together. "How can she stand to be out there with no coat?" Her own was buttoned up to the chin and even her truck still choked, too frigid to run smooth.

She tapped the gas, one eye idly trained on Panties in the mirror. Odd. If Cameron's foggy memory was right this would be the second time in two nights the blonde had been in the back room sanctioned for staff only.

The staff door yawned open.

*Oh?* Jude, joining Panties on the back stoop, wore a glint in his eyes which even at a distance Shaynie recognized. "Ah," she said softly and looked away as they lip-locked. *Oh, what a tangled web we weave.* 'Cause hadn't Cameron said that Panties was with Nelson last night? She fiddled with the defrost, shaking her head. A hundred years ago Nelson had stolen Gray's girl. Fast forward, and today here was Jude, stealing Nelson's. "What good friends they all are to each other." She lifted her foot off the gas. Had her old beast finally warmed up?

It sputtered and hacked.

Scowling, she depressed the pedal again, stole another look in the rearview.

Alone once more and with her tube dress glittering, Panties resembled a life-sized Barbie doll, over-painted, under-dressed, and with no one who wanted to play with her. "Shame on you Jude," Shaynie muttered. "You could have given the silly twit *your* coat."

As if she'd heard her, Panties dug in her too-big hand bag, pulled out an item. Shaynie's eyes widened. Cameron's coat? She stared but as the blonde slipped it on she recoiled. The night shadows, the way they caught Panties' face under that blue motion light...*A corpse.* Shaynie shook away the visual. *Stop with the paranoid fanciful. Just go find Gray.*

Her truck at last cooperated, defrost chugging out delicious warmth. She shifted into gear then shifted back as her cell chirped from in her pocket. Gray! She rummaged for the phone.

Text Message from a Blocked Number.

Now he'd blocked *his* number? Frowning, brought up the message.

<You at work, Clever Faerie?>

"Faerie." She recognized it immediately as a reference back to her Tarot deck and its enchanted artwork. "They suit you," he had said. Smiling, her fingers flew over the keypad. <Persona non grata at Python. Long story.>

A few seconds elapsed, then *Chirp!*

<I like long stories. Call me. I have a story you need to hear too.>

Her fingers clicked. <Give me your number.>

Chirp!

<No. You know where to find it.>

## CHAPTER FOURTEEN

Weste's high rise had frosted glass doors and a fine-grained floor gleaming in the entrance. Shaynie looked down at the snow sludge on her boots. Whatever he was going to tell her had better eclipse marching into this perfect building like some gauche cousin heralding from the sticks. Sighing, she christened the outside mat with grime then pulled the door open. Scents, citrus and vanilla, floated in a foyer twice as grand as it seemed from outside. Soaring ceilings, urns of flowers (fresh, not fabric) and wingbacks were arranged *tête a tête* with artful carelessness.

Careless? *Yeah right.* Everything in the place, even that billowing scent, was on purpose. Hopelessly gauche, she was looking down at her last year's coat and grimy boots when a voice spoke.

"May I help you?" A man, whose perfect pitch was as impeccable as his suit, smiled in her direction.

She clutched the hem of her coat—God, it was shabby! —and tried to untangle her vocal cords.

Impeccable, *Security*, prompted her with a bigger smile that forced a squeak from her throat. "C-cameron We—"

He cut her short. "Of course. You'd be Mr. Weste's guest, Ms. Gavin."

Perfect teeth too. Her boots moved, automatic and miserable, each trying to cover the scuffs on the other.

"May I confirm with ID?" he asked.

And of course she didn't carry anything remotely chic like a handbag or clutch. Sighing, she dug out her ancient wallet, flipped it to her driver's.

He glanced at it. "Excellent. Come with me."

With steps as sleek as the hardwood he led them to a massive painting and she stared, shocked, when the canvas split in two to reveal the inner sanctum of an elevator.

The delight in his expression erased a lot of his perfection. "This building is renowned for creative architecture," he remarked, ushering her into the painting. "And Mr. Weste says you're a carpenter."

She nodded, struck dumb. That *painting.* Which of the artists from back in trade school could fashion a similar concept—the Tarot Sun!—for Divinity's antique elevator? Her eyes raced, took in everything. The detailed crown molding. The exquisite light fixtures. And this was just the *elevator.*

It glided to a stop and Impeccable led her out. "Right this way."

She trailed his fine shoes down a stretching hall, then paused behind him when he halted in front of one stately door, waiting as he waved a card over a sensor she could not see. A lock answered with a soft *schick* and he turned, gave her the key. "A pleasure," he said, then pivoted and was back down the hall, an embodiment of discretion and charm.

*Impeccable.* Her lips quirked and, "Pentacles," she murmured. Money. Privilege. Cameron called this place his condo, but "condo" seemed like a throwaway word for such magnificence. Such *surrealism*. "Okay, Weste." She depressed the door latch. "Who waits behind this door? The Lady? Or the Tyger?"

*Nothing.* The word struck her as motion sensor lighting flooded the room. It was like stepping into a black and white movie, and while to her carpenter's eye it was stunning—more vaulted ceilings, acres of glossy floors—, to the rest of her it was…"Hollow," she announced, starting a bit when the word echoed. What little furniture he did have was stiff, angles sharp enough to slice air. Other than that there was..."*Nothing*," she said again, for not one single thing said Ice God with slick whiplash smile, nothing revealed the smart ass who'd sent an orange sex toy, and nothing even said sweetheart who'd made arrangements for her to be here in the first place. "Weste," she breathed. "Where *are y*ou?"

Nowhere. His place was an elegant wasteland.

She slipped her boots off, moved to a white leaflet centered on a table. His promised phone number was printed tidily at the top. The rest read:

Cleaning lady comes Thursdays. Shopper on the mornings of the days I fly back. Other than that it's all yours. Enjoy.

"Enjoy"? She looked around. How? And "shopper"? What the heck was that? She set the note down, dug out her phone.

He answered off the first ring. "So what's the long story? What happened after I left? Did The Agent catch your crazy fan? Or was he content to just whip out his sidearm, blow Rasputin and Cele away?"

Like *he* had room to criticize anyone's oddities, aggressive or otherwise. She cast another look around. "Andrew is who Andrew is," she intoned, absent. "He's never going to apologize for being a cop."

"Well he was sure as hell going to apologize to you for blowing a vein like he did."

Because on top of everything else she'd needed to referee a scrum between her boyfriend and brother? *Whoa. Boyfriend?* She bit her tongue.

*Dontcha mean "buddy"?* "Thanks," she said. "But I prefer my buddies without bullet holes."

"And your brother without busted teeth."

She massaged her temples. "Weste, there is way too much testosterone in this conversation."

"Sorry. I'll try to adopt a more sensitive countenance."

She rolled her eyes.

"I saw that, little Faerie."

She choked, looked around.

"You either stuck out your tongue, curled your lip, or made an evil face at the phone."

"Why, how omniscient of you."

"I am a God. That's why you bow."

"Uh-huh. Just keep telling yourself that. Now what did you lure me over here to tell me?"

A beat of silence elapsed and it struck her for how much it sounded the way Gray's eye scurry had looked. Trepidation sank her slowly to his granite-hard sofa. "Cameron—"

"Remember last night when you said Nelson was the Knight of Swords?" he asked.

"Yeah. And you said Court Jester."

"Right. But...Shaynie, that was before I realized how whacked things really were."

Something—a dread-like something—sank her gut.

"Faerie, last night you said your Dancing Deejay has history with Nelson." He paused. "What's *your* history with Noel?"

She sagged, dread gone. "For the umpteenth time, I don't *have* history with Nelson. Whatever he's told you is crap." And what could Noel possibly have to do with Gray lying? Whoever had been in her apartment—and clearly it wasn't Gray—had also not been Nelson. 'Cause no way would he have Gray's St. Cecelia.

Cameron said "Tonight I heard Noel on the phone and I have no reason to think he was talking about you, yet...I *know* he was talking about you."

"Oo-kay...?"

"And he said, 'I'd screw her just for spite'."

Hellnight. It blew in and blew out, a black breeze. She envisioned an obsidian stone— *take this burden!*—and exhaled, ragged. *We are not talking about Hellnight.*

Yes, you are.

She jolted. Divinity? She searched his windows. He'd said she'd be able to see the morgue from his bedroom. Did other windows show her too?

"It almost sounded like Nelson's fixated with you," he went on.

"Fixated with taunting me? Yes." She peered through a westerly window. Not the right vantage point. "Fixated with me personally? No. Noel and I share a lifetime of mutual loathing."

"Faerie—"

"Cameron, whatever Noel might have told you here's my real history with him in a nutshell: I'm someone he's consistently failed to charm. And he's so arrogant he doesn't know why."

Quiet crouched on the line. No matter. She heard the doubt anyway. "Noel has a cartoon-sized ego," she said. "He's a jealous fool. But he's still far more harm to you than me."

Silence stretched and she could tell he was debating. Wanting to argue. But then— "So what's the long story?" he asked.

Relief. Kind of. She told him about Gray and her apartment.

"Huh," he said. "So Dancing Deejay 'fessed up and then what?"

Then scurry-scurry. "Then nothing."

"Bullshit."

She blinked. How on earth had he become so adept, so fast, at reading her?

"There's more," he said. "I can tell."

*Yes, Weste, you are far from a stunned puck.* She chewed her lip, then— "Gray's lying."

Stunned silence. "Jesus," he said, after several long seconds. "Why the hell would anyone take the rap for something that fu—er—messed up?"

*'Cause he's covering for someone.* "I...don't know. But I intend to find out."

"Nelson?" he said, absently, then corrected himself before she could laugh at the thought of Gray in consort with Noel. "No, your apartment couldn't be Nelson," he said. "'Cause last night I know he was with the drunk chick."

*Panties.* Still— "I thought you couldn't remember."

"I can't. But today, after practice." He cleared his throat. "Let's just say there are no secrets in the locker room."

"You guys regale each other with your conquests in the locker room?"

A lick of silence blistered by. "No, Shaynie. We strip in the locker room. And those nail tracks on his back aren't from any kind of hockey game *I've* ever played."

Chastened, she bit down on her lip.

"And I'm sure it's her who's been calling his cell a million times today too."

Shaynie snorted. Had Panties called before or after her tryst at the back door with Jude? "Well, whatever he's expecting I certainly hope it's not commitment. I don't think Miss Panties is much into fidelity."

"Pffft. Show me a hockey girlfriend who is."

"Ouch. Pretty cold, Weste."

"And pretty true. Incidentally, I prefer it when you call me Cameron."

"And I prefer when you call me Shaynie—even though you rarely do."

He laughed. "Let everyone else call you Shaynie. Or Shaynie *Grace.* I think Faerie suits you better."

I think you suit me better. She grimaced. *Friend,* she reminded herself. *He is my friend.*

"Faerie," he said. "Promise me something."

*Anything,* she thought and bit her tongue. "Wh-what?"

"Stay put. Stay safe."

"Sorry, but I need to find Gray. He knows—"

"He's lied to you. He's dangerous."

*Dangerous.* Hellnight again shivered in her mind, fragments of memory moving like shards of a mirror trying to mend itself, form a picture. "Gray knows," she blurted, not even sure where it came from.

"Yeah," agreed Cameron, oblivious. "Sure sounds like it. But The Agent needs to choke it out of him. Not you."

"But—" Gray. On Hellnight he'd been there, at the party. What *did* he know? What had he seen? Or been part of?

The thought dropped her heart.

"Faerie," Cameron broke in. "If you try to figure this out on your own I'll call your brother myself."

"No!" 'Cause if all this *was* connected to Hellnight....God. She'd have to tell Andrew.

"What do you mean, "no"? He's a *cop."*

"He...no. Cameron, please. No."

"Your so-called friend Gray is covering for your crazy fan and you don't want The Agent to know?"

"I....Cameron, please. I kept *you* quiet this morning."

"Yeah, well, I didn't ask you to."

That hurt. Hurt and she didn't know why. "I promise I won't put myself at risk."

"Damn right you won't."

His tone made her blink. *Uh-oh. Here's the Moon.*

"You'll keep your little tush locked in my condo or security will tell me. And I won't hesitate to bust you to your brother. There. Argument over."

The phone clicked to dead air. "Cameron?"

His name echoed off walls so empty they couldn't even swallow sound. She shrank back onto his cement sofa. Nelson. Hellnight. Gray. They ran together, colors blending to form an indecipherable shade. She called Gray again on her cell.

"Hey! I'm away! You know what to say"'

She waited through another protracted beep. "Gray, I know, okay? I *know.* And right now it's just me asking what the hell really went on, but if you don't call me back, I..." *I won't hesitate to bust you.* "…I'll tell Andrew everything. So please: phone me." She hung up, gazed around at the emptiness. "Cameron, would you *really* rat me out?"

The soulless walls didn't answer. Didn't care. Cameron wasn't in this condo. *No one* was. She brought up the keypad on her cell. <Will you lift my exile if I promise to watch your game tomorrow night with my cards? I've heard how important your 'California countenance' is.> She hit send.

Her phone took forever to chirp, then, <Quit surfing internet gossip and go to bed. You were up all night. So was I.>

A minute ago he'd been concerned. Now cranky? How could he have not turned The Moon? She typed, <I hate internet and I don't gossip. Andrew told me.>

This time the chirp didn't take quite so long. <Wow. The Agent's a real renaissance man. Seems there's nothing he doesn't know. Except about YOU.>

She glared at the cell. "If I write back now things are *not* going to be pretty." She stuffed the phone in her bag. "I need to get out of here."

Easier said than done. His posse of one in that priceless suit downstairs had likely already received word to track her exits and entrances. She slumped back to the sofa and dug out her cell, hit Gray again.

*'The number you're trying to reach has exceeded its mailbox quota,'* answered an automated voice. She stabbed the cell off. The condo was silent, visually echoing nothing, and it struck her how different it was than her little brownstone on Whyte, alive with color and symbols and

her collection of hand-crafted stuff. She longed for it. Longed for—
"Divinity," she said and hopped up. What was she thinking? She wasn't *really* alone. She rushed through the kitchen—a dream with miles of granite counters and slick stainless steel—but noted no fuss, no muss, not even a stale sack of bread on the counter. *What a jail cell.* She padded into a hall. A bathroom on the left was more granite, pewter, and towels hung with military precision. She reached in, mussed them for spite, then sought a sense of direction. Street level. It would be..."Here." She swiveled, opened a door on her right. "Whoa." She rocked back. "What the heck?"

Boxes, towers of them, filled the room, each identical in size and labeled with tidy block script. *Dining, kitchen, living.* "Ah, Cameron. *Here* you are." The colors he liked, the things he collected, photos, memorabilia, everything was clearly taped up and hidden in boxes. "But why?"

Same reason he didn't want to kiss you.

Then she understood. Andrew's rumor was true. Cameron wanted a trade, and the self-described "Superstitious Athlete" believed that if he unpacked his things they might just root themselves to the floor, tether him someplace he did not want to be. So would kissing someone he "liked"— it would complicate things when the plan was really to grab his packed boxes and bolt. "Twisted nobility," she said, and it somehow amplified the condo's ache of "alone."

And made her long for her morgue that much more.

"Divinity?" She backed out of the packed room, chilled. "I need to get out of here."

One last doorway stood at the end of the hall, and as she padded through it soft light from another automatic sensor illuminated a huge windowed wall. Her breath caught. The panorama of the city was visible through the pane, twinkling lights against an inkwell sky, jewels of amber and diamonds in the frost. Mesmerized, she scanned it, searched street level. "Hey." She found Divinity. "There you are. I miss you."

Wind whirled on its roof.

"Weste's locked me up like all of his boxes."

Snow billowed around the morgue, the flakes catching moonlight and creating the illusion that the building, not the snow, was moving. Dancing.

"Look at you," she chided, yet her eyes adored every stone feature. "It's like you think it's *good* he's trapped me here." Her breath, colliding with the cold on the window, raced up the pane to form frost vines. They climbed the glass like prison bars. "Really?" Her brow hiked. "I can't believe you agree with him."

A gale of wind threw snow against the glass and she jumped. "Hey!" She righted herself, stepped back to the window. "You don't have to get mad. I know you like him, but here's the thing—*he's* not here. In fact I'll bet there's even a box in that horrible room labeled 'My Soul'." She waggled her fingers.

Around the morgue snow whirl-whirl-whirled, like belly laughing. She grinned until without warning another ice blast hit the window with a sound like shattering glass. Lurching back, she hit the bed, bouncing hard enough to see stars.

Oh. *Stars.* Not imagined, they were *there,* drifting in a dreamscape painted above, sunbeams and starlight captured on a ceiling-turned-canvas. The mural was beautiful, impossible, yet with every brushstroke the artist had captured light so real Shaynie could *feel* sunshine, warm on her face.

"Creative architecture," security had said. *No kidding.* Her eyes swept the stars. Now why would the artist depict them shining in the sun? And did they form some sort of pattern? Maybe a constellation? She traced their path but no picture revealed itself. Hmm. She counted them. Twenty-two. Then— "There it is!" she exclaimed, what they formed. *Another* twenty-two. A delighted smile filled her face. "Ah, Cele," she whispered. "You should be here to see this *mystère* in a *mystère.*" Twenty-two in twenty-two. Wait. *"I buy things in twos."* Then at his game, when he'd crashed the boards in front of her, his jersey number..."Twenty-two," she said, and stared. "*You* had this done?"

The room, a vacuum, could not reply. She stared at his skyscape. "You lock your soul into boxes but paint your heart on a ceiling?"

Outside, a howl of wind pelted the window with ice. She looked over at it. "Okay," she said. "So he *is* here. And you *wanted* me to see him. Why?"

A spew of ice splattered a Rorschach on the window. A heart. A soft smile found her face. "Yes, I *see* his heart's up there. Just tell me why?"

So no one can reach it.

She gazed back at the twenty-two and heard him, a murmur from that morning. *"I've had enough heartbreak."* His face had held such desolation that she'd felt that answering stitch, sharp in her side. She spoke to his stars. "I get it, you know. But Weste, look what you've done. Stars can't shine in the sun. You've painted a dream that can't happen. What were you thinking?"

The stars remained, Twenty-two trapped in the sky.

She clucked her tongue and plumped a pillow, laid down so she could face them. "There's an old saying: 'Wherever you go, that's where you are.' Meaning if you've trapped your heart where no one can reach it, then even Utopifornia won't help you."

The stars gleamed, brighter it seemed, as though they listened. She gazed at their light. "But the reverse is true, too. Free your heart, and *anywhere* you go is Utopia. Even here."

The stars stopped gleaming, shrank back in their spots. She smiled.

"Ah, you are Weste. Pouting. And stubborn."

His dreamscape drifted, a magnificent mystery.

"But you're sweet, too. And I'm sorry, Cameron, that someone broke your heart."

Star glitter dove, and for a pulse-stroke she felt it, a caress on her cheeks. She reached back, retraced the twenty-two. "You're welcome," she whispered.

Her phone chirped and her heart leapt. Was the penalty he'd dealt over? She brought up the message.

Reading the screen she knew in an instant it was not Cameron.

<I'm not ignoring you. I just can't call. But I KNOW you know, and I can explain. Can I see you tomorrow? In the morning at Divinity? G.>

Her fingers flew, automatic <YES!> and she held her breath until a reply chirped.

<Thank you. I love you. PLEASE don't worry.>

"Don't worry?" She flopped back on the bed.

Stars glittered above, alive and aware.

"If I texted you to tell you that Gray said don't worry you'd still keep me locked up here, wouldn't you?"

The stars ceased their illusion of drifting and stayed put, static and stubborn. She laughed, helpless. "I guess one night won't kill me." She took the pillow and grabbed the end of the duvet. "But not in your bed."

Heat rushed down from the skyscape with enough force that her hair billowed. Shocked, she reached up. Unmistakable warmth radiated on her face. "D-divinity?" she ventured, half fascinated, half afraid. Tearing her eyes from his stars she sought the window. "I-is there something—someone—here?"

*Faerie.*

*That* wasn't the old morgue. Wide-eyed she looked up.

His sky whispered her name. *Shaynie.*

Heart pounding, she stared.

*Stay.* Starlight shimmered, unmistakable movement.

Her breath stopped. His constellation shone brighter, Twenty-two trapped in an endless vista where it did not belong. *Stay.* "I—I know how you feel," she told it. "I'm lonely too."

Sunbeams. They stroked her face and whispered, *his* whisper, *Shaynie. Stay.*

"I…no." She held his pillow. "Even *you* said '*I like you too much for that*'." She looked away.

*Shaynie.* The sky sighed. *Listen to your good buddy Cameron.*

Jolting, she glanced up and the starlight brightened. Lit things. Changed things. Like the pillow she clutched in her arms. Suddenly it had a heartbeat.

*Shaynie.* A pulse— his pulse?— thundered against her. *Stay.*

"N-no." She cast the pillow aside. "You don't want this, remember? *I* don't want this."

A splat of snow hit the window. She glared at it. "Stop interfering! I don't like how he makes me feel."

Liar.

"Okay. I don't like that I *like* how he makes me feel."

His voice rumbled, an echo in memory's ear. *"One good friend."*

"See? 'Friend'." She seized the word, tossed it out to Divinity. "And here's me, not wanting to be 'friends'." She looked down at her lap. "I want—"

*A kiss in the candlelight.*

Startled, she looked up.

It was all his sky needed. A rush of light dove down, and when she gasped, flavor—chocolate—flooded her mouth. The scent of drowning rain washed the air.

Then she felt him.

Heat. Heartbeat. And his mouth— *Stay, Shaynie.* A whisper sweet on her tongue. "Cameron," she breathed, and heard her heartbeat, *his* heartbeat, and above them stars crackled, their sounds issuing words, fragments of all he had said. *Faerie. Promise me. Stay.*

"I—no. No!" Tearing her eyes from the sky she grabbed the pillow—God, it *smelled* of him, rain and chocolate—and pushed herself up.

Could not push herself up.

Starlight held her, heat trapped her, and his voice—*Stay put. Stay Safe*—was in stars that fell and threaded into her hair, tugged her back. Then more words, more fragments, were sunbeams on her face. In her mouth. *We strip Shaynie. Clever Faerie.*

"Weste—"

*Call me Cameron.*

"C-Cameron—" She tore her mouth away from him, away from nothing—'cause there *was* nothing, right? It was her imagination. Except.... She panted. Imagination did not feather her hair like a thunder whisper. Did not have hands that were big and rough and relentless as they slipped under her sweater. *Strip Shaynie. Stay.* Sunshine pulled her back to the bed.

"Kiss me." The plea fell out.

The stars raced, a whiplash smile, then he was there. A mouth soft and hard all at once and a *body....* Her shoulders sank into the bed as he settled over her, heavy. Hot. *Strip.* The word tickled her ear, then he caught her mouth again.

The tastes rain and chocolate were intoxicating. *Stay.*

"Yes," she gasped. "Stay."

The stars soared. *Strip Faerie promise me.*

It could not possibly be her own fingers she felt on her bra. Not *her* palms coursing over her skin. It was muscle. It was man. It was the sandpaper scrawl of stubble against softness and a scent that made her drunk as he touched her, kissed her, whispered with a thunder rumble deep in her ear.

"Cameron," she breathed, shivering as his fingers skimmed her belly. Writhing as they slipped down the powdery insides of her thighs. *Promise me,* he whispered and she opened herself as his constellation touched her, teased her. Then her breath came in gasps. Her back arced, and—

Light. Heat. Rain and chocolate. His sky exploded with a starburst that echoed a cry—*hers? his?*—before blinding light embraced her, rocked her, soothed her with a whisper. *Stay, Shaynie. Stay.*

Stay. Oh yes. Oh, *please.* Quivering, she opened her eyes, breathless to behold the storm-sky she knew would look back at her.

But they did not. Cameron was not there. No one was.

## CHAPTER FIFTEEN

THE MORNING SUN had not yet shone, but Divinity was alive and awake with lavender when she burst through the door. "*You* did that," she said. "*You* orchestrated whatever that was in Cameron's condo last night."

And *whatever that was* had stayed with her as she'd kicked her clothes away (because she was not touching them after he, or *whatever that was*, had stripped them off), then was around her as she'd jerked open a dresser, nabbing the first thing she saw.

A t-shirt. 'Cause no way was she sleeping naked in his bed with *whatever that was*. And no way were his stars going to let her leave, either. So she'd tossed on the t-shirt, shocked that even its saying had mocked her. HOCKEY PLAYERS WALK ON WATER. An obvious play on words that did not feel cute—or coincidental. "You're not a God," she had muttered, "you're an incubus." Then she'd dove into his bed and pulled the covers up over her head.

The scents rain and chocolate tortured her to sleep.

Now Divinity's silence felt as smug as the t-shirt she still wore and, cocking her chin, she challenged the old place. "How did you put him there? I *felt* him."

The furnace kicked on with a purr.

She scowled. "Instead of just having him call back or, better yet, having Gray call me back, you brought Weste there to have *sex?* What, exactly, were you trying to prove?"

"You're safe and sound, Darling!"

Shrieking, she whirled.

Cele, only Cele, beamed in the entrance, ice crystals twinkling on her coat. "Barnabas and I meditated on your safety all night and now look at you! You are glowing!"

She was? She'd have to see it to believe it, look in one of the pieces of glass she'd use for Jude's mirrors.

Cele drifted to the window, lit a candle. "Continue protection," she murmured then settled onto the window seat.

A little hitch tightened Shaynie's chest. That spot. *Their* spot. Their kiss-in-the-candlelight.

No. Last night was your kiss in the candlelight. Or starlight.

"You're smirking," she said to the morgue.

"Smirking?" Cele blinked. "*Non!* I am smiling. And you are glowing."

She brought her hands together, caftan sleeves billowing. "You must have straightened things out with your dearest friend Gray."

The name pulled her out of starlight and back into the cold light of day. "Kind of." She slumped to the window seat and the story unfurled, punctuated by the rhythmic whoosh of traffic on the slick streets outside.

Several vehicles whished by before Cele said "You trust Gray in spite of his lie."

"I know that it's crazy—"

"*Non.* It is not. Darling, when instinct speaks it is never—ever—crazy to listen."

"*She floats,"* came the whisper, from memory, and heaven help her, she wanted to curl into it, be rocked close like last night.

Cele watched her. "What else does instinct say?"

"Hellnight." It came from nowhere, from everywhere, and she shivered. "Andrew said a redneck vandalized my door. My apartment is clearly connected to Gray. But my heart—and my head—they say Hellnight."

Cele nodded. She'd been thinking it too.

It was far from comforting. "What a fool I am," Shaynie whispered and wrapped her arms 'round herself. "I know, better than most people, that every relationship—no matter how transient or shallow—is indelible. I found that out as a teenager, watching Dad's coffin disappear into the ground. At first I panicked, cried—but later in his workshop I picked up his tools and...." An old smile, a wondering smile, filled her face. "He was there. Alive in me."

"*Oui*, Darling. *Jamais sans*."

"Never apart," Shaynie echoed, and her smile crumbled. "So why did I think Hellnight would be any different?"

"You didn't, Darling. You just never dreamed that your lover would hurt you."

She exhaled, the sound jagged. "Yes, Cele. I did."

Cele made a sound of protest. Shaynie held up a hand. "Please understand. I went out that night wanting something wicked. Something wild. Something that would quench every need I'd never met, then be gone. *Gone*." She closed her eyes. "Like it's ever our choice to make something 'gone'."

Cele reached for her hand.

Shaynie squeezed then released it. "Don't give me the honor of victim status. I chose violence. Degradation. A footprint on my soul."

"But beauty and light walk upon your soul too. Sweet *Cheri,* we are *all* defined by our ability to feel both lust and love."

She considered it. "So the Devil lives in us all?"

"Yes." Cele did not blink. "He does."

Shaynie sighed and the protection candle danced.

Cele cupped a hand around it, soothed the flame. "And Darling, remember: our choices—deliberate or otherwise—are made impure with alcohol. *Spiritus contra spiritum.*"

"Oh, I know." She laughed, a sound like ground glass. "I haven't let myself have so much as a nightcap since that night." Her eyes tracked to the place where Divinity's marble bar would be. "And that was once my favorite thing, another tribute to my Dad; brandy in a fine glass and the sweet smell of sawdust as he shut off his tools for the night." She swallowed. "Now I honor him with water. Sometimes coffee."

"*Café.*" Cele wrinkled her nose. "The most depraved of all poisons."

Shaynie laughed again but this time it felt real, felt right. "Cameron would agree with you. But he'd call coffee a 'lah-tay-dah'."

"Ah." Light danced in Cele's eyes. "So this was where the glow came from earlier. I thought 'Imself the God was playing out of town."

"He is."

"Hmph." A smile toyed with Cele's mouth. "No wonder you spurned staying in our Reiki room." She vaulted both brows. "Whatever 'appened with him out of the country?"

"Nothing." 'Cause if Cele—or Divinity—thought she was going to 'fess up to making love to a ceiling, they were both crazy.

Yet around them the old morgue hummed like it laughed up its sleeve, and Cele eyed her. "You," she said, "are lying."

Shaynie made to retort. Cele clucked her tongue. "Answer carefully, Darling. Or perhaps I am supposed to believe that elves dressed you this morning too?"

Oh. Damn. The t-shirt. She crossed her arms over the words. "We're *friends.*" She ignored the way the slogan seemed to tickle her breasts.

Cele's brows arched, but her reply was lost to the door chime. "Coffee!" called a voice. "And calories!"

Jude? Where was Gray? "Saved by the bell," she quipped, aware of the unease in her belly as she rose for the door.

"We are not finished our discussion about your 'Ockey God," said Cele. "You are holding over about him."

"Holding *out.*" Shaynie disarmed the alarm, opened the door. "I'm holding *out* about him."

"Holding out about who? Me?" Jude hurried in, cold smoking from his shoulders as he handed Shaynie a tray of hot coffee and goodies. "Madame Boisvert," he said, and bowed to Cele. "Has Shaynie told you that I'm the latest conquest of her crafting genius?"

"*Non.*" Cele, sulking, waved a croissant away.

"The Banff doors," Shaynie told her, raising her cardboard cup in salute.

*"Poison!"* Cele uttered, a hissed gasp, and Shaynie's mouth quirked. Was she talking about her coffee—or about the creepy old doors?

Jude's dimples popped in his cheeks. "The coffee and croissants are a cover," he said. "I actually came for a look at them."

"Ah...." Shaynie glanced at her watch.

His face fell. "This a bad time?" A glance at her shirt. "You expecting somebody?"

"Yeah. Gray."

His gaze sharpened. "You talked to him? I tried him all night. And?"

*And I cannot Let it Be.* "And he's coming over. Should be here by now."

He peered at her. "There's more."

She said nothing.

He nodded, lips pursed. "Want me to be here when he comes?"

"You don't have to referee." *'Cause it's not like you'd be neutral.*

He didn't reply. Didn't have to. His expression said it all.

She sought a new subject. "Speaking of referees—or lack thereof—fill me in on last night. The Python looked pretty dead without the team in town."

"Yeah." His mouth twisted. "Everyone misses our hockey boys."

Cele cleared her throat. Shaynie shot her a look.

Jude caught it. "Shaynes?" A grin crept across his face. "*Are you* holding out about somebody?"

"No."

His dimples popped. "Is Nelson lucky at last?"

She grimaced. He laughed. "Ah, Shaynie. Sometimes you make it too easy." His dimples were dancing. "Did you know the other night Noel actually offered to buy shares in the Python just so he could show you who's boss?"

*He said, "I'd screw her for spite."* She choked, coffee coming out of her nose.

Cele breezed over, handed her a fresh tissue. "The upended Magician," she said.

Shaynie nodded. Jude, oblivious, guffawed. "And what did you tell him?" she asked.

"To forget it," he said. "Nobody shares my Snake. Or gets to boss you around. That's *my* job."

She did not laugh. Couldn't.

His grin lost its luster. "Huh. I thought that was funny. Could I—uh—see my doors now?"

*Every gutter leads back to the same cesspool.* Last night Cameron's instinct had led them to Nelson. And now Jude was standing there too.

"Shaynes?" he said, and Cele, aware, slipped between them, rested a hand on the crook of his arm.

"Darling," she interjected. "May I see Monsieur Kevlin's doors too?"

A cue to climb out of the darkness. Trading a look with her, Shaynie imagined tossing a clear, colored stone. "This way." She led them to the stairs. "And be careful. These stairs aren't always friendly to people who aren't familiar with them."

The old embalming room seemed darker than usual and despite their illumination beneath fluorescent lights, Jude's new doors, hulking in a corner, looked at a glance to be a tarped, tethered coffin. Starting, Shaynie glanced at Cele and Jude. Did they seem spooked too?

Not one bit.

Suppressing unease she'd never felt before, she moved to the doors, loosened their tarp strap to peel back the cover.

"*Wow.*" Jude ran a finger over the ornate reliefs carved deep into the wood. "These are beyond what I thought."

"The craftsmanship is superb," she agreed. "You're certainly not getting cheated."

"No kidding." He traced an open-mouthed cherub in one upper left corner. "*Love* the screaming babies."

"Seraphim," she corrected. "And I'd suspect she's singing, not screaming."

"Perspective." He grinned, then crouched, eyes level with the carving. The light shifted with him and the way it caught his face....Shaynie shuddered anew. It looked like he leered at the angel, grinning as it screamed.

*Sang,* she corrected; and, "Seen enough?" She flipped the tarp back over the door fast enough to flutter his hair.

"Uh—yeah. I guess." He tried one last peek.

Good God. Her cheeks heated down to the bone. He wasn't leering. He was looking. And he'd paid top dollar for the product. "Jude, I'm sorry. I'm rushing you." She eased the tarp back. "I think I'll inlay the mirror h-here." Good grief. It was all she could do to run a finger down a natural seam in the door. "Then I'll distress it a bit—beat it up." She painted on a big smile. "Make it look like it's been—"

"—through Hell?" he answered, leering again. She recoiled. Then he frowned and was just Jude as always. "Shaynes? You do know this is just The Python in me talking, right? The guy with the gimmick?"

"Y-yeah." She nodded, then "Yeah," she repeated, a bit stronger. "Just... be careful, Jude. When you invite darkness it...stays." She could not look at the angel doors.

He, however, scrutinized them. "Sure," he said. "I'll scream, terrified, all the way to the bank." He wiped imaginary dust from the cherub then glanced at her, sly. "And so will you. After all, "darkness" sells—even if it is as unpalatable as door mirrors with screaming babies or old morgues re-furbished into a New Age lounge."

"Jude, you know I didn't choose here as a stunt. I chose here because it's sacred."

Beneath his fingers, the little angel suddenly screamed. Shaynie jolted. Had Cele and Jude heard it too?

No, again. It was just her scalp prickling. *What is this?* She covertly looked around, then spoke. "The—uh— the dead here, the grieving, they were respected. Cared for. Comforted and even given their beauty back."

Jude pulled a face. "A morgue as comfort?" He affected a shudder. "Word to the wise, Shaynes, that's a tough sell. You'll be further ahead amping up the eerie and ditching the airy-fairy."

So sayeth the businessman. She said nothing and, to her surprise, the angel stopped screaming.

Taking her silence as sulking, Jude splayed his hands. "All I'm saying is that the hospitality industry is competitive. Expectations are high and people respond in funky ways to funky things."

"Well, then I'm grateful, Jude, to have you as a mentor." She mentally tossed a stone. Black.

And he knew it. "Ouch!" He rubbed his chin as if she'd slugged him. "Shaynie, I'm trying to help you, not cut you down."

Because totally missing the point was so incredibly 'helpful'? She stooped, and as she yanked the corners of the tarp tight the little angel's face screamed through the canvas, suffocating. *I know how you feel.*

Jude, watched her, face meek. "You—uh—afraid that tarp might blow off?"

"You never know. Things have been known to move on their own down here." As far as being true, it skated the line. She'd never actually *seen* something move. Nonetheless when the old furnace reawakened, it sounded a lot like a laugh.

Jude's shoulders twitched. "See?" his voice was a titch higher than normal. "This place *does* have atmosphere."

"Yes. An atmosphere that's safer than anywhere I've ever known."

Around them lavender bloomed and when Cele gasped Shaynie looked twice at the expression she wore. She had always assumed it was the discomfort of disbelief. Now she wondered if it was the discomfort of *belief.*

Jude clearly smelled nothing. "You say safe, I say scary, and who knows what customers will think. Still on target to open?"

"Ahead." She glanced at the project Andrew, her "agent," had scored for her. "The bank raised the bar with a few picky demands, but I've had some high ticket sales to balance things out—maybe even with a few bucks to spare."

Cele applauded. "Oh, *Cheri,* your *Père* would be so proud." She caught Shaynie's eyes, held them. "Might I suggest you salute him upon opening? Brandy in a fine glass?"

"He would have liked that." They shared a secret smile that shattered when the doorbell rang out, an ethereal gong reverberating down through the floor joists. Gray. "Excuse me," said Shaynie, and took the stairs two at a time. Her hands shook as she opened the door.

Gray did not wait on her stoop. A uniformed courier did. "Package." He raised a box. "Can I see some ID?"

Second time in less than twelve hours that she'd needed ID. It disconcerted her somehow. "I'm not expecting anything."

The courier hoisted a clipboard. "It's from Andres."

Andres? The name rang vague bells—a tool company? A finishing carpentry store? Not impossible. In the flurry of building and renovating it was within the realm that she'd ordered something now forgotten. She flashed her ID, took the clipboard and signed.

The courier swapped the package for her signature— "Have a good morning"—then loped back to a truck he'd left running.

Andres. Frowning, she tore the bubble-wrap envelope from the package. "Oh!" She sank to the window seat. *"Andres."* The insignia, gold upon a wine-colored box was instantly recognizable. Andres was not a tool company. It was the oldest jeweler in town, a canopied sovereign on Whyte with a more recent, sister store at "The airport," she breathed and tugged the tulle bow from the box.

Lifting the lid, the sound she made was something between a laugh and a sob.

The Tarot Sun, a tiny charm threaded through a chain fine as gossamer, rested on velvet and when she hooked then lifted it with her pinkie it glinted, a quicksilver flash that had her blinking away tears. A note came tucked beneath it, words clearly dictated but in his voice all the same.

You said the Sun would mean you'd made all the right choices. Now it's yours. So the next time your so-called friend locks you up like a prisoner because he thinks you'll do stupid things, show it off, shut him up.

She wanted to laugh. Wanted to bawl. Wanted to throw her arms around him and say *thank you*, say *I love it*, say..."Kiss me."

"Pardon?" Jude, now beside her, laughed. She did too and when she looked up half expected to see a ceiling full of stars.

Jude flicked the Sun. It spun in soft light. "Wow. Some admirer."

"A friend." She opened the clasp, fastened the chain around her neck.

Cele watched her, tongue pressed so firmly in her cheek that it looked like a round little ball. "Divinity brought me protection," Shaynie told her.

"*Non.* Your *friend* sent you joy." Cele lifted the little Sun from where it twinkled on Cameron's t-shirt. "The Sun means blinding happiness."

"She's right," said Jude. "I don't know a thing about Tarot, but I do know this: you are gorgeous when you're happy."

*Gorgeous.* It slapped the smile from her face.

"What?" He stepped back, bug-eyed. "What'd I say?"

"Nothing," uttered a new voice.

They all turned to the entrance.

Gray, a silhouette on the threshold, was backlit by cold sunshine. "You said nothing." He looked directly at Jude. "And thanks a lot."

## CHAPTER SIXTEEN

SHAYNIE LOOKED from one to the other. "What's this all about?"

"He" — Gray jerked a thumb at Jude— "said nothing while your brother shook me down, but he knew damn well who had been in your place. Who *really* wanted to see you."

Nelson? She whirled, stared at Jude.

Gray smirked. "Your cash crop, right Jude? You sold Shaynie, your *friend,* out to—"

"No," Jude broke in, calm, and looked steadily back at her. "Shaynes, do not listen—"

*"Listen?"* Gray slammed the door. "How about we listen to what I heard you say when you and douchebag Nelson were at the back door. What did you say, Jude? *What did you say?"*

Jude folded his arms. "I had drunks in the staff room of my club, Gray. I'm thinking I had a whole lot to say."

"'Just don't hurt Shaynie'." Gray made quotes in the air. "You had Nelson by the shoulders and said, 'Don't hurt Shaynie'."

"No kidding I said, 'Don't hurt Shaynie'." Jude turned to her. "I just told you how he wanted to 'show you who was boss'." He made air quotes too.

Their mirrored image of bickering made Shaynie's head pound, and around her Divinity felt like it pounded too, air thrumming with unmistakable anger. Cele felt it as well. It was in her wide eyes, and undoubtedly the reason she drifted over to the window, lit a second candle. Shaynie turned to Gray. "Explain exactly how Noel Nelson has anything to do with your St. Cecelia in my apartment."

"Thank you," said Jude, and Gray hissed before looking at her, cheeks bright.

"Nelson didn't have Cecelia," he said. "Chrystal did. Protection." A wistful smile met his mouth. "No one needs it more than her."

"Chrystal?" The name meant nothing, although—oh. *He was with the drunk chick.* "You mean *Panties?"*

Jude's burst of black laughter made Gray lunge. He sidestepped him with ease. "Gray, please. You're ready to do combat over Chrystal Johns? Come on. You're worth ten of her."

Gray bared his teeth.

"I should know." Jude's dimples popped. "I've been with her myself."

"You son of a—"

"Stop!" Shaynie shoved them apart. "Do you think *I* give a rat's ass which of you that silly slut has banged?"

The shout and foreign foray into profanity silenced them both.

She pointed at Gray. "You have exactly two seconds to tell me what that...that idiot was doing in my apartment and why the hell you covered for her or I *am* calling Andrew and I *will* have you charged. And her too."

"No! Shaynie, she...she'd lose her career."

Panties had a career? She had no idea what she felt more, disbelief or disgust.

And Gray didn't miss it. "And she's not a silly slu—" He swallowed. "She's naïve. A sheep. But she's not vicious. Not...mean. And I know what she did was wrong and believe me, I'm pissed with her, but to ruin her over some practical joke?"

"A practical joke? Do you hear yourself? She broke into my apartment. She called me! "

"Not *her!* Nelson. And yeah, it was sick. Cruel. But—"

"But nothing. And for the record I don't give a sweet shit about her so-called 'career'." She reached for her bag, her cell.

"Shaynes, wait." Jude grabbed her wrist.

"You're going to defend her now too? My God. She must be one phenomenal piece of—"

"Stop," he said.

She awakened the screen on her phone.

He covered her hand. "Shaynie, please. Think about what you're doing."

"What *I'm* doing? I—"

He placed his fingers on her mouth.

She yanked away, vibrating.

"You just went off about opening Divinity. About making it a success. Think how that will play out if you forge ahead with charges. Because it's not just Chrystal Johns we're talking about. It's Noel too."

*He wants to show you who's boss.*

She untied the ends of Weste's t-shirt from her hip, wrapped her hands in the warm fabric.

Gray's eyes tracked the slogan. "Shaynie," he said, "There's more—"

"Shaynes," Jude cut in, scowling at him. "We could argue all day, but here's the thing: forge ahead with charges on Noel and it's not going to be pretty. He's not just a hometown hero. He's a hometown *hockey* hero. The public will *not* buy your spin."

She heard him but didn't hear him. Her eyes were fixed on Gray. There was more. Okay. Time to no longer *Let it Be.*

"They'll see exactly what Gray said," Jude went on. "A practical joke and you'll be painted as a jealous puck-fuck—"

*"Mon dieu!"* Cele gasped, her first words of the exchange.

"—by the media," Jude went on, pinning her with a hard stare. "Shaynes, you'll be spun as the groupie who got spurned and is now being vindictive because at the end of the day Edmonton isn't just a hockey city, it's *the* hockey city. Piss people off and it *will* make an impact on Divinity."

She sputtered, unable to find, much less form, words. Jude drew another harsh breath.

"Look, I know it galls you to take business advice from me, but for God's sake, listen. I know what I'm talking about."

The wind left her lungs. He was right. She knew it and, by their silence, so did everyone else. "So he...he just gets away with terrorizing me?"

"Yeah. 'Cause on top of everything else the last thing you need is your brother doing what he's longed to do ever since he got a badge—go batshit rogue."

No, the last thing she needed was to hear a slur against Andrew when she was already furious. "The only thing Andrew may do is hold *me* back from going batshit rogue when I get my hands on Nelson. He's *sick* Jude—finding my address? Stalking me? Scaring me?"

He did not argue. No one did.

"But what of the money?" Cele piped.

They all turned.

Small yet giant, Cele stood, her caftan for once looking less quirky than regal. *The Queen of Cups,* Shaynie thought. *"Cheri's* stalker left money. Why? And does she just ignore that too?"

The money. How could she have forgotten? She looked at Gray. "Why did they leave money? What did Panties say?"

"She didn't. Denied everything, in fact, even had the nerve to get pissy. As if St. Cecelia walked there on her own." He dragged a hand down his face. "But as for the money, I may have a guess." He glanced at Jude. "I take it you've never told about the party either?"

The party. Hellnight. Inside, her pulse slowed, a funeral march. Here was the "there's more" he'd been talking about.

Jude said "Gray—," in a tone thick with warning.

"It's okay," she said. "I want to know."

Jude made a rough sound. Gray chewed his lip. "How much of that night do you remember?"

She squared her shoulders. "I remember turning down Steve's ring," she said clearly. "Then I remember diving into a bottle of brandy." What came next was the memory of looking for something rough, something wild, something that would be the antithesis of any encounter she'd ever tried to enjoy with Steve. But these boys she'd grown up with, these fellas who'd always treated her like she was just one of the guys, did *not* need to know that. She looked at Gray. "What do *you* remember?"

"Gray—," said Jude, but Gray waved him off.

"You were exhausting," he said. "Embarrassing. He—" a thumb jerked to Jude "—washed his hands of you right away. Left *me* to run interference."

"And?"

"And you were all over the hockey royalty at the party. Wild boy shopping."

Okay. So maybe they *did* know.

"It was...infuriating."

*Infuriating?* A different adjective than *exhausting*. And Cele noticed the distinction too. It was in the glance she and Shaynie traded. A glance Gray did not miss. "Shaynie you know how I feel about those guys yet there you were anyway, all yes-and-then-no with them. Coy and then come-on. I don't know how many times I gave you shit and you told me to fuck off."

"I told you to—"

"Fuck off. Yes, you did. You said it yourself: you were drunk."

She stared at him.

"Then things got ugly." He looked at the ceiling. "I got the brilliant idea we should dance. Thought it would help to distract you, get you to behave. And it worked—for you."

"For me?"

"Yeah. Noel Nelson not so much. Entitled asshole that he is, he thought you'd bump with him for a buck. Well," A ghost of a smile lit his lips. "You—uh—didn't agree. Made a complete fool of him.

Announced, loud and proud, that he'd *have* to pay you if he expected you to dance—or do anything else—with *him*."

Well.... She rolled her tongue in her mouth. What was it they said about the truth coming out when you're drunk?

"Don't look so cocky." Gray's ghost smile was gone. "Noel wasn't too keen on his teammates laughing at how you'd humiliated him, and trust me—they weren't laughing with you, either. They were laughing *at* you. They made sport of you, Shaynie, you were a joke, and before I could do sweet FA, Noel retaliated. Jerked you close, made a big show of kissing you—lots of tongue—then he took the hundred he'd held out for our hat and crumpled it, forced it down your pants."

Nelson's hand down her pants? Her gut rolled.

Gray said "I'd suspect that leaving you money in your apartment was a way to resurrect that night. He doesn't know that you don't remember."

*Doesn't he?* "Didn't...didn't I do anything to fight back when he put his hand—"

"Shaynie, please. You just said yourself what you'd been looking for. You liked it. Coy then come-on, remember? It was all I could manage to hustle you the hell off the dance floor."

"And *I* grabbed Nelson," said Jude . "Got him looking at somebody new."

Gray gave him a look. "Thanks, Captain Helpful, for stepping up."

"*So* sorry, but I was a little busy dealing with Shouting Steve—"

"Steve?" Shaynie injected. "My *ex* Steve?"

"Shaynie, that's not all," said Gray. "There was also—"

Jude cut him off, a hard look. "The vomit-fest in the back room," he said. "On top of everything else you also power-puked all over the floor."

She sank to the window seat. God, what a spectacle she had been. But what was a little barf in the back room compared to Nelson's hand on—maybe *in*—her vagina? Not to mention what she *knew* had happened after. She swallowed. "Gray—"

He cringed. "Shaynie, I'm sorry. Sorry those hockey players made a fool of you. Sorry Noel messed with you. Took it so far."

He had no idea *how* far. The taste in her mouth was greasy.

"And that I covered for Chrystal..." Gray hung his head.

Jude cleared his throat. "If it's any consolation, maybe now you and Nelson are even," he said. "Cut your losses, Shaynes, let it go. It's not worth Divinity, which, incidentally, is well worth all efforts."

The kiss-up to Divinity fell on deaf ears. She and Nelson were even? He—they—had no idea what more Noel had done. What she'd let him do. She searched Jude's eyes. "All those times at The Python, and then at the hockey game. When Noel would call me his girlfriend. Wag his tongue at me. Why didn't you tell me he'd…" *Left a footprint on my soul.*

Jude's face became stiff. "I'd think the look you're wearing right now is reason enough to say nothing."

"You...you let him taunt me."

"No. *You* let him taunt you. I stayed out of it."

"You thought it was funny."

"Well…yeah. I kind of did. Sorry, Shaynes, but at the risk of sounding callous I've always questioned the logic of you and Gray doing that whole dance thing. And to do it after adding alcohol…what have you learned?"

"What have I *learned*?"

"Oh, save the indignation. I—and you—have been in the club business too long to have sympathy for drunks who whine about the night before when they knew better in the first place."

"Drunks? Jude, this is *me.* I got drunk, but I'm not *a* drunk. You—you know better. You know me."

"Shaynie, no one knew you. Not that night." He jerked his coat on. "And as for knowing better? That was your job, not mine. I will *not* be made to feel responsible for things that *you* did." He flashed a filthy look at Gray. "Great decision, telling her all this." He stalked to the door. "I'll see you both at work."

The door slammed behind him. Gray glared at it a moment then hovered at her side. "This—uh—this necklace." He pointed at her pendant. "Is that from Cameron Weste?"

Her hand came up, covered the pendant.

Gray looked from it to her. "Protection." He snorted. "From a hockey player. Shaynie, you may be wise to take it off."

## CHAPTER SEVENTEEN

Noel Nelson. Hellnight. A mystery finally solved, and no wonder Cameron Weste insisted that they had history. God only knew what

Noel had told him about Python Princess and her performance. Her face burned. And her phone rang.

She checked the screen. *Oh no.*

"Hey, Faerie," he said.

"Hey," she returned weakly, and sank to the window seat.

"You still mad at me?"

Mad? Not exactly. Her belly pitched. "Weste—"

"Uh-oh. 'Weste'. That sounds like a yes. Didn't you get my peace offering?"

She looked down and the Sun glowed, a sweet song against his shirt. She clutched it in her fist.

He said, "I know I was a caveman last night, but I just wanted you to be safe."

She squeezed her eyes shut. "Cameron—"

"That's better. Now hush and let me explain why I feel so shamefaced today."

She blinked. *He* felt shamefaced?

He misread her silent shock. "C'mon," he chided. "I was a complete jerk when we texted."

"You weren't—"

"Yeah, I was. Shaynie, you know that I was."

She tilted her face to the sky and the ceiling shone back, an array of sun sparkles. The effect was common—morning reflecting off of stained glass—and she'd seen it many times. But not until today had the refracted light looked like stars.

"I was a prick in our texts because I didn't know if I could trust you."

That got her attention. Her head snapped back down.

"Faerie, I believe you when you say you don't gossip. And as for hating the internet? It may be crappy business practice, but yeah, knowing you now I can see that too. It was just...Shaynie, only my agent is supposed to know about California. How the hell did you and *your* Agent find out about me?"

"I...God. Who knows how Andrew finds out anything he wants to know?" she said. "He's a detective. And he doesn't always play clean."

"So was he poking around because you're connected to me? Is that all?"

She didn't know that but *did* know Andrew. "If I had to guess I'd say yes."

He exhaled. "So then he—and you—will stay quiet."

"I—yeah. Of course. And Cameron, really—who would I tell even if I wanted to? I don't know anyone who hobnobs in professional hockey circles."

Except Jude who hobnobbed everywhere. She bit her lip and over the line Cameron snorted. "You live in Edmonton, Faerie. The whole city is a hockey circle."

She wrinkled her nose.

"This news could blackball me," he said. "Loyalty is everything."

*Loyalty*? "So does Nelson know?"

*"No!"* It was so explosive that the flame of her protection candle responded, zig-zagging crazily. Astonished, she cupped a hand around it, settled it.

"Shaynie, maybe I haven't been clear: Am I friendly with Nelson? Sure. But we're not friends. We can't be. We're competitors. Ever since Juniors we've wanted what each other's got."

Noel wanted what *everyone* else got. Still— "But not right now. You said you want a trade. And he wants to be Edmonton's golden boy."

"Yeah, but so do I."

Huh? It was a labyrinth impossible to follow.

"Faerie, it's crucial that I'm the hotshot on the team."

"Ah." She nodded, slow. "In order for another team to think you're hot enough to want."

"Right."

"That sounds so—"

"Manipulative?"

"I was going to say mercenary."

"Yeah, that too. But that's hockey. Hell, that's every professional sport."

She sat back. Had someone told her a few days ago that the Ice Gods of The Python outplayed, outwitted, and outlasted each other in covert media manipulation and deal-signings she'd have laughed herself silly. Those overfed egos knew more than how to chase pucks and boobs?

Apparently.

And apparently the whole process was more cutthroat than she would have dreamed. Although— "Why would Noel sewer you if he knew, ultimately, that you're moving on, no longer a threat to his superstar status?"

"I thought you said you knew him," he said dryly. "Because he *can,* Faerie."

Because he can. Same reason he'd hurt her? No. That was because she humiliated him, just like Gray had said.

Cameron misread her silence. "So," he said. "Is all this quiet because you've learned that I want to abandon your beloved city?"

*Sure. Let's run with that.* Anything to quit thinking of Nelson. "What's so bad about Edmonton?" She kept it light. "Is it the snow? The cold? Are you one of those people who thinks Santa Claus must live right next door way up here in the big, bad north?"

"Please. *I* was once a Saskatchewan farm boy. I forgot more about the cold than you'll ever know."

Debatable. Yet she smiled.

"As for Edmonton, it's a great city. A hockey city—"

"*The* hockey city," she quoted Jude.

"Yeah. *The* hockey city. And who doesn't love being a rock star? I just... need more."

"More what? Money? The media says—"

"No, Shaynie. Not money. I want...commitment."

"Commit—you *have* commitment! This city has hung all sorts of hope on you. And the fans—the other night when you scored, didn't you hear them?"

"You," he said, "aren't hearing me."

Oh. *Commitment.* A kiss-in-the-candlelight sort of commitment. "You...can't have that here?"

He didn't answer, and outside a wave of traffic whooshed by. Then another. Then— "Let me tell you about the road," he said. "On the road you lay in your hotel room night after night, counting the days till you can be with the person you left behind. But as you're counting, she's only getting more resentful with every day that you're gone."

"Cameron, that's an—" *Assumption,* had been what she was going to say. He spoke over her.

"So when you are together you try to make up for it. Throw money around like confetti. Plan all sorts of things you'll do in the off season. Vacations. Shopping. Cars."

*Cars?* She blinked.

"Doesn't matter. There's always another road trip coming and there she'll be, alone again, and there you'll be, choking out another goodbye."

How bleak. How bitter. And what bullshit. "Weste, I *watch* hockey. A trade somewhere won't solve road trips. Every team travels."

"Yeah, but if I were here—California—trips would be closer. I could play away and still be able to sleep in my own bed most nights."

With some non-pouty, less greedy woman that Utopifornia would magically plop on the pillow beside him? She rolled her eyes heavenward. The refracted light on the ceiling was gone. How ironic. 'Cause there wouldn't be a sun on any California ceiling. No stars either. "You do know that place is one earthquake away from plopping into the ocean, right?"

He laughed. "Spoken like a true Edmontonian. So, Clever Faerie, now that you're my secret keeper will you still help me?"

*Watch me? Turn a card?* The other night when he'd asked, instinct had told her to say no. Now she knew why. *Goodbye.* "You...you'll want the Ten of Cups." She was shooting for matter-of-fact but failed pitifully. "The Happy Ever After."

"Oh yeah?"

The electricity in his voice stung. "A Ten means completion," she recited. "The end of a journey by the meeting of opposites. For you, home and career."

"In California."

God help her, the name was making her teeth grind, and she cast a defiant look outside, at her Edmonton. And winced. Miserable pedestrians were shielding their faces from blowing snow. "So," she said briskly. "How quick do trades happen?"

"Why?" A thread of amusement lifted his voice. "Anxious to get rid of the guy who's quickly becoming your neediest client?"

*Get rid of.* A mystery of goosebumps danced on her arms. She frowned at them.

"End of February," he said. "Trade day means if you're dealt you fly out that day, owned by someone brand new."

Owned. The concept was creepy, and it reminded her of something she couldn't quite put her finger on. As for the date— "That's only a few weeks away, and ironically, end of Feb was supposed to be my Divinity target date too."

"Supposed to be?"

"I've had a minor setback."

"So then I won't be there to see it open."

The disappointment in his voice was real, and she smiled a bit as she looked around. *Guess he likes you as much as you like him.*

The candle flame stretched, tall and proud. She passed a finger over its heat. "Sometimes your Utopifornia team will play here," she said. "You'll have to come visit." It was an empty offer. He'd never be in town long enough for that. And they both knew it.

Silence stretched, then— "Describe Divinity to me," he said. "Tell me what it looks like in the day."

"Oh. Well." The request surprised her and she stammered. "It's...enchanted." The word fell out, unexpected, but incredibly apt. The entire parlor, awash with stained glass light, was like being in a bath of gratitude stones. Or— "Like being inside of a prism," she said.

"Gorgeous."

For once the word did not make her flinch.

"Shaynie, *you* need to turn a Ten. End your journey."

A few more baseboards and a bit of paint. That, and the damn bar whose status was a revolving door of back-ordered. She sighed. "I did turn a Ten, Cameron. Swords."

"Stabbed in the back. Right. I turned that one too."

She'd forgotten.

"How the hell is *that* Ten a completion?"

"Because it asks, 'What have you learned?'" Jude's words, a living shiver on her skin. She shook it off. "The Ten of Swords means someone's betrayed you, but now you can conquer him because you know he's there."

Nelson? For both of them? It fit yet it didn't.

"But what if it's your own heart that's stabbing your back?" he asked.

She pursed her lips. "Bad choices," she said. *And I've been there.* "Head trumps heart. Your first loyalty's to yourself."

"But what if loyalty's not the issue?" He paused. "What if it's love?"

"Same rule applies. Harden your heart. Use your head."

"Wow." In her ear he whistled. "Faerie, that's harsh."

"This from the guy who's duct taped his heart into boxes?"

"Ouch."

"But painted your soul on the ceiling," she added, softening the blow. "It's beautiful."

"Glad you liked it."

The shard of silence between them felt like a kiss in the candlelight.

"So how do we protect our hearts?" he asked.

Was his voice as husky as her heartbeat felt? Or was that her imagination? "Easy." She placed her palm over The Sun. "My buddy gave me an exquisite necklace. Hopefully he followed his own edict about buying things in twos."

"He couldn't. He had to make that purchase over the phone from a distance, and anyway, what a show-off. Grandstanding like that with a bauble."

"Careful. I think a lot of him."

"And that means more to him than you know."

Her heart shivered into her throat.

"I'd better go, Shaynie."

*Go.* Utopifornia. "Wait." She clung to the phone.

The line hummed, expectant.

"Cameron, have—" she squeezed her eyes shut, leapt "—have we met before?" *Huh? Where on Earth did* that *come from?*

And he clearly didn't know either because a quiver of quiet elapsed, then, "You mean in another life or something?"

She almost laughed. Superstitious athlete.

"Maybe," he said, brightening. "Maybe in the last life you were the student and I was the teacher."

An illicit image rushed in, rushed out, and twenty-two stars seemed to burn on the ceiling.

"Shaynie," he said, "I have to go."

"Wait!" she said again, and another pause, this one more impatient than expectant, hung between them. "What...what's a shopper?"

He half-laughed. "A shop— "

"On your note. You said you have a shopper."

"Oh. My *shopper.* Well. You don't think a God like me buys all his own stuff, do you?"

She gaped, and it was like he could see her because he laughed.

"I'm away too much. If I buy food, it rots. So a shopper fills my fridge on the days I fly home and I get to raid it when I get in at crazy o'clock. Win-win."

Uh-uh. One more personal detail that went without him. Lose—lose. "Oh." Her voice was small. "Guess it's just a little much for me to imagine."

"My *life* is a little much for people to imagine. But not for long. Thank you, Faerie, for turning a card. For helping me say goodbye."

Goodbye. A clot in her throat.

"Now go talk to someone more important than me. Dancing Deejay should be there soon."

"He was—"

"Text me and tell me what he says, okay? 'Cause—" *Scores!* cried his alarm, she heard it "—I have practice. Then a workout. Then sleep before the game."

Down to a science. Because everything was strategy. Just like texting was far less personal than calling. One more way to say goodbye.

CELE WAS IN her divining room, sewing machine whirring amidst a swirl of black organza. She stopped abruptly when Shaynie came in. "Darling!" She stared. "He upset you."

Shaynie slumped to a seat and the black organza caught air, floated up like a storm cloud. "I upset myself. There I was, supposedly wanting to absolve myself of Hellnight and Nelson, and I end up becoming a confidant. God."

Cele pushed the sewing aside, listened.

"What is *wrong* with me?" Shaynie asked. "I am days away from the bank's deadline, days away from my dream, yet all I can think of is one guy who I allowed to degrade me and another who I've known for less time than it takes an acquaintance to develop, much less a relationship. My heart feels like it's in a shooting gallery."

"Ah, but remember, Darling, you *did* turn the Two of Cups."

Shaynie worked the organza in her fingers. "Cameron doesn't want a lover."

Doubt was in Cele's arched eyebrows, and Shaynie hesitated. What Cameron had told her was a secret—yet sharing a secret with Cele was like locking it into a vault. "He wants a trade," she said. "Thinks Edmonton's too remote for where he wants his life to go, 'cause can you believe my Python Prowler wants commitment? Stability? Fidelity?"

"*Oui.* This I can believe. Cameron turned the Death card, *Cheri*. End an old life, begin a new one."

Her heart sank like a burden stone. "He doesn't want someone he has to constantly say goodbye to."

"Mm." Cele folded the black organza out of the shape of a storm cloud. "Sounds like he's forgetting that he'd also be constantly saying hello."

Shaynie blinked. It had not occurred to her either.

"In fact," Cele put the fabric away. "*Au revoir* and *bonjour* are opposites, Shaynie. One more ten. And look." She reached for paper and in spider-web script printed,

Good Bye

Two words in one word. Two more opposites.

Cele watched her face. "So the challenge, *Cheri*, is to show 'Imself the God Cameron the 'good' in good bye." She waggled bawdy eyebrows.

Shaynie's lips jittered.

"The other night the two of you were turning cards."

"Yes."

"And? While you were with him which auger chose you?"

Chose. What a word. "Lovers."

"Aha!" Cele shot two fists to the ceiling.

"Oh, stop." Shaynie scowled. "We both know Lovers mean get a grip on bad choices."

"Nonsense! You know that Lovers mean head and heart. Male and female. 'Good' and 'Bye'. Two opposites that fit together in the most perfect way. Darling, consider the Tens. They surround you!" With that she leapt from her seat, brandished an imaginary sword.

It was difficult—heck, impossible—not to laugh.

"The Tens are riding!" Cele swiveled, caftan billowing, imaginary sword in her hand. "The apocalypse of your lonely exile. And as they charge they have a war cry!"

"Oh? And what do they say?"

"*Bonjour!* Hello!" Cele yanked her caftan, vamped a bare shoulder. "*Monsieur* Weste, I am *très, très* happy to see you!"

## CHAPTER EIGHTEEN

LAUGHTER FELT SO GOOD, so *new,* and as Cele jousted out into the parlor with her imaginary sword, Shaynie giggled along with her and felt the old morgue do the same. Then one of their cell phones rang and merriment vanished.

"Mine," Cele said, after they'd both looked about, and, lifting it, she uttered a greeting in French. Then Shaynie saw her mouth form the unmistakable 'o' of one who's forgotten something. "*Cheri,*" she said, when she'd hung up, "I must depart. I've forgotten a Reiki house call." She floated into a scarlet cloak as vivid as she. "Work hard, Darling!"

Then she was gone and the sunshine and laughter was gone with her.

"Divinity?" Shaynie's voice echoed within emptiness that was suddenly palpable. "Where'd you go?" She pivoted in the parlor, searching, but all that rushed forward were awakened words and images. Hellnight. No longer a mystery. She'd been with Nelson. And not only that—"*You liked it, Shaynie.*"

Revulsion—and shame—made her want to curl into herself. Just as, it seemed, the old morgue had curled into *itself.*

"Divinity?" she said again. "Are you… ashamed of me?"

No scent nor sensation replied.

"Well. I am so sorry that my drunken act of debauchery offended you." Jumping up, she snatched her tool belt from where she'd slung it. "I'm going to work." She paused at the mouth of the stairway, waited for something, anything, to follow. It didn't. She descended into the old embalming room alone.

CRAFTSMANSHIP, NOT DIVINITY, enveloped her, and her planer sang through the afternoon, conjuring pieces of doors into new tables, new life. And she had no idea how many hours had sailed by but when she climbed the stairs the parlor greeted her with stretching shadows, no longer day but not quite night. And still Divinity hid in its silence.

"I'm sorry," she announced, and lit a fresh candle. "Is that what you need me to say? God knows I feel it. And frankly I don't know how you can think I've violated you more than I violated myself. Being with Noel. Letting him—"

Her cell pealed and she blinked in pleasant surprise at the number on the screen. The masonry department at her old trade school. She answered, anxious, then her heart sank: "Shaynie, I'm sorry," the department head stated, an audible cringe in his tone. "We had your marble bar top ready, but the damn thing must have been flawed. It cracked from side to side as soon as we set it, the fissure looks just like a damn snake slithered across it."

She slumped to the window seat as he told her that the replacement had to be shipped from way out East, and numbly said "Yeah, sure" when he asked if she could just be patient a little longer.

"But I don't *have* a little longer," she said after she hung up. "Divinity, tell me: are we fighting a losing battle?"

Nothing responded. "Right," she said, morose. "I forgot you were giving me the silent treatment."

The flame of the fresh candle she'd lit moved. Left, then right.

Like a head shaking *no*? She looked at it, brows up. "Did you just say *no*?"

The flame went perfectly still then stretched up, and around her the air bore a heaviness, a coalescence of— "Presence," she said aloud, and swallowed. "You're present."

Electricity awakened her skin, the undeniable sensation of one being aware of another. She exhaled, a shaky breath that should have disturbed the stretching flame.

It did not.

"I knew it. I've felt you. Heard you. Divinity, I *love* you."

Lavender. It suddenly rolled like a tide.

Tears pricked her eyes. "Thank you," she whispered. "For loving me back."

The flame bop-bop-bopped and she smiled, swiped the wet that had leaked onto her cheeks. "I'm sorry you're ashamed of me. But I guess you know, better than anyone, that the body is sacred, right? And that I gave mine to—"

The flame moved, left to right. "*No*?" The body *wasn't* sacred? Uh-uh. Couldn't be. So— "You mean you're *not* ashamed?"

Left-right, left-right.

She stared, relieved— and fascinated. "So then why the heck were you so mad at me?"

The flame became quiet and she scrolled back, thought about what she'd been saying when Divinity had retracted into its own walls. Nelson. Hellnight. "I'd said it was no longer a mystery. So are you thinking that maybe it is? Jude said he thinks Noel and I are even now, but...we're not?"

The flame slowly, almost reluctantly, see-sawed. Left. Right.

Goosebumps tracked her neck and she glanced at the door, breathed relief. Locked. Of course locked.

"So then I'm right that Nelson is represented for both Cameron and I by the Ten of Swords. He's the one stabbing us in our backs."

Left. Right.

"What? How can everything be 'no'?" Frowning, she tossed a question unrelated and obvious: "Is my brother's name Andrew Michael Gavin?"

The flame stretched. Grew. *Yes.*

Which validated what the flame had already told her: she and Nelson really weren't even, and Nelson wasn't stabbing her and Cameron in the back. "So...who is?"

The flame, perfectly still, was the only light in the now full descent of darkness. She hunched over it. "Whoever it is...will you protect me?"

The light stretched, reaching for her, so close she could feel heat on her cheeks. It struck her as a curious parallel to Cameron's star-ceiling, how it swooped down— "What about Cameron?" she said quickly. "Will you protect him too?"

The stretching retracted so fast she gasped then—left, right, left, right.

"But I thought you liked him!"

S-t-r-e-t-c-h.

"Oo-kay," she replied slowly. "So...can *I* protect him?"

Stretch. One inch. Two. Three—

"All right!" She hopped back. How tall would it have become had she left it? "Tell me how. If you protect *me,* how do I protect Cameron?"

Light swept through the window, a passing set of headlights from outside. The slice of illumination fell into her showroom, lighting a mirror within which she caught her own eyes, a fleeting reflection before the headlights were gone. "A door mirror?" She stared at her reflected self, now a scurry of shadows in the glass. "A reflection would turn him into two opposites," she reasoned. "A right side and a left, and the door would be a portal, would move his left side, his vulnerable side, away. Away from here. Away from Noel Nelson." She looked at the candle. Had she got it right?

It stretched and then leaned, ever so slightly, to the right.

Her eyes tracked its path. The stairwell to the old embalming room, inky in the dark, elicited a shudder that was new. "You—uh—you want me to make a door mirror right now?"

Left-right, left-right.

She breathed, relief, but then the flame leaned again, to the right.

Her throat worked, a dry little click. "Are you telling me to go downstairs?"

S-t-r-e-t-c-h.

"Why?" And, more to the point, why was she afraid? She'd worked downstairs for endless hours. Showered there often. Had even fallen asleep once after a marathon of building had left her too wasted to even ride the old elevator much less take the stairs. Still, she stalled. "Just—uh—just let me text Cameron first. Tell him about the door mirror."

The flame moved, see-saw, see-saw, but she grabbed her cell anyway. <You need a door mirror,> she typed, and the flame was still until she hit send. Then it leaned, once again, right.

The stairwell waited, a dark open mouth.

She shrank from it. *But why?* The embalming room—every room—was her friend. She stood, lifted the candle. "You said you'd protect me."

The flame stretched, skyward and tall.

"Thank you. Now stay with me."

The stairs did not creak in their usual places and by the time her feet met the last riser the silence was so complete she was sure that if she reached out she'd be able to touch it, a bloated emptiness, pulsing and hungry. "Hungry?" she whispered. "What *is* this?"

A tingle raced across her shoulders.

She whipped around, glanced back up the stairs.

Bloated blackness stared back.

*But how?* Before she'd left the parlor she'd flicked a light on.

The silence grew.

"Th-this isn't possible," she said, surprised her breath didn't puff out as frost. With a deep breath turned back, faced the old embalming room. Her gut went bottomless. Along the back wall a shadow crouched, its shape long and narrow. *A coffin! That's a coffin!* She grasped the hand rail, swallowed her scream.

The shape was not a coffin. *Nothing* down here was a coffin. That shape was— "Jude's doors." She relaxed and moved to them, feet chilled by the cement floor. Up close the doors looked more like a stack of lumber than a casket and, feeling foolish, she set the candle down on them.

Its flame died.

*No!* She pulled matches out of her pocket, tried to light one. Could not light one. The sulphur would hit the strike pad and hiss but not light. It was as if that black, bloated silence had somehow swallowed all oxygen and a thought struck her—*the dead don't need oxygen*—and she began shaking. Could barely grasp the chain for the fluorescents overhead.

Light bloomed and the shadows scurried, hiding from everything illumination might reveal.

Or were they hiding from her?

Trembling, she took a step back and her heel struck a power bar. At once her carpentry spotlights flared, bathing light not only on the angel doors but also on the myriad sheets of mirror she'd leaned against each open wall.

They'd been there earlier, the mirrors, when she'd been down here with Cele and Jude, and she'd scarcely noticed them. Now it was as if the old morgue was a funhouse and, glancing around, she could see the profile of one little angel—*screaming baby*—calling out through the thick nylon tarp.

What was this—all of this—telling her? She untethered the tarp, smoothed it back from the carving.

The angel's blank eyes stared heavenward and its tiny mouth was open. "You *are* screaming," Shaynie murmured and placed a finger on the small lips.

Her flesh was a medium, and the angel spoke. "*You want to dance?*"

She screamed. That voice, grating and rough, shot her backward in time to breath—whose breath?!—hot on her face. Whiskers coarse on her skin.

You want to dance?

There was anger there. Derision. *Punishment.*

"Stop," she managed, but it was feeble, and she knew there'd been a time she'd tried saying it before. Then, like now, it came out garbled. Sounded like it was from far, far away.

*"You act like a whore!"*

"Please." More garbling. "Stop."

*"Gorgeous whore,"* said the voice now, silky, soothing, and a tide of images ripped through her senses. Scents like sweat and cologne. Sounds and a song, *Let it Be,* behind that grating voice. Adrenaline sizzled on her tongue and *Stop!* she tried crying, and flailed. This *was* a funhouse. A funhouse straight out of Hell. "D-divinity! Protect me! *Make this stop!"* She clenched her eyes shut, re-opened them.

A vision appeared before her: the hologram Python, slithering across the dance floor. *The Python will either strangle you or swallow you whole.* Gray's voice. Gray. She squinted. Was he smirking or wincing?

The Python blew in her face, stole her breath and—*Oh my God! It* is *strangling me!*

"Faerie!"

A new voice, calling from somewhere beyond the memory of Hellnight.

"Shaynie, show it off! Shut him up!"

The Sun! Her hands scabbered over his t-shirt, locked on the pendant.

The movie screen in her mind went black and its voices all died. The sweat-smell evaporated and all that remained of the hologram Python was a ghost of light when she closed her eyes. "Protection." She clutched the pendant, collapsed against Jude's doors, face to face with the angel.

Pupils popped into its eyes.

She screamed and scampered backward, heels clanging on the body drawers and palms upending a sheet of plywood she'd balanced on saw-horses. Tools clattered to the concrete and fire shot up her arms when her hands lurched out, broke her fall. Around her papers—invoices and contact numbers—drifted to the floor, their flutter whispering a word.

Protection.

"P-protection?" She raised a stinging hand, recaptured The Sun. "From who, Divinity? *You?*" Tears bled down her face. "You—you've hurt me." Her arms ached and she rubbed them, trembling.

The furnace kicked on, its sound a groan like regret, and as warm air rushed around her another memory was reinvented, this one more recent. Being held. Being comforted. Being told, "It'll be okay."

Cameron.

Did the heat ducts breathe his name? Or was that her heart? Did it matter? "I heard it."

The invisible arms responded, body heat and heartbeat. *It'll be okay.*

"Thank you." She closed her eyes. Leaned solidly against nothing at all. "Thank you."

The furnace abruptly cut out and back was the quiet. But no longer menacing. Now it felt as if it were....waiting. She looked at it. *Through* it. "You're *not* angry," she said, a statement, not a question.

The steady buzz of spotlights answered, audible now even though she knew—*knew*—they'd been silent before. She eased up off the floor, swiping sawdust from her jeans, and unpeeling a receipt and business card both sweat-glued to her palms. Around her the quiet perched, wait-ing. Wanting to be understood.

"You don't *want* to scare me."

The spotlights hummed louder. Shone brighter.

"But you do want me scared." She flicked a glance to the angel. "And you want me to see."

Heat duct air blew her hair back, the wisps whispering, *protection.*

The word made her jolt and her foot struck the radio, in a heap with everything else that had fallen. It sputtered with static, then— "Vision is everything," it said.

Cameron. Her heart leapt. That was Cameron. She crouched, jacked the volume.

"When you see clearly every part of you will know where to go. What to do."

A message in a message. Blood roared in her ears, and when a second voice said, "Cameron Weste, folks, on visualization and its importance in the move toward playoffs," she paid little attention.

"If I see, then I'll know what to do," she repeated.

Divinity answered, humming lights and forced air. *Alive.* She gazed around the room and the mirrors, ringing the walls, reflected her movement, caught both her fascination and wonder. "Show me." She opened her palms like she'd often seen Cele do. "What do I need to see?"

The papers in her hands fluttered to the floor, one business card landing face up.

STEVE LONIGAN, FABRICATOR

"Fabricator." The professional term for welder. Synonym for liar.

"Steve was there too," Jude had said of Hellnight, as if it were no more than an incidental detail. But if that were true then why was the hair on the back of her neck standing? She unclipped her phone and before she could hesitate she dialed Steve's unforgotten number.

He answered off the first ring. "Lonigan."

"Hey." Her nerve fled. "It—uh—it's been a while."

One stroke of silence. Then two. Then "Yeah," he said. "Life exciting enough for you?"

Where's the chase, let's cut to it. Same old Steve. Why on Earth did she call him? Then she heard herself speak. "I'd like to hire you," she said, and rocked back, shocked.

Steve laughed. "Hire me? Last I saw, you were the one for sale."

*You want to dance?* A bolt of pain, physical, mental—was there a difference? —shot through her, and over the phone she heard Steve's chastened sigh. "I'm sorry, Shaynie. That was the asshole in me talking."

She couldn't retort. Couldn't do anything. It was like her throat was welded shut.

"I did *try* taking you home that night," he said.

The neck prickle awakened, loosened her tongue. "Why just try?" she asked.

"Because your two gargoyles, Gray Ward and boss man Jude Kevlin, they were all worked up about how pissed they thought I was with you."

"And?" She sounded strangled. "Were you?"

"We were barely in the grave and you had your boobs bare on the dance floor, Shaynie. Yeah. I was choked."

She bit her lip.

"But I still would have looked after you. And done a better job than those two clowns. Christ, they'd practically drowned you by the time I fought my way into the back room. You'd think a beer slinger like Kevlin would know that just because you force water down someone's throat doesn't mean they'll sober up."

*No kidding.* "I—I would have been better off going home with you."

"And you wanted to. Looked right at me for a minute and said, 'Please help me'."

The words immersed her in ice and Steve felt it too, it was in the way his voice quavered. "That was a little eerie. Pissed drunk and couldn't hold your head up one second, stone sober and begging for help the next."

Her heart hammered. "So why didn't you? Help me?"

"I told you. The gargoyles. They had it in their heads I was going to hurt you."

And so they'd "protected" her. She dragged a palm down her face. "They don't know you, Steve. They never did."

He was quiet a moment. "I—uh—I'm seeing someone."

"I'm glad." And she was. Truly.

"How about you?"

Cameron's shirt was reflected in the mirrors and, rumpled as it was, its words and letters were rearranged like an anagram. PLAYERS WALK AWAY. "No," she said. "There's no one."

It must have been sufficient penance because when he spoke again he was clearly cheerier. "What did you want to hire me for?"

*I have no idea.* "My old morgue drawers," she said, her voice working without her. "I'd like them used in a fabrication."

"Of?"

She listened, astonished, to what she then described in elaborate detail. Where had the idea been? Was it her idea at all? And if it wasn't...her eyes skated the room, felt its unmistakable swell of satisfaction as Steve echoed the concept back to her.

"You want the Tarot suits, three-dimensional and life-size, to hang from your ceiling."

"No. Not life size. Beyond life size. They need to be gigantic."

"And another, smaller set for the walls."

Cameron's suggestion of metal wall art. *That* concept had not been a surprise. "Yes."

Divinity hummed.

"Sounds like something my students will eat up."

His students, apprentices from the trade school where they'd met as students themselves—exacting students who'd wanted to conquer every assignment perfectly. The memory made her smile. "Students will be great," she said. "Overachievers."

"Like you."

Uh-oh. She knew that tone. Thought he said he was seeing someone. "And like you," she volleyed crisply. "You're a perfectionist. That's why I called." Good God, was it? "I want perfect."

"You'll get it."

Oh, please lose that tone.

"So do I come get these body drawers or what?"

"No!" Damn. She'd shouted. "No special treatment," she said, quieter. "I'll deliver."

"Shaynie," he chided. "They're heavy. And you're—"

"Perfectly capable. Especially if Andrew helps." There. Nothing like dropping the name of your brother the cop to end things.

Not that it worked.

"Why bug Andrew?" he asked, still husky. "Why don't I—"

The rest was lost as their connection blanked to the brief signal of call waiting. Andrew? Had to be. 'Cause God knew everything else was being conjured. "Hear that?" she asked when their line was restored. "Bet that's my bro now. I'd better go. We'll be by soon." She quickly engaged the waiting call. "Hey. I—"

"My Grandmother used to cover every mirror when someone died, said otherwise their souls would be trapped."

She gasped. Talk about conjured. "W-weren't you just on the radio?"

"Pre-recorded. No mirror, Faerie."

*Superstitious athlete.* She pursed her lips. "Weste, there are lots of tenets about mirrors and many—including me—happen to believe they mean movement, not entrapment."

"Well *I* happen to believe you're messing with stuff you should step away from."

She flicked a glance to the screaming angel. "A mirror on a door is like a visible Ten," she recited, ignoring the carving. "The glass reflects your opposite, the half of you that's backward and facing the wrong way—" Wait. The wrong way? A few seconds ago the saying on his t-shirt had *not* been the wrong way. Its reflection had been perfectly legible, no reversal needed. How was that possible? The question gurgled in her throat.

"And…?" he prompted.

"A-and a door is a portal." She forced herself on. "A medium that moves your opposite half, your negative half, away from you."

"Or traps your dark half to reflect there forever."

A chill whistled through her and the mirrors reflected it, a legion of shivers that raced around the room.

"And what if the person looking in this magic mirror has *only* a dark half?" he said. "What the hell happens then?"

Good God. Was there such a person?

Yes, hissed Divinity, and, "Well?" Cameron said.

"I .. don't know."

Yes you do!

Back was that sense of no oxygen. She swallowed. "I—I guess they'd die."

"No shit. No mirror, Shaynie."

"But *you're* not just a dark half."

"Really? Right now I lie. I manipulate. I convince the media and my team that I want what I really don't want, and tell them vision is everything while all I'm really visualizing is a way out."

"But we—we all have virtues and vices." She did not look at the angel. Could not look at the angel. "Anyone who sees his shadow and light simultaneously is blessed for perceiving himself as whole because then he can accept the Gemini of himself and love it for all it is. He'll move forward in peace."

"Or be trapped with his bad mojo staring endlessly back at him."

A visual of Jude's angel doors hanging opposite each other in The Python flashed behind her eyes. Those mirrors would reflect the Python

Pack and their lust, their debauchery. *Hellnight.* She shuddered, and again the ringed reflection made the room look like it writhed.

"Faerie," said Cameron. "Don't make any mirrors."

Any? "Why?" she asked and moved to Jude's doors, yanked the tarp over the angel. *"I'm* not evil."

"No, but you *are* blind."

The word caught in her ears like a scream

"And Shaynie, if you stare into one of those mirrors too long, I'm scared you'll stay that way."

## CHAPTER NINETEEN

Visible from her brownstone's parking lot, Shaynie's bedroom window softly glowed, lit by the cut glass lamp she'd bought for a buck at a garage sale and always left on. The sight flooded her with peace. Comfort. Tonight was the first and only time she could remember preferring her shabby little apartment over Divinity.

And she couldn't even stay.

Her shift at The Python loomed, only a couple hours away, and, locking her truck, she went inside, mechanically drifted through the motions of make-up and hair. Trudged to her closet to select Python slink. Pushing her carpentry clothes aside empty hangers jangled. A *lot* of empty hangers jangled. She slid a few down the rod and peered. Her jeweled halter, another flea market find, wasn't there. Nor was her amethyst tube dress. "What the—?" More hangers rang emptily and she noted the absence of a sequined t-shirt and a second halter.... gone.

Swallowing, she plucked out a sleeveless turtleneck and black slacks, pulled them on with the taste of bile in her throat. When Andrew and his uniforms had had her look for anything missing she'd never dreamed to check her clothes. What was Nelson doing with her outfits? Or had Panties taken them, believing they'd fit her sky-scraper frame? This possibility lifted revulsion a bit, but not enough to stop her from casting black stones—one for each item gone—before she left for the club.

~

In The Python she flicked the TV on and tuned it to the game, but couldn't see through the bloodbath of spotlight glaring off the screen. "Gray?" she called. They had exchanged a stiff hello in the parking lot, and Shaynie was now keenly aware of how waitstaff eyed them both, clearly curious as to where things stood between them. The redheaded robots in particular seemed interested.

Gray popped up from behind a speaker. "Whatcha need, love?"

Ah. *Love.* He knew the waitstaff were looking too. "The red strobe. Could you angle it away from my station?"

The light bounced up and over, and he blew her a kiss.

She blew one back. There. That should shut everyone up. Plunking a colored stone in a jar she gazed back up at the screen. No Cameron. Yet. Keeping one eye trained on the TV she moved through prep, looking away only when a hand dropped on her shoulder.

Jude's ever-present dimples were nowhere in sight. Still stinging from the morning? Join the club. "What's up?" she asked.

"You and Gray. You—uh—okay?"

"Gray wasn't the one who huffed out of Divinity."

He looked down, wiped an imaginary spot from her counter. "Shaynes, you know I've never had much sympathy for what people do when they're drunk."

"Yeah, well, I've never been one to *get* drunk. Not like that."

He nodded, solemn, yet the memory tugged at his mouth. "You were pretty wild."

"I was stupid. You have no idea how stupid."

He shook his head, ruefulness gone. "No way. Not stupid. No one stupid could come up with concepts like my screaming baby mirrors." He grinned, rubbed his hands together. "Make any progress on them?"

*Don't make any more mirrors, Faerie.* She shooed the iciness of those open angel eyes from her arms. "Kind of," she fibbed. "But mostly I worked on Divinity." *Or rather, Divinity worked on me.*

She chased another shudder by telling him about the body drawers and their new fabrication, frowning at his recoil. "What?" she said. "You just said you're impressed by creativity."

"I am, but Shaynes, are you sure Steve's the right person for the job?"

Steve whose voice had dropped husky? Steve who'd wanted to come over? "Best fabricator I know," she said stiffly.

Jude's eyebrows stretched for the sky, reminding her of the candle flame in Divinity. "Only *you* could charm an old boyfriend into taking on a project."

"Trust me, he was far from charmed." What a lie. The way he'd said her name. On the rare times he'd felt amorous he'd said it exactly the same way. She gnawed her bottom lip, sought escape up on the screen.

*Oh.* Her belly flipped. *Hello Cameron.*

He peered back at her, storm eyes now as familiar as the stars in the sky.

Jude tailed her gaze. "Uh—Shouting Steve know about *him?*"

"There's nothing to know."

"Right." He lifted her Sun with his thumb.

She gently, but firmly, plucked it back. "This is a talisman for his Tarot reader, nothing more."

Jude eyed her, first shrewd, then drop-jawed. "Holy crap. You're *not* being coy."

She shrugged, palms up, a "what do you do?" gesture.

He gawked. "Pussyhound isn't interested in you? What the hell? Did he just discover he was gay?"

"Because only a gay man wouldn't be interested in 'Python Princess'?" She scowled. "Believe it or not, I *am* capable of being just friends. Case in point—look in the mirror."

"Huh. What I looked at was your face when you got his fancy necklace." Again he lifted The Sun.

Again she snitched it back.

He curled his lip at the screen. "Hmph. Add "stupid" to "arrogant." If Weste had half a brain he'd look at you too. See your moony-eyed expression and know he had it all."

She wasn't sure whether to thank him for the compliment or be insulted for both herself and Cameron.

And Jude clearly didn't care. "Want me to tell him just how much he's missing?"

Good grief. He was cracking his knuckles. "Jude," she chided. "Love isn't forced."

He fired another hateful look at the screen.

She looked up too.

Cameron's storm eyes were gone, but the camera still tailed him, a steady bead on his twenty-two. "We need to get ready to open," she said.

Jude stalked back to his spot and she waited until he was absorbed, then pulled her cards out, began shuffling. "Cameron." She rediscovered him on the screen. "Will you end your journey? Have both light and love?" She shuffled, shuffled....

*"Scores!"* cried the commentator, and Cameron's arms flew in the air. She flipped his card simultaneously but could not look at it. Could not tear her eyes from what the camera had captured.

Love. Light. Euphoria.

Sweat dripped off his face. His uniform was bulky and a helmet hid all of his hair.

Didn't matter.

Oh, Cameron Weste. What have you done to me? What have *I* done to me? She looked down at his card. "Oh! Oh, no."

"Shaynes?" Jude aimed quizzical eyes down the length of the bar.

The Three of Swords. She hated this card, hated even touching it. Snagging a snake-shaped swizzle she slid it back into the deck, poking it till just its corner was visible in the stack. "Heartbreak. Oh, Weste." Then it hit her. The night of his reading, all those swords he had turned made her think that somehow she'd influenced his spread. Cele had been quick to correct her: "His energy, Darling. Not yours." A reminder that he, not she had chosen his cards. But today she *had* picked his card. So if this was *her* energy...relief flooded her. Then the card meant exactly what it said. Heartbreak. For her. The Three meant "Goodbye" and that he'd get his wish card after all, have his Sun. Wistfulness met her mouth and she lifted *her* Sun, kissed it. Above her the screen flashed and she looked up.

Noel Nelson looked back.

She dropped the pendant and it swung like a metronome as Jude called out the count-down. "....and we're *open!*"

The night blew by on hot music, hot bodies, and hot hockey. Then when the team won, the sky exploded, a storm of coins pouring into her tip jar.

*Thank you, Pentacle Queen.*

But the cash storm went as quickly as it came. Even a win from the Ice Gods didn't change that it was a weeknight in a blue-collar city. The Python was still hours from last call when the party disintegrated and The Pack drifted to the doors.

Jude shot the signal that allowed her to shut down and as she kicked off her shoes Gray appeared at her side, wordlessly picked up a bar rag.

"What," she said, "are you doing?"

"Penance."

She sighed.

"I hate that you're mad." He scrubbed the counter, didn't look at her. "Not that you don't have good reasons."

And one 'reason' hadn't shown up tonight. She'd kept an eye out, wondering if maybe Panties would arrive wearing one of her stolen halters, but the ditz hadn't surfaced. She reached out, nicked the rag from Gray's hand. "I'm not happy that you lied, but it wasn't you who violated my place, Grayson. It was her."

He nabbed the rag back. "Shaynie, Chrystal—"

Her phone rang and he stumbled back as she dove for it. "Whoa." He laughed. "I think I can *hear* your heartbeat. You expecting a call?"

"I-uh-I did a distance reading," *God.* Her face was on fire. "This will just be my client."

"'Just'?" Gray's brow bounced.

She turned her back, lifted the cell. "Hey."

"Hey yourself." Adrenaline pumped through his voice. "Turn my card?"

Three swords stole her smile. "Um, yeah. Yes. Better keep your stuff packed."

"Oh yeah? *Perfect!*"

'Perfect'. Swallowing a sharp taste she supposed was irony, in her head she heard Cele—*The "good" in "goodbye"!*—and dove. "You know, Weste, you go from heartbreaker to handsome when you flash that victory smile." She shuffled her bare feet. "You—uh—better be careful or you'll wind up with that relationship you want sooner than you planned."

"Not to worry, Clever Faerie. I'm already on it."

Her heart turned a cartwheel, cried out *'Bonjour!'* "Oh yeah?"

"Yeah. She writes a sports column. Cliché, eh?"

She rocked back, bare heels smacking the floor. Who knew those three swords would pierce her so soon? "O-oh." It was the most she could manage.

"Uh-huh. We're going for a late coffee just as soon as I change."

A late coffee. A lah-tay-dah.

Her chest hurt. Her eyes hurt. "Except you'll have juice," she said numbly. "You hate coffee."

He laughed. "Magic *and* a memory. You're like no one else, Clever Faerie."

"I—I need to let you go." Oh, how true. "I'm still at work."

"Whoa. Wait. You sound...what's wrong? When I texted you earlier you said everything about your apartment had just been a bad practical joke."

Yes, right after their conversation about the mirrors he had texted her, apologized again for not giving her a chance to tell him everything that had happened.

She had lied.

"What's going on?" he demanded now. "Is Dancing Deejay still 'joking'?"

She looked askance at Gray who, alarmed, stopped what he was doing, grabbed paper napkins for her cheeks. 'What?' he mouthed. *'What?'* She shook her head. "I-I'm fine," she said.

But it was Cameron who answered. "No, Faerie, you're not fine. You're crying."

"No I'm not." She swiped her nose, silent. Gray was gaping. She turned away, but there was no escaping Cameron Weste, still a rumble in her ear.

"Clever Shaynie...are you *sure* you're telling me everything?"

*Nope. But you're telling me more than I need to know.* "Doesn't matter. I have to go. And so do you. You have a date." She quickly hung up, set the phone as far away as she could reach.

Gray glared at it. "Okay, Shaynie. I'm going to skip saying, 'I told you so,' and instead just ask how hard Weste the hockey puck needs his ass thumped."

She shook her head and a stray tear flew, made a wee opaque plop on the bar. Her cell chirped with a text. *Dammit, stop! Just stop.* Yet she reached for it, checked the screen.

< Shaynie it DOES matter. YOU matter.>

"Not enough." She turned the phone off.

Gray waited, arms crossed.

"I...Weste's just not into me." She fastened on a smile. "You know how it goes."

He assessed her a beat. "Yeah." He nodded. "I sure do."

Chrystal-Panties, the B&E queen. What on Earth did Gray see in her? Yet he was clearly wondering the same thing about her and Cameron. *Bad choices.* She'd been right about The Lovers all along. "Idiot," she whispered.

Gray misinterpreted. "You sound like Jude. You both thought Chrystal was a ditz even before the whole Nelson-apartment thing happened, but

I promise you, Shaynie, she isn't a dummy. She's just an add—" He broke off, chewed his lip. "She's a nurse."

Whoa. Panties was an addict? And a *nurse?* God help the sick.

His shoulders shrank at her incredulity. "Not that it matters for me anymore. Nelson rides again. Why does he always want what I've got?"

Why did Noel want what *anyone* had? "Because he's an insecure loser," she answered. "Instead of just being happy for people, he feels left behind, second-best. That's why he always makes it his mission to conquer." She shot her bar rag into a bucket. "I should have told Cameron that, too." She pulled a face. Who was she kidding? Her services were no longer required to tell Cameron anything.

Gray slumped, a mirror of her defeat. "Can you believe Nelson actually forked out for a flight for her? Crystal's out in California tonight for his game."

So Nelson and Cameron *both* had dates. Who'd get dibs on their shared room? Or would Nelson have enough couth to even find somewhere different to be? "And I took him home." It slipped out aloud. "I can't believe I took him home." And not only that, but Divinity's candle had said his vendetta wasn't over.

"Huh?" Gray frowned. "Took who home?"

"Noel," she replied. "The night of that after party, when I stripper-danced and liked his hand down my pants. I ended up taking him home."

"*What?* No you did not."

She stopped scrubbing the counter.

"You think I let Nelson near you?"

"I—"

"Shaynie, *you* may have wanted to conquer Nelson that night but I—" he whacked his chest "—*I* took you home."

Her jaw dropped. *"You—"*

"Threw you over my shoulder, hauled you out of here, and took you home, thunked your drunken little butt on your bed."

"But, Gray, I—"

"Oh, I know you weren't happy. Made me well aware that if you couldn't have someone you might just settle for me."

"What?"

"Babe, there's a reason me and Jude always kept that night from you. And really, it's not like I *let* you pull me into your bed." He paused, misinterpreting her shock. "C'mon, Shaynie. I love you but I don't *love* you." He laughed, looked puzzled when she didn't, then stopped altogether. "Shaynie—?"

"Gray, I *was* with someone. Someone who…" She looked down at the cleavage she'd hidden. "I must have got up after you left, called Noel—"

"No. Not possible. After I swatted your hands and tucked you into bed—clothed, incidentally—you passed out dead. I waited a few minutes then left, dead-bolted your door and shoved the key back under so you'd find it the next day. Are you sure you didn't dream—"

"No." Her arms made a stiff X across her chest. "This was no dream."

He looked baffled. Then sickened. "Oh, *Shaynie*—"

"Hello!" Jude called. He was tapping his watch, a merry grin on his face. "The last bouncer just left. If we hurry we can be outta here too. Who's up for pizza?"

Shaynie and Gray looked at each other. Jude ambled over. "Oh, you guys!" Her station was still a disaster.

"You go early." She smiled, falsely bright. "We dawdled, but that's not your fault. Go ahead, go home. We'll lock up."

He looked pained.

"What's wrong?" Gray lofted a brow. "Don't trust us?"

Shaynie flinched at the undercurrent.

Jude didn't. "You're family, Gray. I don't think trust is an issue."

Gray had the good grace to look away, and when he did Jude caught her eye. *'Do you trust him?'*

*Yes.* She snapped his keys from his palm and followed him into the back, resisted the urge to do his coat up herself and shove him out the door.

He needed to go. She and Gray needed to reconstruct Hellnight.

## CHAPTER TWENTY

THERE WAS NOTHING to reconstruct. Five buckets of steaming bleach-water later her station was clean, but Gray's story had stayed the same: when he'd left she was passed out, fully clothed, locked in, and alone.

They cashed out with the question hanging over them.

Who had been with her?

Gray insisted not Nelson. "We wouldn't let him within ten feet of you after you humiliated him with that line that he'd have to pay you."

In fact, for all Gray knew, Nelson had had his first go with Chrystal that night.

For she too had been at the party.

"Panties? God." Shaynie rubbed her eyes. "I think the only person who wasn't there was Cele."

"And I could have used her to spell me off," he said, but it was one of those cracks regretted the moment it fell from the mouth. He immediately winced. "Aw, Shaynie. I'm sor—"

"Don't be. You're right."

Drooping, he set his glass in the sink then eased off the counter where they'd both perched, drinking soda and rehashing. "I should have just stayed with you that night. Bunked on your couch."

God, if only. "You did more than most friends would. Gray, I'm grateful."

He offered his hand. "We completely okay again?"

"Yeah." She clasped his fingers.

He helped her from the counter. "Let me follow you home."

"Home? It's morning." So much for leaving The Python early. "There's only a handful of hours till light, so I'll crash at Divinity, get up and get started first thing. I'm within a hair of giving the bank all they want to see." She killed the lights, moved to the back door.

Gray followed, but did not reach for his coat when she shrugged into hers. "Shaynie?"

She looked up from her boots.

"Aren't…aren't you scared?"

Scared? Perhaps she should be. And under normal circumstances maybe she would be. But..."Nothing's as it seems."

A crease marred his brow.

"Gray, up until now I've always called that night Hellnight because I thought—" She took a breath. "I thought I'd gone looking for pain. *Enjoyed* it."

*"Pain?"* He gaped. "You never said anything about—"

She held up a hand. "Tonight you blew that theory. I'm not my own worst enemy. I never was."

"But, Jesus, Shaynie, *somebody* was. Somebody—"

"Hear me out: I never drink anymore. I don't party. And when I walk out the door I always have this." She pulled her taser from her pocket and depressed the trigger. An arc of electrified color left an imprint on the darkness, a coil of green light sizzling, a small yet more vicious version of the hologram python.

Gray stared as she slipped the taser back into her pocket.

"Looking back at all the choices I've made since that night, maybe some part of me always knew that my...*encounter*...wasn't by choice. I don't know. But what I *do* know?" A smile of ice found her face. "Is that never again will somebody hurt me."

Gray's assessing eyes seemed to weigh her words against her body. Then he nodded.

THE STREETS SLEPT, their only sound the sporadic whooshes of other vehicles like hers, headed to work way too early or getting home way too late. She propped her head against her hand, lulled by the rhythmic sweep of streetlights until a horn blared, jolting her from her slump against the driver's door. She cranked the radio up.

Noel Nelson joined her in the cab.

"Weste had his game in the sun tonight, but it's not gonna last. He knows I'm gunning for him."

A commentator broke in, voice dripping with glee. "Noel Nelson, folks, recorded earlier tonight, and what a rivalry he and Weste have generated within the home team! It's amped up the energy and seems even to have yanked Cameron Weste out of that slump that's been dogging him."

"Oh, what good entertainment. What motivation for the *team.*" She stabbed the dial off. Didn't anyone listen to the words Nelson chose? *Gunning for him.* That wasn't competing. That was *hunting.*

She looked up, found Cameron's building. "You're blind too," she said, and her eyes drew a protective circle around his bedroom window. Nelson may not have been her Hellnight assailant but he'd still been the one to break into her apartment and steal her clothing—for God-knew-what reason.

"Be careful, Cameron," she whispered, and wondered, what was he doing right now? A different time zone, a different latitude, he wouldn't even share the same break of dawn. The thought made her inexplicably sad. So did the idea of he and his sports writer creating their own stars in the sky. Sighing, she eased up 105$^{th}$ and made a left onto Jasper Ave, tooled pensively up to 109$^{th}$ and Divinity.

Her old morgue bore stripes.

"Huh?"

She squinted. Stripes, long and straight, looked, for an insanely split second, like a visual echo of the red strobes from The Python. Blinking, eyes and brain trying to reconcile what they were seeing, she pulled in on autopilot, idled at an angle that let her headlights shine onto—

*"No!"* She jammed into park and was out the door even as she killed the engine.

Those marks weren't stripes *or* strobe lights. They were scrawls, hemorrhage red, and what they said...

*"You bastard!"* The word exploded from her mouth and became spirit, an ice ghost erupting against a soot sky. *"You son of a bitch!"* More ice ghosts appeared and when she slammed her truck door another string of blasphemy filled the parking lot, created an iridescent army.

And she did not feel afraid.

And she did not feel alone.

In fact as she assessed the damage—not little words carved into wood this time but a whole sentence, bleeding on her building—all she could feel was rage.

SHAYNIE GAVIN IS AN UNGRATEFUL BITCH

"Oh, no. Not ungrateful." She felt her ice smile to the core. "Not at all. In fact I'm *very* grateful. 'Cause now you've given me more than enough reason to hunt you, find you, pull my trigger and light you up like a goddamn Christmas tree." She flew up the stoop and her ice army raced alongside her, stopping to float as she shoved her key in the lock and jerked the door open.

The alarm shrilled, far more wrath than warning, and as she disarmed it and pressed her familiar finger-kiss to the wall she didn't know if it was she or the building who shook with rage. "This crap stops *now!* I'm nobody's victim. And neither are *you!*"

The furnace roared and the lights flared on faster, she was sure, than her fingers found their switch.

Tonight the basement was not scary but sanctuary as she gathered one of her big work lamps, a bucket, and the caustic cleaner she'd once used to strip the old floors of their formaldehyde and strange stains. She dug a telescopic scrub brush out of a low cupboard and made a second trip down to wrestle the extension ladder onto the old elevator and up. Piling the wares by the door, she unclipped her cell, but before she could speed-dial Andrew, "Shaynie Grace?" resonated from behind the closed entrance. She smiled, bathed in a feeling of both wonder and power.

"Thank you," she told the room, "for bringing him."

Every duct blew hot air.

She opened the door.

Her brother's face echoed her rage. "Same asshole that did the carving?"

"Yes." She hoisted the extension ladder.

He relieved her of it, looked at her hard. "When, exactly, are you planning to tell me the *whole* story?"

Cameron's question except harsher—and easier to take. "About a year ago I got drunk. Stupid drunk. And I pissed a guy off at a party." There. That was everything and nothing in one simple swoop.

"Who was he?"

"I don't know."

"Could you pick him out of a lineup?"

"No."

He drew a hissing breath.

She smiled the ice smile. "Nonetheless, he'd still better pray you find him before me."

Andrew's nostrils billowed twin blasts of frost. "Make it count," he advised. "And when you're asked say he came at you. Say you believed he intended to hurt you. Then keep your mouth shut—but not before you make them call me."

*Batshit rogue.* "Consider it done."

They shared a cold grin, then gathered the cleaning weapons, went outside.

They worked until the streets rang with sound, and it was Andrew, not her, who at last stepped back and said "There. That's all of it."

She climbed down the ladder, took stock.

Divinity was pristine, stone walls blushing with morning light.

A visible thank you. *No need. I'd do anything for you.*

Early sun hit the windows, turned each colored pane into a gratitude stone.

*I love you.* She beamed, and all at once was aware that her fingers had lost feeling. She looked down and couldn't tell if her skin's five-alarm color was from the paint, the cold, or if perhaps her hands were so raw they were bleeding. She forced them into fists, half expecting them to crackle and break.

"Let's put this stuff away and I'll take you home," said Andrew.

"No. I'm crashing here."

"Shaynie Gra—

"Andrew, I have an alarm. And that guy who installed it said I can have the setting extended to the perimeter too."

"And? Will you?"

"Before my head hits the pillow." That and one more thing.

He deliberated, gaze narrow. Then, finally, "Okay. You win."

"Damn straight."

He allowed a small smile. "Shaynie Grace, you do know you're wrong about this asshole needing to hope *I* catch him before you, right?"

They shared an identical gaze and a smile, pure malevolence. She reached up, traced an ankh on his forehead. "Thank you," she said. "For always looking out for me."

"Damn straight," he echoed, and left.

"Now," She turned to her old building, "Let me look after *you*."

She hauled the cleaning supplies in, and once she'd shuddered into jeans and a sweatshirt called the alarm company, grateful for the wait on hold, for it allowed her to warm first one hand, then the other, between her thighs. When at last the rep verified her request, she'd thawed out enough to march into Cele's divining room and make a beeline for what she needed.

A sack of tea lights. A box of salt.

Protection.

She heard it. *Knew* she heard it. "Yes," she answered. "I promise. I swear." She opened the front door.

The last few weeks had been too cold for the snow to form a protective crust of ice, so the candles she set as she paced the building's circumference sank into powder, could not be seen.

Didn't matter. With every tealight she dropped the wind gathered momentum, and the salt she sprinkled between candles should not have been visible yet glittered, iridescent, in the snow. "Protection." She moved in a perfect circle around Divinity. "For this place my heart loves. For this place I know has a soul."

The wind roared between high-rises, and *protection* became a steady hum until she closed the circle and clasped her hands, prayer-like, raising her face to the old morgue. Her breath caught.

The sun, still a slow orb in the east, burned a golden outline around its edges. *An eclipse.* Cameron had described her eyes just the same way on that seeming long-ago night at The Python.

And now here it was.

She reached out, traced the glow with a finger. *Are you me? Or am I you?*

A fury of wind tore her hair back, but it was not cold. Instead, like a twinned breath, the gale matched her exhalations like the sun ring mirrored her eyes. *You. Me.* She stood within the white circle and could *feel* it, a heartbeat, a second pulse.

Divinity. *Inside* of her.

She turned her palms to it and wind roared. Ice blew. The air screamed, "*Protection!*"

*Yes.* She splayed her fingers, spanned her palms. *Protect you. Protect me.*

The windows glowed, a rainbow of gratitude and love, and she rushed up the steps, depressed the latch.

She clunked hard against the door.

"*What—*" She tried the latch again.

Locked. And the wind roaring up her back was no longer warm

She rattled the handle.

No go.

She slumped back. No coat, no keys, no cell, no— "Protection. Divinity, why? *Why?*"

A gust of wind jerked her head back and there, in her periphery, the top corner of a building stood, stalwart in the storm.

*Protection,* the wind blew, and she turned. Faced Weste's empty castle with his stars in its sky.

## CHAPTER TWENTY-ONE

Impeccable met her the moment the doors to the building whisked shut. His face was a twist of urgency. "Mr. Weste called. He said if you arrived you were to get in touch with him immediately."

How? "His key—all my keys—they're locked in my building."

Impeccable produced a new card key with the ease of a sleight-of-hand artist, pressed it into her palm. "So can we call him?" he asked. "Tell him you're in?"

'Cause they would anyway. The last thing they wanted was to piss off one of their wealthiest tenants. "Go ahead." She let the painted elevator swallow her.

She heard Cameron's phone ringing even before she swiped the key over his lock. Dammit. Could Impeccable not have given her just five silent minutes? She let herself in.

"Shaynie!"

She shrieked.

"I know you're there. Pick up."

Her heart skidded back into place. An answering machine. Just an answering machine.

"Shay—" The machine timed out. And the phone started ringing.

"Shaynie, pick up the goddamn phone!"

"I can't *find* your goddamn phone," she shouted back, looking.

"Answer or I'm going to keep ringing the line till you do." The machine timed out. The phone started ringing. She stomped in the direction of its sound, found a cordless, its red message light throbbing like a pulse. *Yeah, right. Like this place has a heart to beat.* "My God, Weste. Would it kill you to reveal *one piece* of yourself?"

"Shay—" The machine began.

She picked up the phone. "You're stalking."

"You deserve it. I texted you all night. Left you dozens of messages."

"Weren't you out on a date?"

"Yeah, and didn't *that* go well. She was a little irritated because I was a little preoccupied, worrying about you."

So his crappy lah-tay-dah was *her* fault?

"Then I get back to my room and oh, perfect. Nelson's flown the drunk chick to town. So I had to haul ass over to the new room he was so thoughtful to arrange—and by this time it's stupid-o'clock—and then, just 'cause that wasn't enough, I get another bout of that crazy flu I had the night I saw you. Freeze to death then pass out in some sort of coma. So now that I've puked my guts out I'll probably be a flu scratch for our matinee game. So much for my so-called card you said was going to get me what I want."

So that was her fault too? She spoke over him when he started to say more. "Last night someone wrote, 'Shaynie Gavin is an ungrateful bitch' in three-foot letters up the side of Divinity. So apologies that I didn't text you or call. I was just a little busy."

His breath whooshed out. "Shaynie," he said. "What the hell's—I am *worried* about you."

Worried. Because he was a good *friend.* A tear snaked down her cheek and she wasn't sure if it was from that word—friend—or from the shock she'd not given herself time to feel.

"Who's doing these things to you?"

*Don't ask. Just call me Faerie again. And don't say you worry about me. Say you think about me.*

"And don't you dare say 'it doesn't matter'."

<You matter>. The last thing he'd texted after telling her he had a date. A Utopifornia date. She opened her eyes, forced herself to inhale the emptiness he called home. Comfort didn't live here. Her *friend* didn't live here. Nor did he want to.

"Shaynie! Who's—"

"I don't remember what he looks like. And I don't remember his name."

He fell quiet.

"All I know is that about a year ago I made a complete ass of myself at a party and when I woke up the next morning I…stung." Her gaze sought the window. Outside, the sky was an endless blank slate. "The stinging was a pain I recognized but didn't recognize. I couldn't place it. And at first I … I couldn't look."

The line remained silent but within it she could hear something. Dread.

"I crawled—I couldn't walk—to the bathroom. And when I was finished, I hurt so bad… I found a mirror. Then I saw. Saw what the stinging was." She paused, and knew, somehow, that he was holding his breath. "Bite marks," she whispered. "Everywhere."

"Fuck!"

She gasped, more at the explosion of sound than at what he said.

"Sorry," he uttered.

"'S'okay. Those bites. They...they weren't the worst part."

His throat clicked. Or maybe it was hers. She said "Cameron, have you ever driven past an accident and knew you shouldn't look, but you just *had* to look?"

"Yeah. Yeah, Faerie, I have."

*Faerie.* It strengthened her somehow. "Well, I took the mirror and I looked. Down there." She closed her eyes, could see it. "Blood," she whispered. "Front and back. Right down to my knees. I …I looked like I'd been painted. I screamed, I think, and I know I dropped the mirror.

It shattered all over the floor and I...I fell too. I had to crawl through the pieces to get to the toilet. To... throw up."

He groaned.

She barely heard him, barely heard anything other than the rasp of broken glass on grout as she lurched, through blood and bright bits of mirror in her memory. "I stayed on the floor for hours, shaking so bad yet trying to clean all that glass and blood up. Crazy."

"No, Shaynie. It's not crazy."

"Then afterward I hid all the pieces on a back shelf in my closet. Now I know *that's* crazy."

"No," he repeated. "You *had* to hide them."

Of course. Because a mirror would have trapped all that darkness. "It didn't work," she murmured. "Hiding those mirrors didn't trap everything. Or anything for that matter. 'Cause now he's back."

"Back? Where's he been?"

"I don't know. Maybe nowhere. Maybe everywhere. All I know is since the night of that party, *I've* been every place but the truth. I've blamed myself—"

"*Yourself?* You were ra—"

"Cameron, don't say the word. I already know it. Now."

"You didn't know it then?"

She sighed, a harsh sound that managed to give her courage. "Let me put that night in context," she said.

"Shaynie, no. You don't have to—"

"Before that party Steve, my boyfriend—my *then* boyfriend— had presented me with a surprise. A tiny, shiny diamond. Very little. Very practical. Something perfect for a woodworker like me. Because *he* was perfect for a woodworker like me."

Miles away in California he sniffed. She couldn't tell if the sound was dismissal or dismay. And it didn't matter. "One look at that ring and I hated it," she said. "Hated practical. Hated sensible. Hated even the thought of a lifetime of being undressed by a prude under the cover of darkness when what I really wanted was...was *stars*."

Stars. *Oh God.* Did he catch it? She hurried on. "But up till then I was the queen of reasonable, and I don't know who was more shocked, Steve or me, when I closed that ring box; but his face..." Her heart contracted. "It was the right thing to do. The *only* thing to do. But once he left, I, The Queen of Reasonable, felt so awful that I cracked a bottle of brandy and chugged half all alone, just to drown the fact that I'd been—" *An Ungrateful Bitch!* She shuddered. "—that I'd called it quits." She jerked a hand through her hair. "And the more I drank, the more I convinced myself that *I* wasn't the bad one. If only Steve had been a little wilder, a little racier, then everything would have been fine. In fact, maybe that was just what I needed to dilute that awful day: raw and racy. Rough sex."

"Rough *sex?"*

It snapped her straight out of guilt, straight out of everything.

"You got *raped* and you thought you'd had rough *sex*?"

Raped. There it was, out loud, and no black stone in sight to cast it away.

"Shaynie," he said. "I've dished out rough sex. Taken it. It might leave bruises but not bites. And it sure as hell never *bleeds."*

"I..." *Dished it out. Taken it.* How? How could one possibly be rough with a body that size?

'Cause he'd let you.

The answer raced, sparks up her spine, and she jerked away from them. God. What was wrong with her? Feeling turned on in the shadow of "raped"?

*Yes!* cried a voice. *I knew you'd like this!*

She gasped, and half dropped, half fell, onto the sofa.

"I'm sorry," he rasped. "I didn't mean to jump down your throat."

"Y-you didn't." That voice. She *knew* that voice. It was the same as the one she had heard in Divinity, the one that said, *"You want to dance?"* Now, *"I knew you'd like this!"* The only difference was that this time it sounded satisfied. Triumphant.

"Oh, my God!"

"What? Shaynie—"

"He...*he* thought it was rough sex."

Cameron made a sickened sound. She ignored it. "It—it's like talking about it dislodged a memory. He said, 'I knew you'd like this,' and the *way* he said it...." Like he'd been wondering what she wanted. Had spent time trying to figure it out.

"How," Cameron grated, "could anyone think that you—"

"Because he wanted me to like it. 'Cause he liked me—the *other* me." 'Python Princess'. Except on Hellnight he'd called her something different. 'Whore'. It had *not* been an insult.

"Shaynie," Cameron interrupted. "Do you know this or are you guessing it?"

Both. And either way she was right. She knew she was right. Her lover, her stalker, he had watched her at that party. Saw her grind, saw her strip. To him it was...*Punishment. Pleasure.* So when he said, *"I knew you'd like this"*... "Cameron," she said, pulse a cannon in her throat, "you said a crazy fan acts like he knows you. You're right. This guy fantasized and—"

"Whoa. Faerie, fantasizing and rape are two different—"

"Not to him. To him it was seduction." Her head knew it. Her heart knew it. But—

*"Seduction?"* The word exploded over the line and she winced, yet—

"Cameron, I thought so too. I told you that up till last night, even I thought—"

"That you'd had rough sex. Made a bad choice. Which is so colossally naïve that it borders on stupid."

"I know it sounds crazy. But..." But the answer was there. So close that even the wind outside blew the snow into fingers beckoning like the old game of charades, asking for more, more.

"Shaynie, use your head."

The snow swirled into chaos, fingers gone.

"Even if by some twisted miracle this sicko thought you and he were acting out a fantasy, then where was he in the morning? Why didn't he stay?"

"I...don't know."

"And why didn't he call?"

Because he was confused. Startled, she glanced out the window. Was that Divinity?

He didn't know if it was punishment or pleasure and he was confused. He's been ashamed.

Her heart stroked out thunderclaps.

"And let's say you were too wasted to give him your number," Cameron went on. "He obviously knew where you lived. If he thought you liked it then why didn't he just come back to your door?"

Her gut curdled. That face—*whose face?!*—waiting as she opened her door—

It *has* been waiting.

That was not her head affirming. Nor her heart. Mouth dry, she looked again out the window.

The sky was a white rage of snow.

"No guy with a fantasy partied with you," said Cameron. "Some sick bastard with a grudge punished you."

*You want to dance?* He was right. Still...*I knew you'd like this!* She was right too. That night had been pleasure *and* punishment. Another Ten, and who knew how much more she'd have remembered if, rather than stuffing the shame, she'd talked about it before time had done its job of eroding even more memory. Of working to "*...Let it Be.*"

"No, dammit! I won't—"

"The song. '*Let it Be*'," she said. "When I woke up it was on repeat. And all this time that's what I've tried to do. I never tried to find him, never tried to fix it. I just moved on. I let it be."

She could no longer hear him breathing. Could no longer hear anything. "C-Cameron? Are you still—"

"Let it Be," he said. "That's The Beatles. I *hate* The Beatles."

It was so random, so absurd, that she laughed, couldn't help it, hoarse and helpless.

He didn't. "You said a year ago. And Dancing Deejay took you home that night."

Had she told him that? She couldn't remember.

"Would he have given your key to—"

"No. Gray didn't give my key to anyone. He pushed it under my door. I remember it being there the next day. I thought I'd dropped it."

"How about your cheap-ring ex-boyfriend? Skinny guy, uptight-looking, right? Was *he* pissy enough to give your key away?"

How did he know what Steve looked like? And why did what he was saying sound more like certainty than speculation? "S-Steve gave my keys back." Had thrown them back, actually. And she'd been shaking when she'd patched that hole they'd made in the wall, had dripped drywall mud everywhere. Never before had she seen Steve's temper. Didn't even know he'd had one.

"No matter," grated Cameron. "Keys can be cut."

"How do you—" She stopped herself. Thought. That certainty in his tone, not speculation. That shushing look from Jude to Gray in Divinity when Gray had been about to tell her more about that after party. The rest of the story had not been that she'd gotten sick on the floor of the staff room. It was— "You, Cameron," she said. "You were there." And what had Gray said? They weren't laughing with you, Shaynie. They were laughing at you.

"I gotta go," he said.

"What—no! What else do you know?"

"I need to—"

"You said we'd never met."

"We didn't meet—"

"Oh, semantics! You know. You've always known."

Several seconds passed then "Yeah." It came out on a harsh breath. "I have."

They made a fool of you, Shaynie.

"You son of a bitch." She unhooked her Tarot Sun and flung it. It made a tiny whish as it slid across hardwood. "I wish that card I'd have turned for you was The Devil. And I hope you *burn* in your goddamn Sun." She stabbed the phone off, flung it too. Then she ran.

## CHAPTER TWENTY-TWO

THANK GOD CELE was already at Divinity when Shaynie burst through the door shivering, and crying. The older woman held her. Rocked her. Stroked her hair and wiped her face, and left her only to scoot briefly to the Ukrainian bakery around the corner. When she came back she had hot soup and fresh bread and insisted Shaynie tuck into it, a mystical parent saying things like, "Eat, Darling. Sleep, Darling."

Shaynie didn't think she could swallow a single bite, yet she did. Believed she'd never be able to turn her head off and close her eyes. She was wrong.

When she woke all the curtains were hung. The place had been swept. Leftover bread that had come with the soup was buttered and Cele made her polish this off too, hovering till she ate every bite.

It did not escape Shaynie's notice that not once in Cele's ministrations was a single word uttered about what Shaynie had shared about Hellnight and Cameron. In fact, even when the question was put to her, direct— "Cele, what do you think?"—her only reply was, "The upended Magician is a skilled trickster and liar."

"Cameron?" It felt right and felt wrong.

"Cameron lies to himself."

Circle talk. It was exasperating, and despite the coddling and the care, Shaynie was relieved when, at her urging, Cele finally slipped on her cloak and drifted to the foyer. Yet instead of depressing the door latch, her hand floated over it. "I am scared for you, *Cheri.*"

Why? The people who hurt her were all out of the country. And besides—

"I'm safe here, Cele. And I know you smell it, too. *Lavande.*"

Lavender. Cele for once did not deny it.

Shaynie looked into her eyes. "Lavender has always protected people from evil." It was a fact she'd researched. "At one time it was stuffed into every crack and keyhole. Into every coffin." She glanced at the stairwell. "You know I've always smelled it here."

Cele was quiet for one long, full second. Then— "Sometimes more than others?" she asked.

Shaynie frowned. "I'm not sure."

"Before or after certain people have been here? Or have been on your mind while *you* are here?"

"I—I don't know. I've never kept track."

"Perhaps you need to, *Cheri.*"

Shaynie eyed the room from corner to corner. "Because this place *is* protecting me."

"*Oui,*" said Cele, and hesitation hung in the lavender scent before she spoke again. "*De la lavande,*" she said, haltingly. "Shaynie, it was not the only scent as you slept." She paused. "Chocolate."

Shaynie's heart gasped.

"Is this too significant?"

Unwittingly, Shaynie's gaze shot to the table—*their* table—and she could taste it, shared chocolate ganache. "Yes," she mouthed, barely audible. "It's the upended Magician."

Cele's forehead darkened, and Shaynie could not discern whether she agreed or wanted to argue. In the end she did neither, just said, "It is dark soon. How will you spend the night?"

"Working. The bank is back in two days and I still have odds and ends—and no bar. I'm going to cheat and use a couple of Andrew's overpriced tables." The idea had occurred in her sleep. "They should be gothic enough to make me look finished."

Cele nodded, darkened brow gone.

"Of course that's only till seven." Shaynie sighed. "Then it's back to The Python."

Nodding, Cele opened her palms to the sky. "*Ramène-la moi! Ramène-la moi saine et sauve!*"

Goosebumps erupted. Cele had just implored Divinity to "Bring her back safe."

SHE HAD WATCHED Cele leave from the open door and now still stood there, gaze fixed on Cameron's building. *'The Sun means you made all the right choices.'* Her hand crept to the place her necklace used to be. "Another lie," she murmured. 'Cause what she'd chosen was *him.* "But now I see."

Except...she didn't.

Cameron's lies—and theories—about Hellnight didn't alter the fact that Divinity was vandalized while both he and Nelson were out of the country. "So who *is* doing this?" Cameron had implied Steve, but every instinct she had screamed, "no way!" She closed the door and moved to the window seat, sank, and began shuffling cards. "Who painted my morgue?" she asked and flipped one.

The Tower.

Traditionally the Tower meant soul-shaking change, yet, '*The deck chooses the dealer'*. She eyed the artwork on the card. The Tower here was depicted as an enchanted castle and in her mind it had always been synonymous with her old loft apartment, the one she'd fled after Hellnight. "The so-called scene of the crime," she murmured, handling the card. There were answers there, the Tarot said so. And if a mere conversation with Cameron, present on Hellnight, could elicit a memory like, *'I knew you'd like this!',* then what could an actual *visit* to her old loft do?

She jumped up, grabbed her coat.

A flood of lavender choked her, so thick she coughed. "It's okay." She swallowed the taste. It made her throat burn. "It's broad daylight." She stroked a gentle hand down the doorjamb. "I won't even be able to go in. But I can stand outside. I can see."

Fragrance waxed and waned as though the place breathed. Lavender. Chocolate.

Her heart contracted. "Weste. *Go away.*" She armed the alarm, flinching when her finger flicked the wrong key and wrung a squeal from the speaker. "Stop!" she admonished. "I'll be fine." She placed her hand on the latch, half-expecting the deadbolt to turn itself shut.

She rushed outside before it actually could.

On the stoop, the air was deep cold and blank-scented. Normalcy.

*Normalcy?* Right. Was it normalcy that made her legs turn to lead as she moved down the steps? Normalcy which, as she approached the now-hidden white circle, pulled her back, magnetized? *Divinity.* She halted at the inner edge of the salt circle. *Please don't worry.* She glanced back.

Stained glass, storm-blue, stared at her.

Shaken, she bolted over the circumference of candles and hustled, feet making rapid-fire crunches in the snow. *Find the Tower. See.*

Her old loft was only a few blocks east, but even by the time she reached 108th the cold had shredded her lungs. She sprinted the rest of the way. Her old place, her once enchanted "Tower", was nestled above a coffee house and used bookstore. She gazed at it; clean lines, huge windows, and caretakers who'd already brushed every flake of today's snow from the steps, exposing masonry that was light-years from her shabby brownstone with its mounds of lumpy ice on the walkway and busted security door.

*Show me the message,* she implored, and raised her face, sought her old window.

Chimes hung there, similar to ones she'd once had. Her brow hopped, and she wondered if perhaps part of her spirit, an unharmed part of her spirit, had remained in this place she'd once loved, guided the new tenant's purchase.

Or maybe it was just a coincidence.

Her gaze dropped from the window. This was crazy. No new memories lurked here. No soul-shaking change. Her old place was just as serene and beautiful as it had been when she'd hauled the last box out, blaming Hellnight on herself, as "colossally naïve" as Cameron Weste had said she was. Her shoulders sagged.

Does it hurt?

Yes. And Divinity was right. She shouldn't have come.

Turning, she collided with a bespectacled man in an overcoat. He harrumphed, earmuffs askew, and bustled away. "I'm sorry!" she called, but he'd caught a lapse in traffic and was already across the street and heading toward her old building, heading toward—

*"Panties?"* she said.

A passing pedestrian stopped, stared at her. She barely noticed. 'Cause that was her, wasn't it? Panties?

No. Couldn't be. Cameron said she was in California.

*Yeah, but Cameron lies.* She peered through breaks in traffic, looked at the blonde.

Except she wasn't blonde. Beneath a wool tam, the other woman's hair was the same sable color as, "Mine," she breathed, and watched her. Hidden in a shapeless winter coat, Panties—if it *was* Panties—was as indiscriminate as every other pedestrian, and her hair was brown. But that face. Cars whizzed by, broke the stare she had fixed. Why would Cameron lie about her being in California?

Although maybe he hadn't. A quick flight back was certainly possible. *Yeah? And why am I still looking to excuse him?* Hoisting on tiptoe, she tried to get a better bead on the woman, falling back on her heels when a second person, obscured by toque and sunglasses, yet striding with an unmistakable gait, joined the lookalike on the sidewalk. *"Jude?"*

He froze at his name, glanced around.

"Jude!"

Again he searched the street, and as he did, the Panties clone turned her back, strode into the neighboring coffee shop. Shaynie stared. "What the—"

"Shaynes!" He'd spotted her and was waving, a grin splashed across his face. "Wait up!" He sprinted after two cars sailed by, jogging toward her with breaths puffing out in white blooms of frost.

"Hey." She looked over his shoulder. "Was that my burglar with you at my old building?"

"A burglar?" His brow crumpled. "At your old—oh, right. This *is* your old place. Hey, you thinking of renting again? Moving closer to the old morgue?"

"No." She peered beyond him again. "That woman with you. Was that Gray's Chrystal Johns?"

"Gray's Chrystal...oh, for—are you kidding me, Shaynes? Gray still thinks he should chase after Chrystal?"

"So that *was* her?"

"My cousin needs to get a serious grip. God. It's like he's obsessed."

"Jude!" She wanted to shake him. "Was that Chrystal or not?"

"Not." He scowled.

She scowled back. "Well, it sure looked like her."

He shrugged. "Lots of women look like Python mannequins."

She flicked another glance to her old place. "Does that mannequin live at my old loft?"

"What the hell, Shaynes?" He glared at her from over his sunglasses. "You a cop? Or just writing a book?"

In other words, *none of your business.* And really, it wasn't, but— "C'mon." She affixed a saucy grin. "I've never ever seen you with anyone." Well, no one other than the ice-cold lip-lock with Panties out the back door of The Python. "Who's the sweetie?"

He slipped his shades back in place. "Should I be flattered or insulted that you've been keeping score?"

Her brow climbed, but he merely fixed his gaze back onto her old place, a visible change of subject. "You know I've always loved this building. Why'd you leave?"

"Too expensive." Not the reason but not a lie. If there was one thing her little dive off Whyte had over the loft, it was rock bottom rent.

He pursed his lips. "Be nice to have both, though, wouldn't it? Divinity *and* this place?"

Heaven and The Tower. *Does it hurt?* She kicked a hard chunk of snow and it skittered across icy concrete. "Practical trumps panache every time. What brings you downtown?"

He laughed, the cold morphing the sound into substance, frozen fire. "What's with the interrogation? You thinking of moonlighting with your brother?"

She regarded him, nonplussed.

He rolled his eyes. "If you *must* know I'm taking care of business."

"'Business'? Is that what she's called?"

"Yes. And let me tell you, 'Business' is sexy, sweet, and the most delicious little morsel I've ever—"

"Okay!" She held up a hand.

He grinned. "Don't ask if you don't want the answer."

Her gaze trickled back to the loft.

"Stop." He fired a playful shot to her shoulder. "Can I walk you back to Divinity?"

"And leave sexy morsel....?"

He steered her away. "Trust me: she's in good hands."

Good God. He was licking his lips. She reached for her collar, did an extra button up under her chin.

He misinterpreted the movement. "Miserable cold, isn't it?" He slid an arm around her waist, gave her a little squeeze.

She slipped him a glance. "You don't look miserable. You look elated."

"'Elated'? What a word. 'E-late-ed'," he emphasized each syllable. "Why not be elated? The city is busy, business is booming—hey, how about when you and me are both wildly successful we leave Edmonton winters to the minions, go soak up sun in the Caymans or Southern California?"

"California? You couldn't pay me to go to California."

"Whoa." He glanced down at her. "*That* sounds like a story."

She scowled. "You a cop or just writing a book?"

He laughed, more frozen fire, and the sound, his face.... *He's in love.* The thought dawned as clear as the air was cold. Yes, so obvious. She cast a glance in the vicinity of the south side. *Ah, Python. At last someone's trumped you. Jude's not alone anymore.*

"Hey." He halted, Cheshire grin gone. "What's that look about?"

"What look?"

"That I'm-so-lonesome-I-could-cry look. Shaynes, what's up—"

Her cell rang. Purred, actually, buried beneath her sweatshirt and coat. "I'm not lonely," she said, yet her chin wobbled as she rooted, found the cell.

The screen said FIRST FINANCIAL. Her feet stopped. Her heart stopped. "H-hello?"

"Shaynie Gavin? Rick Porter. First Financial."

*Yeah. I know.* She couldn't force a single word out.

"Ms Gavin, I know I'm calling on very short notice, but I was wondering—could we meet?"

"Today?" She stayed perfectly still. "My—my deadline is still two days away."

"I'm aware, but...tell me: are you at your proposed property right now?"

*Proposed property,* not *business.* A lead weight dropped her gut. "Just—just down the street."

"Ah. Me too. As you know." He affected a false little laugh.

She did not return it.

He cleared his throat. "Could I drop by in, say, twenty minutes?"

"Why?"

A pause hung, as heavy as the exhaust clouds in the cold. "I'd really rather discuss it in person."

Another weight hit her gut. "Mr. Porter, is everything still all right?"

"Ms. Gavin, really—twenty minutes?"

Her belly sank even lower. "Y-yes. Fine." She hung up.

Jude waited, sunglasses now off and eyes staring.

"Th-the bank." Her lips were frozen. "They want to meet."

"Oh."

*Nice try, Switzerland.* He sounded as apprehensive as she felt. "Jude?" If there was ever a time she needed his expertise it was now. "It's not my deadline. What could they want?"

He flicked a shoulder, a gesture that tried to look offhand yet came off as phony as the banker's laugh. Panic flooded her mouth.

He did not miss it. "Shaynie." He spoke in his sharp voice, his *Python* voice. "You're a professional. Whatever he wants, hear it out. Walk straight into his office, look him in the eye, and roll with whatever punches you're given."

*But I don't know how to roll!* Panic scratched the backs of her eyes, made them wet.

He squeezed her hands. "Call me after. When you get back to Divinity."

"The—the meeting is *at* Divinity."

His eyes widened, only a fraction but enough to make her gut hit the ground. "Oh my God. This is bad. What's he going to tell me? What's gone wrong *now?*"

"Shaynes!" His laugh sounded forced. "You probably forgot to sign a form. To dot an i, cross a t. And now some pencil pusher has his shorts in a twist. You know how banks are."

No, she did not know how banks were. She only knew how her gut was. Heavy. Churning.

"I'll be by as soon as I see you're alone." He stooped, dropped a kiss on her cheek. "Don't worry. But...maybe pull your hair back. Put on a pair of glasses. Try not to look so…"

"So what?" Oh, God. She *looked* wrong too?

"Hot." He cringed, apologetic.

She stared at him in disbelief. How could he joke when—

"Shaynes, go. And trust me. I'm a businessman. I know when things will be fine." He shooed her, but she could not move; and as he walked away it seemed like the swarms of other moving pedestrians on the street were deserting her too.

In fact, as she forced herself to trudge the long blocks back to Divinity it struck her that she'd never felt so alone.

## CHAPTER TWENTY-THREE

ONE FOOT BACK inside the salt circle and the illusion of abandonment vanished.

Andrew was on the stoop, and he turned when she called his name. "Look who appears out of nowhere," he said. "I just summoned you with your gong."

Who'd been "summoned"? A mere wish for support, and here he was, the second time in twenty-four hours. *Thank you.* She climbed the steps, touched the door. "I wasn't expecting you after last night." She unlocked Divinity. "You couldn't have got any sleep."

"Enough." He fixed her with narrow eyes. "You okay?"

"I.... No." She disarmed the alarm and gave him the details—or lack thereof—of the loan officer's cryptic call.

Her brother, unlike Jude, neither dismissed nor invalidated her. "Want me to stay?"

How *professional* would she look if she crumpled with relief? "I'd be grateful." She dropped a colored stone in a jar. "And, by the way, I really *am* surprised you're here."

His mouth quirked. "I had to come. For the drawers."

"The body drawers?" Last night, as they'd scrubbed the bloodstain of paint from outside, she'd told him about hauling the drawers—but she hadn't meant today.

He leaned a hip against the window seat. "I need to get them out of here, 'cause guess who called this morning, woke me up in fact, said 'Hey, I'm dropping by the ex's old morgue, you gonna be around? We could grab a beer, catch up'?"

"Steve?"

"None other."

"I told him I'd deliver."

"I know. That's why I played it like you'd already made arrangements for me to bring them to him today. No need for him to *drop by*."

She swiped a hand through her hair, their shared gesture of dismay. "I feel like I'm always thanking you."

"Nothing you wouldn't do for me."

True.

"Kind of desperate, don't you think, Steve purposely misreading being hired for being hustled?"

*Keys can be cut.* The words tracked a cold path up her spine. "I should cancel that whole body drawer order."

"Nah." He waved a hand. "It's still a good idea. Just let me act as your agent."

She choked.

"What?"

Oh, nothing. It's just that someone else calls you 'Agent' too. And he thinks Steve's sketchy, just like you. Oh, and he also knows I was stalked and then raped, but he lied about that part.

"Shaynie Grace?"

"Last night." She spoke over her heartbeat. "You were right. I haven't told you everything."

He nodded slowly, crossed his arms. "Alright."

The doorbell gonged and killed every word in her throat. First Financial had arrived.

THE LOANS OFFICER, Richard *Just-Call-Me-Rick* Porter, stepped over the threshold the way she would touch a toe into a cold swimming pool. *Scared witless.* It took everything she had not to sneer. "Mr. Porter." She helped him with his coat. "Please meet my brother, Detective Corporal Andrew Gavin."

"A detective?"

His relief was palpable, and she wondered what he'd do if she told him that the big, bad cop was more afraid of ghosties and ghoulies than he was. "Forgive my lack of small talk, Mr. Porter—"

"Rick."

"—but given how quickly you wanted to meet, I can only assume this is bad news." She reached out, discreetly touched wood. *Let me be wrong. Please let me be wrong.*

The loans officer swallowed hard.

Oh, no. She wasn't wrong.

"Do you have a table, Ms. Gavin? A flat surface? I'd like to show you something."

She led Porter to her and Cameron's spot—would it ever be anything else?—and lifted the protection candle, set it aside.

It shocked her when Andrew grabbed matches and lit it. She gawked at him.

He did not look at her.

Porter drew papers from his briefcase, dealt them on the table very much the way she'd lay a Tarot spread.

A Tarot spread straight out of Hell. She stared at the papers—photos, actually—then at Andrew. Their eyes needed no words. The vandalism had never been a childish prank. It had been a tactical trick.

The photos, taken in the dead of night and printed on plain white bond paper should have been grainy. Indecipherable.

If only.

Every scrawled word upon Divinity was exquisitely legible, each its own bleeding wound. "Where did you get these?" she asked.

"They were dropped off. Anonymous."

"Bullshit," Andrew began. She spoke over him.

"Banks have more security cameras than staff. No one saw this guy?"

"Girl," returned Porter wearily. "Woman to be exact. She was tall, but that's all we know. She wore sunglasses, a winter coat and hat—she could have been anybody. *Everybody,* on a day like today. But Ms. Gavin, she's irrelevant. When a business is risky to begin with—and a hospitality venue in a morgue *is*—and then is the target of repeated vandalism—"

"Repeated? Last night was the first—"

He withdrew another picture, *Devil's Whore* carved into her door. "First Financial just *cannot* continue to finance this venture."

She'd seen the punch coming, but the impact still knocked her flat.

Andrew recovered quicker than she. "Can't you see she's being set up? Sabotaged?"

"Of course we see. And we think it's sick. But it hardly matters. The fine print of this loan—of all loans—affords us the right to forfeit a credit risk. And Ms. Gavin, this place is a credit risk."

Deep under their feet the furnace awakened, a rumble of strength beneath her soles. "But how am *I* a credit risk?" She fixed unwavering eyes on Porter. "Over the last week I've taken orders for over six thousand dollars worth of furniture."

"And as your loans director, I'm applauding. In fact, if you re-worked a business plan, eliminated the hospitality part of your proposal, chose a more suitable setting..."

The furnace blasted so forcefully that his photos blew onto the floor. He scrambled for them, suit coat bunching under his arms as he stooped. "As it stands," he said, voice muffled, "we just can't attach funds to a venue that's a target. First, spray-paint vandalism, and then what? Arson?"

A noise unfamiliar came up from the floor. Did the furnace just growl? Porter—and Andrew—cast slow eyes down the stairwell.

Shaynie didn't. "I have insurance," she said calmly.

"Would the policy you hold right now honor a claim if they saw these?" Porter had a tight fist on the photos.

Sunk. From every angle she was sunk. "H-how long do I have to pay you?"

"Ms Gavin, please believe that I take no pleasure in—"

*"How long do I have?* And no 'Ms. Gavin'. Call me Shaynie. That way it feels like you've at least wanted to know me. Although –" she laughed a little "- I'm fairly certain you never have. Now," She folded her arms. "Please tell me when you need your money."

He hung his head. "My manager gave me seventy-two hours. Shaynie."

SHELL-SHOCKED, she and Andrew were still staring at the door when Jude knocked.

He read their expressions without needing a word. "Oh, no."

She looked through him. At the maple parlor she'd resurrected. At the showroom she had built. At all the electrical she'd so painstakingly purchased, and the breathtaking beauty she'd sweated to restore. "I've worked so hard."

Beside her Andrew swallowed, and his eyes, so much like hers, were bright. "There's a place by Commonwealth," he said gruffly. "Cash guaranteed. No questions."

Commonwealth? That's where the pawn shops, soup kitchens, and sex trade workers were. There weren't lenders there. There were loan sharks. Still— "What sort of interest?"

Outside a shaft of light whizzed past the window, the eaves surrendering an icicle, a sword. And, "*Seriously?*" Jude burst out.

She looked away from stained glass.

Jude was glaring at Andrew. "With all due respect, Corporal Gavin, your little sister does *not* belong over by Commonwealth."

Her brother's jaw twitched. "Got a better plan?"

Efforts to stand off against Andrew were rarely successful, but Jude did better than most. "Yeah," he said.

Her brother—and she—hiked brows.

"Earlier, by 109th." Jude fiddled with his sunglasses, perched them up on his head. "I really *was* there for business."

"Okay. So…?"

"So that 'sexy morsel' I told you about wasn't a person. It was our coffee shop—the one I always get scones from. 'A Latte in Common'."

The shop under her old loft? "You bought another business?"

He didn't nod. Didn't say anything.

"Why didn't you just say?"

"'Say'? Right. A successful coup is exactly what you tell someone who's struggling to get her own place off the ground."

"Jude, we're friends."

"And that's why I kept my mouth shut."

He was right; 'cause if she were truly a friend, she'd hug him, pump his hand and say *Way to go!* As it was, all she could do was choke, "My buddy the mogul," and the words tasted—heck, *sounded*—like sawdust.

"'Latte' is a goldmine." He said it the way someone admitted to an A when they'd just heard their pal flunked the course. Then he took aim at her eyes. "There's more than enough room on the books for a second mortgage."

Her heart soared and her stomach fell.

"Want a partner?"

No!

He jolted. So did Andrew. "What the hell was that?"

She wasn't sure which of them asked. For that word, *partner,* it awakened not only a voice from the morgue but also a rush of memories behind her eyes: Her Dad, assessing one of her earliest projects— "Keep building like that, sweetheart and one day you'll be my partner". Then in a heartbeat he'd been gone, unable to offer feedback on the coffin she'd then crafted, made out of aged pine doors. *We'll meet again, Dad. Through an open door.* She'd kept all his tools, and as a teenager used them, honing her skills and feeling his spirit, feeling a legion of spirits, awakened with every piece of beauty she crafted out of reclaimed wood; mirrors, tables, that ornate, heavy wardrobe... "What's this?" Andrew, her then newly appointed legal guardian, had teased. "You trying to find Narnia, Shaynie Grace?" Then he'd pumped a triumphant fist in the air when that piece and every other she'd made sold at a local craft show.

It was at sixteen when she'd first turned the Tarot, astonished at how the cards read her mind. Then, in her twenties, the concept of Divinity had been born, and the morgue had been exactly what she'd envisioned: a living homage to scripture that said *To everything there is a purpose.* A time under Heaven.

She closed her eyes and saw the years, as cards, turn behind them—The Hierophant, The Hermit, The World. Learning, then meditating, then understanding. Those pictures, those years, they were her story. And this place, this amazing, living place, was the backdrop for her story. Her *real* partner.

But now…an ice fist grasped her heart. Now the bank was going to take her away. Her eyes hopped from Andrew to Jude. *More than enough room for a second mortgage. There's a place over by Commonwealth.* "I—I don't know what to do."

*Caution in all dealings.*

Was that the furnace, the boiler, or just her own head?

"Why not turn a card?" asked Jude.

Andrew said "My guy owes me. He won't say no."

At double-digit interest she didn't doubt it. "I— I need to think."

"Absolutely." Jude nodded. "No decision—and this is a big one—deserves any less than your full deliberation."

Andrew's throat clicked, the sound a whole sentence: *Know-it-all bastard.* God help her, she agreed. Where were her gratitude stones when she so desperately needed perspective? Where were those black burden rocks? "I'll do some math," she said numbly. "I'll think."

"Do," said Jude. "And I'll see you in a bit, at The Python."

Of course. Mustn't forget her shift at the multi-million dollar Python.

After he left, she looked around, helpless. "Maybe I really do belong there more than here."

The morgue was quiet, like it mourned. Andrew wasn't. "Like hell. You just belong there tonight. So go home, get ready. I'll take your key and load the body drawers, then look after this place and lock up."

"You'll—Andrew, no. I don't expect—you hate being here."

"It's not so bad, and besides…" He gazed around. "You won't hurt me, will you?"

The old morgue was silent, but the scent—lavender—was everywhere.

## CHAPTER TWENTY-FOUR

SHAYNIE SLID HER COAT ON but hesitated shy of the door. "Andrew," she said, and glanced askance, at the protection candle. "I … I can't go before I tell you everything."

Her brother sat, listened, and as the known pieces of Hellnight lurched out of her mouth an image struck her: bright bits of mirror coming together to reflect a distorted image, some parts clear, others still skewed.

Andrew took the story far better than she'd guessed he would. Aside from a wee bit of recoil (which would have been indiscernible to anyone who did not know him) as she described the bite marks and blood, all he did was peer at her, silent, for one long second, before he spoke, no longer brother but cop. "So you get violated, and months later Divinity gets trashed. Connect these, Shaynie Grace. Make them make sense. Tell me why some richie pro athlete who either hurt you or was *party* to hurting you would now give a damn if you open a lounge that sells furniture and spook-spooks?"

"I...don't know. Spite? Sport?"

He visibly chewed on it. "I suppose." He did not sound convinced. "Seems all we know for sure is that everyone's either bullshitted you or outright lied. You can't trust anyone."

"No kidding."

"Including Gray."

"Gray? He's the only one who's told me the truth."

The look he gave her was classic Andrew The Skeptic. She tackled it with facts. "Did you forget that Gray was with me last night, when Divinity got painted?"

"No, I didn't. It just seems to me he's been with you during a lot of crucial times."

Beside them, Divinity's protection candle burned soldier-straight. Andrew said, "Shaynie Grace, I'm no profiler, but I think—despite the fact that he's a lying sack of shit—that Weste nailed it; this person is looking to punish you."

"And you think that person is Gray?"

"Just a theory to think about: you're escaping The Python before him. Have never given two squats about him, even though he's always had a wild crush on you."

"No, he has *not*—"

"He has access to the drug culture, and on your so-called Hellnight you were drugged."

Drugged?

He read her expression. "C'mon. Do you really think what you described sounds drunk? You know yourself. You go quiet when you're tipsy, get more new-agey than ever. But you don't get—"

"Slutty? I told you: that night I was looking to—"

"Party hard. Yeah. But you didn't, did you? Think about what Steve—*and* Gray—have told you: you were dead weight. Your arms and legs wouldn't work. You don't have a single coherent memory."

Drugged. God. With all the lectures she'd heard at The Python about club drugs, roofies and God-knew-what other vile crap, she had never even considered the possibility. "Too busy flogging myself," she murmured.

Andrew looked at her, brows up.

"Up till last night I never dreamed I was a victim."

"Well, you were, and you are." He pursed his lips, grim. "And once Divinity's back on the books, this bastard might really get cooking."

PUNISHMENT THAT PUT DIVINITY in the crosshairs. Shaynie exhaled, a breath of frustration that took the form of a frost soldier in grim cold that had not abated but instead had grown deeper in the time it took her to finally leave Andrew and Divinity then head back to her south side brownstone to get ready for work. Now she trudged from her building to her truck, head up, eyes open and scanning all she could see. No need. All she sensed— or felt— was the cold and the absence of eyes.

Out of habit, she flicked the radio on as she drove to The Python.

"Violent antics in our team's dressing room are revealing some hush-hush trade rumors. Who wants out of our City of Champions? Find out after this!"

The station cut to a commercial. She poked off the dial. So Cameron's secret was out—and not only to the media. She had also told Andrew, in her recount of Hellnight. He'd been nonplussed. "I told you that, remember?"

"Yes, Detective," she'd replied, then scowled when he'd told her she shouldn't stray from the issue at hand by talking about "Goliath." And so began anew their debate: was Hellnight punishment or pleasure? *I knew you'd like this!* The unforgotten words continued to echo as her vehicle now bucked over the frozen speed-bumps in The Python staff lot, and she could not shake the sense that Andrew *and* Cameron were wrong and that her own instinct was right: whoever stripped her and bit her had thought he'd been pleasing her. *Although,* reasoned a voice in her head, one that sounded much like Andrew.... How did pleasing her fit with vandalizing Divinity and cutting the throat of her funding?

She cut the engine, flopped back in her seat. Punishment. Pleasure. They were connected, but how? She climbed out of her truck.

Eyes.

She gasped, and her breath appeared, a frost soldier. Her hand dove into her pocket for her taser.

No taser. And no eyes. Or at least not just one set of eyes. Over on the curb, dozens of Python faithful were queued up for the club, and as for her taser? In her rattled state she must have forgotten it. "First time for everything," she murmured.

From behind the staff door The Python emitted noise like throaty snarls. She bared her teeth back at it— "God, I hate you"—and pulled the door wide.

The air bled with music, a techno remix of a familiar track. *Let it Be.*

A chill grasped her chest. "No, I won't 'Let it Be'," she whispered. "But you'd like me to, wouldn't you? 'Cause you know everything about Hellnight, don't you?" She shoved the swinging door to the main club open.

The hologram python was waiting, hanging in the air like a visible stench.

"Game on," she told it.

It licked her, blew her hair.

"Shaynes!" Jude, at his station, beamed. "I am *so* glad you're here. We need to talk—"

"Hey baby."

The familiar little-girl voice came from behind them both. Shaynie turned.

Panties, her hair a rich, sable brown, was illuminated by the hologram python.

Shaynie swung around, stared at Jude. "You." Words could barely form. "You lied."

"Shaynes—" He looked stricken, and behind him the phone started ringing. He pointed at one of the red-headed Robots. "Please," he said. "Shut him up."

"Shut who up?" asked The Robot.

He ignored her. So did Shaynie, striding past him to where Chrystal Johns stood. "And you." She jabbed a finger at Panties' chest. "You have the gall to show up here after you and Nelson pulled your sick stunt?"

Panties' saucer eyes became wide, a *tabula rasa* of nothing. "Stunt?" She cocked a lost look at Jude. "Does she mean with Weste?"

Shaynie trembled, and, ignoring Jude's quick "No!", elbowed him out of the way. "Weste, Nelson, I don't know *who* was with you when you broke into my apartment!"

"Shaynes!" Jude grasped her shoulders.

She wrestled free. "Get your goddamn hands off me."

The hologram snake lit the bar, green wind blowing her hair back.

Shaynie caught her tresses in her fist. "First Gray, and now you lie about this…this *slut?"*

"Hey!" Panties covered her exposed chest as if doing so would somehow invalidate the title.

Shaynie glared. "Chrystal Johns, you must be one *exceptional* piece of ass."

Jude choked. One of the Robots snickered.

Chrystal Johns tossed her darkened hair. "Why, yes," she said. "I am. And if you ever doubt it, just ask your boyfriend, the intensely fuckable Cameron Wes—"

A sound—the crack of her flat hand against Panties' cheek—resounded before she even knew what she'd done.

"*Shaynie!"* Jude bellowed, and—

*"Whoa!"* The Robot, the one who'd picked up the phone, slammed it down, then dove, belted an arm around Shaynie's waist.

"Hey!" Gray, streaking through green slashes of light, also bolted up to the bar. "What the hell is going on?" He snaked a protective arm around Chrystal.

Panties wriggled from him. "She—she's crazy!" She pointed a finger at Shaynie.

Shaynie lunged.

The Robot held fast. "Perfect!" she barked. "Stop! You're half her height. You'll get your little ass kicked."

"Not hardly," Shaynie grated, struggling.

"Shaynie!" The Robot hauled her away, speaking low. "Listen: you're tight with Gray again which means you're tight with me. Now chill. Let us take care of this." She whistled and her sister, sidekick, whatever she was, fastened her hand on Panties' arm.

Panties bit her.

Bawling out a string of curses, the Robot sister dropped her arm and Panties scurried to curl into Jude, fingers alive on his throat. "Do you still have our protection?" she gasped, breathless.

Condoms? Was she serious? Shaynie and Gray shared a split second look of disbelief before he lunged.

Then the air exploded. Shattering glass. Splashing booze. Shaynie and her Robot jumped back but not before a bottle of gin smashed and splattered them with the scent of antiseptic juniper. "Holy shit!" said the Robot, and, "Guys!" Shaynie shouted, moving left, moving right. There was nowhere to grab hold of either of them.

"Jude!" cried Panties, and Shaynie looked up to see the other Robot sister, bitten hand wrapped in a bar rag, wrestle Panties into a headlock. Chrystal Johns upended, and *Omigod!* Shaynie squeezed her eyes shut. She had *no* panties on tonight.

The robot sister dragged her, wailing, to the door. Then the image was lost as a trio of bouncers bounded over the bar.

"Knock it off!" barked one.

"Break it up!" grated another.

"Ladies!" bellowed a third. "Scatter!"

Shaynie and the Robot hustled down to her station, where the redhead shot her a grin. "That's a righteous flat-hand you pack. You're a pistol, Perfect."

"And *you* are a pain in the ass."

The Robot beamed as if she'd won a prize. "Wanna grab a drink?"

Drink? Amid this chaos of tangled limbs and broken bottles?

The Robot waved a hand at the melee. "Shaynie, these boys need to duke it out."

Did they? Over the years she'd seen Jude and Gray argue a hundred times. Heck, a thousand. But now...Jude's glasses were broken and his face was bleeding—from the broken lenses or broken bottles, who knew?—and Gray's right eye was puffed shut, purple and tight. "I'll kill you!" one of them bellowed, and Shaynie caught a breath. "I don't know *what* they need."

Above her, on the television, a familiar voice said, "Sometimes guys just need to kick ass."

Startled, she and the Robot looked up. “Holy crap,” said the latter.

Noel Nelson’s battered face was a bizarre reflection of what Gray now looked like, and several teeth were missing from his smartass smile. “But he went too far,” he went on.

*He?* Shaynie turned, faced the screen fully.

The grunts and croaked curses on the floor faded as Nelson held court. “And he should be suspended. Have time off to think. ’Cause in fairness, if *I* was struggling with inconsistent play in a city that only loved me in a lukewarm way, I might lose it too.”

“You pig,” she breathed. “You’re lying. Spinning it.”

“Oh yeah?” The Robot, interested, took a pull from a beer she’d uncapped. “How do you know?”

Good question. “I—” Without warning, the hologram python blasted her, forced the words back down her throat, and behind her, the phone started ringing.

“Hold that thought.” The Robot sprinted for it.

*No thanks.* Shaynie reached for her purse while out of the corner of her eye, Gray clenched a hand on Jude’s throat, yelled, ‘Had enough? *Had enough?’*

“Yes.” She stepped away from them both. “I’ve had enough.”

“Uh—Perfect?” The Robot had the phone in her hand. “This guy is pissed.” She lobbed the cordless.

Shaynie caught it, knees gone to water, knowing without knowing how, just who ‘this guy’ would be. She raised the phone to her ear.

“I was the crazy fan with the fantasy,” he said.

All the air left the room.

“I was the one who watched you. I was the one who wanted you. But I didn’t lie. We did *not* meet on Hellnight. We didn’t have to. One look at each other and we both knew where we were going and what we were going to do when we got there.”

Beside her a bouncer jerked Jude to his feet, and the momentum made him reel and bump into her. She flinched at the streak of blood he left on her shirt.

“You still there?” Cameron rasped. “Or did you hang up again?”

“N-no. I’m still—”

“Nelson knew I wanted you. Hell, everyone knew I wanted you. But he wants what I want, remember?”

Oh, yes. She remembered.

"After you left that night Nelson got chummy with the guy I'd seen bawling you out while your buddies—Rasputin and Deejay—tried getting you sober."

Steve. He'd seen Steve.

"Then you said you woke up to *Let it Be.*"

Her head bobbed, no sound.

"Nelson collects Beatles music. Plays those bastards all the time."

Oh, God. She closed her eyes.

"So how much of a stretch was it to think that maybe Cheap Ring was so choked that he gave Nelson a key so he could teach you a lesson? How out there was it to wonder if maybe Nelson paid him—or some other sycophantic sludge—to paint your morgue while we've been playing away?"

Not a stretch at all. In fact Andrew would be intrigued to hear it.

"But that wasn't how it was," he went on. "'Cause today I wrapped my hands around Nelson's neck and popped a goddamn vessel in his eye. It was the closest I've ever seen a grown man to pissing himself, so when he says he didn't touch you, that he was *never* in your apartment, I believe him."

The hologram hit the bar, a cyclone of light and hurricane wind.

"So there you have it, Python Princess. The whole story. The whole truth. Happy now?"

Would she ever feel happy again? "Y-you could have just told me—"

*"Told* you? After you went on and on about how your rapist was some horny guy with a hot fantasy? Yeah, Shaynie. I'm sure I should have just told you."

"But I never would have thought it was—"

"Yeah, you did think it was me! Or had something to do with me! But nonetheless I still acted as your detective, and know what that's got me? Suspended from today's game. Ordered to submit to a drug test. A ten thousand dollar fine to the League. And that's all fine, but now any hope I had of getting traded might be gone."

"No! Cameron, the wish card—"

"The wish card? Let me tell you what I wish, Shaynie. I wish I'd never set foot in The Python. Wish I'd never wanted you. I wish I'd never even seen you, Python Princess, now get off my conscience. Get off my mind. Let me play hockey, and let me move on."

The line went dead. "I...I'm sorry," she said.

"You okay?" asked the Robot. Above them the TV blared.

"Cameron Weste was overheard saying that he wishes he'd never set foot in cold, northern Edmonton."

"But I never asked him to *touch* Nelson." She looked at the Robot as if maybe she'd understand. "I never asked him for anything."

The Robot cracked her knuckles. "Does someone need their ass kicked?"

"Yeah." She nodded. "Me."

"Shaynes?" A tentative hand found her arm.

Jude's nose was bleeding. His cheekbone was laid open. "Gray just quit."

"I don't blame him."

He aimed a gaze at her purse, wedged under her arm. "Shaynie, please don't walk out on me too. I—I need you." He looked down, kicked a broken bottle aside. "And we open in just fifteen minutes."

She, like he, stared down at the glass and the gore. It looked like an echoed collage of Hellnight. Except— "I didn't make this mess," she said clearly. "You did."

"Aw, Shaynie—"

She turned to the Robot. "What's your name?"

"Uh, Trin. Trinity."

Trinity. It figured. Stifling a mirthless laugh, Shaynie looked up at the ceiling. Green strobes streaked it, neon veins. "Well, Trinity," she said. "You're now tending bar. And I hope you have a five-hundred-dollar night." She turned on her heel.

"Shaynes!" Jude called.

She hesitated, hand on the door.

"We...we're friends."

"Friends?" She turned. Bleeding and blind, he looked lost, and a sharp little poke of guilt knifed her belly. She spoke over it. "You lied to me over a bimbo who—"*...didn't break into my place after all.* She swallowed. "—who you knew very well our best friend cares for. And why? Because you just had to screw some featherhead who'll clearly strip for anything with a dick? Friends." she spat. "Friends don't pull crap like that."

She turned back around.

"Shaynes, Weste! Weste phoned." It was clearly a bid for her to stay, yet the name, Weste, froze her with a new bolt of pain.

"He...he'll probably call back. He was really anxious to talk to you."

"He already has." She swallowed the lump in her throat. "And he told me he wants no part of my drama. Just like I want no part of yours." She smacked a palm against the staff door.

The hologram bellowed.

She whirled, confronted it. *"Fuck off!"* She hit its kill switch.

The snake vanished, but its absent light left a ghostly imprint on the air.

She turned, left it and the rest of The Python behind.

Her truck hadn't been idle long enough to cool off, and as she wheeled out onto Gateway she shoved the reality of her non-existent funding and the fact that she'd walked out on what very well could be a five-hundred-dollar night out of her head.

Divinity. What she needed was Divinity. She crossed the bridge, let the glittering lights of the downtown core absorb her.

Her morgue's parking lot was not empty. Andrew's unmarked, Cele's MG, and a couple of matching cop cars were all parked there. "Oh, no." Familiar dread sank her belly. "What now?" She was out of her truck and up the steps in one fluid motion, tears racing down her face as she opened the door.

"Oh!" She clapped a hand over her mouth. "Oh, my God."

## CHAPTER TWENTY-FIVE

It was finished. Every baseboard fastened. The crown molding all on. Every piece of furniture she had locked up in storage had been hauled in and set out. Divinity, her dream. *Done.*

She blindly slipped her boots off and moved into the display. A wardrobe, one open door draped with jewel-colored scarves, stood next to a chest of drawers carelessly spilling rich sheaths of silk. Candlesticks topped nightstands. Bookcases and door tables held strings of pearls and leather-clad books. She stared at everything, transfixed, until a throat cleared to her left.

"You're so early, *Cheri."* Cele gnawed her bottom lip. "We haven't unwrapped everything yet. We...we wanted to surprise you."

*Surprise?* "Astonish" was a better word. *Finished.* Beyond the showroom the lounge was warmed by more jewel tones; oversized cushions gathered around door tables alive with tea lights in wrought iron holders.

"You were closer than you thought, Shaynie Grace. And you *have* worked hard."

She turned.

Andrew, covered head to toe in some sort of powder, looked like a ghost. She laughed, the sound hoarse. "What happened to—" *you* dried up in her throat. What he leaned on. "The bar?" Perfectly fitted and fastened. "H-how? That countertop had been back-ordered indefinite—"

"Sometimes a visit from a cop can hustle things dramatically." He grinned. "But there was some assembly required." He held up her grinder. "Lucky thing you aren't the only one who learned a thing or two from Dad."

Gratitude was a rainstorm down her cheeks. "I—I don't have enough colored stones. And even if I did there'd never be enough jars. I—" She covered her face.

Andrew approached her, grin wry. "You can't afford colored rocks. You need to start using dirt."

She laughed, gurgly, and smacked him.

He swatted her back. "Stop blubbering and listen. After you left for the shit-pit and I hauled the drawers I picked Mink up, brought him over here."

"Mink? Your Four Pentacles money lender?"

"Yeah. And while he was here I showed him your books." He paused, waited for her explosion.

She didn't give it. "And? What did he say?"

"That he hasn't seen a bona fide paper ledger since the 1970s. And that you should move into the twenty-first century, get your stuff onto computer."

She did not smile. He cleared his throat.

"Twenty-seven percent and the barn board clock in the corner."

Her gorgeous grandfather clock in a loan shark's lair? Her bank account bleeding Twenty-seven percent? With Jude she'd pay regular bank rates. Still...a *partner.* She flopped her head back, looked at the ceiling.

"It's an option," said Andrew. "And could float you until you're established and can make another pitch to a traditional bank."

She chewed the inside of her cheek.

"It would show tenacity, Shaynie Grace."

"Which creates another issue, right? 'Cause no matter which route I go, my *friend* will see I've won the battle once I open these doors."

"Which may not be a bad thing. Upping the ante usually makes predators careless."

*Usually?* That was no guarantee. And to use Divinity as bait?

He read her look well. "It's safe here, remember?"

This from the guy whose rickety belief system held that even the Bible was just a big book of bedtime stories. On any other day she'd have leapt and cheered. But tonight.... "The ante has already been upped."

He, Cele, and two guys she'd barely noticed, cops according to their haircuts but both dressed in civvies, stared at her. She took a big breath. "I found out tonight that whoever called from my apartment wasn't who we thought." She recounted her phone call from Cameron.

Andrew nodded. "Yeah, I know."

She gaped.

He shrugged. "Richie athletes get what they want, and somehow Goliath got my cell number. Called me when I was dumping the body drawers off at Steve's."

"To say what?" she asked, mouth dry.

"First of all, to agree with me that you need your rear kicked for not telling me everything right from the start."

She said nothing.

"Then he told me how he went vigilante on Nelson, but all he found out was that whoever hurt you *wasn't* him."

Oh. So he'd made the call to get Nelson off the hook and ease his own conscience. Not because.... *Be safe Faerie.* She swallowed. "I-I'm glad you have a better impression," she managed, hollow. "You'd like him, Andrew. He—he's not a bad person."

Then why are you crying? He did not have to ask. No one did. "So." Her brother cleared his throat. "How long are you going to ride the fence over your loan options?"

Not long. She'd already burned up some of her seventy-two hours.

"You don't really have time for what the *real* businessman suggested." Andrew's lips jerked, a wicked smile. "That any decision requires your full deliberation."

"Andrew—"

"I couldn't fucking believe him. Seeing a vulnerable moment and turning it into a slick opportunity. *Acting* like a goddamn python, ready to swallow his prey whole the minute it was defenseless and looked like it could make him a buck."

She sighed. "Trust me—Jude wouldn't think he was making a buck. He's never been convinced that Divinity's feasible."

*Yeah, right.* All over his face.

She smiled. "Tell me: is there any man in my life you do like?"

"Yeah. The one who raised you after Dad was killed." He poked a thumb at his own chest.

She shook her head. Smiled.

"And I suppose I can stomach Weste," he added. "Unless you really *would* like me to clobber him with my billy club."

It was only half a joke, but still it chased the wet from her eyes. "My big brother." She traced her customary ankh on his forehead. "I really don't have enough stones to give thanks for you."

"Shaynie Grace, did it ever occur that maybe I don't have enough for you, either?"

No. It never had.

He gave a rare and vulnerable kind of grin. "You're my best friend."

A lump clogged her throat, stopped anything she might say.

"I gotta go." He turned, beckoned his minions. "We set aside a stupid amount of paperwork that needs to get done. Call me when you're ready to go home. Free police escort."

"I love you, Andrew."

"To the moon and back," he said, and he and his cohorts were out the door.

She finger-drew another ankh, a larger one, over the space they had occupied. "So." She turned to Cele. "What do I do now? You guys did it all."

"Monsieur Kevlin's doors? Complete them so you can pay this Mink the Four Pentacles person your brother the Knight of Pentacles found?"

"Or just complete them for Jude. God." She pulled a hand through her hair. "One of my oldest friends, and tonight I get all sanctimonious and rip his face off just because he fought with Gray over some airhead." She sighed. "Then I get here and see how *real* friends treat each other. Treat *me.* Karma." She squeezed the bridge of her nose. "I am dreading it."

"We are all guilty of errors in judgment," said Cele, always Switzerland.

"Some of us more than others," she agreed, and all at once could hear Cameron: *I wish I'd never seen you!* How could the absence of someone who'd been in her life for such a short amount of time make her feel so alone? "Would I sound greedy, childish or just plain pathetic if I said I wished you'd stay awhile?" she asked Cele.

"You would sound honest," Cele floated near her, kissed her cheek. "Now let us unwrap the rest of your things before we both leave."

A crate was still sealed in the corner and two more flat pieces, swathed in Styrofoam, were propped against the back wall. "I can't even remember what I had stored."

"Then it will be like Solstice come early." Cele brandished a box cutter.

Shaynie unfurled swaths of Styrofoam from one of the flat packages, laughing. "Good grief! I must have thought this was going to get in a car accident or some—oh." The Styrofoam fell away. "Oh."

*"Mon dieu!"* Cele stopped to stare.

The piece, a door mirror, boasted a narrow glass frame with green ivy vines embedded in the pane. "I can't believe I forgot this." Shaynie recalled now, with clarity, the old farmhouse she'd scavenged the door from, a rotting building that had been squatting in a wheat field, the stalks glowing in the fall sun like a legion of Wands. She'd known even before walking through the door that she'd discover something precious inside, and there had been the ivy door, a piece of beauty within utilitarian barrenness. Haute couture amongst starched gray pinafores. Not belonging, yet completely belonging. Inexplicably. Ethereally.

Kind of like a ceiling alive with impossible stars. Or like a man who flashed a slick whiplash smile while inside he ached for commitment. For forever. *Right side, left side. Dark and light. See them both. End your journey.* "Let me move on," he had said, the last thing he had asked of her. The last thing she could give him.

"Your Wish," she whispered.

"Darling?" said Cele.

"I need to wrap this back up." Shaynie gathered the sheeting. "There's somewhere it belongs."

"Ah."

Shaynie heard but did not listen to the warning chord in her voice.

"You wish to deal an Ace of Cups, *Cheri?* A gift of love?"

*"Oui. Amour."* It didn't hurt so bad when she didn't say it in her own language. "Will you help me haul this to my truck?"

"No."

Shaynie blinked. An expression had found Cele's face, ripples on a placid ocean. "Ivy," the older woman said. "It is not the best choice."

"But—" Shaynie skated a thumb over one leaf. "Isn't ivy—" *Love.* "—commitment? It's in every traditional bridal bouquet."

"*Oui,* yet—"

"And the way it creeps, the way it winds, ivy represents the journey of a soul and its spiral toward love, its true self." She didn't know if she'd actually learned that part or whether it was blind instinct talking. Or *singing.* She could give Cameron his true self. *His right side, his left side.* A little thrill took flight in her belly.

"Shaynie!" Cele barked.

She jumped, thrill gone.

"Ivy does not wind, ivy wraps. Clings and binds and becomes a living part of anything it attaches to."

"Yes, yes. Like commitment."

"*Non!* Like entrapment."

Entrapment? Prickles danced on her spine. *Trapped.* The reason he'd refused a door mirror in the first place. "B-but doesn't it depend on intention? If I give this door in the spirit of a wish—"

"Darling, even a gift given in love can be toxic."

*I knew you'd like this!* Shaynie clasped her own cold hands. "Then what if it was a request for forgiveness? A way to end things in peace?" God, listen to her. She was begging.

"If absolution is your desire, ask for it."

*Get off my conscience. Off my mind.* "I…can't." She looked away. "He won't listen."

Silence stretched until Cele broke it. "It is time I departed," she said.

Shaynie's jaw dropped. "You really won't help me?"

"I *am* helping. I am saying no." She drifted to the door.

Shaynie trotted after her. "Cele, *please.* Look at the size of that mirror. There's no way I can lift it on my own."

"I know," she said and reached out, hugged her.

She smelled of black licorice and warm cider. Good things that somehow made Shaynie want to stamp her foot, have a tantrum.

And Cele knew it, for she smiled. "You will thank me, Shaynie. Ivy either lets one soar or be strangled. And you do not want to take that chance. Never open a door you cannot shut." She left in a swirl of ice air and frost, and the morgue fell quiet.

*Almost* quiet.

A sound, rustling leaves, slipped through the silence behind her. Shaynie inched around.

A face gazed out of the ivy mirror. *Her* face, yet…its eyes. *Dark side. Light side.*

*Soar. Strangled.* Did she just say that? Or had the figure in the mirror? Magnetized, she moved to it, reached out, and again let her fingers bump over the inlay of ivy.

The etched glass writhed beneath her touch and she gasped. *That* had been the sound. Not leaves rustling. Leaves *growing.*

She met her own eyes. "Cele wouldn't help me. Will *you*?"

Her gaze stared warmly back. "An eclipse," Cameron had called it. "Gold behind green. Sun on a meadow." Not exactly. That gold light in her eyes wasn't sun. It was the ring of candles—the protection—she'd placed round Divinity.

And when her reflection smiled they all started on fire.

SHE DID NOT SO MUCH drive as coast the two blocks to Cameron's condo, inching over every bump and frost heave. Braking in the fire lane, she raised a hand to Impeccable, visible through the glass doors. He came out, coatless yet gracious in the vein-chilling cold. "Does the building have a loading dock?" she asked, and not only did he supply a valet but also a crew of the best-dressed custodians she'd ever seen. "They'll look after the lifting, Ms. Gavin." He glanced in the bed of her truck. "How in the world did you ever move this on your own?"

She had no idea.

He escorted her into the building, led her upstairs to where the custodians met them at Cameron's door, the ivy mirror affixed to a dolly. "Can you manage from here?" he asked.

*Absolutely,* said the woman sheathed in the mirror. Shaynie's neck prickled as she nodded.

She had no clue what force propelled her through the door and into his bedroom, nor did she know where the strength came from that lifted the mirror from the dolly to its stand on the floor.

But she liked it.

The power tasted like chocolate, lit the room like twenty-two stars in a sky, and as she stared at the hot-eyed, red-lipped woman in the mirror, it was like hearing a stranger she somehow knew. "Welcome home," her mirrored image said, and the glass ivy caught starlight and crawled, Shaynie watched it creep across the floor. Up onto his bed. There it would be able to wind about his wrists, bind him, prone…

Wait. *Bind* him?

Her breath caught, and as it did, her eyes, reflected in the mirror, became huge. Became *hers.*

Ivy clings. Ivy binds.

Oh, God. Cele was right. Just like Jude's little angels, this ivy was *alive.* "And I brought it here."

*"I knew you'd like this!"*

And now Impeccable and his crew were gone, and she knew, instinctively knew, that whatever force had allowed her to lift the piece on her own was long gone. "So now what?" She backed away from the glass. "I don't want him bound and strangled. I want him to soar." She looked up, found his stars. "Cameron, I swear."

*Faerie. Promise me.*

"Promise you. How?" Outside his window ice crystals rode an iridescent sky. Their presence dropped her heart back into place. Salt. Those ice crystals looked like salt. That, and her sack of tea lights—she'd forgotten them there this morning, left them lying by his phone. She bolted out of the bedroom, halting on his slick kitchen tiles.

Different.

She looked around. Not a thing was out of place, everything was still barren, yet something was different. Something was off. She grabbed her bag of tea lights—

No salt.

"Dammit!" Where the hell did it go? She whipped a gaze around, panicked, then reason seeped in. His housekeeper. He'd said she'd be by, and that was likely what was different too; she had been here, had put things away. "Oo-kay." She whipped a likely cupboard open.

A flurry of items plop-plop-plopped to the counter. Crackers. Pasta. Several cans of soup. Hissing, she scooped them up, stuffed them back on the shelves. Way-too-full shelves.

*"My shopper comes on the days I fly home."*

Oh, no. He'd said that too. Heart hammering, she pivoted, yanked open his fridge.

Full.

She shrieked, slammed it shut. *Get out!*

She had to run.

*No!* She froze fast to the floor. She had to protect him!

It was no choice at all.

She began batting open cupboards, not bothering to pick up things that fell out. “Salt!” She bounced up on tiptoe, crouched way down low. “Cameron, where is your salt?” Normal people kept it with their spices. But guys weren’t normal people. Not in kitchens. And apparently housekeepers weren’t either.

“I’d fire her,” she muttered. Every cupboard stood open, cans of soup rolled around on the floor. And no salt. She glanced at the door—*He’s coming!*—, then began to yank open drawers.

The first one clattered—silverware. The next was food wrap and tinfoil. A sob of frustration choked her, but then she jerked open the next and, “Yes!” A box, *her* box, lay there on its side. *“In a drawer?”* She grabbed it and ran, started pouring salt and dropping candles the moment her feet hit his bedroom.

The circle she made was snaky and uneven.

But still a circle.

“Protective circle,” she panted. “Here where you’ve allowed yourself to be present, to be stars, you are safe in this circle, Cameron, *not* strangled. You’ll soar.” She closed the ring and glanced furtively, fearfully, at the mirror.

It reflected a sweaty, frantic version of...her. Just her.

“Oh, thank God. Thank God.”

Never open a door you can’t shut.

“But I *did* shut it.” Weak-kneed, she smiled up at the ceiling.

Twenty-two stars rode the sky.

“There, my Ice Deity. The good in goodbye.” Her smile died. “And now, I’ll go.”

Starlight fell into her hair. *Shaynie.*

She froze.

*Faerie.*

The whisper did not so much come from above as around.

*Stay.*

Her heart bloomed and broke and she looked up, traced his number, alive in the sky. “Cameron Weste,” she whispered. “I will miss you.”

*Shaynie,* breathed the starlight, winding in her hair. *Stay.*

"Stay?" she breathed back. "What if that was my wish? A wish on twenty-two stars." Her eyes touched each point of light. "Would it come true?"

*Promise me.*

She closed her eyes. If she *did* stay and he came home, right now, what would he say?

"I wish I'd never seen you!"

It was like being grabbed by the ankle and yanked out of the sky. Had she gone crazy? To think he'd be turned on—or even remotely glad—to see her now, standing uninvited in his bedroom? "But I'm glad I saw you." She blinked pain from her eyes. "Glad for even the time I don't remember seeing you." She dug in her jeans, found a stone. It was valentine red, and she squeezed her eyes shut then held it up, showed his stars. "I am grateful, Cameron Weste. Even for what might have been." She touched the stone to her mouth— "The good in goodbye"— and placed it on his pillow.

Then she ran.

## CHAPTER TWENTY-SIX

If she stayed at Divinity she'd haunt her window until light came on in his condo then torture herself, wondering if he was looking down trying to see her too.

She called Andrew and he tailed her to her brownstone, came in to make sure nothing was wrong.

Nothing was.

"Want me to stay?" he asked.

"I'm okay." The solitude of her apartment, shabby yet alive with jewel colors, wind chimes, and jar after jar of bright stones, had never felt more like home.

"Call me first thing." He helped her push a bookcase over the sliding glass doors to her small balcony before he left, and she slid a barn-board buffet across the front door after she'd locked it. Then she crawled into bed, cell phone by her pillow. *Ring. Please ring.*

It didn't. Silence settled, and it wasn't until streaks of morning painted dawn in her bedroom that her phone, buried now beneath blankets, pealed. She scrambled for it.

JUDE KEVLIN.

It was tempting to just let it ring, but she sighed, touched the screen. "Hey."

"Hey," he returned, baleful. "We—uh—we're twenty-four hours into your seventy-two."

Eighteen, actually, but who was counting?

"Made a decision?"

'Cause there was no more time for her *full deliberation.* Still—"It's complicated."

"Not a bit!"

His enthusiasm made her cringe. She'd had no right to make him feel like he now needed to suck up.

"Just think Shaynes. No crazy interest, no more worries, and buy me out when you can. And if you want to."

He sees a slick opportunity to make a buck.

She fired a hand through her hair. Why be snarky over an offer she should fall on her knees for?

Caution in dealings.

She cleared her throat. "I just hate using my friends," she hedged.

"So we *are* friends?"

She massaged her forehead.

"Shaynes, I'm sorry about Chrystal."

"It's none of my business who you're with."

"Yeah, but you were right; I lied." He sighed, ragged. "I just wasn't prepared to tell you about her. Not after you thought she was in your apartment."

"Well, now I know that she wasn't."

Silence, then—"Shaynes?" he ventured, quiet. "Did you ever think that maybe Gray could explain everything about your apartment?"

Cameron had skated around it. Andrew had come right out and asked. Now Gray's own cousin was pointing the finger.

And he read her silence well. "Tell me he's not being completely erratic. Look what he did to *me* last night."

She began to protest that he'd kind of deserved it. He spoke over her. "Shaynie," he said. "He 'fessed up to a relapse."

"No, he 'fessed up to a slip." God. Semantics on slippery ground. Still— "Whoever's messing with me isn't Gray. It's...a crazy fan."

"Huh?"

"Long story." She crossed her fingers.

Either it worked or he knew enough not to argue. He shifted subjects. "Heard from Weste?"

"Yeah. Last night, remember?"

He audibly winced. "But nothing after? No callback? No text?" He trailed off, sounding hopeful.

"Sorry." She was proud that it came out disaffected.

He wasn't fooled. "What an idiot," he spat. "Stay put, I'm coming over. I'll bring coffee and something fattening."

Sugar, the Jude Kevlin fix-all. "I'm okay. Really. And anyhow, I need to hustle. Finish my work orders so I can get paid and take an *independent* bite out of my debt."

"Well…alright." It teetered out, uncertain. "Don't forget to set time out in your day to schedule a visit with me to my bank."

"Jude—"

"Just looking out for you, Shaynes. Just trying to make *something* right."

Memory carried her back to a teenage Jude Kevlin, standing on her doorstep with not coffee or scones but instead orange pop, her then-favorite. Her Dad had just died and orange soda was a sixteen-year-old boy's way of saying he was sorry. He had no idea that she'd never been able to choke down orange soda again. Didn't know that in that moment its taste—even its smell—became synonymous with her Dad being gone.

All he knew was that he'd tried to "make something right."

"I'm glad you called," she said softly.

"Me too."

"Tonight at our usual stations? Or am I fired for insubordination?"

"You kidding? I get rid of you and I'll be spinning music *and* mixing drinks all alone. See you at seven."

She hung up and immediately scrolled to her voicemail.

No messages. No missed calls. No Cameron. *Of course* no Cameron.

She took extra long in the shower. Was painstaking with her hair. Brushed her teeth, made her bed, did anything and everything to avoid going back to her cell to see that no one had called.

No one had.

His t-shirt still hung on her chair. She tossed it on. "Stay with me. I miss you."

Out in the living room, she flicked on the TV, shattered the too-quiet. A veteran home team player, whose face she recognized but name she couldn't place, spoke Cameron's name. She listened.

"Cameron Weste is *not* getting suspended." He swiped his sweaty brow with a towel. "He only did what anyone would do when they're antagonized over and over, strung out from the road, and dealing with a slump we've all been through."

The interviewer gaped at the camera, affected incredulity. "You're condoning how Weste lashed out at Nelson?"

The veteran hissed. "I'm saying that sometimes in this business tempers flare. And players—*real* players—don't bitch and moan about it."

Meaning Nelson wasn't earning himself any points for whining about his beatdown. And meaning that the team's allegiance to Cameron wasn't as "lukewarm" as he'd implied.

"Weste's an asset," confirmed the veteran, as though he had heard her. "Any team would be lucky to have him."

Doublespeak; the words were an additional plug for the desired trade that was now in the open. Her belly flipped, bittersweet. The protection circle. It was working already. "Soar, Cameron." She turned the TV off. There were gratitude stones in a drawstring sack on her coffee table and she reached for them, dumped a few in her hand.

A rat-a-tat bang on her door made the stones jump into her jar, a waterfall of musical clicks.

Bang-bang-bang! Again.

*Coffee and something fattening.* "And apparently no doesn't mean no." She sighed. "Jude?" she called.

"In his dreams."

Her breath disappeared and out in the hall the floor creaked, audible through the paper-thin door. Weste.

"Well?" he said.

"J-just a second." She tried moving the buffet from the door, but her hands—her everything—were shaking so bad it took three tries to wrestle it out of the way. Then unlatching the chain, fumbling with the deadbolt, it was like trying to do a puzzle with fingers too clumsy, too weak.

And her heart. It was going to beat her to death. She opened the door.

He was big, but she'd forgotten how big. And handsome—God, he was handsome—but she'd forgotten how chiseled his face really was. How storm blue those eyes really were.

"Nice t-shirt," he said.

*Oh, let me die.* Her arms criss-crossed over the smart-aleck slogan. "H-how did you know where I live?" She could think of nothing else.

"I went to Divinity. Cele made me a map."

*Bonjour!* She heard the cry, and, fighting a crazy desire to laugh, looked at the floor.

He stuck a finger under her nose. "You forgot this."

A silver flash, her Tarot Sun. She'd thought of it last night after she'd raced from his condo, of how she'd not retrieved it. Now it caught delicate sunlight, hanging from his knuckle. She slipped it off, careful not to make contact. "Thanks," she whispered.

"Welcome." He did not sound one bit gracious.

She unclasped the chain and re-fastened it, grateful to have something to do.

He watched her. "So is this the part where I thank you for your dark gift or the part where I apologize for blaming you because I got myself into trouble doing something you never asked me to do?"

Her arms moved this way and that on his shirt. "Would—would you like to come in?"

She did not expect him to say yes. Did not expect him to shrug his jacket off and kick his shoes to the side then follow her, one massive shoulder hitting a wind chime and sending it into song.

He winced and reached for it. She did too, and this time their skin did connect. Electric. She jerked away. "I-it's okay," she said. "I just…don't do minimalist quite as well as you."

He glanced at the buffet, awkwardly slid to the side.

"It's usually somewhere different. I had it across my door. Protection."

The way he glared at it, as though it had done something wrong, she stooped on impulse, flicked a black rock in a jar.

His gaze followed the sound of its click. "You left one of those."

No, she'd left him a red kiss on his pillow, beneath his stars. "Yes." Her voice cracked. "I was thankful."

He sighed, and she hated the pity in the sound.

"It's just something I do." She shrugged as though it didn't matter. "The colors are gratitude stones. They show that I'm grateful."

He looked at them, looked at her, then stooped, picked up the jar of black rocks, the question in his eyes.

"Those are burdens," she said.

He eyed them. "It's fuller than the gratitude jar."

"No, it—it just seems that way."

He hiked a brow.

"Look around," she bade softly.

He scanned the room and she watched him take in the dozens of jars, some large, some small, all winking with rainbows of light. "Clever Faerie," he rasped. "Are you magic?"

The little flutter shimmering inside hurt. "No." She shook her head. "Not even close. I just know to hang on to what I'm thankful for."

He shook the burden stones, made them clack. "And these?"

"I cast those away."

"Get rid of the things that hurt you."

"Yes." She met his eyes reluctantly. Fleetingly.

He sank to a seat before her. "You look sad, Shaynie."

Tenderness. It hurt so much more than anger. "A little." She avoided eye contact. "I have a lot of burdens these days."

He made a sound. Nodded. "Am I one of them?"

She made an indiscriminate movement with her head and reached past him, over his shoulder, fussed with a cushion that had bunched up when he sat.

He followed the path of her hands. "You make this chair?"

A neutral topic. *Thank God.* "It's not a chair. It's a throne."

He laughed. "Oh, so many directions, so little time. *A throne?* Fit for who exactly? A god like me?"

"In a way." She continued to fiddle with the cushion.

He grasped her wrist. "Shaynie, look at me. Talk to me."

*Oh, those eyes.* They made her want to start talking and never stop. Start *running* and never stop. What hurt more, having him hang up in her ear or having him here now, trying to make nicey small talk like *friends?* "Th-this throne comes from the altar of a church near my old place," she said. "A group of nuns worshipped there, and in the summer their hymns used to come through my window. Angel sounds."

"And this is how you thanked them? By stealing their altar? Wicked faerie!"

A tiny smile tried her lips. "The church got condemned, you delinquent. Too old and decrepit. So were those nuns when I hunted them down, asked permission to scavenge this wood. Frail little birds." She smiled, carried back. "They came with me, and while I took my crowbar to their altar, they sang, just like they used to. And in that moment they were *not* old. Their wings were new-born. They soared."

He said not one word. Her face got hot.

"Believe me, I've heard every jeer you can imagine from Gray and Jude. Andrew too. So you're in good company if you think I'm a flake."

He grunted. "What I think, Shaynie, is that sometimes the things you say sound just like prayers."

*Oh.* Her heart stopped. "Cameron?"

"Yeah?"

"Last night, did...did you mean what you said? That you wished you'd never seen—"

"—Python Princess? Yeah. I meant it."

"O-oh." Her heart free-fell. She stepped back.

He caught her hands. "Why would I want to see *her* when all I crave is you?"

## CHAPTER TWENTY-SEVEN

SHE HAD NO IDEA who moved first. No idea who uttered the incoherent little whispers that slipped, feverish and breathy, into each other's mouths.

"Ached."... "Dreamed."... "Missed you."

She whispered it. "Oh, I missed you."

When he stood, her feet left the floor. "Where?" he asked.

Aloft against his chest, she pointed, blindly, to her bedroom.

He buried his face in her neck. "Burdens." He abraded her soft skin with stubble. "Ever since I hung up the phone."

She soothed him, hands in his hair, slipping through short strands of silk. "I should have stayed in your room."

"You did. When I got into bed, you were there. I laid there feeling like everything that touched me, touched you."

"Ah." She trailed a finger down his cheek. "I know what that's like."

Shades of old sparkles leapt in his eyes. She jacked a brow. "And you knew that when you made me stay there."

The whiplash smile was wicked, wild, and in one fluid motion her t-shirt—and his—were whipped off, the wind lifting her hair as he flung them. She bounced dizzily as he dropped her to her knees on her bed.

Eye-to-eye, his smile was gone. "Shaynie, what have you done to me?" His hands rushed over her back. "I work out like crazy just so I can forget you, skate and skate and skate. But when I hit the shower, you're there, I feel you, all slippery under my hands. Under my mouth." His lips fell to the curve of her neck. "You taste the way pearls look."

Oh.

"Your voice stays in my ear and sings me to sleep, Clever Faerie, did you know that?"

No. She didn't know that. Didn't know anything. But what she felt… *everything.*

His lips moved against her ear and she jolted, her silver Tarot Sun flashing between her breasts.

He bent, put his mouth on it.

She cradled him there, and when he slid free she moaned protest, but he shushed her, kissed her, sought with his hands until he found her bra.

She shivered as the wisp of lace slid away. Shivered again when he pulled back, looked at her…. "My fantasy," he breathed, then descended.

Heat. *Hunger.* So wet, so warm, and she clung to his shoulders, hands racing over bulky muscle and smooth skin. She cried out when her flesh, peaked and pulsing, disappeared into his mouth. Quaked when his words hit her skin.

"God, I've wanted this." He dragged his mouth away. "I've wanted *you.*"

She yanked him down.

Feasting.

Tongues and teeth and breath, a co-mingling of gasps that sounded like starvation. Like satisfaction. She pressed into him and he answered, grinding against her. Growling in her throat, her fingers flew to his jeans.

He brushed her away, mouth locked on hers, and her knees left the bed as he lifted her, tugged at her.

There was a chill, then a sound—the slump of her jeans hitting the floor—and while part of her marveled, *how did he undress me?* another part, a bigger part, reveled in the freedom of her uncovered skin. Her *accessible* skin.

She tore her mouth away, hands roaming the planes of his face, holding him still so she could fasten their eyes. "I touched you every night." She needed to say it, he needed to know. "Did you feel it?"

"Like flying. And I couldn't catch my breath." He caught her mouth, pulled her into him.

He was hot. Hard. And that scent, *his* scent, the scent of her dreams... her head spun and she had to break free, gulp air. "Please," she whispered.

"Look at me."

She opened her eyes.

A perfect storm looked back. "Please what?"

Love me.

She didn't say it, but for the space of a heartbeat wondered if he heard it, because the look on his face, it took her breath away, and when he pulled her close and his hand slithered down… "Let me show you," he whispered.

Oh. Oh, *God…*Her cry split the air and her head fell back, hair swishing her bottom as his fingers probed—

"Yes."

—parted—

"Please."

—penetrated—

"Cameron—!"

"Ah, Shaynie." His breath tickled her throat. "You *do* want me."

She couldn't answer. Couldn't breathe. Could only feel, stroke after stroke until.... Starlight. Sunbeams. They crashed before her, light into light.

"Yes, my Faerie, now show *me.* Show me, show me, show me…."

She tried forming his name, but her only sound hurtled out like a sob, and she soared higher and higher—*I can't stop. Can't stop. I—"… can't stop."*

"Don't want you to." He kissed her, drank every cry, kept their mouths fastened and feasting until her quakes became slower and she became still.

Still. Stay, Faerie.

*Yes.* Her body, his body, sweat-slick and wrapped together, one rhapsodic heartbeat.

His mouth lingered on her bottom lip, teeth raking it gently. "Ready to come back to me now?"

She found his eyes. Beautiful storm eyes. "I never left you."

"Not true." He slid his fingers through her hair. It was wildly plastered against her cheeks and his chest and he combed it, straightened it. "Everything about that road trip was hell."

"Uh-uh." She shook her head. "Not everything." She raised her Tarot sun.

He held it between thumb and forefinger.

"I waited for you," she said, and as it slipped out she didn't know quite what she meant, quite what it was she was trying to say, and when a flash of pain—regret—lanced his eyes, the breath she drew was so sharp it hurt.

"Shaynie." He dropped the Sun. It twinkled against her skin. "This. You and I…" He drew a rough breath. "The last thing I want is for you to wait."

"It's not your choice."

Hunted. Haunted. The expressions chased shadows on his face. "You... you told me you don't make good choices."

She held up The Sun. "And you told me to show this off, shut you up."

The Smile. It raced through his eyes and she loved it. She loved *him.* She cupped the back of his neck, pulled him down. "Now let me," she whispered, and her free hand slithered down his chest, over his belly.

He clamped huge fingers 'round her wrist. "Stop."

Rejection stung from the inside out.

"Faerie," he chided. "You think I don't want to lay you down and touch you till the sun comes up tomorrow?"

"And let me touch you?" She wound her arms around his neck.

Another flash, like a gasp of pain, made his throat work. He leaned his forehead against hers. "The boarding call for our next charter is in just a couple hours."

She stiffened. Another road trip?

"Just a short one," he said, as though he had heard her. "Calgary, then back in the morning. Arena schedules are crazy. We have to work around everything else they host too. It's…" He broke off, spread his hands. "…it's my life."

His life. And the way he looked. Like he was waiting for the shoe to drop. For her to blow up. Sulk and swear. 'Cause 'goodbye' was resentment and bitterness and betrayal all wrapped into one neat, female package. *But not from me, Mr. Weste.* Stretching up she kissed his nose. "A flight that leaves in just a couple hours yet you're here, half-naked and a solid thirty minutes from the airport. You must have thought frustration would give you a little aggressive edge out on the ice tonight."

Sound rumbled from his chest. "Wicked faerie."

"Wicked? I'm not the martyr who gave and didn't take."

He tried setting his jaw, but his mouth twitched. Then he laughed. "Shaynie," He kissed her nose. "If you don't know that what just happened here was the most selfish thing I've ever done, then you truly are as naïve as you don't look."

"Told you I wasn't Python Princess."

He grinned.

"And, for the record, you can be selfish with me anytime you like."

His grin flickered then faded. "Faerie." He cupped her cheeks. "You have no idea what you're asking me for."

"Cameron, I know *exactly* what I'm asking you for."

Something drifted in his eyes. Something that looked like a wish. It took everything she had to lift his hands from her face. "But for now? You need to get out."

His storm eyes blinked, wide blue.

"You think you're the only one who has to work?" She slipped past him, climbed off the bed. "I need to pull off the deal of a lifetime today."

He frowned. "A deal—"

She pointed to the door. "Bathroom's down the hall, Ice Deity. Go make yourself presentable. You have a plane to catch. And I need some privacy to—uh—reassemble myself."

His gaze skipped over her skin. "Want help?"

"Hmph. What's that hockey saying? 'You miss a hundred percent of the shots you don't take'? You're too late, Weste."

He stared at her, tongue rolling in his cheek.

She crossed her arms over her breasts. "Get lost," she stage whispered.

Grinning, he stooped and grabbed his shirt, ambled into her teensy washroom like he owned the place.

Her eyes traced a Celtic love knot over the breadth of his shoulders before she wriggled back into her jeans and tossed his t-shirt back on, hugging it around her as she moved to the door. She retrieved his jacket from where he'd slung it. God, it was thin! Chrystal Johns needed to cough up his real coat.

His presence cast a shadow, and when she looked up, he looked lost. "Wow," he said. "You really *are* kicking me out."

"'Cause you really do need to catch a plane." She primly handed over his jacket.

"Do I get my shirt back, too?" His eyes skipped over the saying.

She protected it with her arms. "What was I supposed to do? Sleep in your bed naked?"

"That *was* the fantasy."

"You manipulated me."

"Uh-huh. One of those shots that I took."

She wanted to glower but could do nothing but grin. "Come." She pushed the barn board buffet completely away from the door.

His gaze tracked from it to her necklace. *Protection.* Neither of them needed to say it. He reached for her Sun pendant.

She covered his hand, then frowned. Something in the gesture, something in the unspoken word, "Protection"...she had seen something, heard something, just like this. Keeping their hands knotted, she held very still.

"Faerie?"

The memory—or was it just déjà vu?—vanished on his voice.

"Does The Agent have any clue who this guy is?"

"No." She didn't want to talk about it. Didn't want Hellnight between them. There was already enough that would keep them apart.

And he knew it, too. It was in the way he pulled her into him.

She rested her cheek on his chest. "Ever wish you could just freeze in a moment and not remember anything like being worried or scared?"

"Uh-huh. There are a lot of things I don't want to remember right now."

"Tell me."

"My flight. My life. The fact that I love what I do."

The wish card. Did he want to forget that too? She looked up, and again his face held a caught-in-both-worlds look, like he didn't know whether to be hurt or be happy. She tightened her arms, gently rocked them back and forth.

"He scores!" cried his phone.

"You know," she said. "I really detest that thing."

"And yet it's so accurate." He grinned.

She regarded him. "Hockey, Weste? Why not comedy?"

"So you could throw tomatoes at the stage?"

"Definitely. Now come."

"You're seriously going to walk me out?"

"Of course. I'm a gentleman that way."

He laughed and plucked her keys, gallantly locked the door behind them, then swept her down the corridor. No glossy hardwood or silken walls here. Even if the carpet *were* clean, it would still look like mud, and above them jaundice-colored stains crept over the ceiling.

"Place could use a little paint," he mused.

She stopped mid-stride, stared at him.

"What?"

He thought a relationship would meet certain death because of time spent apart but that a rotting building could be resurrected by *paint*? "And you say *I'm* 'colossally naïve'." She wanted to hit him and hug him. Laugh and cry. Instead she reached up, ruffled his hair, then pushed on the door. *Locked?* "The security deadbolt is fixed?" When had *that* happened? And—she looked down—the steps had been shoveled too. "Either someone got a raise or this dump is out to prove you right, that it is a decent place."

He patted the doorjamb as though it were a buddy, then trailed her outside.

Wet snow whispered from a warming sky. Still, he shivered when he tucked her under his arm. "I'll try to get your coat back," she said.

He shrugged. "I can afford a new one. Just need a spare minute to shop. Maybe next road trip. God knows there's always lag time."

Spare time on road trips hundreds of miles away but mere minutes free when they were in the same city? God. *Did* she resent it? Already?

She chased the question away, trudged with him to his vehicle, a truck like hers yet nothing like hers, they were a visual ten sitting side by side, her old half-ton's faded paint and rust dots—*age spots*, she corrected herself quickly—giving away its years while his was slick, shiny, and clearly brand new. "Nice ride."

"I could afford that, too." He eyeballed hers. "Want one?"

"I hope you're joking."

"Not if you don't want me to be."

"Well I *do* want you to be."

He lifted a careless shoulder. "I won't apologize for having money and liking to buy people things."

"And *I* won't apologize for not *needing* money or 'things'."

He said not a word, but she knew his expression. Had seen it many times on Tarot clients. A face that wanted to believe, but just couldn't. Usually the lack of faith made her feel sympathetic. Today it just pissed her off. "Your boarding call must be down to less than an hour." She briskly pulled her mitts from her pockets.

He grabbed her hands before she could put them on. "So kiss me goodbye, stubborn Faerie."

Goodbye. His definition of pain. *I don't think so.* "We're not saying goodbye." She wiggled out of his grasp. "This is just, 'See ya'."

"Ah. And, 'See ya' doesn't rate a kiss? Thought you said you were a gentleman."

"I am. And I didn't say, 'No kiss'." She stretched up. A little peck would be a sweet, 'See you soon'. A quick kiss would say, 'See? This is easy'.

Except it wasn't easy. And it wasn't quick.

Their mouths met and the sky exploded, sunbeams and starlight. She clung to him. *Okay. You were right, I was wrong. Please don't go.*

He made a harsh sound, a greedy sound, a sound not like skin hunger but *soul* hunger; yet as snowflakes drifted, the kiss drifted too. Slowed, and became silky. Became soft.

When they broke apart, he was as wide-eyed as she felt. "You lied when you said you weren't magic," he whispered.

She shook her head but knew she now wore his look too, hurt and happy, and this time there was nothing either of them could say that would make laughter chase it away.

"Shaynie." His forehead fell to hers. "I don't know if I can go where this will take us."

"I know."

"I'll hurt you."

"Then I'll have chosen to be hurt."

He closed his eyes.

"Cameron, please don't make the choice for me."

He lifted his lids, looked at her.

*Looked* at her. A sheet of cold found her back. *Eyes.* Out of nowhere they'd returned. Were behind her. "You need to go," she said. Thank God her voice sounded calm.

He wasn't fooled. "What is it?" He looked over his shoulder.

*Not behind you. Behind me.* An eyeless angel. A shudder scored her spine and she hid it by briskly rubbing his arms. "Your flight. That's it." *Now, go!*

Doubt rippled over his face.

She stepped back. "Cameron, look at this snow." It was all she could do not to turn around, search the street behind her. "The highway'll be a mess and the airport is—"

"—twenty minutes away. Yeah, I know. But—"

"But, nothing. You need to go."

The breath he blew out gave her enough time to shoot a covert glance behind her.

Eyes. Still watching.

Her heart tripped into overtime.

He captured her waist. "Goodbye. There. *I'll* say it." He pulled her close.

"No!" She stepped back. No more kissing. No more touching. Someone had already seen way too much. "Cameron...see ya."

Hurt. Happy. Again, both floated through his eyes.

She grabbed his hands, helpless not to, and as she squeezed them she prayed that whoever was behind her could not see. Because whatever she was sensing it was more than just Eyes. It was *rage.*

## CHAPTER TWENTY-EIGHT

SHE RUSHED CAMERON into his truck—"You'll miss your boarding call!"—and held her breath until his taillights were barely visible. Then she bared her teeth in the direction of Eyes. Look *me* in the eye, you coward.

Behind her a horn blared, shredding nerves that already seemed to jitter under her skin.

"Shaynie!" It was Steve, hopping from a vehicle he'd parked haphazardly in the tenant lot.

She shrank back. *Good God.* Cameron had called him skinny, but when had he become skeletal? And so *pale*? "Hey there." Blindly, she reached back, opened her truck and perched on the driver's seat.

*Eyes.* Did they still watch from across the street or—

She assessed Steve, one finger over the panic alarm on her key fob. "What brings you by?" Damn it, if there was ever a time she needed her taser—where the heck *was* her taser? "I didn't know you even knew where I lived now." *Keys can be cut,* Cameron had said. Her gaze scurried between Steve and where she'd sensed the presence across the street.

"I didn't," Steve said. "Kevlin told me, last night when I was at The Python looking for you."

Why thank you, bigmouth Jude.

Steve approached, leaned an elbow on the side mirror of her truck. She swallowed a gasp. Up close he looked even more ghoulish.

"I wanted to show you that I almost have your Tarot suits ready," he said.

*Tarot* pronounced like *carrot*. "It's—" The correction died on her tongue. He'd unfolded a piece of paper he held and she gasped. Heck, even the Eyes across the street seemed to sink back in their sockets. "Stephen," she croaked. The picture, of her suits, was phenomenal. "They're enormous," she breathed. And seamless. Even appeared, despite the grainy quality of the photo, to have luster. "Stunning," she said, eyes traveling their presence. He'd gone so far as to even add colored glass to bejewel them. "You're amazing. And so fast!"

He beamed so bright that the sunken pallor of his cheeks lit up.

The contrast stole her smile. "Stephen." She examined him. "Are you okay?"

His brow puckered.

"You're pale. So thin." Good grief. She sounded like an old clucking Baba. Still— "Are you sick?"

His mouth hitched, an expression she knew. "Heartsick, maybe." He grinned, lopsided. Hopeful.

*Oh, damn.* "I thought you said you were seeing someone."

"I am. But she...she's not you, Shaynie"

She closed her eyes.

He grabbed her hand. "I loved you."

"Steve." Gently, carefully, she slipped her fingers away. "Tell me something—what's my favorite TV show?"

"Your favorite..." He trailed off, endless silence.

"Trick question. I hate TV shows. That's why I always keep it on sports. How about my Sun Sign?"

"I—well, your birthday is this month, February..." Another acre of silence elapsed.

"Pisces," she supplied. "How about my eyes?" She closed them. "What color?"

"Blue," he said immediately, decisively. "They're blue."

*No. They're an eclipse.* She opened them, looked at him.

His cheeks went pink. "So is this why you wouldn't take my ring? 'Cause I couldn't answer questions about eyes?"

*Eyes.* A shiver scurried up her spine. "No. I didn't take your ring because I couldn't have answered those questions about you, either. Steve, I'm not who you think I am. Who you assume me to be."

"Oh, yeah? So then who are you, Shaynie?"

Someone magic. Someone's Faerie. Someone who says things that sound just like prayers. "Someone you really aren't in love with."

Anger. Disappointment. They twitched on his face, but something else was there too. Relief. She seized it. "And you *know* it's good that we're done."

He didn't agree, but...she smiled a little. He didn't argue either.

The crook of his arm rediscovered her mirror. "Know what I do know?"

"Let me have it."

"That you're right—you're not who you were acting like the night we broke up." He looked down, looked sheepish. "And I knew it that night. Despite what I said the other day on the phone."

"And that was why you were going to rescue me even after everything with the ring." And why Cameron was wrong. No way had Steve given a key to Nelson. Or anyone else.

"Yeah," he said gruffly. "And you wanted me to rescue you, like I said. But the gargoyles, they had it all under control. One of them even laughed in my face, told me how glad he was that you'd dumped my 'loser ass'."

"*What?*" Gray or Jude said *that?*

"Oh, waltz them off the pedestal, Shaynie. They're childhood buddies, not angels."

But not asses either. At least she'd never thought they were. "Which of them said that to you?" she asked hotly.

"Oh, Christ. Why does it matter now? And who knows anyway? I never could tell those two apart."

'Cause while he could gaze at a hunk of metal and see—then create—the most amazing art, he had no clue how to look at anything else.

But then again, maybe that was why he could create such amazing art. It was one hundred percent of his focus. She glanced again at the picture of the suits, besieged by an irrational yet irresistible urge to climb into the photo, physically touch those magic pieces.

"Jude and Gray look exactly alike," Steve went on, taking her quiet as argument.

She rolled him a look. "They resemble each other, Stephen. They're cousins, not twins."

He frowned. "Well...one has a goatee. It was that one."

Neither Jude nor Gray had ever worn a goatee. And she didn't need to say it. He grinned, red-cheeked. "Maybe you never noticed," he tried.

She shook her head, laughed a little.

He did too. "Well at least you can't say you're the only one I'm not real observant with."

"You are *completely* oblivious. Except for..." She gazed, enraptured, at the picture.

"Yeah." His smile dwindled, and he folded the page, crumpled it.

She winced. That hurt. Somewhere between her heart and her gut, Steve crumpling the photo hurt.

"About these," he said, unaware that she'd just placed a hand over a wounded spot in her middle. "You asked why I look like shit. Can...can I be honest?"

Her brow leapt.

"It's these things. I want rid of these things. Like, yesterday."

"'Rid of them'? As in pick them up and pay?"

"Yeah. As soon as they're done—a day, hopefully not two. Would you?"

The better question was, could she? No. Not without either Mink or Jude. "I...well, you're quicker than I thought. Why's it so important to get them out? What's it got to do with—"

"Because, Shaynie, I can't eat, can't sleep, nothing, with these damn things on my property."

Her eyes felt huge.

"All your other weird crap, it never bothered me before, but these—"

He unfolded the picture, and the way he recoiled—it mirrored the way she leaned into the photo. *I want you.*

The suits gleamed.

*I need you.* Still—pick them up? "Steve, I—" *Don't lie.* Shame singed her cheeks. "I can't. I'm a little strapped right now, so—"

"So owe me. Make payments. Whatever."

She gaped.

"A few minutes ago you said I worked fast." He swallowed, Adam's apple bobbing. "That's not it. Me and my students—we're not working any differently than we normally do. It's these body drawers, Shaynie. It...it's like they're making themselves."

*Promise. Protection.* The whisper, a breath across the river, tickled her ear. Had Steve heard it too? She searched his face.

His cheeks were brick red. "I know I sound crazy—"

"No. You don't." Heart pounding, she tracked a gaze back to the picture.

Sopping wet from the snow that had melted against it, the suits nonetheless gleamed, so luminous that she knew if she touched the photo she'd *feel* them. Smooth. Warm. "Enchanted," she whispered.

"Nuh-uh," said Steve. "Not enchanted. More like pissed off."

She dragged her gaze from the photo.

"One of my students swears that when he worked on the pentagram, it bit him."

"Pentacle," she corrected and looked back at the picture. The suits glowed.

"Whatever. I want them out."

"And I can pay you—"

"Christ, Shaynie, just have them. Please."

He *was* terrified. *His eyes.* She froze. *Eyes.*

"What?" His gaze skittered around. "Shaynie, *what*?"

The Eyes. They were still present. Except...a smile slithered over her face. This time they weren't watching. This time they were running.

This time *they* were scared.

"Sh-Shaynie?"

She captured his dark-ringed gaze. "Don't worry," she said, and knew, beyond a doubt, that if she could see herself she would look like that Ivy Mirror Shaynie. *Luscious. Lethal.* "My Tarot suits aren't going to hurt you."

But they were going to hurt someone. She just didn't know who. And didn't know how.

## CHAPTER TWENTY-NINE

Climbing Divinity's stoop, she wagged a finger. "You scared Steve."

The old morgue, had it had shoulders, would have shrugged.

She opened the door and lurched backward. Her own reflection was waiting. The Ivy Mirror. Cameron had said he'd stopped at Divinity, that Cele had made him a map. He'd failed to mention that he'd brought his mirror back in the process. Breathing away the shock, she righted the hem of her coat.

Her reflection did not move.

She went utterly still and Ivy Shaynie, before her, stared back, trapped in the glass.

*Trapped?* Her head jibbered. *She's not trapped.* "She's free," she croaked.

The reflection smiled, and its features...*My God.* Her own cheeks were not that creamy. Lashes not nearly that sooty. And that smile.... *Luscious. Lethal.*

"Darling?" Cele drifted from the vicinity of the divining rooms to the door.

Shaynie kept one eye trained on her twinned image as she shrugged off her coat and slung it over the mirror.

Cele waited, a ream of paper in her hands. "A *dossier* from the Knight of Pentacles' Mink," she said.

*That* was the contract? It was a tome. Had to weigh at least a couple pounds. Shaynie took it, began flipping through its preachy legalese. "Thanks," she murmured and sank to the window seat, eyes caught by the words PROPRIETOR SHALL and the long list of black bullets thereafter. And she'd thought this option would keep *her* in control? She flipped page after page, the document as compelling as any bestseller but for all the wrong reasons. With every bullet the decision she leaned toward gained firmer ground, and for the first time since she'd started bartending, she couldn't wait for the day to be over, for her shift to start. Never had she needed The Python more than tonight.

JUDE LOOKED SO PREOCCUPIED when she approached him at his station that she was hesitant to tap his shoulder, afraid she'd startle him. He startled her instead by speaking before she could: "Have you heard from Gray?"

She hadn't. Although when Andrew had been by to share that nothing had turned up on her vandal and/or the accomplice who'd delivered the pictures to the bank, he'd said he was going to track Gray too, ask him for more details on Hellnight. "Good luck," she'd said. "Gray had a blow-out with Jude and now it seems he's in a snit with everyone. Hasn't returned a single text or call." And she'd tried, especially after wallowing in the misery of that loan shark contract. Feeling crappy had reminded her that Gray felt lousy too. She'd tried calling, knowing that whatever they said to each other would turn everything around, make it bright.

"Shaynes," Jude said now. "He's missing."

"Missing?" Dread lanced her stomach. "As in—"

"As in, he's screwed off with every track he's ever mixed, and all his equipment."

*Oh.* Missing from *The Python.* "Jude, he's angry. You know how he—"

"His apartment looks abandoned too."

Lead reinvaded her belly. "So where do you think he—" A sight over his shoulder snagged her voice. *"What* the *hell?"*

Panties, wearing a team jersey fashioned into a mini-dress, shimmied over to Jude's end of the bar, a change belt affixed to her waist.

Facing Shaynie's incredulity, Jude seemed to shrink. "She...lost her job," he mumbled.

"So you brought her here? And you wonder why Gray's taken off?"

The hologram python roared at the bar, and, "Forgive me, Shaynes," Jude said starchly, "but I'm *not* in the mood to have my moral inventory taken."

She bit her tongue so hard she tasted blood. *Don't blast him. Not tonight.* "Well." She kept it light, gazed around. From Panties the barmaid to Gray's darkened stage, how on Earth would they salvage this night? "Maybe I should read The Python's cards."

"Please. I don't think I've sunk to witchcraft just yet."

*Alrightie, then.* She turned on her heel, stalked to her station. "Temperance," she muttered. "Grant me patience." No music meant no money. Clubbers came for the atmosphere, and Gray made it what it was. She pointed the remote at the TV, awakened the game.

The team was just arriving at the opposition's arena, and the camera, accompanying them, lingered on each suit and tie who strode by. "Oh," she uttered. *A God,* Cele had said. "Yes indeed." The suit he wore was tailored, 'cause nothing off a rack fit a frame that big. That defined. She stared at the screen. *Look at me, Cameron.* He didn't. His eyes were fixed on his phone.

Beneath her counter her cell chirped. She dug it out.

<My countenance is frustrated>, said the screen.

Laughter danced from her mouth. She typed, <Whose fault is that?>

*Chirp!* <Look in the mirror>

A mirror? The memory of Ivy Shaynie scored a tremor up her spine. <Find your own mirror. You did not take what was freely being given>

"Shaynes?" said Jude.

<But I will>, answered her screen, and when she looked up he, now facing the camera, shot The Smile.

*And you say I'm wicked?* Her eyes lingered on the screen.

"Perfect?"

She ripped her gaze from the TV. Trin and Jude were both waiting. "Me first." The redhead flapped a scrap of paper scribbled with drink orders.

Blushing, Shaynie read it. Trin hunched over her counter. "Shaynie?" she murmured, out of earshot of Jude. "I'm worried about Gray."

The look she wore, different than Jude's, was one Shaynie had felt on her own face more than once. "Oh, Trin." Her heart sank. Gray's disappearing act was far more than a tantrum over Jude and Panties. "Please tell me that it was just a slip and not a relapse. Is he using?"

"No! Well…I don't know." Trin chewed her lip, debating, then—"Here's the thing," she said. "Anything Blaze and I do is strictly recreational. But around Gray? We do nothing. He's too preachy and—" She smiled, the veneer of hard-ass chick gone. "We like it. We like *him.*"

"Me too. Heck, I love him. He's been my buddy since I was thirteen." She pulled out her phone, used the keypad. <Hey, The Python misses you—but not more than me and Trin.> She held it up so Trin could see then hit *send.*

Trin looked dubious, and Shaynie nodded at the expression. "He *is* stubborn," she agreed. "But he's not stupid. Let's assume he's just going to his meetings."

"He will be," said Trin, but with more hope than conviction. Shaynie reached down, dropped a colored stone she hoped would carry a wish: *Please don't let Panties and Jude and Nelson derail more than a dozen years of clean and sober.* Above her the TV blared. "Scores!"

Her gaze shot up.

Noel Nelson was on the screen, arms in the air.

"Noel!" cried Jude. "Way to go!"

The Python Pack, a modest mob despite the lame music—Jude's iPod plugged into speakers—cheered, and Shaynie was carried into the rhythm of mixing, pouring, and popping bottle caps. "Scores!" the TV cried again, minutes later, and as she loaded Trin's tray she glanced up, saw Cameron's arms in the air.

"Yes!" Her arms flew up too, and "California, here we come!" she cried on impulse.

Delighted coins rained from the sky. *Thank you, Pentacle Queen.* She laughed, caught up in the moment. *And thank you, my Ice Deity.*

Her tip goblet sang.

Jude sauntered over when there was a lull. "Little Miss Rich. You scooped every customer."

"Must've been the witchcraft," she quipped, then bit her tongue. *Don't shoot your mouth off. Ask him. Ask him now.* She squared her shoulders and cast a steadying gaze over the dance floor. Yikes! Panties, change belt askew, teetered on her high heels, still trying to take drink orders. "Jude," Shaynie clucked, "go rescue her. She's drowning."

He glanced over, shrugged. "She wanted the job."

Mr. Sensitivity. No wonder he'd never kept a girlfriend.

"So?" He watched her. "Have you made a business decision?"

Ah, business. His *real* girlfriend. "Yes." She nodded, but the chin she tried to keep straight wobbled and she was suddenly unable to see anything other than the water in her eyes. Nonetheless— "Hey, partner," she managed.

Jude snapped his fingers over their heads. "Trin!" he barked. "Now!"

Trin ambled over, gyrating to music that had switched tracks to the mournful *Hey Jude.* "What?" she asked, simulating a pole dance. "You want me over here to dance to your theme song?"

Shaynie coughed out a watery laugh but Jude scowled. "Grab your sister," he said. "We're breaking."

Reality returned the moment they hustled into the back room. "Shaynes." He shook his head as she haphazardly tried to stop sniffling. "It's just money."

"Just money"? Right. Only someone wealthy could miss the whole point.

"I'm not taking Divinity away from you," he said. "I'm giving it to you."

"Y-you'll need me to…come to the bank." She swallowed, tried to sound like his definition of 'professional'. "Bring my legal land description, my ledger and—"

"No need."

Her mouth snapped shut.

"I already talked to the bank and for the amount you need? My loans officer didn't even blink. He'll just stretch my line of credit."

"O-oh." Her face burned. *Colossally naïve.* Wasn't that what Cameron had called her? Although— "There *is* something you need to know before you sign for any loan or line of credit."

"Oh?" He waited, face a combo of cocky amusement and superiority that made her glad, suddenly, that she really did have something to say that would shock him.

"Divinity is a credit risk," she announced. "And not just because it's New Age or set in an old morgue."

His eyebrows climbed, just a hair.

"I have a stalker." She held his gaze. "From the night I broke up with Steve. The night I got so drunk at that party."

It worked. His eyes grew huge behind his glasses. She raised her chin. "That same guy also raped me that night."

"What? He ra—"

She waved him off. "Don't fret. I'm fine. But this guy...whether he's playing some sadistic game or has a crazy vendetta, he's the reason I lost all my funding."

He was wordless, so incredulous she had to break eye contact. There was a sticky splotch on the floor, possibly a far-reaching splash from last night's brawl. She toed it, shoe making a small sticking sound in the silence.

"I—I had no idea you'd been so scared," he said finally.

Her cell chirped and they both flinched. She brought up the message.

<You won't be alone tonight>

Her heart screeched to her throat until she saw the name of the sender—*Cameron Weste*—, then she smiled. <Why?> she typed, <Are you coming home?>

A second elapsed. <I wish. I texted The Agent. He said he has a cop following you from The Python to my building tonight. You won't be alone.>

Andrew had told *him* that but not her? Although…she checked her voicemail. It was blinking. *Oops. Sorry, big brother.* Her cell chirped again. <No stealing any t-shirts tonight either. Your sexy underwear is all you need.>

Sexy underwear? She didn't own a single pair that weren't yawn-white cotton. Including the ones he'd stripped off her today.

"Shaynes?" said Jude.

She held up a finger, typed <Beauty must be in the eye of the beholder.>

An answer appeared instantly. <Beauty was under my hands this morning. Beauty will be in my dreams tonight.>

*Oh.* The ball of her thumb caressed the screen.

"Uh—Shaynie?"

<Stop making my knees weak>, she typed. <I still have to work.>

*Plink!* <Your deal of a lifetime?>

Her smile withered. Jude cleared his throat. "You done?" he said dryly.

*More than you know.* "Yeah." She palmed the phone, but when it chirped again she could not resist a quick peek.

Not Cameron. *Gray.*

<I do NOT miss The Python and it's poisoned YOU>

She gasped. Jude frowned. "What?"

"Gray," she said, but before she could get more out, her cell chirped again. Neither Cameron or Gray, *Steve Lonigan*, read the screen, and the message: <Burning midnight oil! Will have these #$%# suits finished VERY soon!> had an uncharacteristic happy face icon flashing right after it. She shook her head but then the screen darkened, its blackness reflecting *her* face.

Or, rather, a version of her face.

Ivy Shaynie gazed out of her cell. *Protection,* she mouthed, and on the heels of the whisper every snake in the staff room hissed.

## CHAPTER THIRTY

When she woke beneath Cameron's starscape she grabbed her cell from his nightstand.

No new messages. Gray hadn't responded to her repeated callbacks and no Cameron this morning, either.

She set the phone back beside a book, clearly new. *Tarot For Fools.* Grinning, she picked it up, delighted to see it already had underlined passages, but shivering when she saw one circled picture. The Devil. And he'd underlined words in the text below it. *Obsessive. Manipulative. Greedy.* A note was scratched in the margin. *Shaynie's stalker. WHO?* He'd underscored it.

"I wish I knew," she said. Andrew was no closer, either. Last night it was he, not some anonymous cop, who'd stayed on her bumper all the way to Divinity, and he'd accompanied her inside when she went to fetch clothes, interested in all she could tell him about the brawl that had seemed to send Gray underground.

"Funny that your boss didn't tell me any of this when I saw him yesterday," he said.

"Why did you see Jude?"

"I wanted the guest list to your Hellnight party. Of course, he didn't have one. Said all his guests that night were *discreet word of mouth*." He said it mimicking Jude, a superior-sounding drawl, and she grimaced. There was no time like now to 'fess up to accepting Jude's line of credit.

Andrew polluted the air with his own inventive brand of profanity when she did. "Mark my words, little sister: he's a mercenary bastard." Slamming into his unmarked, he then inched along behind her, hunkering in the fire lane of Cameron's high rise until Impeccable, seeing them through the window, emerged to wave them down to the belly of the building, where tenants parked.

Membership, apparently, had its privileges.

A quick ankh in the air for Andrew, then she'd ridden the elevator into the sky, mentally casting colored stones.

The first thing she'd noted was that the condo had lost a bit of its vapidity. Subtle differences softened its edges, such as crumbs on the counter. A plate in the sink. A sweatshirt tossed on the back of the sofa.

Her sleep had been deep and dreamless. And now she hated to leave, but...

Jude's money had not come without strings. Last night, in the midst of taking exhaustive notes about the terms of his offer and a repayment regime, she'd asked one more thing of him—"Please keep this bail-out quiet until Andrew nails my stalker to the cross."

'Which is hopefully tomorrow,' he'd replied, then quickly added, "And not because I want to announce an active partnership. God. Like I'd have time for that."

The fatigued hand he'd pulled down his face made her feel guilty, so when he'd said— "Shaynes, tomorrow I have an appointment for *Latte* at the décor store—*Creative Cucina* in the mall— but it's right when my loans officer gets in, and since you're on such a tight deadline..."

How could she say no? "I'll go to the mall for you," she'd promised and there went any fantasy of waiting for Cameron in bed. "God, Shaynie," she grumbled to herself now, "be grateful."

THE MALL LOT was madness and she had to park eons from the door. A crowd and *Creative Cucina*. How lovely. The sole time she'd visited

*Cucina* she'd actually been with Jude, on a quest for Python stemware. His wealthy background had preceded him through the door and the hoity salesclerk had fawned over him. Not so much over her. One sour look and Shaynie had wondered if she'd forgotten deodorant or something. Now she was going back. "The things I do for money," she muttered.

*Whore.*

She shuddered to a stop within the beehive of people crowding into the mall. Whore. Everywhere she went, everywhere she turned. She visualized a black stone—*Take this burden*—and her cell rang. Cameron? Side-stepping a mom with a stroller, she lifted it. "Hey—"

"The Python makes you do things you wish you wouldn't."

"Gray! Where are—"

"Shaynie, shut up and listen. Run. You've—"

"Hey!" A second voice on the line spoke over him. "What are *you* doing with a phone? Hello?" This was spoken into the receiver, then, "Call's over," the voice said abruptly, and the next thing Shaynie heard was a click.

"What the—" She scrolled to 'last number'. Unfamiliar digits, not Gray's phone, nonetheless she hit redial. A computerized voice met her ear. "The cellular customer you are trying to reach is away from their phone. Please try aga—"

She hung up, brought the keypad up. <Run where, Gray? And why?> Then, in caps, <WHERE ARE YOU?>

The reply field stayed blank, and her phone did not chirp all the way down the concourse to *Creative Cucina*. The store was ensconced behind a gilded door. In a *mall.* She rolled her eyes. Only this snooty place would *discourage* window shoppers. She slipped inside.

"Mrs. Kevlin!"

Oh, perfect. Now when she corrected this beaming sycophant, she'd look like Jude's shack-up or something. Still— "It's Ms. Gavin," she corrected. "Jude's colleague."

Ah, there it was, the no-deodorant look. "Well. How can I help *you?"*

Not missing the tiny inflection on *you,* Shaynie lifted her chin. "I'm here in Jude's stead. He had an appointment to choose stoneware and linens for his latest venue, *A Latte in Common."* She affixed her own hoity stare. "You do have the samples ready?"

The saleclerk's mouth formed a small, perfect 'o'.

Ivy Shaynie came alive. "Is there a problem?"

"He...an appointment? Mr. Kevlin?" The salesclerk click-click clicked her computer mouse, eyes racing the screen. "There...there's nothing."

What? She'd better not have gotten out of Cameron's bed for *nothing.* "It's not like Jude to be mistaken."

"No, it's certainly not! Mr. Kevlin...." The salesclerk wrung her hands, snatched the mouse again. Click, click, click. "No," she said miserably. "Nothing. And I have no idea what sort of samples he wanted..." she trailed off.

Ivy Shaynie shone a benevolent smile. "Mistakes happen. I'm sure he'll understand."

"I'll call him!" The salesclerk's head bobbed. "Assure him that his time—your time—will be compensated! Perhaps free stoneware or stemware—"

"I'm sure he'll be thrilled," said Ivy Shaynie, and turned, glided back out the door.

Eyes.

They were a trickle on her neck and she froze, scanned the mall concourse, gaze tripping over fountains and palm trees.

Unknown faces surrounded her, a sea of colors and cultures. None familiar. None interested.

Except she could feel them. Eyes, in the direction she'd come from. *So I'm trapped!* 'Cause the mall was huge. Finding a different exit meant she'd be literal acres from her truck, and without her taser...

*"Run,"* Gray had said.

Suddenly it had a whole new meaning.

She rushed, broken chatter, gurgling fountains, and tepid mall music all a blizzard in her ears. *Run.*

Eyes. They too gathered speed behind her, she felt them, and, breaking into a jog, she apologized, absent and breathless, to the countless shoulders she jostled. *He's watching.* She jutted in front of two entwined teens. *Behind me!* A marble walkway broke the path of a mid-running fountain in the concourse and she pitched over it, ducked into the first store she saw.

"Welcome to *Body Chocolate."* A perky salesgirl shoved a leaflet into her hand. Shaynie stared blankly down at it. *Undies!* delicate script shouted. *3 for $10!*

She closed it in her palm, felt it become damp with her sweat as she melted deep into the store. The Eyes were gone and her breath rattled.

She leaned against a bin alive with a festival of color and a placard like the flyer—*Undies! 3 for $10!*

A smile, jittery and strained, twitched on her mouth. Sexy underwear. She lifted a pair with saucy pink frou-frou on the fanny.

Eyes.

She dropped the panties, plunged deeper into the store. *Now what? Now where?* Where to go when there was *nowhere* to go?

Change rooms, at the back.

She reached out, blindly jerked what felt like a bathrobe off a hanger. A silky chemise came with it.

"Uh—excuse me?"

She whirled, the night things in her hands.

A second perky salesgirl pointed at the chemise. "Isn't that luscious?"

Luscious. Lethal. Wind dried up in her throat.

"It'll be stunning on you, but—" the salesgirl's nose wrinkled prettily "—not *that* size." She looked, pointedly, at Shaynie's breasts.

She curled her arms over herself—*Stop watching me!*—and beseeched the bank of fitting rooms at the back. "H-how about I check the size in a change room?" *Please. Let me hide.*

"Of course!" The clerk ushered her to the back of the store. "I'll knock and check your measurements when you're ready—and keep the next size on deck just in case."

"Yes. Sure." She threw herself into the change room, rocking back as her own frantic image encircled her from wall-to-wall mirrors. *A fun house.* She collapsed onto the bench seat. *With a perky salesgirl anxious to measure my boobs.*

Meaning she couldn't just sit there, for God knew how long, hiding. Weak-kneed, she rose, began shucking her clothes, freezing when a thought occurred—*Will she make me step outside to get measured?* A wave of panic knocked her breath away. Reason brought it back. *No. Of course not. That's why this room's big enough to fit two.* Exhaling, she toed her socks off, slipped the chemise over her head.

It *was* luscious. Slithered like quicksilver when she moved. But—she grimaced. Perky salesgirl was right. The satin ribbons lacing the chemise were strained, taut, and as she pulled a face at her busty image there came, unsurprisingly, a soft knock on the door. The ultra-efficient, "next size on deck." She cracked it open.

An enormous set of fingers clamped over her wrist, and before she could scream, before she could do *anything,* a second reflection appeared, eyes snaring hers in the glass.

Storm eyes.

Her legs went to water. He pulled her upright and snarled. "It wasn't bad enough that you drove away just as I got home and was dying to see you?" He slipped in quickly, locked the door. "Did you have to taunt me by bringing me in here, too?"

She tried to answer, but every word was drowned by the tide of adrenaline rushing through her body. She plastered a palm on the mirror so she wouldn't collapse. "*Y-you* were following me?"

"Like you didn't know it. You looked right at me. Twice."

No, she'd looked right *through* him. 'Cause what she'd felt—someone, something, else. Wasn't it?

"C-Cameron, you s-scare—"

"Scared you?" He jerked her back, against him. "That's not all I'm going to do to you."

Adrenaline raced back, the shock of sensation making her head swim. His mouth found her ear. "That flight yesterday to Calgary was torture." His hands raced up her sides. "The flight home this morning was worse. I could feel you. See you. God, Shaynie, I wanted to *taste* you."

She turned her head, sought his mouth.

He pulled away. "Walking wet dream." He yanked the satin chemise laces. She spilled into his hands.

"Oh!"

"Shh," he hissed, primitive, bestial, and licked her ear. "I dreamed all night long."

"S-so did I." He was cupping her, thumbs swirling, hot and rough. Her knees failed.

"I had you every way possible."

She matched his expression, feral and fierce, in the mirror. "I *let you* have me every way possible."

He growled and shoved the chemise down. It shimmered, a pool of quicksilver on the floor and "My turn," he uttered, and one hand jerked her panties—*ripped* her panties—while the other dove. "Ah, Shaynie." His fingers shivered against slickness. "I love how I could drown in you."

The sound of his zipper sizzled, then—

He clamped a hand over her mouth, caught her cry.

He was bigger than she'd thought. Hotter than she'd dreamed. Her feet lifted from the floor as he plunged, breath harsh in her ear. "Yes. Take me. *All* of me. Drown me, Faerie. *Drown me.*"

Pleasure. Pain. So full she thought she'd die. So full she'd never known she'd been empty up until this moment. This *perfect* moment.

His lips were fire on her ear. "God, I love watching you."

Watching her. Touching her. Filling her. Her head spun, and as her orgasm tore through her she broke free, gulping air as brutal shudders stole her breath.

His voice hissed— "Shh"—then a jolt shot through him and he jerked against her. *Inside* her. "S*haynie…*"

*"Yes!"* Her head fell back, mouth open on his throat. "*You* show *me.*"

"Anything," he panted. "Everything." He delivered one last, splitting thrust.

A scream very nearly ripped itself from her throat.

A satisfied scream.

"Hush," he whispered, still convulsing but softer now, slower.

She was quaking, breath resounding like uneven sobs.

"Faerie!" he admonished, mouth close to her ear. "We have to be quiet." He held her, face buried in the side of her neck. "Okay?" he breathed when the last of the shudders stopped.

She nodded, turned into him.

He eased away.

"You're leaving me again?"

"For the time being? Definitely." He reached down, zipped his jeans.

She watched him, wide-eyed. "H-how are you going to get out of here?"

"Very—" he cracked the door "—carefully." He slipped outside.

Her legs were water as she pulled on her jeans, and her hands vibrated as she stuffed her ruined undies into her purse. She carried everything else out to the till.

The perky salesgirl, a measuring tape draped around her neck, was trapped between a preachy mother and an embarrassed teenage daughter. She caught Shaynie's eye with apologetic dismay. "Sorry I didn't get back to you. Did that size work?"

"Perfect," she said, and the word prompted an image of Trin, laughing hysterically and giving her a lascivious thumbs up. Still shaking, she dug for her credit card. That chemise was worth far more than the two twenties she'd plucked from her tip money. She was a lunatic to buy it.

But no way could she leave it behind now.

"Uh..." The cashier stammered before her.

Shaynie raised her eyes.

"Your—um—your boyfriend already paid for this."

"Pardon?"

"And the bathrobe. He said to tell you, 'surprise'."

*Surprise?* No kidding. Speechless, she accepted the chemise—and bathrobe—wrapped in embossed tissue and slid into a bag. Bought and paid for, every direction she turned. *Whore.* The word was like a rotten breath, and when the cashier beamed, said, "He forgot his change," she could barely mumble a thank you as she crumpled the bill alongside the coins in her palm.

He waited on a bench outside the store, an Adonis beneath the forced palm trees. She marched up to him, kicked him in the shins.

"Ouch! What the hell was that for?"

"You, Cameron Weste, are the spawn of Satan."

His eyes danced. "That's not what you said a few minutes ago."

"A few minutes ago I didn't say anything! How could I? I was busy trying not to get caught!"

"No, *I* was busy making sure we weren't caught. *Noisy.*"

She glowered. He grinned, then stood, towered over her. "Come here."

The evil eye didn't work. He captured her, pulled her close, and the wall of his chest smelled of chocolate and rain. She closed her eyes and breathed him in. Breathed *them* in.

"My Faerie." His lips moved in her hair. "You stop my heart."

He opened her palm, placed it over his chest. "Kiss me." He raised her face.

Stars flashed, and the entire universe whirled into one silken kiss. Then reality was back, the bag in her hand. "Cameron." She rattled it. "That...that stuff in the store, why did you do that?"

"Seriously? You need a biology lesson, Shaynie?"

She flinched. What they'd just shared was a lot more than biology—wasn't it? "Not *that.*" She avoided his eyes. "This." She hoisted the bag. "I...I didn't need you to pay for this."

He went utterly still, then she knew. And as she looked up, his storm eyes mirrored her horror.

He had not bought *anything.*

## CHAPTER THIRTY-ONE

SHE LOCKED A VICE GRIP on his hand and turned them back to *Body Chocolate.*

A light popped. “Weste! Hey!” A second flash blinded her. “Cameron Weste!”

Oh, damn! Those lights she’d seen when they’d kissed hadn’t been exploding stars—they’d been cameras.

A reporter with a sidekick photographer elbowed his way near them. Cameron swooped her backward, shielded her behind his arm. “Hey.” His voice came alive with whiplash charm. “Now’s not the best time.” He stepped away, and Shaynie, by default, stepped with him.

“It’s always a good time,” said the reporter, and the proximity of his voice told her that he too had stepped. “Any comments on the trade rumors? Chatter says you’re disenchanted.”

“You were just snapping pictures.” *Step, step, step.* “Did I look disenchanted?”

“Ah. You in love, Weste?”

Cameron laughed, and as they took another step it struck her that she couldn’t tell if the sound was fake or not. “Edmonton’s a hockey city,” he bandied. “What’s not to love?”

The stock answer rattled her. So did a second photographer, now at their other side. “Cameron.” She tugged his sleeve, kept her head down.

He glanced, then, loud enough for all to hear, said, “Happy to chat more, fellas” *Step, step, step.* She followed, face hidden in his sleeve. “Go ahead and set up a press conference with my publicist.” They’d managed to move to the other side of the concourse. “Ready?” he murmured.

For a big man he was incredibly agile—*athlete,* she reminded herself, running to keep up—, and the crowd parted, intimidated by his size and speed as they barreled down the mall. He skirted them around shoppers and perfumed kiosks, racing down to where the number of shoppers dwindled near the in-house amusement park. He grasped her wrist. “Down here!”

She whipped one last look over her shoulder.

No reporters. No Eyes.

She didn’t think.

A tiny gelato shop was tucked beside the mouth of the park and they ducked into it, rushed to a booth at the back. He whipped a ball cap out of his coat pocket and plopped it on his head backward, hiding his neck from passersby before dropping into the seat across from her. "You okay?"

No, her chest was on fire. Her heart was going to explode.

"Sorry," he said. "I didn't know I was being followed too."

She rested her head in her hands, caught her breath. "I can't stay here. I need to get back to *Body Chocolate,* find out who—"

"Shaynie we *can't* go back with media crawling around, and you can't go alone." He rummaged in his jacket.

"What are you doing?"

"What we need to do anyway." He drew out his phone and a series of chimes rang out—"Damn messages"—as he hit speed dial.

"Gavin," said the voice on the line, and Shaynie gaped. He had *Andrew* on *speed dial?*

Cameron held up a silencing finger, then delivered an abridged version of events to her brother. "I will," he said when he'd finished, then raised the phone between them. "Did I leave anything out?"

Yeah. The part where you ripped my panties off in public and ravished me mindless. "N-no."

"Hear that?" he said into the phone, then, "All right." Hung up.

She stared. "How much have you and my brother been talking to each other?"

"A bit. He's on his way. We're supposed to wait here for him." He hitched a thumb toward the gelato counter. "Want something before he comes?"

Was he kidding?

"Faerie, we need to look like customers, not fugitives." He got up, kept his height hunched as he ordered, and shoved money across the counter. "Keep it," he told the portly little server who'd been about to make change. Shaynie shivered. Her stalker had left *his* change too. *He said to tell you, "Surprise!"*

Cameron pushed a creamy concoction toward her. "It isn't our chocolate pie from Divinity but it's something."

Frost curled atop the ice cream, small versions of the cold soldiers who'd stood with her at Divinity. "I'm afraid," she said, more to them than him.

He reached across the table, lifted a loop of hair that had fallen over her face. "The Agent's coming." He tucked the hair behind her ear. "He's going to go to the store first."

The store. The sex. The *Surprise!* "Why?" she said, low. "Why scare me? This guy has violated me. Sabotaged me. Humbled me. He's won, I've lost. Why does he insist on scaring me?"

"Because he doesn't think he's won."

She peered at him.

"Shaynie, when you told me about Hellnight and said your rape was attempted seduction, I argued—but you were right. And I should have listened, because it's exactly what I said from the start."

"A crazy fan." Punishment. Pleasure.

Divinity, when she'd petitioned it for answers, had said the same thing. Still—

"Hellnight," she said. "Andrew was right too when he said it was months ago. So where's this guy been? And why get aggressive now? What's changed?"

He splayed his hands and she reached for them. Touching him was as natural as dreaming. As breathing. Then it occurred. So obvious. So incredibly *natural.*

"You," she said. "Cameron, *you're* the difference."

He stiffened. She held fast to his fingers. "None of this started until you and I started."

"Whoa. We didn't start until yesterday."

"Oh, please. The sex happened yesterday. But *we* happened on Hellnight. I just couldn't remember. And this person…he knew I couldn't remember. Was glad that I couldn't remember. But then you and I reconnected, and it…rocked his world."

"Because he'd prevented it on Hellnight," he said, following the thought through.

She nodded and, piecing it together, a sinking sensation dropped her belly. She was relieved when he interrupted, asked "What do your cards say?"

"The Devil," she answered, absent. "And an army of Swords."

"An army?"

Something in his voice pulled her out of dread. *An army.* Like the frost soldiers that had surrounded her at Divinity. Like the tiny curls wafting off the ice cream. "Nothing's as it seems," she murmured, and in her head she turned cards one by one. "On the surface Swords mean challenges. The Devil means lust. But they could also mean—"

"Weapons. War."

Yes. They could.

"So maybe all this time they haven't been warnings. Maybe they've been advice."

Why had it never occurred before? "Protection," she whispered. Her cell chirped and she jolted, placed it on the table before them. *Steve Lonigan*, read the screen. She brought up the message. <Suits are done. Bring a truck TOMORROW NOON.>

Because he wanted them out of there. She typed, <I'll be there>

Cameron raised a small calendar to his cell phone, too. "I'll come." He swiped a finger over noon the next day, highlighted it.

She raised her eyebrows.

"I don't trust him."

"It's not—" *him* was lost when her cell rang. She answered it, leaning forward so Cameron could hear.

"Hey." Jude's voice. "*Creative Cucina* just called. Looks like I sent you on a goose chase. Shaynes, I am *so* sorry."

"Not your fault."

"You still at the mall? If yes, I'll come over with your check. Rain you some Wands."

"Pentacles."

"Whatever. Anyway, I thought we could celebrate with lunch, maybe set *you* an appointment up with *Cucina*. I was going to anyway, to surprise you. But now—"

"No." It came out so forceful even Cameron sat back. "I...I really don't need any more surprises."

"Oh," Jude's voice in her ear was small. She cringed.

"But thank you. You...you're worth a truck full of colored stones. Heck, a *mine* full."

He was quiet.

She closed her eyes. "How about dinner tonight instead of lunch? Before The Python?"

Cameron made a choked sound. "But I don't play tonight!" he hissed.

She opened her palms, helpless. In her ear, Jude said "Perfect!"

She hung up and Cameron's cell rang before he could spit out the hurt she could see on his face. He flashed the screen.

Noel Nelson.

Ice rolled down her neck. He too held the phone so they both could hear. "'Bout time you turned your damn cell on," said Nelson.

Cameron grunted.

"Management's freaking out, trying to get a hold of you."

"Oh? For what?"

"For a meeting they've scheduled in your honor. Trade Day's looming, Weste, and they want answers from anyone who's even breathed the words 'outta here'."

He rolled his tongue in his cheek. "You *helping* me, Noel?"

"Just being decent."

Then why so surly? And clearly Cameron wondered too, 'cause he said, "Where are you right now?"

"Where—who cares where *I* am? The better question is where are *you?* You going to show up for the honchos or not?"

He met her eyes from across the table, and in his gaze was an echo of everything he'd told her about his trade. "Yeah," he said. "I'll be there."

Inside her, something died.

"I'll tell them," Nelson replied. "And let them know I tracked you down. *I* like being a hero too."

No kidding. She listened in on the when and the where, then looked at her watch. Tight timeline. He needed to go, and in leaving he'd be one step closer to being gone for good. "You'd better take off," she said, when he hung up the phone.

"No. I won't leave you."

*Yeah, right.* "Andrew's on his way."

"And I promised I'd stay until he gets here."

"Cameron—"

"I won't leave you, Shaynie. Not until I have to."

A double meaning, and when he linked their fingers, the feelings—*hurt, happy*—were so strong she could taste them. She contemplated the table. Felt him do the same.

"I'm still here now," he said finally, quietly. "Spend the night with me tonight."

Love me then leave me. Three Swords pierced her side. "I can't. I'm working. And even if I wasn't..." She raised her gaze, looked at him.

"No place safer than my condo."

A deliberate misunderstanding. She softly smiled. "Ice Deity. You know that's not true."

Color rose on his cheeks, guilty red.

"Stop that." She raised their clasped hands, moved her mouth on his knuckles. "My choice, remember? But—" She tried to smile. "That doesn't mean I'm impervious to pain."

"Me either," he said, and happy was gone. Hurt was all that was left.

"Hey." Andrew joined them. Their hands scurried to their sides.

"You'd better go," she said to Cameron.

"I've still got a couple minutes."

She glanced at her watch. No he didn't.

"My choice," he murmured.

She tore her eyes from his as her brother dropped into their booth. "Were you able to get to…" *Body Chocolate.* God. She wasn't saying it to a cop. She was saying it to her brother.

"Yeah." He didn't look at her, obviously not too keen to choke it out himself. "I've got that info and...more."

She and Cameron stared at him.

"Yesterday I got a lead in the case."

"What? You didn't tell—"

He held up a hand. "Because I wanted to be sure. And now..." He echoed their shared gesture, a hand through the hair. "Look at this." He opened an envelope he'd brought, slid a photo across the table to her.

Steve's picture of the Tarot fabrications. "Given everything that's happened I thought a visit with ol' Steve was worth my while," said Andrew.

She nodded. "Okay. So...?" She opened her palms, lost as to how the suits were relevant.

"So when you and Steve looked at this picture, all you saw was this creepy shit." He jabbed a finger at the Suits. "Look harder. At the window."

Behind the fabrications, in the background, was a ground-level window. She looked into it.

A shadow peered back. She recoiled, and Cameron's legs, under the table, stretched out, feet finding hers and offering comfort.

"Recognize him?" asked Andrew.

The shadow in the window was just that, a shadow. But its posture, its stance.... "It—it's grainy," she said, desperate.

"How about now?" Andrew pushed a second photo, an enlarged version of the first, over.

She closed her eyes.

"You profiled him yourself, Shaynie Grace. Both of you, actually. A 'crazy fan'. The behaviorist at the Detachment agrees. Except he calls him a 'Borderline Personality'."

"Obsessive?" said Shaynie.

"Uh-huh. 'Cause he's afraid you'll abandon him. Nothing triggers a Borderline more than thinking they're not getting attention or being left behind."

"Or being replaced by someone new," Cameron interjected.

Andrew nodded, grim. "And they're notorious for impulsive violence, which is why you two need to stay the hell away from each other. At least for right now."

And with the trade deadline approaching, maybe forever. She looked down at the figure in the picture. You're jealous of Cameron? *That's* what this has all been about? What a waste. I won't even have him for long.

"Shaynie Grace." Andrew followed her gaze to the picture. "If you're feeling like a fool, you're not alone."

She hadn't been. Hadn't quite got there yet. Still, she lifted her eyes to her brother.

He looked bleak. "I said just the other day that he was likable and I meant it. There was once a time I defended him, too. Christ, I remember being a kid and going toe-to-toe with our old man, thinking he was being unreasonable when he gave you what I'm certain was the only rule you ever had. You remember?"

*"That boy is forbidden from this house, Shaynie!"* Oh, yes. She remembered.

Andrew kept his voice low. "The more I thought about your profile, the more everything you'd told me fit. Then I saw this photo and—"

"And at the store, *Body Chocolate?*" It wasn't important to blush about it now. She wanted to hear it all. Understand it all.

"They thought it was a good likeness to the guy who paid for your things."

*"Run, Shaynie."*

Why? she wondered now. Were you right behind me?

Her cell rang, and all three of them collectively flinched.

"Answer it," Andrew barked. "Speakerphone."

She depressed the button.

"Sh-shaynie?"

Not an oft-heard voice but still one she recognized. "Chrystal Johns?"

"C-can we get together? There....there's things you need to know. About the stuff that's gone on with you. And...Gray."

Of course. Who other than Gray?

## CHAPTER THIRTY-TWO

SHE SCRAWLED Chrystal Johns's address onto a napkin Cameron shoved at her.

"I'll go with you," said Andrew, when she hung up.

She nodded. "And you need to go." This she directed at Cameron.

He rose, righted his ball cap. "Call me. And if I'm still in my meeting, *promise* you'll leave me a message."

"I will." Their eyes locked, and every moment from the mirror in *Body Chocolate* shuddered between them. He trailed a finger across her palm.

Then he was gone.

Andrew cleared his throat. "He'll break your heart, you know."

"The Three of Swords. I know."

They left her truck at the mall and took Andrew's unmarked to Panties' address on the south side. Andrew flanked her as she buzzed the security entrance.

It rang. And rang.

"Damn her," Shaynie breathed, and jerked out her phone, dialed the number Panties had called from.

It too rang and rang.

"Let me try." Andrew punched the number into his cell. "She might pick up from a number other than yours."

The resounding purr remained unanswered.

"She's decided to turtle." He led them back to the visitor lot. "Nine witnesses out of ten chicken out."

"Dammit!"

"Shaynie Grace, what could she possibly tell us that we don't already know?"

He had a point.

"And if you're thinking, location, forget it. I'll find Gray. And you won't be out of my sight till I do." He traced a clumsy little ankh on her forehead.

She smiled, helpless. "How does one pay a big brother back for all the stuff he does?"

"Cough up some more of those gold-section hockey tickets you offered last week."

"Pfft. You're asking *me*? Talk to your best buddy on speed dial."

A smile slanted his face. "Goliath comes with perks. Maybe I should trump up some kind of charge against him, detain him in the country." He slid her a look.

Her smile fell flat. "His honchos would probably override anything you came up with."

"And he'd want them to?"

"Yes."

"Huh. Told you I should have beat him with my billy club."

Jude bailed on dinner—*Sorry! Got a meeting about Latte!*—and Cameron replied to her voicemail via text. <Want to hear everything, but am in phone conference with my agent. I'll call as soon as I can. >

Except he didn't, and by the time she was dressing for The Python, she'd tortured herself, visualizing his new condo in fabled Los Angeles or maybe the funky Bay Area. Ignoring the few Python costumes that had been left by Eyes, she plucked a somber black t-shirt from her closet, paired it with jeans. Turned out to be the same outfit her brother wore when he strong-armed his way into the club shortly after she got there.

"Lord, Lord." Trin said, looking at him and fanning herself with her tray. On any other night the way her eyes stripped him would have made Shaynie laugh. Tonight it didn't even conjure a smile.

And Trin was no fool. "Hey." She set her tray down. "You've been a million different places in just a few seconds. What's up, little Perfect?"

"Gray." Not a lie, but not the whole truth.

Trin sighed. "Me too. Heard from him?"

"No." Another lie. God. The Seven of Swords. Weapons and war. She hated it. All of it. Still—

"What about a dealer, Trin? Is there anyone you know who'd help him hole up?"

"Perfect, I told you before: I don't think he's using."

Shaynie sighed but didn't argue. There had once been a time when she'd defended him too, ignored the most obvious evidence. Only when he ratted himself out had she finally accepted it. But then, like now, she wanted to know—*Why?*

"'Cause it helps me not worry, Shaynie," he had answered. "And nothing else helps me not worry." Then he'd smiled, lopsided like she loved. "'Cept you."

Now the adjectives Andrew had shared from the behaviorist bled in her ear. *Obsessive. Dependent.* She wanted to bawl.

Trin said, "Although," with such heavy weight that it pulled her out of any gloom. "There *was* one night when he *said* he'd been drugged." At Shaynie's look of surprise Trin's head bobbed. "And he acted like it. too. All slurry, zoned out, and pissed off." She laughed a bit. "Not that he could do anything about it. He tried to get a grip but almost flaked out altogether."

"Flaked out? As in unconscious?" That symptom and others ricocheted off one another: Cameron's "*crazy flu*", then his passing out like he was in "*some sort of coma*". And then there was Andrew's assessment of her: *You didn't act drunk, Shaynie Grace. You acted drugged.* One common denominator linked them all.

"What?" Trin watched her face.

"He was given—or tried for effect—a sedative." She shot a filthy look over at Jude. "And I know exactly who the dealer is." *She's a nurse.* And now she'd been fired. No kidding. Someone probably caught her pilfering pharmaceuticals. No wonder Chrystal Johns had decided to turtle. She'd bury herself if she told all she knew because it would be as much confession as disclosure.

Jude, feeling her glare, came over. "Hey," he said. "Sorry I ditched our dinner plans. I—"

"Did you know Crystal Johns had been dealing roofies?"

His jaw dropped, but whether it was shock that she'd said it or shock that she knew was beyond her. And either way she carried on. "'Cause Gray let slip long ago—" back on the night when he'd told her that Panties the Python Doll was really a *nurse* "—that she was an addict, so is it prescription stuff she's hooked on and dealing? Anesthetic drugs that knock people out?"

"I—" Jude's mouth opened and closed as he visibly tried to keep up. "Is that why Andrew barged in here tonight? To bust Chrystal?"

"No," she said abruptly. *Say nothing to no one.* That had been Andrew's parting shot after they'd sat in Divinity following the non-meeting with Panties. *Too many people already know way too much.*

The 'too many' had not included Cele, who'd lit a candle in the old embalming room as Andrew efficiently converted a whiteboard Shaynie used to sketch furniture designs into a place they could list all they knew—and all they didn't.

The list was surprisingly more one-sided in favor of what they were aware of versus what they weren't, but one unknown still trumped all. Where was Gray? And, *why?* her head nagged.

"Shaynes?" prompted Jude.

She looked at him. He loved his cousin like she loved Andrew. No matter how bad they'd fought, she would not win loyalty if he had to choose. "My brother's here because of my stalker." She glanced away from his eyes. "He wants to scan the regulars."

"Our bouncers can do that."

"But they're not cops. And they're not Andrew. You know he's protective."

*"Protective?"* He laughed. "Is that what you call shadowing your every move?"

"Andrew and I are tight, Jude. It tends to happen to orphans. No one's around to give a damn, so you end up giving an extra damn about one another."

"Whoa, Shaynes." He grimaced. "I'm sorry. All I meant was that he's the quintessential big brother. Never been too crazy to let anyone close."

*Yeah, well Cameron certainly hasn't had any problems.* She bit her tongue, grateful when a shadow dropped over her station. Andrew. Speak of the protective Devil.

Except it wasn't Andrew. Noel Nelson, locked in the orbit of the hologram python, waxed from chalk-pale to neon green. "Can we talk?" He directed it to Jude, eyes skittering to her with unmistakable direction. *Get lost.*

She hiked a brow. "Like I'm interested in anything *you* have to say," she lied, and took enough steps away to stay within earshot. Andrew, parked at a nearby table, nodded approval.

Nelson spoke in a harsh whisper. "Where's Chrystal?"

"Wish I knew." Jude polished a glass. "Wish I knew where *everyone* who's bailed on me is."

Shaynie reached for her cards, and, as she shuffled, tracked Nelson out of the corner of her eye. He grimaced as though in pain. "Jude, I need to see her."

What for? Was he looking to knock Cameron out again? Scowling, she shuffled her cards hard, the deck rat-a-tatting.

Jude examined the glass he'd shone. "Chrystal's not here, Noel. But then again, neither's your rival, Weste."

Jude thought Panties was with Cameron? God. He really *was* in the dark. She kept shuffling and listening.

A blue strobe lit pallor on Nelson's face. "She's a human being, Jude."

Shaynie frowned.

"No," Jude replied. "She's a fox. Wears dumb blonde then takes it off like you and I would wear a hat. The only thing she likes better than cock is cash, and believe me, she's not worth either."

Shaynie's head, like Nelson's, snapped back. "Human being," said the latter, again.

Jude rolled his eyes. "You sure know how to pick 'em, Noel."

Shaynie flipped a card.

The Knight of Swords. Bad news. Nelson. She glanced at him again. "Human being," he said a third time but to no one. Jude had walked away.

Taking a cue from Andrew's jutted chin, she moved to where Noel stood abandoned, examining him. Beyond the sweat sheen on his face there was more, a defeat in his eyes she knew. Had felt. Grief. Finding out your friend was someone you'd never banked on.

"Noel—"

He snared her eyes. "Why," he said, "are you still here?"

She rocked back. Wasn't that Gray's line?

"Shaynie…" Nelson's mouth worked. "You need…. Watch your back."

She disguised an answering flinch. "Okay. Who am I watching for?"

"Cameron."

She jolted.

"You and him.... You're making a mistake. A big mistake."

"Really?" God help her not to sound strangled. "Since when is friendship a mistake?"

*"Friendship?"* A shadow crossed his face, neither a smile nor a grimace, but both. "Shaynie, you don't make good friends. You never did."

Trin, loitering near, went still.

"Your *friendship* with Weste.... Cut the ties. Walk away."

"Why?"

"Because! You…he.... You'll get hurt."

"Hurt how?"

"Dammit, Shaynie!" His eyes skittered. Sweat shone on his upper lip.

God. She narrowed her eyes. Maybe he was looking for Chrystal for a *fix.* She planted her palms on the bar. "Straight up Nelson, what's this about? Chrystal Johns? Cameron's trade—"

"Cameron's *trade?* So it *is* going to happen?" His face flooded with relief. "That would be perfect! 'Cause Cameron, he...he needs to get the hell out of here."

"Why? So you can—"

"And Shaynie, so do you." He turned then, swallowed up by dry ice and strobe lights.

She stared after him, hands unwittingly seeking her cards. She flipped one and The Magician faced her, right side up. Not a cunning trickster. Someone who had all the answers.

## CHAPTER THIRTY-THREE

"THAT'S TWICE IN ONE DAY I've been told to run," Shaynie said, and Andrew, leaning on the bar where Nelson had been, nodded, out of breath. He'd bolted out after Nelson, had tried questioning him in the parking lot, but Noel had stonewalled him, first with circle talk, then with the threat of a lawyer.

Few things pissed her brother off more than suspects with lawyers.

She fixed him an ice water and spared a tight smile at Trin who watched them both, big-eyed. "Okay," Andrew said. "So now we need to sort out how Nelson and Gray are linked."

"They're not. God, Andrew, you know their history. You remember Jen."

"Yeah. Wonder if anyone ever told *her* to run."

Shaynie grimaced, and her phone chirped, a text. Andrew jutted his chin to its sound. "Check it."

Cameron Weste.

Her brother read her eyes. "No. Not him. Not *now.*"

She scowled and so did Trin, who spoke suddenly— and loudly. "No, I won't," she announced. "I won't stock your damn liquor for you, Perfect. Go in the cooler and do it yourself. I'll open your station. I'm going to be taking your place once you quit here anyway."

Their eyes met and shared a sparkle before Shaynie bolted to the cooler, cell tucked in her jeans. She hit speed dial as soon as she was sequestered behind the fridge door.

"Been waiting for you to call," Cameron growled. "And The Agent told me that if I dared show up at The Python, he'd kneecap me."

"Right now I'm the only one he wants to kneecap. Gray's still MIA." She dropped to a pallet of beer. "But I do know that Chrystal Johns is a dealer. Maybe Gray's dealer. And Nelson was just in here, frantic to find her."

A pause hung on the line. "Well," he said slowly. "I guess Noel wouldn't be the first player to get caught up in cocaine."

"Not cocaine. Sedatives. And I think you've had a taste of them too."

He listened without contradicting, but when she finished, said, "So he drugged me. Why?"

*Why. So many whys.* "I don't know," she confessed.

He released a breath she could hear.

"But that doesn't change that it happened, so...be careful, okay? It's one thing for just me to keep my head up, but..." *But so much to say. So much to feel.* And here she was, trapped in a beer cooler on a cell phone.

"You trying to protect me, tiny Faerie?"

Protect him. Love him. Yes. All of it.

"I miss you tonight, Shaynie."

And soon they'd go from missing each other tonight to missing each other *every* night. *The big trade.*

She swallowed past the lump in her throat. "T-tell me about your honchos."

"Not much to tell. They sat me down, said, 'Weste, you're an unrestricted free agent. You gonna bail?'"

Like Gray. Like Panties. It was a strange sort of parallel. "And you said—"

"I said, 'that's not what I'd call it'."

Semantics again, which told her nothing other than that she'd dropped from the stature of confidant to being with the ranks of the media he'd parlayed with this afternoon in the mall.

His voice rumbled in her ear. "After your shift, use your key. Come over. Be with me."

"And what do I do with Andrew?"

"Tase him."

She laughed, helpless. "Kind of tough to do without my taser."

"Please Shaynie," he said, serious. "I miss you."

Then why move away from me? "Cameron—"

The door to the cooler groaned and a shadow fell over the liquor. "Perfect," said Trin. "Gray just called me."

Her heart stopped. "Cameron, I need to go."

"But—"

"I'll miss you too." *Dammit! Wrong tense.* Did he catch it? Did she want him to? "Soon," she said, and ended the call.

Trin closed herself in the cooler. "He said he was trying to call you but couldn't get through. And I recognized the number that came up—it belongs to a guy I used to know. Gray...he must have borrowed his phone."

In other words, another user. "Andrew needs—"

"To know? He does. I just told him. Told a *cop.*" She tittered, the sound uncharacteristically uncertain, uncharacteristically small. "Imagine. My dream lay is a cop."

She was hysterical. So much that she was straying from the point. "Trinity!" she cued her, sharp. "*What* did Gray say to you?"

"He—" Trin's chin jittered. "Shaynie, he sounded crazy."

Borderline Personality. She swallowed. Nodded. "Tell me."

"He..." Shivering, Trin's shadow sketched darkness on the wall. "He was babbling about this place—The Python—as if it were real."

*"The Python will either let you soar or be strangled."*

"And...and he does that sometimes, but this time—" She broke off, mouth working. "This time he said you'd *slept* with it."

"What?"

"And that he'd 'tried to drag you away by the hair'." Trin made air quotes.

Shaynie sank back to the pallet of beer cans. She'd slept with The Python? The Python was Gray's code name for enemy. So...a hockey player? And he'd dragged her away by the hair? That had to be what he meant by his rescue on Hellnight.

*Rescue?* Right. Then why did she wake up to bruises and bite marks? In her mind's eye she saw the flash of horror the mirror had reflected before it dropped and shattered and when she spoke her mouth felt full of those broken shards. "Anything else?"

"Yes. He kept babbling that somebody was going to end up dead again."

## CHAPTER THIRTY-FOUR

"Dead *again*?" asked Andrew. They'd made it through her shift and now sat in her brownstone, soft lights bouncing off jars of colored stones.

"Think he meant Jen? Gray's always blamed Nelson for her car wreck."

"Pfft. Jen drove herself off that cliff when she found out she'd be a teenage mama."

"Of Nelson's baby."

"Or Gray's baby."

She spread empty hands and he chewed his lip before saying, quietly, "Shaynie Grace do you think he meant *Dad*?"

Oh, not *this* debate, not now. Still, she knew better than to argue a truth against a belief. "I don't know what he meant." And had it been a statement, or a threat? A *death* threat. From— "Gray. God, Andrew. He *did* do this. My *friend—*"

*You don't make good friends, Shaynie.* Nelson's voice, alive in her head, and for once he hadn't sounded like a smart ass. He'd sounded sad. "You know, tonight Noel Nelson told me I make crappy choices," she said.

"Yeah, well, Nelson's an idiot who needs to get traded a far sight quicker than Weste. Maybe he'd finally grow up if he actually left home."

Spoken like a true ally. "Loyalty is everything."

"Go to bed. And think about the good friends you do have. Like that scary redhead. Christ. She looks like she could kick *my* ass."

She smiled shakily. "Be nice. She thinks you're hot."

"Please. I *use* handcuffs, I don't want to wear them. *Bed!"* He took out his phone. "And I'm going to call my constables, see if they've ferreted out any locale on the cell Gray used—and if any of them are places Nelson went after The Python."

She traced their ankh between them, left the room.

Sleep, when it came, was fitful, and when she woke Andrew was raiding her fridge.

"Mother Hubbard," he teased.

"I need a 'shopper'."

His mouth twitched. "No locations last night, and Nelson didn't go anywhere except his own condo. As for your Goliath, he called me already, at stupid o'clock. Said he was up for morning skate and that I should get my lazy ass out of bed too. I gave him a bare-bones account, then told him to stay away from you. For today," he added, around a mouthful of bread.

"He didn't call me." Of all things, it wasn't important. Yet it was everything.

"Because he knows how to listen," said Andrew. "If there's one thing a pro athlete can do very well, it's take orders. They've had coaches telling them everything from how to skate to how to shit since they were kids. Being bossed around comes naturally to them, which, incidentally, should make you very happy." Grinning, he plopped a dollop of jam onto a fresh slice of bread, stuffed it into his mouth.

She returned a weak smile. No point telling him he'd been right yesterday, that Cameron would break her heart. She sighed, wondered what the honchos had *really* told him about California.

ANDREW TAILED HER to Divinity. "Stay put with Cele until I say otherwise."

She stood within the white circle. "You'll call me?"

The look he gave her let her know it was stupid to ask.

Cele rushed to the door when she opened it. "*Cheri*!" She looked beyond her. "The Knight of Pentacles, where is he?"

"Headed to his Detachment. Why—"

"All is well, Darling!" Cele called, and the floor creaked, spilled a large shadow out of her divining room.

Shaynie flew to him and their silk kiss was eternity.

Around them Cele flitted, a delighted little bird. "She's happy her charm worked," Cameron whispered, when they finally broke free.

Shaynie frowned.

"You know," he said, "that little thing she made me with your hair, to bring what I wanted close to me."

"That was my hair?"

"You didn't know?" He laughed. "I knew right away."

And he'd worn it anyway. It'd had nothing to do with playing better hockey.

He wrapped her close, her back to his front. "Cele," he said. "We're going out on a date."

"*Non!*" Cele stopped flitting. "That was not the deal. The Knight of Pentacles—"

"—isn't here. You made sure. C'mon, *Mère.*"

*Mother.* Cele's brows snapped together.

"It's not like we can even go far," he said. "Or for long. We have to pick up the welded body drawers in a half hour. All we want is twenty minutes alone."

Cele glowered.

"Please?"

She was powerless. And he knew it. *"Merci,"* he said.

Cele scowled. Shaynie sought her eyes. "Thank you," she mouthed.

"*Vous avez l'air belle en amour,"* she replied, growing soft.

You look beautiful in love. Shaynie's cheeks lit.

"What did she say?" Cameron found his shoes. "My French isn't that good."

"That she approves," she fibbed. The L-word danced way too close to commitment. And commitment was California. The trade. The honchos he did not want to talk about. The honchos she did not want to hear about—not for their twenty stolen moments, at least.

Outside the temperature had soared and the world was melting, a symphony of running water and promise of spring. He looked over his shoulder at Divinity's closed doors. "It's fantastic in there, Faerie. Cele gave me a tour. Looks like your deal of a lifetime worked out."

"Uh-huh." She didn't want to talk about knuckling to Jude's funding either.

Still he waited, clearly hoping she'd say more.

She didn't.

He cleared his throat. "How are you going to manage a grand opening without escalating Gray?"

*Escalating.* Such a mild word for what Gray had said would happen. *Dead.* And why? To keep her away from The Python—whatever or whoever that was—he'd destroy Divinity? Kill her? Confession or not, it still made no sense. "I won't open until Andrew says Gray's caught," she said. "Up till then I'll just keep status quo. Although—" A sardonic little twist moved her mouth. "Who knew I'd be stuck at the one place Gray himself nagged me to get out of, just to now keep him at bay?" It had been one more sticking point she and Andrew just couldn't agree on: Gray would know that sabotaging Divinity would trap her at The Python.

"'Course," Andrew had said, "he wants you close to him."

"But he's not there," she'd replied

"Yeah, but he could come back at any time. Whereas he'll never be part of Divinity."

Because at Divinity she'd be completely independent.

She stopped, feet squelching in the wet snow.

"What's wrong?" said Cameron.

Probably nothing. But maybe something. That word, *independent,* its mirror, its opposite, was *dependent.* A connection, an answer, crouched at the back of her mind.

"Faerie?" tried Cameron.

She blinked, and he was gazing down at her, storm eyes wary and worried.

*Twenty beautiful minutes.* She shook the word *dependent* away. "Wondering where we're going on our date," she said; and, *Gray?* she called, to wherever he might be. *What were you really trying to say?*

Cameron eyed her, dubious, then pointed. "Down there."

"The river valley?"

"Well...yeah." He rushed them across the street to a set of wooden stairs leading to the valley below. "I've only seen it from my window. I want to see it with you." He took her hand, then the stairs, two at a time.

She galloped after him. "Hey! Slow down!" Wind caught her hair. "Cameron, when you run, I fly!"

"Oh. Right." He eased up, red-faced. "Bull in a china shop. Just like in the mall."

Where-oh-where was the smart aleck who'd once sent her a goofy orange sex toy? Who was this vulnerable, sensitive man? His dark side, his light. Superficial and serious. Right from the start she'd seen one and sensed the other. Loved them both.

He, oblivious, was scanning the area, whistling. "Wow. No wonder so many guys on the team go running down here."

Andrew did too. The valley was renowned for runners—though she had always wondered why anyone would want to see its pageantry fly by at warp speed. Especially on a day like today: February sun and hoar frost. "Glitters like a diamond mine," she murmured.

He nodded.

"And in the fall, when all the leaves turn, then it's a firestorm." Her feet crunched, led them through the snow. "Cele performs a ritual then, on Halloween. Comes down just before midnight and lights candles for those who have passed, lets them sail on the water."

"Huh." His gaze tracked the length of the North Saskatchewan. "Wonder if she'd light one for my Dad."

An orphan, like her? Somehow it wasn't a surprise. She reached up, stroked shadows she'd felt herself from his face. "How old were you?"

"Sixteen. Playing out east on a US team. Living as a billet."

So without family, friends, or even community when his Dad died. And, again like her, he'd been just a kid. She took his hands.

He clucked his tongue. "Get those tears out of your eyes, Faerie. It was a long time ago."

*Liar.* His face said it was yesterday. "What did he think of you playing hockey so far away?"

"Loved it. Worked his butt off so I could afford to go. I owe him—owed him—everything."

"And you never got to see his reaction when you made it pro."

"Nope."

"I am so, so sorry." She raised their linked fingers to her mouth.

"I take it your Dad never got to see your morgue or the amazing things you make, either."

She blinked. "Oh, of course he sees. Just like your Dad sees you. It's you and me who don't see them."

The befuddlement he wore made her laugh. Made him laugh too. "Tell me about him," he said.

"Quid pro quo," she answered, and for the next several minutes their fathers became the light in the hoar frost as they crunched through the snow.

"Your Dad sounds quite a bit like The Agent," Cameron said, when she had run out of stories.

She smiled. "Andrew would disagree but secretly be thrilled to hear it."

"How did he die?"

"Ah…" Her smile shrivelled. "That part is nothing like the so-called Agent. Not real noble."

"Pfft. Nobility's overrated."

Out on the river, ice floated. She fixed her eyes on a piece. "On a good day, I call what happened a work accident. Although Andrew will forever disagree." *Do you think he meant Dad?* She shuddered, and river ice shifted. She watched it.

"My brother will spend a lifetime chasing demons because he can't admit the simple truth—our Dad was a wonderful person, an amazing father—but also a falling-down drunk."

He was so quiet she swore she could hear the melting snow.

"One night he was out in his shop as usual—and had tipped one too many, also as usual. The cops said he must have fallen, and the coroner concurred. His blood alcohol level made falling way more likely than standing. Anyway, his head wound matched a corner of his work bench. A stupid accident when he was stupid drunk."

Silence swallowed sunshine, and on the bank of the river, a branch, bobbing in the lapping water, looked for a split second like a stiff grey hand, reaching out for forever.

Or maybe waving goodbye.

She looked away.

Cameron watched her. "Your Dad is why you judged yourself so harshly after getting drunk on Hellnight." His words sliced the quiet. "Why nothing other than your own fault ever occurred to you."

"He shoots, he scores," she said, and out on the water a crack of ice resonated, made both of them jump. "May I take a shot too?"

His permission hung in the quiet.

"Losing your Dad is what's made goodbyes so hard, not the bimbo who cheated on you and used you for trips and cars. Although I don't suspect she helped."

He did not argue.

"You think that when you go away, bad things happen. People hurt you. Sometimes even disappear."

He said not one word.

She led him to a park bench. "Sit," she commanded.

He obeyed, and her mouth twitched. Maybe Andrew had been onto something with that taking orders thing. "You need to forget the word 'goodbye' and what you think it means. 'Cause if you can't see the person who loves you even when they're not there? Then you're not looking hard enough."

Another sheet of ice cracked, made them both flinch. "Shaynie," he growled, "do you think I *like* that you turn every belief I've ever held on its head?"

"I don't care whether you like it or not. I'm right."

A scowl and a laugh fought it out on his face. Laughter won, and in one fluid motion he was up, and she was over his shoulder.

"Hey!" She flailed.

"Shaynie Gavin, you lied when you said you weren't magic."

He whirled in a disorienting circle, but she could still see the snow bank. She grasped his pant legs. It didn't help. The melting snow made a slumping sound as she landed in a heap.

"Uh-oh." He laughed, flopped down beside her. "Now you're mad."

She sputtered. Glared.

"Aw, Faerie." He trailed a finger down her nose. "Don't be mad." He lowered his head.

God, he could kiss.

Silken hair, the scent of chocolate, and above them hoar frost glittered, a living recreation of his ceiling of stars.

He spoke first. "Stay with me tonight."

"What...what about California?" There. She said it.

A mask, atypically remote, fell over his face. "You just said goodbye doesn't exist."

"It doesn't. But—"

"Tell me, Shaynie—which Tarot card means faith?"

*Shaynie?* What happened to *Faerie?* As for *faith*— "The Star." *Stars. God.* "Why?"

"Because." He rose, brushed snow from his jeans. "Sounds like maybe you need it."

She hopped up too. "What do you mean, I need—"

"You say goodbye doesn't matter, but what's the first thing you do when I ask you to stay? Start resenting goodbye."

"'Resenting'? No, I didn't—"

"Maybe not with words, but—"

"Words? *Words?* You're talking in Tarot riddles! All I did was ask about California!"

"And all I asked for was faith."

Faith? Since when?

"I think *you're* the one who's scared, Shaynie."

"No, Weste. I am *not.*"

He flicked a shoulder, then turned back the way they came. "We need to go get your body drawers."

She sputtered behind him, baffled palms to the sky.

"You'll need two trucks to haul them," he said. "I'll follow you in mine."

He took the stairs two at a time, this time without taking her hand.

AT DIVINITY, she scribbled the address of Steve's shop on a scrap of paper. He took it, a half-cocky, half-grim *I was right* look hanging on his face.

It was all she could do to not tell him that his smugness reminded her of Nelson. She let loose the moment he was gone. "He is a walking ten. All yes then no, can't stay but won't go, and *I'm* the one who's afraid? He asked me for faith but didn't tell me what the hell to believe in!"

Cele, having bounced looks between them, began dealing cards. "What would you *like* to believe in?"

"Love." No question.

"*Oui*. Love. And? Is that not what he's asking for?"

"Why are you taking his side?"

"I am not taking his side." Cele swallowed what looked like a laugh. "I am taking *Love's* side."

"Hmph. Well. He has that already."

"Ah, yes. So beautiful. But Darling, have you *said* this to your 'ockey god?"

"Please. I'm as transparent as glass. I don't need to say it."

"Shaynie! We are talking about a man. They need it spelled out."

Shaynie dropped to their window spot. "He wonders how someone would tolerate being alone week after week while he's out on the road. But I'd do it. Figure it out. Make it my life. And if he didn't want to make it *his* life, then I'd pack up, go with him."

Silence fell. She and Cele stared at each other, each shocked by what she'd just said. "You would give up your home, *Cheri*? Your dream?"

A rush of air raced from the heat ducts, lifting her hair. Divinity. *Would* she give it up?

"Cele, if Cameron asked me...I don't think there's anything I wouldn't do for him." Cringing, she petitioned the walls. *Forgive me*. "Maybe that does scare me."

"*Oui*. You should be scared." Cele straightened the row of cards she had dealt. "Love is, after all, the biggest leap of faith."

## CHAPTER THIRTY-FIVE

Steve's shop, out near Refinery Row, was as close to the country as Edmonton got. She parked by the loading dock, waited for Cameron to pull up beside her. They hadn't spoken when they left Divinity. He, like she, didn't seem to know what to say. "I should have asked Andrew or Jude along," she ventured now. "Being a game day, you're probably supposed to be home, sleeping." There. Ice broken.

He consulted his watch. "Still an hour till naptime and *no,* you can't join me."

She rolled droll eyes.

"I'm a working man, Faerie."

And so, *spend the night with me, say goodbye,* was tabled. For now. She opened the shop door, the acrid sizzle-scent of welding rods hitting her like a wall. "When you get home, put your jeans and jacket in a bag for your housekeeper." She wrinkled her nose. "Otherwise this smell will permeate everything. Your hair. Your bedding. Shower before your nap."

"Why? You don't want to smell your old boyfriend on my pillows?"

Ah. *Spend the night.* There it was. "Not particularly. And I don't want to apologize for *having* an old boyfriend, either." She raised her voice over the roar of generators. "Hey! Stephen!"

Steve's torch spat an arc of sparks before he lifted his visor. But his answering grin fell off his face. "Huh." He eyeballed Cameron. "You brought muscle."

And what on Earth had possessed her to bring muscle? Stifling a sigh, she moved to a series of shapes and bumps beneath a weathered canvas. "These my suits?"

Steve grunted, a sound she supposed was a yes. She pulled the tarp from one end.

Every molecule of air left the room.

The sword was massive. Luminous. But that wasn't what robbed the breath from her lungs.

It was vibrating.

She reached for it and a shudder, long and slow, responded from inside. It was like an echo, *a greeting,* and the sword answered with a perceptible zing. *My God.* Her mouth dropped in wonder. *It's singing.*

"Cameron?" she whispered, but her voice sounded as though she were speaking through water. Cold river water, thick with ice and darkly winter-colored.

Beside her, or behind her, she wasn't sure, she could vaguely hear Cameron and Steve, their tones clipped and way too polite. No matter. They were talking to each other, not distracting her from the sword which now pulled her, magnetic, to its razor's edge. *Luscious. Lethal.* The words flew through her head. So did one other.

Protection.

Air hissed through her teeth, and, caressing the blade with one hand, she used the other to jerk a second canvas loose.

The Pentacle, the piece Steve said bit his student, gleamed, and beside it the Wand's metallic leaves writhed with living lustre, much like the ivy had around Cameron's mirror. *Yes.* Hissed a thought. *Strangle. Then soar.*

She jolted. Was that *her* thought? And if not.... She peered at her reflection in the Tarot sword.

Ivy Shaynie peered back.

She smiled and reached out, one hand wrapped around the sword's hilt, the other under its blade.

*Yes,* hissed more thought. *Protection.*

"Hey!"

A voice. Steve's voice. But insignificant. Unimportant.

"Shaynie, don't try to lift that! Creepy thing turned out *far* heavier than its material should be."

Heavy? It wasn't heavy. She effortlessly raised it, its five-foot length as long as she.

"What the—" Steve broke through whatever separated them and was in her face, ogling her. "How the hell can you—"

"Faerie," Cameron also broke through. "Your *hand.*"

She looked. Blood seeped from her palm, made a greasy smear on the blade. *Does it hurt?* No. It didn't. In fact her face, *Ivy Shaynie's* face, beamed. "Cameron," it said. "Could you back my truck up to the door? I need to get these home."

"No."

Steve, not Cameron, spoke. Wrenching her eyes from Ivy Shaynie, she said, "Pardon?"

He folded his arms. "Can I speak to you a moment?" He sliced Cameron a look. "In private?"

Leave the sword? Her fingertips massaged her blood into the blade.

"Faerie?"

Cameron's voice, quietly unnerved, pulled her eyes to his. "I'm okay," she said, and felt Ivy Shaynie's smile on her face. "My truck...?"

He turned for the door, but as she followed Steve, she felt him linger.

Steve slouched against a counter in the corner. "What's the problem?" she asked.

"I want to be paid."

"Wha—but you said, 'free'. Stephen, we *shook* on free."

"No, we shook on you trotting out a sob story about having no money, about losing the old morgue. And now I see you're banging a fucking millionaire?"

Her head snapped back. "I'm not his concubine, Steve. Not a whore."

He shrugged the word off as though it meant nothing. "Well, whatever you are, you can't have your pieces until you cough out the cash."

He named a figure. Her jaw dropped.

"By the end of the day, or they get hauled to the junkyard."

"Why, you vindictive son of a—"

"Take it or leave it."

"Take or leave *this.*" She swiped her bloody hand down his face. "And ask yourself, Steve—do you really want to do this to me?"

He half-laughed. "Now you're threatening me?"

"No. Not *me.*" She gazed, pointedly over at the Tarot suits.

All of them had started to vibrate.

And this time he saw it too.

"They won't let you get near them, much less allow you to haul them away."

He blanched. She smiled. "I'll have them before the end of the day." She turned.

Cameron was half in and half out of the door. "We're leaving," she said.

He rounded on her the minute they were outside. "I respect you, Shaynie, and that is the only reason I didn't call you on your bullshit while your old boyfriend had a tantrum like a jealous ass. You said you pulled off your deal of a lifetime. And now Cheap Ring says you're broke?"

"I'm *not* broke." Correction: *Jude* wasn't broke. And now she really needed to access that check he'd promised before Steve called her bluff and hauled her suits—her *Protection*—to the landfill.

Cameron loomed over her, arms across his chest. "It took everything I had to keep my mouth shut in there. But now we're alone, Faerie. Start talking."

Swallowing hard, she told him everything—her yanked credit. Mink the loan shark. Jude the silver spoon. The reality of being both in debt and indebted.

He summarized it neatly when she was all done. "So you were a sell out."

"No, I was a *survivalist*. And it's not like I had much choi—"

"Oh, bullshit!" He swiped a hand through his hair and the gesture, its context, struck her. It was something he had picked up from her. "Shaynie you know, full well, that I, like your old boyfriend just said, am a 'fucking millionaire'."

"So that makes you fair game to ask for money?"

"Is that what this is? A game?"

"I—no! That's not what I meant."

"So what the hell *did* you mean?"

"That I don't want our relationship to cross that line."

"That line? Commitment?"

"Commitment? Since when is gold digging in the same category as commitment?"

"Relying on someone to help you, asking him, that's trust, Shaynie. That's commitment. That's faith."

Whoa. Since when?

"I would have given it—given anything—freely."

That hurt. Why did that hurt? "I—I give *me* freely. I don't need trips or trucks."

"This wasn't a trip or a goddamn truck! This was *Divinity.* Your dream that means everything to you. And I could have given it to you because I thought I meant something to you."

*"You do!* Cameron, I—"

*Love you* was lost as he turned, dug his keys from his pocket. "I need to go. I'm on a schedule and I play tonight."

She stared at the breadth of his shoulders. "Do...do you want me to come to your game?"

He did not turn around. "I don't know."

Guess that's a *no.* She shuffled through the slush to her truck.

## CHAPTER THIRTY-SIX

At Divinity, he waited long enough to watch her climb the stairs and open the door. Then he was gone.

Cele, in the showroom, was ushering an unknown woman through the furniture display. Shaynie raised her eyebrows. "Reiki patient," Cele murmured, leaving the woman to browse a moment. "She would like her cards done. Do you think you're ready?"

For a distraction? For something she actually felt competent at? "Definitely."

Cele beamed. "I knew this, of course, so I readied your divining room."

*"Merci."* Her first paying Tarot customer. Butterflies filled her belly as she spread out her scabbard. Anxiety. *Good* anxiety. The kind that came with diving into something new, something right. Beckoning the customer in, she smiled, encouraging, and asked her to call her question into the deck.

Cup after Cup turned up in the reading, and as the querent hovered on the edge of her seat, Shaynie grinned. "The question you called, was it all about love?"

The woman's cheeks went electric, and around them Divinity shone, a smile that came straight from its soul. "Let's talk about the person the cards say is coming into your life."

Divinity hummed.

CELE GLOWED like a proud parent once the querent was gone, and Shaynie laughed at her smug expression. "It's been so long since something went right, I forgot what it feels like."

"So celebrate, Darling. A phone call to your beloved." Cele peeked at her. "Share the success you just had?"

Share the *dream that means everything to you*. Shaynie swiped a hand through her hair. "The only phone call I need to make is to Jude," she said, and, ignoring Cele's crestfallen face, she dug out her cell.

He answered off the first ring. "Hey, nothing like keeping your friend in the loop after you and the cop barrel out of the club last night, leaving me wondering if you're okay."

She massaged her forehead. "It—uh—it's been a long day."

"Huh. Well. Since you're on the phone, that must mean you're safe. What do you need?"

Because she wouldn't be calling unless she wanted something? And yet.... *If the shoe fits....* Guilt deflated her, made her feel sleazy. "I—uh—about our deal—"

"Oh, right!" She could almost see him pop a palm against his brow. "I said I'd have your check, then bailed on dinner. Sorry, Shaynes."

*He* was sorry. God. She *was* sleazy. "I...I can't tell you how grateful I am," She rummaged in her bag of stones and found an orange one. Generosity. She plunked it into a jar. "Hear that?"

He laughed. She did too. Then said "Can you believe I've got to shuck out a chunk of your coin *already* today?"

"Shaynes, I grew up in a family that ran businesses. I'd believe you if you said you had to shuck out big chunks of coin every *hour* of a day."

How glum.

"But I'd also believe it if you said you made big coin every day too," he said brightly. "What's up?"

She gave him a somewhat sanitized version of Steve and the suits, editing out Cameron.

"Ah. A deal with an ex. Do I really need to turn this into a business lesson lecture?"

"No need. Seems I've already done the field study."

He chuckled. "Tell you what: *I'll* go pay Sulking Steve—with *your* money, don't huff!—and I'll arrange to have your stuff hauled out of there, too. No sense you going back and giving him the chance to up the ante and become an even more unreasonable dickhead."

Plunk-plunk-plunk, went more stones in the jar. "Hear that?"

"Yes, Shaynes. I hear that. Love you."

"I love you too."

She heard him beam, then, "Hey." He cleared his throat. "Heard from that other guy we love?"

Ice lanced her spine. "No. You?"

"Nothing. But after what you said about Chrystal last night, I was sort of hoping he'd give you a call."

"Oh?" Something—instinct? Reflex?—made her slide to the edge of her seat. "Why?"

"Because..." He paused, and she felt the weight of it. "I poked around after Nelson's histrionics—you heard what he said, right? That Chrystal was missing? Well, turns out he's right."

She relaxed. That was all? It was nothing she and Andrew hadn't concluded last night, that Gray and his dealer had made themselves scarce. She said as much.

Jude paused again, this time longer and heavier. "Remember how Jen disappeared too after she chose Nelson and not Gray?" he asked then.

A shadow fell over her heart. "J-Jen *died,* Jude. An—"

"Accident? Shaynie, cars don't drive themselves off of mountains."

Andrew had implied it. Heck, Gray himself had implied it: *Somebody's going to end up dead again.*

"What a coincidence that it happened right when Gray was so mad that she'd cheated," said Jude, and, when she said nothing, went on. "Gray hates disloyalty."

*He says you slept with The Python*, Trin had said. And then there was Andrew: *A Borderline can't stand rejection.* There was no air in her throat.

"After all," Jude continued. "Look what he did to me the other night."

She found her voice. "Look what you did to each other. You—"

"Shaynie, he threatened to kill me."

She'd heard the words, hadn't known which one of them said it, and now Steve's voice rewound in her ear. *I never could tell those two apart.*

"People who get too close to people Gray thinks are his don't seem to fare well," said Jude.

*Do you think he meant Dad?* Andrew had asked, and new horror seeped into her belly. No. *No.* That was *Andrew's* histrionics. Their *Dad fell.*

"And now Chrystal Johns..." Jude trailed off.

It was hard to talk around the thick dread in her mouth. Still, she was a cop's sister. "Jude, I know he's like a brother, but if you hear from him—"

"I'll call *your* brother."

Silence hovered on the line, the absence of sound sounding a whole lot like grief.

"Hey." He broke it, shaky. "Could you do me a favour in exchange for meeting with Steve?"

"Absolutely."

"I—uh—I really want my mirrors."

The mirrors. His eyeless angels. She fought back a shudder. It was a small price to pay.

THE STAIRS CREAKED like companions as she descended into the old embalming room but once her feet hit the concrete, silence swallowed air and Jude's doors circled her, the eyeless angels staring and blind, their little mouths neither singing nor screaming.

They were laughing.

And one of the doors, with its centre cut out and ready for glass, looked as though it had a wide, gaping mouth.

Also laughing.

"I didn't catch the joke," she said aloud.

Laughing. She could hear it. Dry-mouthed, she forced herself to unfurl Styrofoam wrap from a glass sheet of mirror. "Measure twice, cut once," she stated aloud, for there was comfort in making noise. *Human* noise. She hoisted the mirror, yelping when its edge cracked the cut in her hand. *Don't bleed on it!* The possibility filled her with revulsion and she brought her hand to her mouth, sucked on the wound while to her left the furnace chugged on. Its noise was still not loud enough to cover the scraps of laughter spattering the air. *Shut up!* she thought, and shot a hand to the radio, cranked it on.

"With trade deadline approaching, a surprise rumor has surfaced: seems Noel Nelson has joined the likes of Cameron Weste in possibly wanting out of our City of Champions."

*What?* Slack-jawed, she and her mirrored selves gaped at one another.

A commercial kicked in. "Tired of break-ins and being on guard?"

Stunned, she swung her gaze to the radio.

"What you need is protection!"

Shaking, it took her three tries to slide on thick coveralls, three more to fasten glass-grinding goggles on her face. "Protection," she said clearly, and gazed at the ceiling, the walls. "I hear you. I believe you. Please help me."

The furnace roared. And in the space of a second all the little eyeless angels went blind.

She worked all afternoon, fitting mirror after mirror into doors and, with the radio cranked over the whine of the glass grinder, she hung on every word the sportscaster said. "We're all stunned at the news of native Edmontonian Nelson's rumored request for a move. Nelson has always maintained a wish to play his career out as a hometown hero."

Since they were kids. So what had happened? Why was Nelson now hellbent on getting everyone—including himself—out of Edmonton? Surely not because of his liaison with Chrystal Johns and how they'd spiked Cameron's drink. By now that sedative was long out of Cameron's system and, really, other than one crappy game its efforts at sabotage had fallen flat.

Or had it?

*Nothing's as it seems.* Laughter sprinkled the air yet again, and when her cell rang she reached for it, grateful to speak over the phantom sounds. "Hello?"

"Concierge has a ticket with your name on it. And one for The Agent too. Don't come alone, it's not safe. I'm busy with pre-game. Gotta go." He hung up.

She scowled at the cell and, as if by command, it rang again. "You know," she answered. "Being a snippy jerk isn't the best way to ask me out."

"I haven't even said anything yet," said her brother.

Her face started on fire.

"But even if I *was* being a snippy jerk, it looks like protecting you pays off. We're going to the game with some gold section tickets. Cameron just called me."

'Cameron', not 'Goliath'. She stuck her tongue out. "I'm not going."

"You are *not* serious," he said, and, at her silence, growled. "Shaynie Grace, you can't stay alone."

A tide of lavender billowed down the stairs, and she glanced up to find Trin on the treads looking atypically meek and impossibly small. "I'm not alone," she said into the phone. "Divinity just brought me a friend."

Andrew made a sound she guessed was profanity but came out sounding more like a grumble.

"Andrew, I'm *fine.* Trin's here. But you go. Take a date. Have fun." God knew he needed to—after she'd hung up with Jude she had called him, shared everything Jude had implied. He'd been all cop in taking the info but she knew him and could hear, crouching between the lines, his old question: *Do you think he meant Dad?* And now… she truly didn't know. "Andrew," she said gently, again. "Go to the game. 'Cause remember— life is meant to be lived."

A stroke of silence elapsed, then "I'll pick you up right after."

She smiled, relieved, and drew their ankh in ground glass dust after hanging up. She turned to Trin. "Welcome."

Uncertainty fell from Trin's face and, grinning, she loped down the rest of the stairs.

They creaked happily.

"I invited myself," she said, apologetic, "I explained that to the little lady who let me in upstairs. I—uh—just had to see what rescued you from The Snake."

Bull. She'd invited herself because after last night and everything about Gray, she was worried. Still— "A Python is far more deadly than any mere snake," Shaynie corrected, dry.

Trin rolled her eyes. "Nice Jude impersonation. The first time he said that to me I told him that The Python was really just a trumped-up version of his own penis."

Shaynie spat out a mouthful of now-cold coffee. "And what did he say?"

"Ah, Perfect. What *could* he say?"

No one wore disaffected better than Trin. Shaynie toasted her with the cold cup of coffee. "The 'little woman upstairs', Cele, calls The Python 'The Poison'." She pronounced it with French inflection.

Trinity grinned. "What a freaky little French woman. I like her."

They beamed at each other. "Want a tour?" Shaynie asked.

"Hell, yeah!"

They took the elevator up and she told Trin, once they got out, her plans to improve it, and how she now wanted to paint its doors like a picture.

"Go with a landscape," Trin advised. "One that looks like you're able to walk into it, like a fantasy."

*Like a sky full of stars.* "Another dimension," Shaynie murmured. "Because that's what Divinity is."

Trin nodded, and wandered into the showroom.

The way she studied the furniture reminded Shaynie of her toughest woodworking instructors, and she found herself holding her breath until, "Unbelievable," Trin breathed, crouching eye-level with a credenza fashioned out of old window panes and doors. "Perfect, what the hell have you been doing, wasting yourself slinging beer at The Snake?"

Echoes of Gray. "Earning money," she said, and cleared sadness from her throat. "Buying this place was cheap, but everything I've done with it? Not so cheap."

"Ah," Trin nodded, and paused by the window seat. "Now *here's* a spot."

*The* spot. *Their* spot.

Trinity tracked a gaze up the length of stained glass. "These windows remind me of eyes," she murmured. "Eyes that know lots but are still really kind."

Shaynie felt the place glow. "Yes," she agreed. "And they're glad you're here."

Trinity laid her fingers on the window casement. "This building, the way it feels. It's like it loves you, Shaynie. Like it *is* you."

A subtle shaft of sun brightened the stained glass.

"See?" Trin said, thrilled and hushed.

Shaynie offered a silent benediction to the ceiling and walls.

The responding pulse was unmistakable. Trin's eyes were huge. "Can…can I tell you something?"

"Of course." Shaynie sank to the window seat.

"Today when I came to the door there was something, a *measuring* sort of something, that hung in the air. For a split second I almost believed the place was deciding whether or not it should let me in. Do—do you think that's possible?"

"Well," Shaynie thumbed through her deck, found the Judgment card. "A morgue *is* the last place we're seen before we move on to final judgment."

"Or punishment."

Shaynie blinked, startled.

"Perfect, don't you get the feeling that if this place *doesn't* like you, there's hell to pay?"

Divinity malevolent? She couldn't imagine.

*Oh yes you can.* The thought, not her own, rode through the air upon images. The welded Tarot suits. Ivy Shaynie. "I—I won't deny that unexplainable things happen here," she said neutrally.

"Unexplainable?" Trin jacked a brow. "No way. I think this place knows exactly what it's doing."

On the air a sound drifted. Laughter. But this time the laughter wasn't *at* her, it was *with* her, and when her cell rang she half-expected a disembodied Ivy Shaynie to hiss in her ear.

Jude spoke instead. "Mission accomplished," he said. "Not only am I sending someone by to pick up my mirrors, but I also have your welded Tarot suits."

The laughter around her was deafening.

## CHAPTER THIRTY-SEVEN

"YOUR HONEY SCORED a hat trick and you were too busy pouting to see it." Andrew picked her up after the game, still chomping on an arena pretzel.

"You have crumbs on your coat," she said dryly. "And what was wiser, going to the game or making money? I got Jude's mirrors done *and* Trin got a reading."

"You charged her? I would have read her future for free." He placed a hand on his forehead, squinted his eyes. "I see a mug shot. I see jail—"

"Stop." She swatted him, softening as she recalled Trin, holding her breath as Shaynie turned cards.

"So?" Trin's eyes had darted from one augur to the other. "Am I gonna have a stroke? Get hit by a bus? Drop dead?"

"No, no, and stop being ridiculous." The entire spread was Wands. "Trinity, are you thinking of starting a business?"

"Please. I don't have a pot to piss in."

"But the cards say a work endeavor. A very successful work endeavor."

"Right. The only 'successful endeavor' I can hope for is that some drunk accidentally tips me a winning lottery ticket at The Snake."

Shaynie laughed. "Why on earth did you ever start there in the first place?"

"Same reason you did—Gray told me I'd make big money."

Gray. She had wondered how long it would take for them to circle the drain and be back at him.

"He always told me not to stay in The Python too long," Trin said wistfully. "He said The Python will promise the moon but—"

"Make you pay with the stars. Yes. I know."

"Shaynie Grace?" Andrew broke in now, disrupted her recall. "You're pretty quiet."

She started, abruptly back in the now. *Quiet.* No kidding. Her cell hadn't rung with a call nor chirped with a text. Apparently Cameron wanted to be quiet too. A payment of stars. Seemed she'd already written the check. "Stress," she murmured obliquely.

Her brother nodded. "You have your fair share."

They cruised without speaking for a few moments, the sound of his unmarked whooshing through slush strangely lulling. When he parked in her lot she gave him the keys to her apartment, then stayed beside him as he swept through the rooms.

"Your truck overnight at Divinity might be a magnet for Gray," he said. "He'll think you're alone and come calling."

"Maybe." It was part of a plan Andrew had texted her from the game: she'd leave her truck at Divinity as though she were there too, while one of the young constables he'd brought to haul furniture the other night would stay in the morgue. The young uniform had met them at Divinity when Andrew arrived to pick her up and he could not have made it clearer that he hoped something creepy would happen. It wouldn't. Divinity had glowed with gratitude as she and Andrew left, and she'd known the young cop would be sheltered there.

Now Andrew flopped onto her sofa, put his feet up on her coffee table. She curled into the throne she'd come to think of as Cameron's. "Nobody in Gray's circle of twelve steppers will talk," he announced.

She was surprised he'd even been able to ascertain names. Twelve step groups were notorious for anonymity.

He rolled deadpan eyes when she said so. "The rank 'Detective' means I know how to do more than eat donuts, Shaynie Grace."

"Or pretzels." She grinned. "And what about the cell phone pings, Detective? Haven't any of those given Gray's locale away?"

"General area's the best you get with a throw-away cell, and believe me, that's all these druggie losers ever have. Anything with a GPS component would have been fenced for more dope."

"God." She swiped a hand through her hair. "When will this *end*?"

"Patience. One thing my guys did gather from a flophouse on Boyle is that the shit-rat whose phone Gray used to call Trinity is in detox."

"Detox as in the clinic just up from Divinity?"

"Yeah."

So close. She swallowed. "And? Did you talk to this guy in detox? Ask him where Gray is?"

"You kidding? Those do-gooder addiction counsellors guard those losers like Dobermans. We can't even get a client roster without a warrant."

"But you're getting a warrant, right? To go see this guy?"

"How, Shaynie Grace? All I've got to accuse him of is lending his phone. Where's the probable cause? More important, what's the crime? This isn't the movies, you know."

"I don't watch movies," she said sulkily.

"Detox is a short stay for druggies. They clean 'em up and spit 'em out. This loser will be out on the street within twenty-four to forty-eight."

"Not always. Gray wasn't when he went there."

Her brother looked at her, sharp.

She forced herself to look him in the eye. "When we were kids I brought him here, to the city. For detox."

"All the way from *Jasper?*"

"Yes."

"How old were you?"

"Sixteen. I—uh—borrowed your car."

"You borrowed my...." He did the mental calculation. "You said you were going to a folk festival in Banff. You *lied* to me, Shaynie Grace?"

Her gaze hit the floor. "Yes."

Several seconds twitched by then "Well. That explains it."

"Explains—"

"Why he hasn't targeted me. It's the piece I've been missing. I'm as close to you as anyone—"

"Closer," she said. "In fact, Jude and I had a little set-to last night when he made a crack that you're so protective no one could ever get near me."

"Oh did he now? And you said?"

"Damn straight."

His mouth flickered, an Andrew smile. It healed things. "Apparently I didn't work hard enough."

She opened her palms, a *what-do-you-do?* gesture.

He grinned a bit. "I've wondered why Gray wouldn't feel more threatened about you and me, but the whole detox story explains it; you betrayed my trust once for him. That's proof enough he's more important."

It made some sense, but..."So then why did he never trash things between me and Steve? Why did he never care that I became friends—good friends—with Jude?"

"As I recall, he never left your side when Jude was around."

True. Except for the times Jude gave him money which she'd known very well Gray used for dope. *I can't say no to him, Shaynes.* In retrospect it seemed like it had happened far more than it had appeared at the time.

"As for Steve," Andrew went on, "who rode your ass constantly about how he was dorky? Not compatible? That you should look for someone new?"

Again, all true. Still— "Steve *wasn't* compatible." It sounded defensive. And ridiculous. She slumped in her seat. "Listen to me," she said.

"I sound like a lunatic. But...I miss him. Even after all of this, I...I just want my friend back. Isn't that crazy?"

"No, Shaynie Grace. It's human."

ALONE IN HER BEDROOM, she pointed the remote at her small TV. *Your honey scored a hat trick.* It was on the highlight loop, and an announcer crowed, "Cameron Weste with his third goal of the game" Hats rained on the ice. A smile skipped on her heart. *Way to go, Ice Deity.*

Her cell chirped. She pounced on it.

<Didn't see you at my game>

Just words on a screen, still she could hear the reproach. And the hurt. She used the keypad. <Serves me right that you got that hat trick>, she typed. <The camera loves you>

An eternity of silence ticked by, then, <Divinity tomorrow, 10am. Goodnight>

"No, Cameron. It's not a goodnight." She ran her thumb over the screen. "I'm not with you." She took the cell into bed with her, tucked it by her cheek. Maybe it would help conjure a ceiling of stars to sleep to.

## CHAPTER THIRTY-EIGHT

THE YOUNG COP who'd stayed at Divinity met her and Andrew at the door, disappointment in his slumped shoulders. "The place was dead all night."

"No pun intended," said Shaynie.

The kid constable and her brother stared at her. "Sorry," she squeaked but couldn't help the spring in her step. An armed guard, veiled threats, Gray himself could not deflate her. Not today.

"Keep your phone close," said Andrew, and left with the uniform.

She lit every candle. Checked and re-checked herself in every piece of looking glass except the ivy mirror. Hair? Down. Makeup? Subtle. Clothes? Not carpentry garb but not a slinky Python costume, either. She hoped the dress she wore straddled the line between sexy and sweet. *You stop my heart,* he'd said. "God, I hope so." Trade deadline was only one day away. "And I don't want to pay stars."

The door latch rattled at nine forty-five and her heart stopped, but Cele, only Cele, swept in, all cloak and fur.

"'Imself your 'ockey god is very demanding," she grumbled, and frost swirled around her feet, as rattled as she.

"Cameron called you?"

*"Oui:* 'Get up! Get moving! My Faerie is going to need you today'."

"*What*? Isn't *he* coming at ten today?"

Cele waved both hands in confusion. "I 'ave no idea. All I know is *I* am to do as I am told: 'Get ready for coffee and *petit gateau.*"

"Coffee and cupcakes? What on Earth—" The doorbell gonged.

Two white-clad women—bakers—swooped inside before Shaynie could invite them, the scent of vanilla rolling in with them. One handed Cele two urns—"One's coffee, one's tea"—while the other plopped a stack of boxes in Shaynie's arms. "Careful with these."

Shaynie peeked through the cellophaned window on the top box. Cupcakes, capped with soft-colored frosting and piped insignias that said Fuss. *Fuss? No kidding.* "Is there something I should sign?"

"Nope. All looked after. Congratulations!" The women beamed, then were gone.

"Congratulations?" Shaynie and Cele, half laughing, looked at each other.

"Ah, that 'ockey god." Cele clucked. "Full of *mystère.*" She set the urns on the bar then went to the window seat table, flipped a card. "Aha, *Cheri!* The Four of Wands!"

"A happy surprise?" Shaynie rapidly laid linen and set cupcakes upon trays, instinct driving her. "*What* is he up to?"

The door chime gonged again.

"We find out." Cele rushed to open the door.

The first thought in Shaynie's head was, *Sirens.* The women on the stoop looked just like sirens, and as they filed in, Shaynie knew exactly who they were. Hockey wives. Breezing past, they loaded her arms with coats and wraps that even her thrift store eye recognized as Prada. Gucci. *God!* Louis Vuitton.

"Thank you for hosting." One Siren, clearly the leader, sized her up with eyes that missed nothing. "Weste said this would be a private party."

He had? "Uh—yes." Shaynie's head bobbed. "Definitely."

"And any card readings will be private? Confidential?"

"Absolutely. Always."

"And the furniture—prices include delivery, right?"

Delivery? She had no access to delivery! But there was only one right answer. "Certainly." She crossed her fingers behind her back, saw Cele do the same.

The all-encompassing eyes sized her up. "Trish." A graceful hand was extended.

She met the perfect manicure with her own work-battered fingers. "Shaynie."

Trish smiled as though a test had been passed. "I know your name. 'Shaynie'."

Shaynie swallowed but did not break her stare. 'Trish'. A name not too different from 'Trin'. In fact with the same access to the wardrobe and the aesthetics endless dollars could buy, Trin could *be* Trish. Steel beauty. Women who would chew a mere puck bunny up.

Would she chew her up too? She lifted her chin a fraction.

Trish said "Your run in with the media? Ignore them. Avoid them."

Her run in.... God. Had this perfect creature heard about the reporters at the mall? About *Body Chocolate*? Her face burned.

If Trish noticed, she didn't care. "Reporters move from player to player like fruit flies. Weste will lose his taste soon enough and then they'll find a new meal. But it works faster if you starve them. Give them nothing to talk about and they'll abandon you."

In other words, eliminate public displays, and for God's sake no more public sex. "Duly noted."

Trish nodded, then turned to the sirens. "Shop first, readings after?"

They swarmed the showroom, perfect hands plopping onto mirrors, chairs, tables and *étagères*. Some haggled, most didn't, and as Cele filled out sold tag after sold tag, Shaynie plopped stone after stone into gratitude jars.

"You do take credit cards, right?"

"Absolutely."

Their readings took all afternoon, and when they abandoned half-eaten cupcakes and retrieved their fabulous coats, Divinity was a beautiful disaster. Shaynie collapsed at the window seat. "Do I look as depleted as the rest of this place?"

"Yes, Darling." Cele gathered leftover cupcakes and frosting-streaked linen.

Shaynie rifled through scratch notes she'd made with the sirens. "Look at these special orders! It'll take a day– *a whole day!*—just to sketch that one design. Did you overhear what it is? A dining room suite!" She squeaked, a little sound of delight. "I've never made a whole set before. Eleven pieces. And she loves old wood, and wants chicken wire imbedded between the glass on the cabinet doors. Won't that look phenomenal?"

"Country chic," Cele smiled. "Now, is it her friend who wants an *étagère* made from her husband's old 'ockey sticks?"

Shaynie giggled. "A trophy stand. How on earth will I pull off old hockey sticks without it looking tacky?" Who was she kidding? She couldn't wait to try. She re-read her notes. "I'm going to need a day timer for all these design appointments. And a digital camera too. Oh, and now I *have* to break down and get a computer. Learn about internet." She shuddered. "Did you hear how many of them wanted my email address? To keep track of what they'd ordered?"

"Yes, Darling."

She knew she was babbling. Just couldn't help it. "*Look* at this place." Furniture was jostled this way and that. "They bought every piece I have!"

Well...*almost* every piece. The Ivy Mirror still stood without a sold tag, and she had watched as the hockey wives moved up to it, then away. Some had worn expressions of vague alarm, and one Siren, only one, achingly beautiful, had paused before it and said "I feel queer when I look in this."

"It's 'cause you're pregnant," her sidekick had replied. "Again. You guys gotta quit honeymooning after every road trip."

"You crazy? I love the honeymoon."

Her companion grinned, wicked. "Me too."

And so the Sirens understood "the good in goodbye". So much that they could sum it up in a few saucy sentences. *Ah, Weste,* She had watched them, enchanted. *You have no idea of the capacity for love.*

And enchantment had apparently worked both ways. Before they left, Trish approached her. "We'll need you at Halloween. We—the wives—do a charity event every year. Tarot will be perfect."

"Oh. Well." *Cameron's not staying!* "I'm not exactly a wife."

"Yet." Again those eyes looked her up, looked her down, and left her with a curious sense of having been stripped and accepted all at once.

"Darling?" Cele broke into reverie. "You're going to need to arrange delivery." A smile danced in the words. "You promised."

Ah, yes. The non-existent delivery. "I should make Cameron sort out delivery."

Cele laughed. "'Imself would likely be 'appy to."

Yes, he would. She knew he would. Just like he'd be thrilled to hear that Divinity had been a whirlwind of turned Tarot cards and melted credit cards. "I love him." It bubbled out, helpless.

"Yes!" Cele shot a fist in the air. "She says it!"

"This was the grand opening I'd dreamed of, and he knew it. Created it. He...I *love* him."

"So *tell* him, *Cheri*. You know you can make this work."

"Every bit as well here as Utopifornia. Better, even."

Cele reached for her phone. "Call him! Right now."

"Put your damn phone away, Shaynie Grace."

Both she and Cele whirled to where Andrew had silently entered the foyer. Shaynie scowled at the old building. *You need to stop doing that!*

Her brother stomped over, smacked a newspaper down hard enough to send Tarot cards fluttering. "What part of 'keep a low profile' is a foreign language to you?"

The paper, The Sun, boasted a cover photo: a couple lying in the snow, lip-locked and lost to the world. The headline read, LOVE CHANGES EVERYTHING?

## CHAPTER THIRTY-NINE

SHE DROPPED to the window seat, thumbed to where the accompanying story hid between pages. A subtitle—TORN BETWEEN TWO LOVERS—rode the space between two more pictures, another of the two of them, this time outside *Body Chocolate,* and one more, again of Cameron but this time with a different woman. Chrystal Johns. With her dyed-dark hair and come-hither clothing, she could almost pass for The Python Princess, and in the photo she was all over him, mouth on his jaw, hands on his bare chest. Her eyes were closed, but his.... Shaynie peered. His were gazing straight into the lens.

Kind of.

Murky and vacant, she knew the expression in an instant. Had seen it before. Her own eyes, peering back from a broken mirror.... "He's drugged."

Andrew snorted, a sound that implied she was reaching, looking to excuse him from being with another woman.

*I'm asking for faith.* The words slipped into memory's ear like a song.

She tapped the newspaper. "Detective Gavin, meet the elusive Chrystal Johns. This picture would have been taken when she flew down to California to meet Nelson. The night after which, Cameron thought he'd had the flu." *And told me later he'd dreamed of being with me.* She glared at the brunette Panties in the picture. Is that what she and Nelson had been banking on? That Cameron would think she was her?

Although it looked like it had worked.

Andrew grunted. "A *guy* being slipped a roofie?"

"What athlete wants to look like he's more into drunken sexcapades than playing hard for his team? This picture was taken before the trade rumors hit the media. Before Nelson knew anything other than the fact that Cameron was stealing all of his coveted limelight."

"So he leaks this picture *now?* Shaynie Grace—"

"How do you know it was leaked now? He may have given it days ago. Media are like fruit flies," she quoted Trish, the head siren. "The tastier the story, the more they swarm and look—" She pointed to the home team insignia over her picture, the California state seal over Panties. "They've turned this into a competition between two teams, not two women. God. Like he needed this."

*The California hottie or the Edmonton sweetheart?* read the article. *Weste needs to make a choice, and either way things look a lot more complicated than hockey.*

Andrew frowned. "I don't know. Doesn't it seem a little coincidental that you're being stalked and suddenly you're a billboard for the whole city to see?"

"Andrew, *think*—this would be why Nelson was so frantic to see Chrystal when he came to The Python. He knew this story was finally going to break and he knew she could sink him if she spilled the truth. Drugging a teammate? He'd be lucky to carry the sticks for a pee-wee team if that got out."

Andrew said nothing and she thought she'd hit it home. But then—"I can't shake that the stalker's connected somehow."

*Stalker,* not *Gray*. One more way to remind her he was *not* her friend. "There's no way Gray would hook up with Noel. He's never got over how Noel stole Jen."

*Stole* Jen. And Jude thought Gray killed her. She twitched, cold shoulders.

"I wonder," said Andrew, "how detached from reality is Gray? *Would* he maybe align with Nelson now that *another* Nelson—Cameron Weste—is getting close to the other woman he loves? You?"

Talk about reaching. And from the twisted way he held his mouth, he thought so too. "Sometimes things are what they are," she offered. "'Cause I may not understand Gray—*clearly* I don't understand Gray—but I do know he'd never pair up with Nelson."

"Yet this Chrystal Johns has paired up with all of them."

Cameron too. Or so the picture would have one think. *I'm asking for faith.*

Yes, Cameron. And here's me giving it.

Andrew pulled a hand down his face. "I have half a dozen cops trying to dig both Johns and Gray out from wherever they're holed up." He consulted his watch. "And speaking of, it's shift change at detox. I'm going over. You never know how they might respond to charm."

"You? Charm?"

She was shooting for levity, but Cele, emerging from her divining room, wagged a finger. "Everyone loves when the Knight of Pentacles turns up, *Cheri.* Do not discount your Andrew."

Beaming with a rare grin, he stepped to stand next to her. "I think I love you."

Cele rose on tip-toe, kissed both his cheeks. He blushed like a school boy. "Make sure she behaves." He tossed a thumb Shaynie's direction, then was gone.

Cele eyed her, baleful. "You will not listen," she said.

"Yes, I will." From the window she watched Andrew's unmarked pull out into traffic. "But only until my brother can't see me in his rear view."

GRAY COULD BE WATCHING. *Waiting.* Still, as she slipped out the back service door, he was not whom she thought of. *I love him.* Storm eyes. A slick whiplash smile. Her heart fluttered as she eyed the back alley. She could drive to Canada Place, park underground, then access the sub-level walkways specifically designed to offer shelter from Edmonton winters. Using them, she could then double back and emerge at street level only a block north of Cameron's high rise, all unseen. "All I'll need is The Moon," she whispered. "To be the thing that hides in the shadows." She glanced left and right. Nothing. No one. She sprinted for her truck.

Her shoes stopped in the snow. *"No!"*

The driver's window—perfectly intact when she and Andrew had arrived this morning—was now a shattered chrysanthemum of broken glass, and a weapon, a hammer, hung like a calling card from the frame. *"Goddamn you, Gray!"* She grabbed her cell. Andrew may as well pitch the idea of going to detox. Their quarry was clearly on the loose. Finger on speed dial, she reached with her free hand for the hammer.

The hammer.

Her cell slipped from her fingers and into the snow, for her carpenter's touch recognized the hammer in an instant, knew its shape, knew its weight. Knew immediately what the stains were on the wood handle near its base. Deep red wine splotches.

*Red wine? That's not red wine. It's brandy. In a fine glass.*

Heart in her ears, she saw her father, his fine glass raised in a toast. "You are my sunshine." God. He really had looked like The Agent. She drew a gurgling breath and was back there, fourteen and standing next to her Dad's dead body, Andrew's arm around her as he spoke—shouted, really—at the cop he would one day become, filled with hotheaded defiance. "*Our Dad was not drunk! Someone killed him!*"

"You were right," she breathed. All that time, all *this* time.... *But why? Why?* She stooped, and it was like watching someone outside herself reach for her phone. How would she tell her brother? What would she say? A wave of dizzy emptiness washed over her and she had to smack a hand upon the door of her truck, forget her phone. Her vehicle's cold, tangible presence grounded her as it came to her then, the why. *"A Borderline hates rejection, and when he sees someone getting close to you…"*

No one had been closer to her than her Dad.

And more words rushed back, Gray's words, from long ago: "Your Dad doesn't like me and Jude does he?" She'd shrugged it off. What father of a teenage daughter *did* like teenage boys?

Who knew she should have considered what teenage boys thought of Dads?

*"People who get too close to people Gray thinks are his don't fare well."*

And what was close to her now? Divinity, which he'd tried to sabotage. Cameron, who.... "*Somebody else is going to end up dead.*"

An ice fist gripped her gut. Cameron. A love affair that hadn't even tried to be subtle. It had combusted like the firestorm she'd referenced when they'd walked in the river valley, an explosion of dizzy color and heat.

And commitment. And faith. For while Cameron was still too scarred to believe what she felt, Gray—who knew her as well as or better than anyone—had seen it right from the start, on Hellnight when he'd *dragged her away by the hair.*

A burst of rage bolted through her and she gripped the driver's door of her truck. What lay there, visible through the broken glass, knocked all her anger away. This morning's newspaper, the same one Andrew had smacked down in front of her, had been tossed on the seat, and she reached for it, jagged glass snapping and breaking off into the snow. The picture in this copy had been defaced. "*Somebody else is going to end up dead.*" She stared down at Cameron's face, scrawled out as if a child had had a tantrum with a Sharpie marker. *Someone else. Dead.*

Her gut went to water, and when her phone rang, still buried in the snow at her feet, she knew who'd be calling.

Dead.

No one knew where Gray was. Andrew and his constables hadn't been able to find him.

The phone rang again. She clutched the paper. *People who get too close to people Gray thinks are his don't fare well.* Her Dad, when she'd found him, had bone and brain matter on his ball cap. Horror bloomed as a picture—Cameron, blood and brain on *his* ball cap—splashed up in her mind.

Down at her feet, her cell kept on ringing.

And in her head, images kept ringing. Gray. Cameron. Her Dad.

Now the hammer, this newspaper, they were more than a threat. They were a promise.

*So what do I do?* Desperate, darting, her eyes sought Divinity.

The morgue's back door blew open, and on a rush of warm air, the building spoke a word that pulled her inside. *Protection.*

## CHAPTER FORTY

In the end, the lies she told Cameron rolled off her tongue far slicker than she would ever have imagined. Still, she'd clung to the pitch of his voice after she managed, numbly, to pick up her cell, say "Hello?"

"You sound pretty distant, my Faerie. Didn't the WAGS redeem me?"

"W-wags?" she echoed but didn't really care what it meant. She just wanted him to keep talking. Maybe then she wouldn't have to.

"Wives and girlfriends." He laughed. "So, tell me, who's pregnant? Having an affair? Going broke? It had to be in their cards."

In the cards. Of course. The answers were always in the cards. *Oh, thank God.* 'Cause left on her own, she'd never be able to do it.

"Cameron?" She leaned back against the wall, felt Divinity hold her up. "Let's—let's talk about the cards."

Apprehension hung in the silent way he did not answer, and she knew then that he'd already anticipated what she was going to say. *But he doesn't know why!*

Blood. Brain matter. She let horror guide her, and the lies poured forth. "The wives turned one card more than any others," she said, and this part was true. The Two of Cups, the love card, had appeared so many times she'd started to expect it as she'd turned spreads. "Three of Swords," she lied. "Heartbreak. It showed up every time they asked about love, commitment...fidelity."

He did not say a word.

She went for the throat. "And the Three was always surrounded by Pentacles." She affected a little laugh. "As if it's possible to buy your way out of someone else's bed. Although, maybe for some of those women, the way they spend money—I guess maybe it *is* possible." She paused. "But that's not me."

"I know that's not you. Shaynie. Listen, if this is all about yesterday at the welding shop...let's talk in person. I'll come ov—"

"No!" No *way.* He'd see the truth in her eyes. Someone else would see him. And then—*Bone. Brain matter.* Her gut lurched. Her head raced. *What do I say?*

More lies rode to the rescue.

"Case in point was this morning's newspaper."

"The news—oh, for...Faerie, you *know* that was a set up!"

Oh, yes. He saw the truth. And knew she saw it too.

But lies were so easy.

"Yes, but Trish—you know Trish, right?"

"Chief WAG. Yeah. What about her?"

Anger had crept into his voice, and she was grateful. It was far, far easier to endure than his hurt. "Trish said this would happen. How the media are like fruit flies, how they ruin things—"

"Oh, Christ, Shaynie, *Nelson* ruined things. He just left here, practically bawling and carrying on, 'I'm so sorry, man'. Snivelling about how we both needed to take a trade, get out of here—"

"He's right."

Stunned silence. She swallowed cold air, forced herself to keep talking. "Cameron, everything that's happened—Chrystal Johns, our fight about money, then the cards the wives turned.... Don't you think it's like prophecy?"

"No! No, Shaynie, I do *not* think—"

"You've said all along what the strain of being away does to relationships. You lived through someone cheating on you, but from what I saw today in those cards it could just as easily be *me* wondering who's getting wild with you."

"*What?* Shaynie—"

"Tomorrow's trade day, and Cameron, you want that wish card. You want the happy-ever-after. Increase your odds. Take the trade. Take California."

Silence and her pulse pounded. *End it! End it!*

"So that...that's *it?*" he rasped. "We're done?"

Done. *Goodbye.* Tears held at bay scored her cheeks.

"Well?" he asked.

"W-we we're done, yes. But remember, you...you got the wish card. The Sun—"

"Yeah. And three fucking swords." He hung up.

SHE TOLD MORE LIES to Cele after she hung up the phone. "Cameron's coming," she said, faking demure by ducking her head. It hid the tears. "We—um—we'd like privacy…?"

Cele had hesitated but only for a moment, and when she left she was clucking but oblivious. "Stay safe with your 'ockey God, *Cheri,* and do not tell the Knight of Pentacles."

Andrew. He'd go vigilante when she told him about the hammer and the note.

And Gray would go vigilante right back. *I've done it before.* Bone. Brain matter. Cameron. Her brother. No one was safe.

The alarm panel blinked. She blinked back. Correction. So long as she stayed here, alone, everyone was safe. Stomach churning, she locked the doors, wrapped the hammer in the newspaper, and hid them in her divining room trunk. Tomorrow she'd go to the Detachment, make sure other detectives were there to temper her brother when she showed him everything. Tomorrow. After Cameron was safely on an airplane and gone.

Gone.

She turned off all the lights and blindly rained stones in a jar. Black for burdens, colors for thanks. 'Cause it was good that fear had turned her belly ice cold, good that it had made her pulse pound. Nothing hurt when it was numb, and she could hear nothing but heartbeat. It was good.

THE SKY WAS AN INKWELL when her cell woke her. CALLER BLOCKED. She shot up. "Hello?"

"Trade's done. But you owe me one thing."

Trade. Done. And he'd wiped her number from his cell. Blocked his own. "I...I owe—"

"My Sun. I want it back."

His Sun. Her necklace. Her hand came up, closed over it, and though the gesture took the mere work of a second, it struck her how automatic it was and how often, unconsciously, she had reached for the pendant. How holding it had become reflex to anxiety. And heartache.

"Shaynie?"

Not Faerie. That was gone too. And now her little Sun.... She looked down at the silver shard of light between her fingers. *Protection.* The Sun was California. California was protection. One more symbol that would take him away. "I—I'll bring it over. Give it to security." Impeccable could take it upstairs, deliver it—

"No. You still have a key. I want that too."

## CHAPTER FORTY-ONE

WHEN HE OPENED HIS DOOR all he wore was sweat, jeans, and a light in his eye she did not recognize.

"I turned every belief on its head for you."

She swallowed hard, looked away.

What she saw only drove the swords deeper. Pictures. Books. His things. *Him.* He'd unpacked. He had given up California.

He'd been going to stay.

He watched the comprehension play out in her eyes. "Guess it's a lucky thing agents can sweet talk their way in and out of deals real quick-like isn't it?"

Lucky? She wasn't sure she even knew what it meant anymore.

"The Sun." He stuck out a finger.

Her pendant. The first time she'd slipped it on she had been sitting in their spot in Divinity, then after, when she'd angrily tossed it onto this once-barren floor, he'd brought it back, said *All I crave is you.* Her heart collapsed, and her hands slipped on her nape, unable to unfasten it. *I can't!* She could feel him, storm eyes, body heat. The scents of rain and chocolate. And around them everything was...*Cameron.* A condo he'd decided to live in. For her. Because she'd turned every belief on its head. Because he loved her. *And I love him. I can't do this! I can't—*

"It's my card," he said "Not yours."

A shock of pain whistled through her, and her hands scurried to unclasp the chain, refasten the closure. The little Sun winked light as she hung it on the end of his finger. "E-every joy," she whispered. "Every dream. Every moment of love you've ever dreamed. I—I *am* grateful you got the wish card and The Sun, Cameron." How could tears feel like fire? How could words feel like they *bled?* "G-goodbye." She turned.

*"Goodbye?"* He jerked her around and her shoulders hit the door.

She gasped, shock and pain chasing tears.

"Goodbye means you'll always be with me. Haunting my side even when you're not there. Isn't that what you said goodbye means?"

*Always?* She raised her eyes, found his. *Oh, yes. Oh, please.*

He made a sound—pain, rage—and knotted a hand on her jacket. Her knees buckled as he jerked and the staccato clatter of buttons rained onto the hardwood. He threw her coat. It made a black puddle on the floor. "No goodbye," he spat, and kicked it. It whished across the room as he grasped her collar, gave another yank.

Fabric gave way. Icy air met her skin. She shrank into herself. "Camer—"

"Shut up, Shaynie." His mouth dove.

Their silk kiss, except hotter. Wetter. *Angrier.*

She gasped in his mouth, and her feet left the floor. The next thing she saw were his painted stars, racing the sky.

"One night." He tossed her on the bed. "I didn't want your goddamn necklace. I wanted one night."

He advanced, and her breath evaporated on a sound, a whimper she remembered as terror, *old* terror, squeezing its way out of her throat. She scampered to the top of the headboard, ruined dress slipping down her hips, pulling her panties down too.

He watched, an animal flare in his eyes. "God, you're gorgeous."

*Gorgeous whore.* Her heart froze and his mouth moved, a vicious version of the whiplash smile. "Come here."

No! She shrank back. Don't do it! Don't touch him! Don't—!

"Come." He moved, a pulse stroke away. "Come Shaynie."

Shaynie, not Faerie, yet she could not stop her hands from betraying her, starving and cold.

He connected them, fingertip to fingertip. "One night," he said, softer. Gentler. "Let me give you what you gave me."

Which was...? Her gaze trembled in his.

"Everything," he whispered.

Wet pricked her eyes and a tear escaped. Floated down her face.

"Don't." He caught it. "Shaynie, don't cry."

Shaynie again. Seven blades—trickery, deception—flashed in her head.

He climbed onto the bed. "Everything." His mouth nudged her lips. Coaxing. Kissing.

Oh, kissing.

She tasted chocolate and tears, hers, leaking into the corners of their mouths.

He groaned. "Don't cry." He laid her down. "Shaynie, let me touch you. Let me give you everything."

His hands were huge. Heavy. Heavenly. And his mouth....she ached. *Craved.*

"Oh, yes, Shaynie. You like that, don't you?"

Something in the question made her heart darken.

He slipped down between her thighs. "You'll *love* this."

*This.* A long, melting lick down her belly. Oh. Oh, *God.* She melted into the bed, into him.

He laughed against her skin. "See? That feels good, right, my Faerie?"

Faerie. Finally. Her heart slid out on a sigh and she arched her back. Arched her *hips.*

She felt his smile on her thigh, then...*"Oh!"* Tongue. Teeth. Feasting noises. So intense she wanted more. So intense she had to get away.

"No." He grasped her hips, held her still. "Feel it," he muttered, and his tongue flicked.

Her blood thrummed. "More," she gasped.

"Yes," he hissed. *"Feel it."*

The muttered breath almost took her. Almost. She raised herself up... up—

He jerked back. "There, Shaynie. What you gave me. Everything. *Nothing."*

Seven swords. She uttered sound—feral, fierce—and shoved him back.

He landed with a grunt and his tongue taunted her, flicking air.

Snarling, she dove for it.

The silk kiss was raw. Enraged. And when she broke it, she was panting. "You like torture?"

"I must."

Ivy Shaynie was a reflection in his storm eyes. Skin hunger sizzled there too. Panting, glaring, they attacked, raking nails, brutal teeth, and fingers fisting into each other's hair. "My God, Shaynie." Trembling, he jerked her to the edge of the bed. "You *do* like it rough."

Her bottom teetered half-on and half-off the bed, and with a snarl she jerked him down, jerked him into her. Her cry scarred the air. *Pain.* "C-cameron!" they'd gone too far.

He thrust again.

*Pleasure.* "C-cameron—"

"You wanted me, now take me. *Take me*!" He jerked her legs higher, buried himself deeper.

"Cam—" *Pain.*

"Take me!"

*Pleasure.* "Cameron!"

"Take me!"

A tide snagged her, tossed her, and someone cried out as first she, then he, shook with shudders. Then—

Blood roared in her ears. Ragged breaths tore holes in the silence.

"Shaynie."

She didn't want to answer. Didn't want to know that love could feel so much like rage. So much like hurt.

*I knew you'd like this!*

"Shaynie."

In silence she held him, deep inside, and closed her arms around him too, a protective circle with her fingers just meeting across the breadth of his shoulders.

"Shaynie," he said, a third time, then broke free.

A cold thread of air slid between them and the bed rose as he lifted his weight. Slowly, carefully, she lifted her lids.

No anger. No hurt. What she saw etched on his face...horror. "You..." He swallowed, audible. "You have bite marks."

She looked. Red abrasions, some purpling, littered her shoulders. Her breasts.

"I hurt you."

"N-no." She touched the marks, almost in wonder. "You...had everything."

"Everything? Shaynie. I took—"

"I *gave*. My right side. My left. My dark and my light. A ten—"

"No. A mirror. And here it is, trapped and looking back at me." He swore, ripped a hand through his hair.

"No. Cameron—" She tried to sit, but her arms, her *everything,* stung.

He didn't miss how she winced. "God, look at you. At what I did. No better than Gra—"

"Don't. Don't say that name. Don't invite him here."

He flinched from her tone.

She looked at him evenly. "What we just had is yours. Mine. You didn't take any more than I gave, and, Cameron, I...I'd give you *anything.*"

Anything. The word echoed between them, and instant comprehension, instant questions, raced through his eyes. "Shaynie—"

"H-hold me." *And don't ask. Don't ask!* "Cameron, please, I—I hurt."

He hesitated. "Please." She couldn't look at him. Held her breath.

Groaning, he gathered her close. She closed her eyes against his chest. *I wanted one night.* Yes. And this was it. Then California. Protection. The Sun. "T-trade day is tomorrow," she whispered.

He didn't answer. Didn't need to.

"California is far away." From her. From Gray.

Silence slid by, so long that when he spoke, she was startled. "You said if I looked hard enough I'd see you even after we said goodbye."

An ocean hit her eyes. "Yes."

He nodded, and more silence slipped by as he rocked her, just like that day in Divinity when he'd surprised her, hiding in the back room before he'd charmed Cele into letting them go out, have a *date.*

They'd never actually had a real date. And now they never would.

"I'll miss you, my Faerie, when I say goodbye."

She closed her eyes.

"But not tonight."

One night.

He tilted her face back.

His whiplash smile broke her heart for how it lit her up.

"Come." The bed sank, and body heat bathed her as he laid them back down, wrapped her close.

She stayed, her back to his front, grateful to at last let agony silently course down her cheeks.

When she woke he was gone.

## CHAPTER FORTY-TWO

He must have refastened The Sun around her neck while she slept. She lifted it to her mouth, moved her lips against its warmth. In the distance her phone was ringing, the peal muted but still recognizable. She pushed herself off the bed—God, she really did ache—shoving the sheets away when they clung to her hips, beseeched her to stay.

Her coat was still a spent puddle on the floor. She rifled through the pockets. Andrew, said the cell screen. She lifted it.

"Listen and do not interrupt," he said. "Are you close to a land line?"

"I—yes. I'm at—"

"Don't tell me. Just call me back." He hung up. She picked up Cameron's phone, instinct driving her to block his number before she dialed.

Her brother answered with no preamble. "Chrystal Johns was found washed up on the shore of the North Saskatchewan."

Her gasp was sharp. He spoke over it.

"She was discovered a few feet from where you and Goliath were photographed."

Where she'd seen that branch that had looked like grey fingers. Her blood slowed, ice cold. "H-how long has she—"

"Medical examiner says a couple days—"

"A couple *days?* That would be right after she talked to me about—"

"—Gray. Yeah, I know. And you know. But when I told everyone else, they thought his motive sounds awful flimsy." The breath he drew reminded her, inexplicably, of a wrecking ball. "But they think *your* motive sounds awful compelling."

"Me?"

"You and her have been painted as rivals. You already had a cat fight in The Python. The banker from your old mortgage ID'd her as the person who brought him the picture of your vandalism—"

"But *I* didn't—"

"I know that! But the other D's don't. You look guilty as hell, and now more than ever I need to find Gray Ward, nail his fucking balls to the wall."

*"End it or I will. I did it before."* "A-Andrew, he...he's dangerous."

"No shit."

"No! I mean..." Bone. Brain matter. "He did kill Dad."

He didn't ask how she knew. Didn't say anything at all. But his silence ached with rage and sorrow that seemed to bleed. "I'll find that fucker," he rasped, finally. "But while I do, you hide, understand? *Hide.* I don't care where and I don't care with who, but you duck for cover—*do you understand?"*

"Yes, but—"

"And no cell phone. They're going to be looking for pings, looking for you."

But Cameron. How would she hear from Cameron?

"Shaynie Grace," said her brother. "I can't lose you too. Promise me, 'kay? Promise me you'll stay safe."

*Play safe.* She'd said it to Chrystal Johns on that long-ago night when she'd made her the turkey martini, back when Chrystal had been nothing more than an empty-eyed Barbie doll in skyscraper heels and fluorescent undies. *Oh, you twit!* Tears burned her eyes. *You poor, silly twit.* In her mind's eye she saw her, skin blue beneath the Python's back door light, looking for one split moment like a corpse before she'd teetered away, Cameron's stolen coat in her bag.

Cameron's coat.

"Andrew?" she rasped. "Chrystal Johns—what was she wearing when she was found?"

He didn't answer. But she knew. "Symbolic," she said softly.

Andrew said nothing, then—"And Gray's chain," he added, quiet.

St. Cecelia. She held her breath.

"It's how she died. He twisted it into a garrote."

Her gut rolled, and her hand clasped The Sun Cameron had replaced around her neck. Protection becoming a murder weapon. "My God," she whispered.

"I need to go," said Andrew. "But please—"

"I'll hide."

His breath whooshed, relief. "Promise, little sister. 'Cause I love you to the moon and back." He hung up.

Naked, frozen, she couldn't move. *Protection.* So twisted. Gray had killed the lover who'd jilted him with St. Cecelia, his protection.

Her cell rang and she jolted, searched out the screen. Cameron. Her heart tripped and instinct grabbed for it. Andrew's warning made her throw it back down. *They're looking for pings, looking for you.*

"I have to play safe," she said aloud, and Panties, dead Panties with her dumb blonde smile seared her memory anew, asking for that stupid turkey martini. Dressed like a Barbie doll out in the cold. Painting herself all over Jude, fingers fluttering over his face and neck, asking "Do you have our protection?"

She froze.

Protection.

*The Python will strangle you or swallow you whole depending on what it needs.* Gray's mantra had always made Jude laugh. But now.... Her jaw dropped. *Do you have our protection?* St. Cecelia. "Panties didn't mean condoms."

On the couch, where she'd tossed it, her cell began ringing anew.

Cameron, again, it would have to be, and as she stared at the phone she could hear him: *Maybe the Devil and the swords haven't been a warning. Maybe they've been advice.* Because up until that moment, she had been looking at them backwards—just as she had looked at *protection*, at The Python, at Gray, all backwards. "Oh my God."

She raced away from her ringing cell, bare feet pounding back into Cameron's bedroom. The Devil. He made sense. Protection also made sense. And The Magician was no longer upside down.

"And neither am I."

Last night's clothes were ruined. Thank God. Because—*Hide, Shaynie Grace.*

"Yes. I need to." She rifled through Cameron's dresser, found sweats and a long-sleeved shirt. An impressive collection of ball caps hung in his closet, and she snagged one, sized it so she could jam her hair underneath. A pair of sunglasses had been carelessly tossed with some change on his bureau. She took those too, then paused, looked down from his window.

Divinity was a sentry below, vacant, yet she knew better. Andrew's colleagues would have it under surveillance. May even get a warrant to bust down its doors. "Stay safe," she whispered and traced an ankh over its colored windows, so much like benevolent eyes.

*Protection,* it breathed back, for it understood her, had always understood her, just as she had understood *it* when she'd paid, with orphan's benefits—*orphan's benefits! Money from a dead man!*—to save it from a wrecking crew.

To protect it.

"But not entirely, right?" she asked, looking down. "I didn't protect you entirely, did I?"

*The Python will promise the moon but expect you to pay stars.*

"But I promise too," she whispered, and righted Cameron's ball cap. "I won't pay any more of our stars."

She left the high rise through the back tenants' exit, her brother's plea meeting her outside, riding harsh February wind. *Hide.*

"I will, Andrew." She pulled the brim of the ball cap down. "But I'm also going to *find.*"

## CHAPTER FORTY-THREE

She blended into foot traffic on Jasper Ave, just another cold pedestrian hustling under the cement-colored clouds drifting over the sun.

Detox was a quick two blocks north, and she traversed the distance cloaked in Cameron's too-big clothes, hiding in plain sight as she approached the inconspicuous little clinic she'd been to once before, all those years ago. "You can hide there from your demons, Shaynie," Gray had said. No kidding, she thought now. The same barricade wicket still blocked the entrance from the ward, and when the young woman in an old-fashioned nurse's cap glanced at her, Shaynie knew what she saw—a drug user, swimming in ill-fitting clothes and with a face still smeared with yesterday's makeup.

Hide.

*You bet, Andrew. How am I doing so far?* "My friend Gray Ward is a patient here," she announced.

The nurse did not reply, unable, Shaynie knew, to confirm or deny.

"You can't tell me anything, but I know you can pass on a message."

Eyebrows rose, just a fraction.

"Tell Gray that I'm glad he's been hiding. That—" *Not Shaynie! You can't say Shaynie!* "—that his dance partner is glad he's been hiding." She paused. "Then tell him that I'm going to The Python."

A large clock on the wall stroked out seconds. "Sounds like street speak," the nurse said.

"It's not." Blood thrummed in her ears. "Gray will know it's not."

"The Python is a club."

"Gray knows exactly what The Python is." She found the woman's eyes. "Please tell him that now I do, too." She spun on her heel, dove back out into the cold.

Walking in Cameron's bulky clothes felt like a swim through thick water. They hid her real gait and allowed her to pause, unrecognizable, at 109th. She glanced at Divinity, wondered how many cops were watching while she stood right there, mere meters from its protective white circle. *Stay with me,* she begged.

Snow responded, swirling to become her frost soldiers. Nodding at them, she mentally cast a clear, colored stone, then stepped up her pace. Her truck remained parked out back, its wrecked window inviting in snow and its presence likely inviting more surveillance. Didn't matter. She didn't need it. The Python was not across the river. She could easily get there on foot.

*A Latte in Common,* the coffee house at the base of her old Hellnight apartment, looked, with the eastern sun rising behind it, as though it were ringed with hellfire. "How appropriate," she murmured, and smacked the door open with a flat hand, sending the overhead chimes into a jangling frenzy.

A wide-eyed barista jolted behind the front counter.

"Is the owner available?"

A fuzzy frown creased the barista's brow. "I am the owner."

"I mean the new owner."

The brow crease deepened, a furrow.

"Uh-huh. That's what I thought." Shaynie pivoted. *Things aren't what they seem.* Not exactly true. Things were exactly how someone had made them seem. Slithering through the cracks the times he'd been caught. Like that morning when instinct had brought her back here, to her Hellnight apartment. What she'd seen had been real, but what she'd heard was a quick cover story, an elaborate lie, and why on Earth would she doubt it? *Eyeless angel, you've been blind.*

A rush of images flew into place. A spitefully cold walk home down Whyte Ave after that hockey game. Money left on her table after that vicious verbal jab that he'd never seen anyone more obsessed with making a buck. A fake appointment at the mall for a new business that did not exist. Crippling *her* business just so he could ride to the rescue.

A promise of the moon, a payment of stars.

Blind.

Sort of. It was like she'd been staring at a tapestry backward; some of the picture had made sense, but not all. Now, turned, the image was clear and things like a drugged Cameron missing their lah-tay-dah were understandable. A vandalized business losing credibility to all except one investor made perfect sense. Even Andrew's words about Gray were bang on: "If Divinity looked like a target, it would be too scary to operate. So you'd stay at The Python. With him." With *him.*

Not Gray, and oh, yes, *keys could be cut*—and stolen easily from the safe place she put them shift after shift.

She raced up the stairs to her Hellnight apartment, hiking Cameron's baggy sweats up from where they swam round her ankles, making her stumble. *No more stumbling. I'm nobody's victim and I'm no longer blind.*

The door to her old place was ajar. She pushed it wide.

A scream lodged in her throat. Her own face—dozens, *hundreds* of her own face—stared back at her. From teenage back in Jasper to her in her Python costumes obliviously tending bar, the entire apartment was papered with her picture. And with the eyeless angel mirrors that had taken all of her nerve to build.

*"Trapped with your bad mojo staring back at you into infinity."*

Her throat clicked, and the sound was enough to stiffen the shoulders of the figure she recognized from where he stood with his back to her, facing the window.

"Where did you spend the night, Shaynes?"

The night. *One night.* Holding Cameron deep inside of her, his skin salty-sweet on her tongue.

Jude turned around. "I asked you a question."

His pupils were like two dead insects and his fingers, flexing, looked like they slithered.

The Python. It had never been a place, it had always been a *person.*

"That hammer should have told you what to do, but you didn't listen. You weren't at your apartment on Whyte last night. You weren't at your old morgue. *Where the fuck were you?"*

*Oh, God.* Her heart thundered. What had she been thinking to come here alone? Her pictures, the mirrors, all her eyes seemed to stare back at her, terrified.

Jude stalked up to her, grasped a handful of Cameron's loose sweatshirt. "Did you want just one last night, Shaynes? One last night for him to touch you? Fuck, to *dress* you?"

He shook her, and her teeth chattered.

"You let him fuck you even after I showed you what a pussy hound douchebag he was? Screwing big-mouth Chrystal Johns in California even after he gave you this?" He dropped the sweatshirt, grabbed The Sun. "I *hate* this."

Her neck sizzled as he yanked the chain, jerked it off. The Sun made a helpless little swish as it hit the floor.

*Protection!* She looked at the little silver pile as it whished away. Oh, God. Now what?

"Nelson was supposed to bring you that picture immediately, but the chicken shit got cold feet. 'Weste's angling for a trade,'" he mimicked, voice cruelly accurate. "We don't need the picture'. Even though I helped him back when he needed it. I shut Jen up *completely* when the stupid bitch got knocked up and was about to ruin his career."

*I've had to make decisions for him.* Did Noel even know? Had that been why he'd been so greenly sickened in The Python the other night when he'd told her to run? Had he figured it out? *I loved Jen.* He'd said it for years, a mantra she now believed. A wave of compassion made her weak.

Jude plucked the thoughts from her eyes. "Nelson's a pussy. Didn't want the fucking kid but has bawled about it ever since. 'My poor Jenny,'" he mimicked, again cuttingly spot-on. "Some thank you."

Thank you? For killing someone? Her gut churned. "M-my Dad—"

"Way worse than Andrew the Asshole. Wouldn't let me get near you. Cornered me, the old fuck, and told me stay away. I showed *him* who was going to stay away."

That hammer. Her Dad's precious blood. Bone and brain on his ball cap. Before that night, that awful night, she had kissed that ball cap a hundred—a thousand—times. "'Night, Dad."

*"You are my Sunshine."*

She sobbed, and a shock of pain stung her face.

"Shut up!" Jude's palm glowed rage red, she caught a glimpse of it before her left eyelid puffed, blocked her vision.

"Always locked in the shop with your Dad. Even when I'd drive four hours just to see you. Didn't you want a life?"

A life? Being with her Dad *was* her life.

But not the life Jude had wanted. She stepped back.

He stepped forward. "I had one night too." He reached out, ran his fingers into the hair at her nape.

Cameron's ball cap fell to the floor.

"Look." He directed her eyes away from the cap and up, to the wall of photos. Centered in the collage was a shot of her, sleeping—*No! not sleeping! Drugged! I was drugged!*

"You were so *beautiful.*"

Beautiful? Bite marks seethed in the photo, livid on her throat. On her breasts. Had she looked that way this morning? When Cameron clasped The Sun back in place?

"You'd just dumped Steve," Jude crooned. "Cut the loser loose, but then you danced like a slut in my club!" His fingers curled in her hair. "I didn't know what to do with you! You just wouldn't *behave."*

*Behave.* As in, let him make decisions for her, much as he'd always done for Nelson.

"So what could I do other than knock you out? But then…" His eyes softened. "I was worried—what if I gave you too much?—so I came here to check on you."

"W-with my stolen key!"

He tightened his grip on her hair. "And you looked so beautiful. And I thought about the way you'd danced in The Python, what you'd wanted."

His smile carved the breath from her throat.

"Shaynes, I couldn't just Let You Be."

Her belly lurched.

"But afterward you couldn't even remember!"

She cried out.

Startled, his eyes went from dead bugs to doting in an instant. "I hurt you," he said. "I hurt you and I felt so..."

The shame on his face terrified her, somehow, more than anything.

"Maybe it was better you didn't know," he whispered. "But Shaynes, I was sorry." He folded her into him. "So, so sorry."

Her stomach pitched. His shirt smelled of liquor and dry ice. Of The Python. *'Cause he* is *The Python!*

"But now look. It's better. I made our place beautiful with you. Just you." He extended an arm, swept an arc over all the pictures. "And did you see the cards?"

The cards, Tarot cards, tacked between the pictures and the mirrors.

"I don't know what they mean, but you'll teach me, right?" His lips were on her ear and he held her, back to front, like she loved Cameron to do.

Cameron. Her heart gasped as her eyes lit on The Two of Cups, tacked into the wall. *Oh, Cameron, my Ice Deity. I love you. Where ever you go, no matter what happens, keep me in* goodbye. *Please know how I'll always love you.*

"I'm going to make love to you Shaynie. Right here. Right now." He turned her to a bed he'd positioned in the middle of her old living room floor.

"Beautiful, right?" He walked her to it, kissing the spot behind her ear.

Her skin slithered.

"And look, Shaynes, you didn't even see what I put up top." His fingers curled back in her hair, tugged her head back.

Her gaze flooded with shock.

"Told you I'd pick them up for you," he chuckled.

From the cathedral ceilings the welded Tarot suits looked as if they floated on air. "H-how…?"

"Fish line," he answered. "See? I can be artistic too."

"F-fish line?" But Steve had admonished her to put the sword down. Had seemed baffled by how it turned out to be so…

"Heavy," she managed. "Jude, th-they're too heavy." The Pentacle, as if in answer, jogged a bit on its wire. "F-fish line isn't strong enough."

Above them, over the bed, the sword began spinning, a slow circle.

"They're fine." Back were the dead insects, beady in his glare. "Look at them. They're dancing for you."

Dancing? Or testing the air for sturdiness?

The Wand, suspended by one of the leaves Steve had fashioned, jittered. Then—her breath caught—it glowed. Shining and lit to life with the luster she'd first seen in the picture, the picture where she'd known.... *Protection.*

Her gaze jumped to the Pentacle. It also glowed.

So did the Cup and the Sword, pearly and perfect. Luminous.

Then came scent. Lavender. "D-do you smell that?"

"I smell you." He slid his nose down her arm, inhaling deeply.

Her gut went to oil.

"Shaynes, I have loved you all my life. I'm so sorry you don't remember our special night. Our beautiful, beautiful night, right here."

But she did remember. Bruises. Bite marks. Blood.

"When you left this place, you broke my heart." His hands slid up under her sweatshirt, *Cameron's* sweatshirt, and found her heart.

Her skin clenched and she sent a gasping glance to the suits. *Help me!*

Scent soared. Lavender so strong she could taste it, breathe it, acrid in her nostrils.

Jude murmured in her ear. "I hated everything that came between us. Needy Gray. Your meddling father—"

"Dad—"

He jerked her hair back, and for the first time she saw it, clenched in his free hand.

Her missing taser.

"Shut up about your Dad. You're better off without him. Look at all you've accomplished on your own."

The suits—or something—hissed. She swallowed, stock-still.

"Although all the time you spend in that fucking old money-leeching morgue..." He trailed off, speculative, it seemed. "But now we own it together."

One of the suits—the Pentacle?—growled, unmistakable. She held her breath.

"*Without* Pussyhound Weste." His hand, on her breast, clenched.

A whistle of pain sailed through her teeth.

He misread it. "Weste's a whore, Shaynes!" He twisted her breast. She screamed. "How could you?" He twisted again. "How could you let him make you dirty like that? And how could you say, 'California here we come,' the other night in my club?"

The tripwire. Oh, God. A throw-away statement she'd barely meant had been the tripwire.

He yanked her hair back, demanding answer, and her eyes bulged. But any gasped reply was lost to a low rumbling.

Thunder? In February?

"It's our turn now," he said, softer, and his grip eased. "You're not going anywhere. And when we make love, you'll remember. Your beautiful eyes will be open and you'll see."

*See.* Murky shadows emerging from the ceiling. From the walls. And a low rumble—*was* that thunder?—alive in her ears.

"L-let me go." She was going to pass out. Was that why her vision was grey, why she was hearing things? Because she was going to faint? "Jude, let me—"

"I can't. Shaynes. I—I know I've scared you, but I...I've been so afraid that you'll go."

"But I..." Shadows stormed her eyes. *Think!* But how? That rumble! It was drowning her thoughts. *Replacing* her thoughts. "I—I'm dirty," she blurted, and had no idea where it came from.

"I know." He nodded. "Let's get rid of him." He grasped the hem of her sweatshirt.

*"Cameron!"* She clung to it, automatic.

Jude roared, and a sizzle met her ears before her entire being jolted, the sensation like being shoved under jittering water then jerked back out. The taser. He'd just used her taser and she'd fallen, a twitching heap at his feet.

"Get up," he said calmly, and by his changed stance she had the disoriented sense that some time had passed, but no clue how much. "And take that filthy sweatshirt off."

Reality—fear—coursed through her stomach, made it loose. "I—" *Think!* "I need to shower."

He stilled, suspicion palpable.

But the rumbling was palpable too. Louder, a singing noise now that formed one word. *Protection.*

"Shower," she said again, stronger. "Let me shower. I can't..." She climbed to her feet, glanced at the bed in a way she hoped he saw as shy, not shrewd.

"Shower," he repeated it. *Tasted* it.

She held a breath she could almost see, hanging and begging between them.

"Okay. I'll help you."

"No!"

His fingers flashed out, clenched in her hair, the taser cocked in his other hand.

"J-Jude, please. I—I just want to clean up. I want to be—" The word she needed was phlegm in her throat. She swallowed it, a slippery lump. "Be *gorgeous* for you."

He relaxed. Chuckled. "Shaynes," he chided. "You already are."

"N-no." She forced out a laugh. It too tasted of phlegm. "I—I'm filthy. H-he made me filthy." Locking gazes, she pleaded, prayed he wouldn't see the heartbeat in her eyes. Or the lies.

He lingered on her gaze for a lifetime of seconds. Then he stooped, kissed her mouth. "Don't be long."

She wanted to swipe the kiss off but couldn't. Wanted to run and had to force herself to walk, steady, not too eager. The bathroom was an ensuite in her old bedroom.

And her closet was in her old bedroom.

She shut the door behind her, shaking all over once she was alone.

*Turn the taps on!* The command, couched in the rumbling, propelled her, and as she cranked the shower to full strength it seemed the rumbling sighed with relief. *Now the closet.*

"Yes," she whispered. "I know." Leaving the water rushing, she silently padded to the wardrobe, opened the door.

She choked on a scream. Her Python clothes, her missing costumes, were waiting there, all glitz and slink. Shaking, she shoved them aside, stuck her hand deep in the back, feeling for the shelf.... Slick sensation met her fingers, a glossy surface, lethal edges. The broken pieces of mirror, hidden after they'd shown her Hellnight horror, bite marks, bruises, and blood.

"You had to hide them," Cameron had said, and now she knew why, knew what the Tarot had always known. The Devil. Swords. *Weapons. War.*

She chose the biggest piece and, holding it carefully, pulled the sleeve of Cameron's too-big sweatshirt down over her hand to the fingertips.

Jude waited beside the bed, and a ripple of surprise that she'd returned was in the way he straightened.

"I changed my mind," she told him, and Ivy Shaynie, reflected in one of the eyeless angel mirrors, smiled, heaven sweet. "I didn't want you to wait."

Pleasure bloomed on his face, and when he opened his arms he did not see the jagged edge coming.

The air curdled with agony as the mirror met its mark, and his ruined eye, a scarlet socket, managed to somehow look shocked as she drove the glass home.

*"You bitch!"* He dove for her.

She raised the slice of glass but his blood made it greasy, and as he knocked her backward the piece of mirror slid from her grasp, shattered onto the floor.

"Hockey whore," he panted. *"Little bitch!"*

His fist met her face, and stars burst in her eyes, tiny pinpricks of light which were also like wee silver mirrors.

"You want dirty? You want filth?" Blood gushed from his eye as he trapped her, one hand on her wrist, the other reaching for his pants.

She kicked, scratched, and when she cried out, *"Help me!"* she caught the gaze of one of the eyeless angels on his mirrors, saw its little mouth frozen in a round, worried 'o'.

For the rumbles and shadows had at last taken form.

*Hundreds* of forms.

Opaque figures, her frost soldiers, emerged from the floorboards, the walls. Walked out of thin air. The dead. Now she could see that the soldiers were the dead, *all* of the dead who had ever been nurtured and restored within Divinity's walls.

They were terrible. They were beautiful.

True eyeless angels, their lids long since glued shut to prevent them flying open. Their mouths silenced by discernible stitches that kept lips from parting and giving the illusion that the dead could speak.

Yet they *could* speak.

Silent, deafening, the dangling Tarot suits vibrated with their roars as they moved *en masse,* their last, best outfits starched stiff and crackling, some collars open and revealing the black Y stitches on the wrecked flesh beneath.

Terrible. Beautiful. *Feral. Fierce.* She sought their eyeless glares. "Help me!"

"*Help* you?" Another flat hand. Another starburst of pain. "I'll *kill* you."

A dead roar shook the floorboards and raced through the Tarot suits.

Her eyes widened, and she knew then, what would happen.

*Weapons. War.*

The Cup shook loose first, crashing to the floor and making the floorboards quiver. The Wand zinged and bounced as it landed. The Pentacle spun on one side like a coin tossed in water, like a wish, before it too crashed on the floor.

The dead roared, triumphant. Shaynie looked straight up.

The sword made a dizzy half arc before the fish line snapped, and, *"Get off!"* she screamed, shoving Jude.

Too late. The blade whistled down and he slumped onto her chest with a wet sounding grunt.

She struggled and the sword's blade poked through him, sliced her skin.

He looked at her, and for a moment his uninjured eye held a bewildered sort of shock. "But I loved you," he said, then blood lurched from his mouth, splashed her face.

She shrieked and scrambled free, off the bed and onto the floor.

Silence fell. The dead army was gone. Ivy Shaynie was gone. All that was left was Jude's body, face down on the bed, a Tarot sword tall in his back. Betrayal. The image of the Ten of Swords.

*But I loved you.*

So much that he'd carried her pictures with him since childhood. So much that he'd never had a girlfriend since the day they had met. Her memory flashed, a cherub's smile. Dimples in the cheeks. *"Love you Shaynes."*

Loved her? He'd possessed her. Isolated her. Raped her body and her bank account, killed her father....

She scooted across the floor, away from the bed and his body, terrified that somehow he, like the army who'd risen to rescue, would somehow awaken from death.

To love her. To punish her for not loving him.

"Shaynie!"

The cry came from the door, and when she looked, a scream gurgled on her lips. *Jude!*

Her eyes darted back to his corpse. Back to the door.

No. Not Jude. Gray—*God, Steve, they do look alike*—racing toward her. "Oh, Shaynie," he babbled. "My sweetest friend Shaynie. I put it together. I think I'd always put it together. I always knew he...."

*The Python is evil.*

"His head went to really dark places. But he had a way of making you believe that what he believed was always right."

*"I had to make decisions for him."* .

"And you...your dad...Jen. Shaynie, I—I didn't want to believe. Used dope so I didn't *have* to believe. But then you told me about Hellnight, and I already knew about Chrystal and drugs—and that I'd given her St. Cecelia as protection. Then she asked about protection with *him*...." He buried his face in his hands.

She stared at him. Could do nothing more than stare at him.

"He knew that I knew. The night after that fistfight. And I knew what he was capable of, what he'd already done, and I—" He rocked, back and forth. "I was a coward. I've *always* been a coward. Hiding behind dope. Hiding behind your skirt. This time I hid in detox. Fooled them into thinking I'd had more than just one little slip. But I still tried to talk to you, Shaynie. Warn you."

*Run, Shaynie.*

He put his head in his hands. "I'm sorry. Oh, Shaynie, I'm so sorry."

She rose, unsteady on her feet. She heard him. Understood him. But didn't know how to speak. What to say.

"Shaynie Grace." Another voice from the door.

The expression of bone-melting relief on Andrew's face was all it took to pull an internal trigger. She slipped to the floor, finger tracing a shaky ankh in the air before all the pictures, every mirror, all the eyeless monstrosities watching her were swallowed, blissfully black.

## CHAPTER FORTY-FOUR

LIGHT. It burned and she fought it.

"There, there."

The fingers that had opened her eye soothed her cheek, their touch cool. "Her pupils are normal. The bruising is bad. There's a popped blood vessel in her right eye, but those always look worse than they are. It will heal."

She tried opening her eyes. Only one would obey.

"I'm prescribing an anti-inflammatory for the contusions and swelling. A painkiller too. She had those jolts of electricity from the taser, and most people recover fine, but trauma complicates things. I'd like to keep her overnight for observation, try a tranquilizer along with the analgesic. It will calm her from fighting us like she has."

She had? She tried sitting up, focusing. The person speaking, a white coat, a doctor, smiled. "Why hello there. You're going to join us." He flicked a look to her blind side. "You're next of kin, right?"

She turned. Andrew.

"Want to help me help her up?" asked the doctor.

Her brother slipped a hand behind her back. She clung to him.

"'S'okay, Shaynie Grace," he whispered.

His eyes were red. Had he been crying?

"I'm right here and you're going to be okay."

His voice was thick. He *had* been crying. She tried taking his hand but recoiled. Her fingers! A shriek caught in her throat. They were caked with dried blood. *Jude's* dried blood.

"*Ne vous inquiétez pas*, my darling, my *Cheri*. We will clean you."

Cele, on her other side.

Shaynie looked at her. "The Poison," she croaked.

*"Oui."* Cele nodded. "The *Poison*" She collapsed in a chair, began weeping.

"You're a brave soldier, little Perfect."

A third voice. Trin. She peered at her through her one good eye.

She'd been crying too.

The doctor spoke. "I'm going to leave you with family," he said. "Have a nurse arrange a room on the ward." The rings on the curtain rod rattled as he brushed the drapery aside and strode to where she could see a nurse's station and other gurneys. This was Emergency. A cubicle in Emergency. "Which hosp—"

"The Royal Alex," said Andrew. "It was closest."

Closest to her Hellnight apartment. Closest also, to Divinity. She tried nodding acknowledgement but dropped back onto pillows, lids fluttering shut.

A new voice invaded.

"Cameron Weste stunned the city with his big trade today!"

She shot up from the bed.

A TV screen above the nurse's station was blaring.

"We don't know what to make of this!"

"Shut it off!"

"Shaynie Grace—"

*"Shut it off!"*

"Shaynie Grace, calm—"

"—shut it off, shut it off shut it— "

"Listen to her!" Trin yanked the curtain closed, sent the curtain rings jangling. "Christ almighty, have a heart." She gathered Shaynie close and rocked her, crooning. "'S'okay, little Perfect. 'S'alright."

No. It wasn't all right. Nothing was all right. "Shut it off!" she sobbed, and knew she was hysterical. Couldn't help it.

Andrew, on her right side, her blind side, made an exasperated sound. "I'm going to go find the doctor. Get that tranquilizer *now."*

"And I am looking for Barnabas," said Cele. "Darling, Reiki. You need Reiki."

The curtain rattled again. She shrank against it.

Trin held her tight.

"Get me out of here," Shaynie mumbled, against her.

Trin stopped rocking. "Oh, little Perfect, I can't—"

"*Please.* Get me out of here, get me away. Trin, please. *Please.*"

The sounds from the television were still audible, and she could pick out Cameron's pitch, his thunder rumble, giving an interview. His big trade. His goodbye. She clung to Trin, cringed away from his voice. "*Please.*"

The sound Trin made was the misery of indecision.

Shaynie looked up at her. "My Divinity. My old morgue.... It'll help me. Heal me. It..." She swallowed. "It understands goodbye."

Trin pulled a face, but Shaynie knew she'd agree before she even spoke to say, "We'd better hurry before those two come back."

~

Colorless ward rooms raced by as they whished down the corridor, Trin running, Shaynie in a wheelchair. "Your brother will arrest me."

"I left him a note." *Divinity,* scrawled on her chart. She'd tossed it on top of her gurney.

"He scares me."

"He'll understand. He'll blow up and be mad, but he'll understand."

She needed help getting into the passenger side of Trinity's car, was shaky, and Cameron's sweats kept tangling round her ankles. Bloodstained, and with a tear from the sword over one knee, they were all she'd had to pull on under her hospital johnny. That, and Trin's coat the latter had sacrificed before they burst out into the cold parking lot.

"My God, Perfect. *Look* at you."

"I have clean clothes at the morgue."

Trin cranked the heat, but Divinity wasn't far enough away for the vents to warm up to more than cold air. "Do you even have a key?" She pulled up, parked.

"I won't need one." The old building would let her in just as it had always tried keeping Jude out. She recalled now that every time he'd come, the door would be locked even when she'd been sure that she'd left it open. And that one time the alarm had even gone off when he'd gone inside. Signs. All signs. *Protection.*

She stepped from Trin's car on fawn's legs, wobbling and grasping the frame of the door when a crack of thunder filled the air, *real* thunder, not the rumble of voices. Amazed, she watched a sizzle of lightning span the sky. A thunderstorm in February? Winter lightning wasn't unheard of, but that didn't make it any less bizarre.

A second bolt of lightning lit the looming high rises. Lit *Cameron's* high rise. Her heart rocked as she looked up, up, up to his window.

Or what used to be his window.

Another jagged line of lightning jittered behind his building, and the image.... The Tower. The lightning-struck tower. The *change.* The goodbye.

"Trin?" Her voice sounded displaced, as if from a dream. "You go into Divinity. Wait for Andrew. I—I'll be there soon." She started walking.

"What?" Trin yelped. "Where are you—"

She turned to her and felt the lightning, an electric back drop. "I need to say goodbye." She looked over her shoulder, at his condo. "I need to *feel* goodbye."

*"Perfect!"* Trin raced after her, Shaynie could feel her. But when her hand clamped onto her shoulder she also felt something else.

Movement, an emergence out of the ground and the air. Shadows shifted, and as the frost soldiers surrounded them, Trin's eyes grew huge. Shaynie winced, able to almost feel the terrified scream boiling behind her friend's lips. "You need to let me do this," she told her.

Trin released her and the soldiers shrank back, but she wondered if they were not part of the strength it took to get her across the street and up his block.

Impeccable let her in, fine features startled. "Ms Gavin! Are you all ri—"

"No," she said. "Not really." She smiled, wan. "Would you—"

"Of course!" He took her arm before she could raise it, ushered her into the picture-elevator, then down the elegant hall. He didn't need to ask if she had her key, let her in with his own.

"Thank you," she managed.

The condo crackled with silence. With vacancy. She slid her shoes off and soundlessly crept across hardwood, sleek and shining. The personal items she'd noticed last night—the pictures, the casual mementos—were still where he'd set them. Would movers pack everything? He wouldn't be able to. The wish card—the trade—meant he was already owned by a brand new team. Had been launched onto the first available flight to The Sun. Ignoring the clench in her chest, she moved quietly—God, everything was so quiet!—into his bedroom.

If glitter had a sound it was made by his stars. They pulled her inside, and she traced their pattern, twenty-two. Had it hurt to leave them behind? She touched the bed, noticing absently that it had been made. How long would he keep his housekeeper employed now that he'd gone away? Would it be she who directed the movers to anonymously box and ship all of his private stuff?

She sank to the bed. God, her head hurt.

Above, the stars whispered and shone, a sparkle soft on her cheeks. *Stay, Faerie.*

When her tears came, they were hot. Somehow heavy.

*Faerie, stay.*

She closed her eyes and starlight, sunshine, trickled down her cheeks with the tears. *Goodbye.* She couldn't say it. Could barely think it, and above her, the stars understood. They shone warmer, stronger, touching her as though they too, protested *goodbye.*

*Oh, my Cameron. My Ice Deity.* Her lips tried to say it, but no sound came out.

The stars soothed her, cupped her face and stroked it, careful of her injuries. Soft on her cheeks like a mouth. *God.* They felt *just like* his mouth. A sigh slid from her throat, and scent, rain and chocolate, bloomed. *Cameron. I love you.* Another tear fell.

Something caught it.

"I have looked *everywhere* for you."

Her lids flew open. A storm sky looked back.

"What the *hell* were you thinking?"

She squeaked, half expecting outside's lightning to flash in his eyes. "H-how did you get in here?"

"How did I—I'm *supposed* to be here! I *live* here. You, however, are supposed to be in the hospital—" With a sound like a growl he broke off, and she sat in stunned silence as he dug out his phone, poked speed dial. "Hey Andrew."

Andrew. Not The Agent. And she remembered Andrew no longer called him Goliath, either.

"Guess who I found?" he said, and scowled at her, listened. "Yeah. Yeah, I *will* tell her you're pissed." Pause. "Yes, I will happily tell her that she should shake in her boots from the blast you're going to give her." He glared at her, pointedly, then listened a moment more. "No," he said, then and his face softened. "You don't have to worry. She's not going *anywhere* now." He hung the phone up.

She swallowed, audible.

His jaw twitched, and a hundred—a thousand—yelled thoughts struggled through his eyes, and she held her breath, waited.

He said none of them. Finally just slumped, forehead in hands. "Do you have *any idea* how scared I was?"

Nope. She didn't have any ideas at all. "C-Cameron—" she reached out. He jerked back.

"Don't. Do *not.*"

She gasped, stricken. He glared.

"I am not finished being really fucking *furious* with you."

"But I—"

"You went after him? Faerie, you knew what he'd done. What he was capable of. And you went after him all alone?"

But she hadn't been alone. Ivy Shaynie. The Dead Army. But it didn't matter. What he'd called her. What he'd just called her— "Camer—"

"Last night, *our* night....did you not think, after our night, what it would feel like to lose you?"

Lose her? Wait a minute. *Cameron Weste's big trade! Goodbye.* "I-is that why you haven't left yet?"

Confusion flickered on his forehead.

"You—" She reached for him again. Was relieved when he let her. "The TV is all over your big trade."

His brow jumped a bit.

"I—I thought you'd have flown out. Been gone."

His frown deepened. "Didn't you just say you watched the TV?"

Confusion. Her turn.

He scooped the remote from the dresser, aimed it at the screen.

He, like she, kept the station on sports, and the day's highlights had cycled, repeating the words she had heard in emergency, "Cameron Weste stunned the city with his big trade today!" She flinched.

He turned it up.

"We don't know what to make of this, and of course we're employing the word 'trade' very loosely."

She peered at the screen.

"A deal had been inked that would see the sniper move to California—"

"I like how they call me a sniper," he said dryly.

She shushed him.

"—but in a shocking last-second move he traded himself back to Edmonton, and to the tune of half his salary."

Sound squeaked in her throat.

"And if that wasn't enough, he bargained for a 'no move' clause that will see him remain in Edmonton. For that he forfeited another half of his already sliced salary."

Her jaw dropped.

"Sure hope you can sell a lot of furniture, Faerie."

She swatted him, absent, automatic, transfixed by the camera which cut to his digitized image on the screen.

"We understand you're staying for personal reasons," called out a reporter.

"Personal, professional, my future is here."

"Ah. Care to tell us future's name?"

"Yeah. Divinity."

She caught a gasp in her hand.

"I turned cards yesterday," he said.

She turned to him, stunned.

"After you said we were through. I needed answers. I'd bought my own deck, and so I turned cards, asked all about you. Guess which card was the first to turn up?"

Speechless, she shook her head.

"Heartbreak. Three of swords."

Tears reawakened. Rushed to her eyes.

"That was a gut punch. But then I turned the next one. Seven Swords."

The liar's card. Lies. "I—"

"They both made sense as soon as I saw you. You—" He broke off, swiped a hand through his hair. "—you really are a lousy liar, my Faerie."

"So you...you knew?"

"That you were lying about us? Yeah. The minute I saw you, I knew. And after, when you laid in my arms crying and thinking I couldn't hear, I absolutely knew. Why do you think I raced out of here this morning without even waking you? I needed to turn my deal around."

"B-but last night you asked if I'd stay with you even though you were saying goodbye."

"Because living *here,* I'm going to be saying goodbye to you far more than I'll ever say hello."

No, he'd say hello just as many times. Did he still not see that? But now was not the time to argue it. They had time. Lots of time. She reached up, tentative as though he might still disappear, and stroked his face. "You gave half your salary. Half of the half of your salary. I—I can't believe your team took advantage of you like that."

"Ah." A ghost of the old whiplash smile moved his lips. "Spoken like a true WAG."

"Do not, *ever,* refer to me as something a dog can do."

His laughter was every good memory. Every sweet moment. "Shaynie Gavin, you are *not* my WAG. You," He brought her hand to his mouth, "are my Faerie."

Every inch of her glittered like the stars in his sky.

"And if you'd just say three little words, then that pay cut, the goodbyes, you scaring me to death, they'd all be worth it."

Three words? "You—you're my Sun."

He pulled a face. “Not exactly the words I wanted, but—”

She placed a hand on his mouth. “You’re my Sun, and I’ve loved you since that night you found me after we didn’t have our lah-tay-dah. Maybe even before. Cameron, you’re my Sun, my wish card, you...you’re my everything. I love you. I love you.”

“Love you.” He slid his hands in her hair, groaning when she winced from her bruises. “My Faerie, my Shaynie, say you’ll say goodbye to me for the rest of my life.”

“No.” She shook her head and her smile felt like The Sun. “I’ll say hello to you for the rest of mine.”

## EPILOGUE

He left on a road trip early the next morning, and when he returned ten days later most of her bruises had healed. The scarlet spot that had inked her right iris was gone. And she was grateful because eyes—paparazzi eyes—followed her to the airport when she went to meet the team’s chartered plane. The reporters cheered, cat-calling when Cameron jumped out of queue to run to her. Were delirious when, with a whiplash smile, he dipped her down low in front of the cameras and silk-kissed her, slow and long.

Trish, the head Siren, denounced them as crazy. Edmontonians did not. The city fell in love with their love, and everywhere they went they were comped, coddled, and catered to.

Divinity came alive with more customers than she could have dreamed of, and, backlogged and busy, she needed to approach her old tech school, arrange to take students on an apprenticeship regime.

Steve Lonigan helped her with the paperwork. Vouched, as a certified instructor, that she too would be an excellent member of the school’s trades faculty.

Noel Nelson re-negotiated with Edmonton, and the media were sour about his modest salary hike in comparison to Cameron’s willingness to play for less than what most rookies made. Shaynie was not too impressed either, so when offers for endorsements started pouring in she waded through bids with Cameron—Nike and Reebok, Adidas and Cooper—, laughing till tears rolled when, buried in the offers, was an undergarment company, pleading with him to pose.

He folded his arms, peered at her dry. "Think *this* is funny?" He showed her what they were willing to pay.

"Oooh." Her eyes widened. "They *do* think you're a sexy thang." She tweaked his nose.

He tweaked hers back. "Read the fine print, Faerie. They'll double it if you pose with me wearing their girly-girl line."

She vaulted a brow then slowly, slyly, she met his eyes, mirrored his whiplash smile.

They made feverish love in the elevator after the photo shoot.

Andrew gave them both shit when their barely-clothed underwear ad hit the magazine stands—"Is *nothing* sacred to you two?"—but Cele roared, bawdy delight, and had Shaynie make a frame for the picture. Barnabas hung it in her divining room.

Sobriety came in the form of Gray, arriving one afternoon at the old morgue. "You've been requested to be present at the reading of Jude's will," he said.

Andrew growled. Cameron bristled. Divinity's furnace awakened with a roar.

"Come with me," she said.

Cameron assumed she meant him and so he attended, hand locked on hers, a contract lawyer he'd hired flanking her other side.

Neither of them saw Divinity's army, shadow figures hovering as the will was read.

Jude had left her The Python. A hand reaching out from the grave. She approached an ashen-faced Gray after the reading. "Do you want it?"

"Are you nuts? I want a clean start. A *pure* start. I'm sorry, Shaynie, but no. No way."

Trin was not quite as reticent. Cameron's contract lawyer drew up the papers, and when she bought it for a buck she already had a new name in mind. *Holy Hell.*

"The cards said you'd be starting a business." Shaynie smiled, and was grateful when Trin understood why she skipped the grand opening. Cameron didn't have a game. He wasn't out on the road. They spent the entire night talking. Laughing. Filling his condo with jar after jar of clear, colored stones.

ϰ

## AFTERWORD

Though set in the very real City of Champions—Edmonton, Alberta, Canada—Divinity & The Python is a work of fiction and as such I have taken great geographic liberties with the placement of downtown streets, their proximity to the river valley, and have also randomly scattered several imaginary businesses hither and yon, such as Has Beans on Whyte, Body Chocolate in the mall, and, of course, Divinity, the old morgue, downtown. In addition, the nameless hockey team that frequents The Python is fictional too, and play for a professional league which exists only upon the pages of this book (and, unluckily for Cameron Weste and Noel Nelson, their league has a far more demanding, rigorous, and totally unrealistic schedule than any real professional sports league I've ever heard of).

## ABOUT THE AUTHOR

Bonnie Randall is a Canadian writer who lives between her two favourite places—the Jasper Rocky Mountains and the City of Champions: Edmonton, Alberta. A clinical counsellor who scribbles fiction in notebooks whenever her day job allows, Bonnie is fascinated by the relationships people develop—or covet—with both the known and unknown, the romantic and the arcane.

Divinity & The Python, a paranormal romantic thriller, was inspired by a cold day in Edmonton when the exhaust rising in the downtown core appeared to be the buildings, releasing their souls. It is Bonnie's first novel.

## ABOUT PANVERSE PUBLISHING

Panverse Publishing is an independent press dedicated to publishing original work, both fiction and nonfiction, by new writers and established professionals. Our titles are readily available in both print and digital formats from Amazon, Barnes & Noble, and other online retailers, and in print from your local bookseller. You can read about current and upcoming titles at our website at http://www.panversepublishing.com

Reader support and word-of-mouth is vital for independent publishers and their authors. If you enjoyed this book, please help spread the word by telling friends, mentioning it on social media, or posting a review online. Thank you so much.

Panverse Publishing. Story. Wonder. They're back.

CPSIA information can be obtained at www.ICGtesting.com
Printed in the USA
LVOW13s0924111013

356393LV00004B/14/P